"In his third book of *Tales,* Maupin watches his characters with a sharp eye and describes them with a sharper tongue, but his bemused irony is tempered with such obviously genuine affection that the result is both uplifting and urbane."

Philadelphia Inquirer

"The abrupt violence in this once-lighthearted novel reads as much more dangerous—and true—because we've been fooled into going along with what seemed to be a joke. Maupin is a mask-wearer, like many of his actors. He is also capable of compassion, of making us care about and care for the players. They may behave indecently but they are innocents; the villains live in the larger world beyond Barbary Lane."

Los Angeles Times

"Maupin has a genius for observation. His characters have the timing of vaudeville comics, flawed by human frailty and fueled by blind hope."

The Denver Post

"Like those of Dickens and Wilkie Collins, Armistead Maupin's novels have all appeared originally as serials. It is the strength of this approach, with its fantastic adventures and astonishingly contrived coincidences, that makes these novels charming and compelling. Everything is explained and everything tied up and nothing is lost by reading them individually. There is no need even to read them chronologically."

Literary Review

NOVELS BY ARMISTEAD MAUPIN

FURTHER TALES OF THE CITY

Armistead Maupin

HarperPerennial

A Division of HarperCollins*Publishers*

This work was published in somewhat different form in the *San Francisco Chronicle*.

FURTHER TALES OF THE CITY. Copyright © 1982 by The Chronicle Publishing Company. All rights reserved. Printed in the United States of America. No part of this book may be used or reproduced in any manner whatsoever without written permission except in the case of brief quotations embodied in critical articles and reviews. For information address HarperCollins Publishers, Inc., 10 East 53rd Street, New York, NY 10022.

HarperCollins books may be purchased for educational, business, or sales promotional use. For information please write: Special Markets Department, HarperCollins Publishers, Inc., 10 East 53rd Street, New York, NY 10022.

First Perennial Library edition published 1982. Reissued 1989.
First HarperPerennial edition published 1994.

Designed by Cassandra J. Pappas

LIBRARY OF CONGRESS CATALOG CARD NUMBER 81-4805

ISBN 0-06-092492-6

96 97 98 RRD 10 9

For Steve Beery

Surely there are in everyone's life certain connections, twists and turns which pass awhile under the category of Chance, but at the last, well examined, prove to be the very Hand of God.

SIR THOMAS BROWNE
Religio Medici

Further Tales of the City

Home and Hearth

THERE WERE OUTLANDERS, OF COURSE, WHO CONtinued to insist that San Francisco was a city without seasons, but Mrs. Madrigal paid no heed to them. Why, the signs of spring were everywhere!

Those Chinese schoolboys, for instance, sporting brand new green-and-yellow baseball caps as they careened down Russian Hill on their skateboards.

And what about old Mr. Citarelli? Only a seasoned San Franciscan could know that this was *exactly* the time of year he dragged his armchair into his garage and opened the door to the sunshine. Mr. Citarelli was infinitely more reliable than any groundhog.

Here on Barbary Lane, the vernal equinox was heralded by an ancient scarlet azalea that blazed like a bonfire next to the garbage cans. "My goodness," said Mrs. Madrigal, stopping to adjust her grocery bag. "It's you again, is it?" It had also bloomed in August and December, but nature was always forgiven for offering too much of a good thing.

When Mrs. Madrigal reached the lych gate at Number 28, she paused under its peaked roof to survey her domain—the mossy brick plain of the courtyard, the illegal lushness of her "herb garden," the ivy-and-brown-shingle face of her beloved old house. It was a sight that never failed to thrill her.

Dropping the groceries in the kitchen—three new cheeses from Molinari's, light bulbs, focaccia bread, Tender Vittles for Boris—she hurried into the parlor to build a fire. And why not? In San Francisco, a fire felt good at any time of year.

The firewood had been a Christmas gift from her tenants—a whole cord of it—and Mrs. Madrigal handled it as if she were arranging ingots at Fort Knox. She had suffered too long under the indignity of those dreadful pressed sawdust things they sold at the Searchlight Market. Now, thanks to her children, she had a fire that would *crackle*.

They weren't really her children, of course, but she treated them as such. And they appeared to accept her as a parent of sorts. Her own daughter, Mona, had lived with her for a while in the late seventies, but had moved to Seattle the previous year. Her reason had been characteristically cryptic: "Because . . . well, because it's The Eighties, that's why."

Poor Mona. Like a lot of her contemporaries, she had capitalized The Eighties, deified the new decade in the hope that it would somehow bring her salvation, deliver her from her own bleak vision of existence. The Eighties, for Mona, would be the same in Seattle as in San Francisco . . . or Sheboygan, for that matter. But no one could tell her that. Mona had never recovered from The Sixties.

The landlady's ersatz children—Mary Ann, Michael and Brian—had somehow kept their innocence, she realized.

And she loved them dearly for that.

Minutes later, Michael showed up at her door with his rent check in one hand and Boris in the other.

"I found him on the ledge," he said, "looking faintly suicidal."

The landlady scowled at the tabby. "More like homicidal. He's been after the birds again. Set him down, will you, dear? I can't bear it if he has bluejay on his breath."

Michael relinquished the cat and presented the check to Mrs. Madrigal. "I'm sorry it's so late. Again."

She waved it away with her hand, hastily tucking the check into a half-read volume of Eudora Welty stories. She found it excruciating to discuss money with her children. "Well," she said, "what shall we do about Mary Ann's birthday?"

"God," winced Michael. "Is it that time already?"

Mrs. Madrigal smiled. "Next Tuesday, by my calculations."

"She'll be thirty, won't she?" Michael's eyes danced diabolically.

"I don't think that should be our emphasis, dear."

"Well, don't expect any mercy from me," said Michael. "She put me through hell last year on *my* thirtieth. Besides, she's the last one in the house to cross The Great Divide. It's only proper that we mark the event."

Mrs. Madrigal shot him her Naughty Boy look and sank into the armchair by the hearth. Sensing another chance to be picturesque, Boris dove into her lap and blinked languidly at the fire. "Can I interest you in a joint?" asked the landlady.

Michael shook his head, smiling. "Thanks. I'm late for work, as it is."

She returned his smile. "Give my love to Ned, then. Your new haircut looks stunning, by the way."

"Thanks," beamed Michael, reddening slightly.

"I like seeing your ears, actually. It makes you look quite boyish. Not at all like you've crossed The Great Divide."

Michael showed his appreciation with a courtly little bow.

"Run along now," said the landlady. "Make little things grow."

After he had left, she permitted herself a private grin over this Great Divide business. She was sixty now, for heaven's sake. Did that mean she had crossed it twice?

Sixty. Up close, the number was not nearly so foreboding as it had once been from afar. It had a kind of plump symmetry to it in fact, like a ripe Gouda or a comfy old hassock.

She chuckled at her own similes. Is that what she had come to? An old cheese? A piece of furniture?

She didn't care, really. She was Anna Madrigal, a self-made

woman, and there was no one else in the world exactly like
her.

As that comforting litany danced in her head, she rolled a
joint of her finest sensemilla and settled back with Boris to
enjoy the fire.

Michael

FOR ALMOST THREE YEARS NOW MICHAEL TOLLIVER HAD been manager of a nursery in the Richmond District called God's Green Earth. The proprietor of this enterprise was Michael's best friend, Ned Lockwood, a brawny forty-two-year-old who was practically the working model for the Green-collar Gay.

Green-collar Gays, in Michael's lexicon, included everyone who dealt with beautiful living things in a manly, outdoorsy fashion: nurserymen, gardeners, forest rangers and some landscape architects. Florists, of course, didn't qualify.

Michael loved working in the soil. The fruits of his labors were aesthetic, spiritual, physical and even sexual—since a number of men in the city found nothing quite so erotic as the sight of someone's first name stitched crudely across the front of a pair of faded green coveralls.

Like Michael, Ned hadn't always been a Green-collar Gay. Back in the early sixties, when he was still a student at UCLA, he had paid his tuition by pumping gas at a Chevron station in Beverly Hills. Then one day a famous movie star, fifteen years Ned's senior, stopped in for an oil change and became hopelessly smitten with the lean, well-muscled youth.

After that, Ned's life changed radically. The movie star wasted no time in setting up house with his newfound protégé. He paid for the remainder of Ned's education and incorporated him—as much as propriety and his press agent allowed—into his life in Hollywood.

Ned held his own quite well. Blessed with a sexual aura that bordered on mysticism, he proceeded to win the heart of every man, woman and animal that crossed his path. It was not so much his beauty that captivated them but his innate and almost childlike gift for attentiveness. He listened to them in a town where no one ever listened at all.

The love affair lasted almost five years. When it was over, the two men parted as friends. The movie star even helped subsidize Ned's move to San Francisco.

Today, in his middle years, Ned Lockwood was handsomer than ever, but balding—no, bald. What remained of his hair he kept clipped short, wearing his naked scalp proudly in the long-haul trucker tradition of Wakefield Poole porno movies. "If I ever start raking my hair over from the back and sides," he once told Michael earnestly, "I want you to take me out and have me shot."

Ned and Michael had gone to bed together twice—in 1977. Since then, they had been friends, co-conspirators, brothers. Michael loved Ned; he shared his romantic exploits with the older man like a small dog who drags a dead thing home and lays it adoringly on the doorstep of his master.

And Ned always listened.

"You wanna go to Devil's Herd tomorrow night?" asked Ned. "They've got a live band."

Michael looked up from the task at hand. He was boxing primroses for a Pacific Heights realtor who had fretted far too long over a choice of the pink or the yellow. The realtor eyed Ned bitchily, then resumed his fussing:

"Of course, there *are* some potted fuchsias on the deck and those are sort of purplish. I mean, the purple might not even *go* with the yellow. What do you think?"

Michael shot Ned an apologetic glance and tried to remain

patient with his customer. "All flowers go together," he said evenly. "God isn't a decorator."

The realtor frowned for a split second, perhaps determining if the remark had been impertinent. Then he laughed drily. "But some decorators are God, right?"

"Not around my house," smiled Michael.

The realtor leaned closer. "You used to know Jon Fielding, didn't you?"

Michael rang up the purchase. "Something like that," he replied.

"Oh . . . if I hit a nerve, I'm sorry."

"Not a bit." He smiled nonchalantly, hoping he didn't sound as feisty as he felt. "It's been a long time, that's all." He slid the box of primroses in the direction of his inquisitor. "You know him, huh?"

The realtor nodded. "We did a fly-in together once. Gamma Mu." He tossed out the name like bait, Michael noticed, as if *everyone* had heard of the national gay millionaires' fraternity.

Michael didn't bite. "Give him my best when you see him," he said.

"Right." The realtor simply stared for a moment, then reached over and stuffed his business card into the pocket of Michael's coveralls. "This is who I am," he said *sotto voce*. "You should come over one night. I have a Betamax."

He left without waiting for a reply, passing Ned in the doorway.

"What about it?" asked Ned.

Michael looked at the realtor's card long enough to read the name, Archibald Anson Gidde, then dropped it into the trash can. "Sorry, Ned, what did you say?"

"Devil's Herd," said Ned. "Tomorrow night?"

"Oh . . . yeah. Sure. I'd love to."

Ned checked him out for a moment, then tousled his hair. "You O.K., Bubba?"

"Sure," said Michael.

"Did that guy . . . ?"

"He knew Jon," said Michael. "That's all."

The A-Gays Gather

ARCH GIDDE WAS A MESS. TWENTY MINUTES BEFORE his dinner guests were scheduled to arrive the yellow primroses were still in their tacky little plastic pots. And Cleavon—damn his lazy, jiveass soul—was still in the kitchen, dicking around with the sushi.

Arch bellowed from the bedroom. "Cleavon . . . *Cleavon!*"

"Yo," replied Cleavon.

The realtor winced at himself in the mirror. *Yo,* for Christ's sake. Harold had never said yo. Harold had been campy, to be sure, but never, ever disrespectful. Arch had lost Harold in the divorce, however, and Rick was too selfish (and far too shrewd) to part with a competent servant who was both black *and* gay.

"Cleavon," yelled Arch, "I cannot stress too strongly that the primroses *must* be potted before the guests arrive. I want four of them in that elephant planter and four in the box on the end of the deck."

A pause. Then another yo.

Arch Gidde groaned out loud, then pushed up the sleeves

8

of his new Kansai Yamamoto sweater from Wilkes. It was embroidered with a huge multi-hued hyena that draped itself asymmetrically across his left shoulder. Is it too much? he wondered.

No, he decided. Not with the sushi.

The guests arrived almost simultaneously, all having attended a cocktail party thrown by Vita Keating, wife of the Presto Pudding heir.

They included: Edward Paxton Stoker Jr. and Charles Hillary Lord (the Stoker-Lords), William Devereux Hill III and Anthony Ball Hughes (the Hill-Hugheses), John Morrison Stonecypher (sometimes referred to as The Prune Prince) and Peter Prescott Cipriani.

Conspicuously absent was Richard Evan Hampton, Arch Gidde's ex; the Hampton-Giddes were no more.

"Well," cooed Chuck Lord as he swept into the living room, "I must say I approve of the help."

Arch smiled reservedly. "Somehow I thought you might."

"He's not from Oakland, is he?" asked Ed Stoker, Chuck's Other Half.

"San Bruno," said Arch.

"Pity. Chuckie only likes the ones from Oakland."

Chuck Lord cast a withering glance at his lover, then turned back to his host. "Don't mind *her*," he said. "She's been having hot flashes all week."

Arch did his best not to smirk. Chuck Lord's addiction to Negroes from the East Bay was a matter of common knowledge among the A-Gays in San Francisco. While Ed Stoker stayed home, popping Valiums and reading Diana Vreeland's *Allure*, his multi-millionaire husband was out stalking the streets of Oakland in search of black auto mechanics.

And whenever Ed asked Chuck for a divorce (or so the story went), Chuck would recoil in genuine horror. "But darling," he would gasp, "what about the baby?"

The baby was an eight-unit apartment house in the Haight that the two men owned jointly.

9

"Guess who I saw at the nursery today," said Arch over dessert.

"Who?" asked The Prune Prince.

"Michael Tolliver."

"Who?"

"You know. The twink who used to be Fielding's lover."

"The cripple?"

"Not anymore. Jesus, where have *you* been?"

"Well, pardon me, Liz Smith."

"He practically groped me in the greenhouse."

"Where *is* Fielding, anyway?"

"On a ship or something. Handing out Dramamine. Too awful for words."

Peter Cipriani passed by and dropped a magazine into Arch's lap. "Speaking of too awful for words, have you checked out Madame Giroux this month?" The magazine was *Western Gentry,* and the object of Peter's disdain was one Prue Giroux, the society columnist. Arch turned to the inside back page and began to read aloud to his guests:

" 'This morning, while talking to the charming and delightful black man who parks cars in the garage next to L'Etoile, it occurred to me how truly blessed we are to live in a town that's just chock full of so many interesting races, creeds and colors.' "

Tony Hughes moaned and rolled his eyes. "The stupid twat thinks she's Eleanor Roosevelt now."

Arch continued: " 'As a simple country girl from Grass Valley . . .' "

More groans from everyone.

" 'As a simple country girl from Grass Valley, it gives me such joy and fulfillment to count myself among the friends of such well-known black people as Kathleen Cleaver, wife of the noted militant, and such distinguished Jewish persons as Dr. Heinrich Viertel (author of *Probing the Id*) and Ethel Merman, whom I met when she came through The City plugging her fabulous new disco album.' "

This time there were shrieks. Tony jerked the magazine out

of Arch's hands. "She didn't say that! You made that up!" Arch yielded the floor to Tony, who obviously wanted to continue the reading.

Almost unnoticed, Arch slipped away from the table to deal with a situation which may have reached crisis proportions: Cleavon had not shown up with the coffee. *And Chuck Lord had not returned from the bathroom.*

Purple with rage, Arch listened outside the bathroom door, then flung it open ingloriously.

Cleavon was seated on the black onyx sink, holding one nostril shut while Chuck Lord spaded cocaine into the other. Showing not the slightest trace of remorse, Chuck smirked and returned the paraphernalia to the pocket of his Alexander Julian jacket.

Arch eyed his guest murderously. "Come back to de raft, Huck honey. You are missed."

When Chuck was gone, Cleavon climbed down from the sink and sucked the crystals noisily into his sinuses. His employer was livid but controlled. "We are ready for coffee now, Cleavon."

"Yo," said the servant.

Out in the dining room, Peter Cipriani brayed a drunken riddle to the returning Chuck Lord: "Hey, Chuckie! What's twelve inches and white?"

"What?" came the wary reply.

"Nothing," shrieked Peter. "Absolutely nothing!"

Arch Gidde could have died.

True Prue

PEOPLE SAID THE MEANEST THINGS ABOUT PRUE GI-
roux.

Her willowy good looks, they said, had gotten her
everything she had ever wanted but respect. When
people spoke of her divorce from Reg Giroux, it
was Reg who had always been "the nice one." He had also,
by the strangest coincidence, been the one with the forty
million dollars.

Prue had some of that now, thank God. Plus a Tony Hail
townhouse on Nob Hill. Plus enough Galanos gowns to last
her through all of the Nancy Reagan Administration, even
if—knock on wood—it lasted eight years.

The real secret of her power, however, lay in her column
in *Western Gentry* magazine. It didn't matter, Prue had discovered, if your blood wasn't blue and your wealth was all ali-
mony. So what if you slipped up and pronounced *Thaïs*
"Thayz" or applauded after the first movement or held a
black tie function in midafternoon? If you wrote a social column, the bastards would always let you in.

Not all of them, of course. Some of the old-line San Mateo
types (she had taught herself not to say Hillsborough) still

regarded Prue from a chilly distance. The young lionesses, however, seemed grimly aware that their niches would never be secure without at least nominal recognition by the society press.

So they invited her to lunch.

Not to dinner usually, just to lunch. When, for instance, Ann Getty threw her February soiree for Baryshnikov at Bali's, it wasn't really necessary to include Prue in the proceedings; the guests simply phoned her the juicy particulars the morning after.

Prue didn't mind, really. She'd come a long way, and she knew it. Her penchant for dubbing herself "a simple country girl from Grass Valley" was no affectation. She *was* a simple country girl from Grass Valley—one of seven children raised by a tractor salesman and his Seventh Day Adventist wife.

When she met Reg Giroux, then president of a medium-sized aeronautical engineering firm, Prue was still a fledgling dental hygienist; she was, in fact, flossing his teeth at the time. Reg's friends were horrified when he announced their engagement at the Bohemian Grove summer encampment.

Still, the marriage seemed to work for a while. Prue and Reg built a sprawling vacation home in the Mother Lode country which became the site of many lavish, theme-oriented costume galas. At her Pink-and-Green Ball Prue played hostess to Erica Jong, Tony Orlando and Joan Baez, all in the same afternoon. She could scarcely contain herself.

That, eventually, became the problem. Complacent in his aristocracy, Reg Giroux did not share or comprehend his wife's seemingly insatiable appetite for celebrities. Prue's weekly Nob Hill star luncheon, which she had grandly labeled "The Forum," was so universally scorned by the old-liners that even her husband had begun to feel the sting.

So he had bailed out.

Luckily for Prue, the divorce coincided conveniently with the arrest and conviction (on indecent exposure charges) of *Western Gentry* society columnist Carson Callas. So Prue invited the magazine's editor to lunch and made her pitch. The editor, a country boy himself, mistook Prue's studied elegance for patrician grace and hired her on the spot.

She was her own woman now.

13

*   *   *

Prue's three-year-old Russian wolfhound, Vuitton, had been missing for nearly a week. Prue was frantic. To make matters worse, the man at Park & Rec was being annoyingly vague about the crisis.

"Yes ma'am, I seem to remember that report. Where did you say you lost him again?"

Prue heaved a weary sigh. "In the tree ferns. Across from the conservatory. He was with me one moment, and the next he was . . ."

"Last week?"

"Yes. Saturday."

"One moment, please." She heard him rifling through files. The jerk was whistling "Oh Where Oh Where Has My Little Dog Gone." Several minutes passed before he returned to the phone. "No ma'am. Zilch. I checked twice. Nobody's reported a Russian wolfhound in the last . . ."

"You haven't seen any suspicious Cambodians?"

"Ma'am?"

"Cambodians. Refugees. You know."

"Yes ma'am, but I don't see what . . ."

"Do I have to spell it out? They eat dogs, you know. *They've been eating people's dogs!*"

Silence.

"I read it in the *Chronicle*," Prue added.

Another pause, and then: "Look, ma'am. How 'bout I ask the mounted patrol to keep their eyes open, O.K.? With a dog like that, though, the chances of dognapping are pretty high. I wish I could be more helpful, but I can't."

Prue thanked him and hung up. Poor Vuitton. His fate lay in the hands of incompetents. Somewhere in the Tenderloin the Boat People could be eating sweet-and-sour wolfhound, and Prue was helpless. Helpless.

She took a ten minute walk in Huntington Park to calm her nerves before writing the column. When she returned, her secretary reported that Frannie Halcyon had called to invite Prue to lunch tomorrow "to discuss a matter of utmost urgency."

Frannie Halcyon was the reigning Grande Dame of Hills-borough. She had never even communicated with the likes of Prue Giroux, much less summoned her to the family estate for lunch.

"A matter of utmost urgency."

What on earth could that be?

The Matriarch

SOMETIMES FRANNIE COULDN'T HELP WONDERING whether there was a curse on Halcyon Hill.

It made as much sense as anything when she stopped to consider the horrid consequences that had befallen the members of her family. At sixty-four, she was the sole surviving Halcyon, the last frayed remnant of a dynasty that had all but capitulated to death, disease and destruction.

Edgar, her husband, succumbed to "bum kidneys" (his term) on Christmas Eve, 1976.

Beauchamp, her son-in-law, perished the following year in a fiery crash in the Broadway tunnel.

Faust, her beloved Great Dane, passed away shortly thereafter.

DeDe, her daughter and Beauchamp's estranged wife, gave birth to half-Chinese twins in late 1977 and fled to Guyana with a woman friend of questionable origin.

The Jonestown Massacre. Even now, three years after the event, those words could pounce on Frannie from a page of newsprint, prickly and poisonous as the fangs of a viper.

Edgar, Beauchamp, Faust and DeDe. Horror upon horror. Indignity upon indignity.

And now, the ultimate humiliation.

She had finally been forced to invite Prue Giroux to lunch.

Emma appeared on the sunporch with a tray of Mai Tais.

"A little refreshment?" asked Frannie.

The columnist flashed her syrupy little-girl smile. "It's a teensy bit early for me, thanks."

Frannie wanted to kick her. Instead, she accepted a drink from Emma with a gracious nod, sipped it daintily, and smiled right back at this hopelessly common woman. "By the way," she said, "I find your column . . . most amusing."

Prue beamed. "I'm so glad, Frannie. I do my best to keep it light."

"Yes. It's very light." Inside, Frannie was raging. How dare this creature address her by her first name?

"As far as I'm concerned," Prue continued, obviously developing a familiar theme, "there is far too much ugliness in this world, and if each of us lit just one little candle . . . well, you know."

Frannie saw the opening she needed. "I suppose you know about my daughter."

"Yes." The columnist's face became a mask of tragedy. "It must have been awful for you."

"It was. It is."

"I can't even imagine what it must have been like."

"Most people can't." Frannie took another sip of her Mai Tai. "Except maybe Catherine Hearst. She comes to visit sometimes. She's been terribly sweet. Uh . . . do you mind if I show you something?"

"Of course not."

The matriarch excused herself, returning moments later with the evidence, now tattered almost beyond recognition. "These used to be DeDe's," she said.

The columnist smiled. "Pompons. I was a cheerleader, too."

"DeDe sent for them," Frannie continued, "when she was in Jonestown. She used them when she was at Sacred Heart, and she thought it would be cute if she had them in Guyana for the basketball games." She fidgeted with her cocktail napkin. "They found them with her things . . . afterwards."

"She . . . uh . . . led cheers in Guyana?"

The matriarch nodded. "Just as a lark. They had a basketball team, you know."

"No," said Prue carefully. "Actually, I didn't."

"DeDe was a *doer*, Prue. She loved life more than anything. I have verified for certain that she and the children weren't among the dead in Jonestown . . . and in my heart, my most basic instincts tell me that they made it out of there alive."

"When?"

"I don't know. Earlier. Whenever."

"But didn't the authorities presume . . . ?"

"They presumed a lot of things, the fools! They told me she was dead, before they even checked to see if her body was there." Frannie leaned forward and looked at Prue imploringly. "I know you've probably heard all this before. I called you here, because I need you to help me publicize a new development."

"Please," said the columnist, "go ahead."

"I spoke to a psychic this week. A very reliable one. She says that DeDe and her friend and the twins are alive and living in a small village in South America."

Silence.

"I'm not a hysterical woman, Prue. I don't normally subscribe to that sort of thing. It's just that this woman was so *sure*. She saw everything: the hut, the mats they sleep on, the villagers in the marketplace, those precious little twins running naked in the . . ." Frannie's voice broke; she felt herself coming apart. "Please help me," she pleaded. "I don't know who else to turn to."

Prue reached over and squeezed her hand. "You know I would, Frannie, if there was any way to . . . well, surely the newspapers or the TV stations would be better equipped to handle this sort of thing."

The matriarch stiffened. "I've talked to them already. You don't think I would call you *first*?"

*　　*　　*

What was the use? This ridiculous woman was like all the rest, humoring her as if she were some sort of senile old biddy. Frannie dropped the matter altogether, hastening her guest through lunch and out of her house without further ado.

By three o'clock, she was back in bed, drinking Mai Tais and watching the little "belly telly" that DeDe and Beauchamp had given her after Edgar's death. The afternoon movie was *Summertime* with Katharine Hepburn, one of Frannie's favorites.

During the "intermission," a pretty young woman offered shopping tips to viewers: where to find good factory seconds in the Walnut Creek-Lafayette area. Frannie turned off the sound and poured another Mai Tai.

When her gaze returned to the television, she nearly dropped her drink.

That face! Of course! It was Edgar's old secretary. Frannie hadn't laid eyes on her for at least four years. Since Beauchamp's funeral, probably.

What *was* her name, anyway? Mary Jane something. No . . . Mary Lou?

The matriarch turned the sound up again. "This is Mary Ann Singleton," chirped the young woman, "wishing you bargains galore!"

Mary Ann Singleton.

Maybe, thought Frannie. Just maybe . . .

A Daytime Face

FTER ALMOST TWO YEARS OF BEING A WOMAN IN
television, Mary Ann Singleton was finally a
woman *on* television.

Her show, *Bargain Matinee,* attempted to up-
date the old *Dialing for Dollars* afternoon movie
format by offering inflation-fighting consumer tips to Bay
Area viewers. This was, after all, The Eighties.

The movies, on the other hand, were firmly grounded in
The Fifties: comfy old chestnuts like *Splendor in the Grass* and
The Secret of Santa Vittoria and today's feature, *Summertime.*
Movies that used to be called women's movies in the days
before ERA.

Mary Ann's shining hour was a five minute spot interrupt-
ing the movie at midpoint.

The formula was fairly consistent: dented cans, factory seconds, Chinese umbrellas that made nifty lampshades, per-
fume you could brew at home, places you could shop for
pasta, new uses for old coffee cans. Stuff that Michael persisted in calling "Hints from Heloise."

Mary Ann was faintly embarrassed by the homebody image
this format compelled her to project, but she couldn't deny

the delicious exhilaration of the stardom it brought her. Strangers stared at her on the Muni; neighbors asked her to autograph their grocery bags at the Searchlight Market.

Still, something was wrong, something that hadn't been cured by becoming a Woman on Television.

A real Woman on Television, Mary Ann felt, was a glamorous hellraiser, a feminine feminist like Jane Fonda in *The China Syndrome* or Sigourney Weaver in *Eyewitness*. A real Woman on Television was invariably an investigative reporter.

And Mary Ann would settle for nothing less.

Immediately after the sign-off she left Studio B and hurried back to her cubbyhole without stopping in the dressing room to remove her makeup.

It was five o'clock. She could still catch the news director before he mobilized for the evening newscast.

There was a note on her desk: MRS. HARRISON CALLED.

"Did you take this?" she asked an associate producer at the next desk.

"Denny did. He's in the snack bar."

Denny, another associate producer, was eating a microwaved patty melt. "Who's Mrs. Harrison?" asked Mary Ann.

"She said you knew her."

"Harrison?"

"That's what it sounded like. She was shitfaced."

"Great."

"She called right after your show-and-tell. Said it was 'mosht urgent.' "

"It's *Summertime* is what it is. The drunks always call during the tearjerkers. No number, huh?"

Denny shrugged. "She said you knew her."

Larry Kenan, the news director, lounged back in his swivel chair, locked his fingers behind his blow-dried head, and smirked wearily at the Bo Derek poster he had pasted on the ceiling above his desk. Its inscription, also his doing, was burned indelibly on Mary Ann's consciousness: FOR LARRY WITH LUST—NOBODY DOES IT BETTER. BO.

"You wanna know the honest-to-God truth?" he said.

Mary Ann waited. He was always disguising his goddamned opinion as the honest-to-God truth.

"The honest-to-God truth is you're a daytime face and the public doesn't wanna see a daytime face on the six o'clock news. Period, end of sentence. I mean, *hey,* what can I say, lady? It ain't pretty, but it's the honest-to-God truth." He tore his gaze from Bo Derek long enough to flash her his "that's the breaks, kid" grin.

"What about Bambi Kanetaka?"

"What about her?"

Mary Ann knew she had to tread softly here. "Well . . . she had a daytime show, and you let *her* do the . . ."

"Bambi's different," glared Larry.

I know, thought Mary Ann. She gives head on command.

"Her GSR's were dynamite," added Larry, almost daring Mary Ann to continue.

"Then test *me,* " said Mary Ann. "I don't mind being . . ."

"We *have* tested you, O.K.? We tested you two months ago and your GSR's sucked. All right?"

It stung more than she wanted it to. She had never really *believed* in Galvanic Skin Response. What could you prove for certain, anyway, by attaching electrodes to a guinea pig audience? Just that some performers made some viewers sweat more than others. Big fucking deal.

She tried another tack. "But I wouldn't have to be on camera all the time. I could research things, investigate. There are lots of subjects that the regular reporters don't have the time or the inclination to cover."

Larry's lip curled. "Like what?"

"Well, like . . ." Think, she commanded herself, think! "Well, the gay community, for instance."

"Oh really?" he said, arching an eyebrow. "You know all about that, huh?"

Mary Ann puzzled at his inflection. Did he think she was a lesbian? Or was he just toying with her again? "I have lots of . . . contacts there," she said. A lie. but what-the-hell. Michael had lots of contacts there; it was practically the same thing.

He smiled at her as a policeman would smile at a runaway child.

"I'll tell you the honest-to-God truth," he said. "The public is sick of hearing about faggots."

The Man in Her Life

IF LARRY KENAN WAS AN ASSHOLE—FOR THERE WAS NO LON-
ger any doubt about that—Mary Ann's paycheck at least
provided certain amenities that made life in the city
considerably more graceful:
   She ate at Ciao now.
She drove a Le Car.

She wore velvet blazers and button-down shirts over her
Calvins—a look which Michael persisted in labeling as "Ivy
Lesbian."

She had stripped her apartment of all furnishings that were
either yellow or wicker and installed gun-metal gray industrial carpeting and high-tech steel factory shelving.

She had canceled her subscription to *San Francisco* magazine and started reading *Interview*.

She had abandoned Cost Plus forever.

Still, she couldn't help but feel a certain frustration over the
progress of her career.

That frustration was only heightened later that night when

she watched a particularly compelling episode of *Lou Grant,* one featuring a scrappy woman journalist in her struggle to uncover the truth.

It was almost too painful to endure, so Mary Ann turned off the set and marched into the bathroom to Sassoon her hair. Sometimes a shower was the best of all possible sedatives.

Her hair was shorter now than it had been in years. Waifish and sort of Leslie Caron-like with just the vaguest hint of New Wave. Anything more pronounced would have been pressing her luck with the management of the station.

As she towel-dried her new do into place, she found it extraordinary that she had ever endured the rigors of long hair in the first place. ("You kept trying for a French twist," Michael was fond of recalling, "but it kept going Connie Stevens on you.")

After searching in vain for her rabbit slippers, Mary Ann knotted herself into an oversized white terrycloth robe and climbed the stairs to the little house on the roof of 28 Barbary Lane.

She paused for a moment outside the familiar orange door, peering out through an ivy-choked window at a night full of stars. An ocean liner slid past aglitter with lights, like a huge chandelier being dragged out to sea.

Mary Ann heard herself sigh. Partly for the view. Partly for the man who waited inside.

She entered without knocking, knowing he was already asleep. He had worked a double shift that day, and the crowd at Perry's had been more boisterous and demanding than usual. As she expected, he was sprawled face down on the bed in his boxer shorts.

She sat on the edge of the bed and laid her hand gently on the small of his back.

The most beautiful part of a man, she thought. That warm little valley just before the butt begins. Well, maybe the *second* most beautiful.

Brian stirred, then rolled over and rubbed his eyes with his fists the way that little boys do. "Hey," he said throatily.

"Hey," she replied.

She leaned over and lay against his chest, enjoying the heat of his body. When her mouth sought his, Brian turned his head away and mumbled a warning: "Moose breath, sweetheart."

She took his chin in her hand and kissed him anyway. "So?" she said. "What if the moose is cute?"

Chuckling, he wrapped his arms around her. "So how was your day?"

"Shitty," she said, speaking directly into his ear.

"You spoke to Larry Kenan?"

"Uh-huh."

"And?"

"He still wants nookie before he'll negotiate."

Brian jerked away from her. "He *said* that?"

"No." Mary Ann smiled at his alarm. "Not in so many words. I just know how he operates. Bambi Kanetaka is living proof of *that.*"

Brian pretended not to understand. "I find her most incisive myself."

Mary Ann goosed him.

"Incisive and perky. A winning combination."

"I'll do it again," warned Mary Ann.

"I was hoping you'd say that," grinned Brian. "Only slower this time, O.K.?"

Remembering Lennon

THE BEAUTY OF BEING A WAITER, BRIAN USED TO THINK, was that you could dump the whole damn thing tomorrow.

There were no pension plans to haunt you, no digital watches after fifty years of service, no soul-robbing demands for corporate loyalty and long-term commitment. It was a living, in short, but never, ever a career.

He used to think.

Now, after six years of working at Perry's, he'd begun to wonder about that. If it wasn't a career now, when would it be? After ten years? Fifteen? Is that what he wanted? Is that what *she* wanted?

He rolled away from her and stared at the ceiling in silence.

"O.K.," said Mary Ann. "Out with it."

"Again?"

She laughed at his joke, then snuggled up against his shoulder. "I know pensive when I see it. So what are you pensing about?"

"Oh . . . the bar, I guess. I think it may be time for that."

"I thought you hated tending bar."

He winced. "The *state* bar, Mary Ann. As in lawyer?"

"Oh." She glanced over at him. "I thought you hated that, too."

There was no quick answer for that one. He *had* hated it, in fact, hated every boring, nerve-grinding minute he had ever been Brian Hawkins, Attorney-at-Law. He had sublimated his hatred in the pursuit of causes—blacks, Native Americans, oil slicks—but the "old ennui," as he had come to call it, proved as persistent and deep-rooted as the law itself.

He still cringed at the thought of the singing fluorescent bulb that had tormented him for hours on end in the grass-cloth-and-walnut conference room of his last law firm. That fixture came to symbolize all that was petty and poisonous about life—if you could call it that—in the Financial District.

So he had fled his profession and become a waiter.

He had also become a rogue, terrorizing singles bars and laundromats in a frenzied and relentless search for "foxes." He had simplified his life, streamlined his body and subjugated the "old ennui."

But now something different was happening. The woman he had once described as "that uptight airhead from Cleveland" was easily the love of his life.

And she was the one with the career.

"I have to do *something*," he told Mary Ann.

"About what?"

"Work," said Brian. "My job."

"You mean your tips aren't . . . ?"

"It isn't the money." His voice had an edge to it. His flagging pride was making him cranky. *Don't take it out on her,* he warned himself. "I just can't go on like this," he added in a gentler tone.

"Like what?" she asked cautiously.

"Like your dependent or something. I can't hack it, Mary Ann."

She studied him soberly. "It *is* the money, then."

"It's one thing to go dutch. It's another to be . . . I don't know . . . kept or something." His face was aflame with self-contempt and embarrassment.

Mary Ann laughed openly. *"Kept?* Gimme a break, Brian! I paid for a weekend shack-up in Sierra City. I *wanted* to do

that, you turkey. It was as much for me as it was . . . oh, Brian."
She reached over and took his hand. "I thought we'd gotten
over all that macho stuff."

He aped her mincingly. "I thought we'd gotten over all that
macho stuff." It was so petty and cruel that he was instantly
sorry. Examining her face for signs of hurt, he made the
maddening discovery that she had already forgiven him.

"What about John?" she asked.

"John who?"

"Lennon. I thought you admired him for becoming a
househusband when Yoko . . ."

Brian snorted. "It was John's money, for Christ's sake! You
can do anything you goddamn want when you're the richest
man in New York!"

Mary Ann stared at him incredulously. Now she really was
wounded. "How could you do that?" she asked quietly. "How
could you cheapen the thing that we shared?"

She was talking about the Memorial Vigil on the Marina
Green. She and Brian had spent six hours there mourning
Lennon's death. They had cried themselves dry, clutching
strawberry-scented candles, singing "Hey Jude" and smoking
a new crop of Hawaiian grass that Mrs. Madrigal had named
in honor of the deceased.

Brian had never before—and never since—made himself so
vulnerable in Mary Ann's presence.

Afterwards, he had tacked this note to her door: HELP ME,
IF YOU CAN, I'M FEELING DOWN, AND I DO APPRECIATE YOUR
BEING 'ROUND. I LOVE YOU—BRIAN.

He was feeling down all right, but it had more to do with
mid-life crisis than with the passing of a Beatle.

For, on the day that John Lennon died, everyone in Brian
Hawkins' generation instantly and irrevocably turned forty.

"I'm sorry," he said at last.

"It doesn't matter," she said, leaning over to kiss his shoulder.

"I'm just . . . edgy right now."

"I could sleep at my place tonight, if you need the . . ."

"No. Stay. Please."

She answered with another peck on the shoulder. "Do me a favor," she said.

"What?"

"Don't become a lawyer on my account. I'm a big girl now. I don't need any dragons slain on my behalf."

He looked into her radiant face. Sometimes she understood him better than anyone. "Right," he murmured. "I'll get by with a little help from my friends."

And sometimes she made him say the corniest things.

Cowpokes

CROSS TOWN ON VALENCIA STREET, MICHAEL AND
Ned were sharing a Calistoga at Devil's Herd,
the city's most popular gay country-western bar.
What Michael liked most about the saloon was
its authenticity: the twangy down-home band
(Western Electric), the horse collars dangling from the ceiling, the folksy Annie Oakley dykes shouting "yahoo" from
the bar.

If he squinted his eyes just so, the dudes doing cowboy
dancing could be grizzled buckeroos, horny claim-jumpers
who were simply making do until the next shipment of saloon
girls came in from the East.

True, the beefcake cowboy murals struck a somewhat citi-
fied note in the overall scheme of things, but Michael didn't
mind. Someday, he believed, the homoerotic cave drawings
in San Francisco's gay bars would be afforded the same sort
of reverence that is currently heaped upon WPA murals and
deco apartment house lobbies.

"Oh look!" a sophisticated but hunky workman would cry,
peeling back a piece of rotting wallboard. "There seems to be

a painting back here! My God, it's from the school of Tom of Finland!"

The band was playing "Stand By Your Man." As soon as they recognized the tune, Michael and Ned smiled in unison. "Jon was big on that one," said Michael. "Just as a song, though. Not as a way of life."

Ned took a swig of the Calistoga. "I thought it was you that left him."

"Well, *technically,* maybe. We left each other, actually. It was a big relief to both of us. We were damn lucky, really. Sometimes it's not that easy to pull out of an S & M relationship."

"Wait a minute. Since when were you guys . . . ?"

"S & M," Michael repeated. "Streisand and Midler. He was into Streisand. I was into Midler. It was pure, unadulterated hell."

Ned laughed. "I guess I bit on that one."

"I'm serious," said Michael. "We fought about it all the time. One Sunday afternoon when Jon was listening to "Evergreen" for about the three millionth time, I suddenly found myself asking him what exactly he saw in . . . I believe I referred to her as 'that tone-deaf, big-nosed bitch.' "

"Jesus. What did he say?"

"He was quite adult about it, actually. He pointed out calmly that Bette's nose is bigger than Barbra's. I almost brained him with his goddamned Baccarat paperweight."

This time Ned guffawed, a sound that told Michael he had struck paydirt. Ned was the only person he knew who actually guffawed. "It's the truth," grinned Michael. "Every single word of it."

"Yeah," said Ned, "but people don't really break up over stuff like that."

"Well . . ." Michael thought for a moment. "I guess we just made each other do things we didn't want to do. He made me alphabetize the classical albums by composer. I made him eat crunchy peanut butter instead of plain. He made me sleep in a room with eggplant walls. I made him eat off Fiesta Ware.

We didn't agree on much of anything, come to think of it, except Al Parker and Rocky Road ice cream."

"You ever mess around?"

"You betcha. None o' that nasty heterosexual role-playing for *us*. Lots of buddy nights at the baths. I can't even count the number of times I rolled over in bed and told some hot stranger: 'You'd like my lover.' "

"What about rematches?"

"Once," said Michael grimly, "but never again. Jon sulked for a week. I saw his point, actually: once is recreation; twice is courtship. You learn these nifty little nuances when you're married. That's why I'm not married anymore."

"But you could be, huh?"

Michael shook his head. "Not now. Not for a while. I don't know . . . maybe never. It's a knack, isn't it? Some of us just don't have the knack."

"You gotta want it bad," said Ned.

"Then, maybe I don't want it bad enough. That's a possibility. That's a distinct possibility." Michael took a sip of the mineral water, then drummed his fingers on the bar in time to the music. The band had stopped playing now; someone at the jukebox had paid Hank Williams Jr. to sing "Women I Never Had."

Michael handed the Calistoga back to Ned. "Remember Mona?" he asked.

Ned nodded. "Your old roommate."

"Yeah. Well, Mona used to say that she could get by just fine without a lover as long as she had five good friends. That about sums it up for me right now."

"I hope I'm one of 'em," said Ned.

Michael's brow wrinkled while he counted hastily on his fingers. "Jesus," he said at last. "I think you're three of them."

House of Wax

PRUE GIROUX AND VICTORIA LYNCH WERE KINDRED spirits.

For one thing, they were both handsome women. For another, Victoria was engaged to the ex-husband of the woman who was engaged to Prue's ex-husband. Bonds like that were not easily broken.

Today, Victoria had called to share a secret with her spiritual sister.

"Now listen, Prudy Sue, this is cross-your-heart stuff, definitely not for publication, understand?" (Prue's closest friends always addressed her by her childhood name.)

"Of course," said Prue.

"I mean, eventually of course I would adore for you to give it a little publicity in your column, which is part of the reason I called, but right now it's just in the embryonic stage, and we don't want to kill the baby, do we?"

"Of course not," said Prue.

"Well," announced Victoria, sucking in breath as if she were about to blow a trumpet fanfare, "yours truly is in the process of organizing the world's first society wax museum!"

34

"The . . . come again?"

"Now, shut up a sec, Prudy Sue, and hear me out. I met this absolutely divine little man at the Keatings' house in Santa Barbara, and it seems he's fallen on rather hard times lately, which is too tragic, because it turns out he's descended from the Hapsburgs or something. I mean, he's got the prominent lower lip and everything. Anyway, Vita told me he used to work at Madame Tussaud's, where he was their principal designer . . ."

"Ah, yes. I have one of his gowns."

A pause, and then: "You do *not* have one of his gowns, Prudy Sue."

"But that mauve cocktail dress I wore to . . ."

"That's a Madame *Gres,* Prudy Sue. You do not own a Madame Tussaud. Madame Tussaud's is a wax museum in London."

"I knew that," sulked Prue. "I thought you said . . ."

"Of course you did, darling. Those French names all sound alike, don't they? Now . . . where was I?"

"He used to work at Madame Tufo's."

"Uh . . . right. He worked . . . there, and he's terribly aristocratic and all, and he thinks that it's just a damn shame there's never been a wax museum for society figures. Think about that, Prudy Sue! We have wax museums for historical people and show business people and sports people, but nary a thing for the movers and shakers of society. It's shocking really, when you stop and think about it."

"That's a good point," said Prue. "I never really . . ."

"And if *we* don't take the initiative on this, who will? I mean, that's what this little man said to me, and I was absolutely *floored* by his insight. Our children can see for themselves how short Napoleon really was, for instance, but where can they go to look at a replica of, say, Nan Kempner. Or Sao Schlumberger. Or Marie Hélène de Rothschild. These people are *legends,* Prudy Sue, but they'll be lost to posterity forever, if we don't take decisive action now. At least, that's what Wolfgang says, and I think he's dead right."

"Wolfgang?"

"The little man. He's such a dear, really. The wax figures

usually run about fifteen thousand apiece, but he's offered to do them for ten as a sort of a public service. He wants me to scout locations for the museum, which is a damn good thing, since he was leaning towards Santa Barbara when I talked to him, but I think I convinced him to move it here. That way, see, we can have a San Francisco wing as well as an international wing."

"I see."

"I thought you might, darling." Victoria giggled conspiratorially. "God, isn't it fabulous? We'll get to donate our old gowns and everything. Plus Wolfgang can make marvelous paste imitations of your emeralds, and . . . well, I'm just positive we can raise the money in no time."

"Have you talked to Denise yet?"

Victoria chuckled. "I'm way ahead of you, Prudy Sue. I think she's good for fifty thousand, *if* we put her in the international wing. Ditto Ann Getty. That one may be a little tougher to pull off unless we stack the board of directors, but what-the-hell, we'll stack the board of directors."

Prue finally managed a laugh. "You haven't told Shugie Sussman, have you?"

"God no! We hadn't planned on a Chamber of Horrors, darling! On second thought, let's do—have you seen Kitty Cipriani's latest facelift?"

Prue laughed even louder this time. Then she said: "Oh Vicky, thank you! I've needed to laugh more than anything. I've been so depressed over Vuitton."

"Over . . . ? Oh, your dog."

"It's been almost two weeks now. The Park & Rec people haven't seen him anywhere. I don't know what to do except . . ." Prue's voice trailed off as the melancholy swept over her again.

"Except what, Prudy Sue."

"Well . . . I thought I might go back to the park and . . . wait for him."

"That's an awfully long shot, isn't it. I mean, *two weeks,* Prudy Sue. It's not very likely that he's still . . . ."

"I *know* he's there, Vicky. I can feel it in my bones. I know he'll come back to me, if I give him the chance."

Even as she spoke, Prue knew how she sounded. She

sounded like poor old Frannie Halcyon, still believing against preposterous odds that her long-lost daughter would return from the jungles of Guyana.

But stranger things had happened.

No Big Deal

ON HIS WAY HOME FROM PERRY'S, BRIAN STOPPED AT a garage sale on Union Street and bought an antique Peter, Paul & Mary album for a quarter. Also available: two Shelley Berman albums, an early Limelighters album featuring Glenn Yarborough, and the soundtracks of *Breakfast at Tiffany's*, *Mondo Cane*, and *To Kill a Mockingbird*.

Somebody's youth, in other words.

There was nothing like a stack of dog-eared record albums to remind you that the past was just so much dead weight, excess baggage to be cast overboard when the sailing got tougher. Or so Brian told himself.

Nevertheless, he lit a joint upon returning to Barbary Lane and crooned along euphorically while PP&M sang "If I Had a Hammer," "Five Hundred Miles" and "Puff the Magic Dragon."

Had it really been eighteen years—Christ, half his life!—since Nelson Schwab had cornered him during Hell Week at the Deke House to impart the privileged information that "Puff" was really an underground parable about—no shit!—smoking marijuana?

Yep, it really had.

He fell into a black funk, then snatched the record off the turntable and shattered it with the hammer he kept in the tool box under the kitchen sink. Inexcusable symbolism, but somehow richly satisfying.

So much for the iron grip of the past.

Now, what about the present?

The *Chronicle* "help wanted" ads were so dismal that Brian postponed any immediate career decisions and trekked downstairs to help Mrs. Madrigal plan Mary Ann's birthday party. He found the landlady installing a Roach Motel in a dark corner of her pantry.

Looking up, she smiled defeatedly. "I told myself I would never buy one of these dreadful things. Those TV commercials seem so sadistic. Still, we can't love absolutely all of God's creatures, can we? They haven't found their way up to your place, I hope?"

Brian shook his head. "The altitude's too much for 'em."

Mrs. Madrigal stood up, wiping her hands against each other as if they were sticky with blood. She cast a final glance at the grisly Motel, shuddered, and took Brian's arm. "Let's go sit in the sunshine, dear. I feel like Anthony Perkins waiting for Janet Leigh to check in."

Out in the courtyard, she ticked off a list of prospective delights for Mary Ann's upcoming celebration: "A nice roast of some sort with those baby carrots that she likes . . . and some ice cream from Gelato, of course, to go with the birthday cake. And . . . well, I guess it's about time for Barbara Stanwyck, isn't it?"

"A movie?" asked Brian.

Mrs. Madrigal clucked her tongue at him. "Miss Stanwyck, my dear boy, is my heartiest specimen yet." She pointed to the edge of the courtyard where a sensemilla plant as big as a Christmas tree was undulating softly in the warm spring breeze.

Brian whistled in appreciation. "That stuff knocks your socks off."

The landlady smiled modestly. "I didn't name her Barbara Stanwyck for nothing."

They previewed Miss Stanwyck. Then they wandered down the hill to Washington Square and sat on a bench in the sunshine, docile and groggy as a couple of aging house cats.

After a long silence, Brian said: "Does she ever talk to you about me?"

"Who? Mrs. Onassis?"

Brian smiled languidly. "You know."

"Well . . ." Mrs. Madrigal chewed her lower lip. "Only about your extraordinary sexual prowess, that sort of thing . . . nothing really personal."

Brian laughed. "That's a relief."

The landlady's Wedgwood saucer eyes fixed on him lovingly. "She cares about you a great deal, young man."

Brian tore up a tuft of grass and began to shred it. "She told you that, huh?"

"Well . . . not in so many words . . ."

"It only takes three." His voice was tinged with doubt, more than he wanted to show. "I don't know," he added hastily, "maybe it's just her work or something. She's so obsessed with becoming a reporter that nothing else seems to matter. I don't know. Screw it. It's no big deal."

Mrs. Madrigal smiled wistfully and brushed the hair off his forehead. "But it is, isn't it? It's an awfully big deal."

"It wasn't before," said Brian.

The landlady's eyes widened. "Oh, I know how that can be."

"I want this to work out, Mrs. Madrigal. I never wanted anything so bad."

"Then you shall have it," said the landlady. "My children always get what they want." She gave Brian's knee a friendly shake.

"But *she's* one of your children," said Brian. "What if it's not what *she* wants?"

"I expect it will be," said Mrs. Madrigal, "but you must be patient with her. She's just now learning how to fly."

40

Ah, Wilderness

AT LEAST TWICE A YEAR THE SAN FRANCISCO GAY
Men's Chorus made a point of retreating to the
wilds of Northern California for a weekend of
intensive rehearsals and camping-around-the-
campfire camaraderie.

The "wilds" were always the same: Camp Eisenblatt, a
summer camp for Jewish teenagers which leased its sylvan
facilities to the one-hundred-fifty-member homosexual choir
during the off-seasons. And *this* season was about as off as it
could get.

"What a pisser!" groaned Michael as he stared out at the
driving rain. "I was gonna start on my tan line this weekend."

Ned laughed and clipped an olive drab jockstrap to the
clothesline strung across one end of the baritones' bunkhouse. "Cowboys don't have tan lines," he said.

Since the theme of this year's retreat was "Spring
Roundup," the western motif was in evidence everywhere.
Even their name tags were affixed with swatches of cowboy
bandannas: red for the first tenors, tan for the second tenors,
dark blue for the baritones, dark brown for the basses and
royal blue for the nonmusical "chorus widows" who had

come along to make sure that their lovers didn't have too much fun in the redwoods.

"Just the same," said Michael. "I liked it better last fall when we had the luau and the eighty-degree weather."

"And the sarongs," added Ned. "I thought we'd never get you out of that damn thing."

Michael inspected his fingernails blithely. "As I recall, there was a first tenor who succeeded."

"Well, shift fantasies," suggested Ned. "Pretend you're in a real bunkhouse. You've just come in from a long, hot cattle drive and the rain is cooling off the livestock."

"Right. And my ol' sidekick Lonesome Ned is about to dry his jockstrap with a blowdryer. Listen, pardner, I don't know how to break this to you gently, but *real* bunkhouses don't have REBECCA IS A FAT SLOB written in pink nailpolish on the bathroom wall."

Ned smiled lazily. "Jehovah moves in mysterious ways."

After a long morning of wrestling with Liszt's Requiem and Brahms' Alto Rhapsody, the chorus converged on the Camp Eisenblatt dining hall for a lunch of bologna sandwiches and Kool-Aid.

Later, Michael and Ned and a dozen of their compatriots gossiped jovially around the fireplace. There were so many different plaids in the great room that it looked like a gathering of the clans.

"Hey," said Ned, as he warmed his butt in front of the gas-jet embers. "I almost forgot. I got a call from _____ this week."

"No kidding," said Michael, his voice ringing with unabashed fandom. It was almost inconceivable that someone he knew got personal phone calls from movie stars. Even if Ned *had* been this movie star's lover.

"He's royally bummed out," said Ned. "They canceled the musical he was gonna tour with this summer."

"He sings?"

Ned shrugged. "When you look like that, no one notices."

"Tell him to come with us," offered Michael, meaning the

chorus's own nine city summer tour. "God, wouldn't that knock 'em dead in Nebraska?"

"I think he'll survive," said Ned. "He still gets two million a picture."

Michael whistled. "Where does he spend it?"

"On his friends mostly. And the house. Wanna see it?"

"Uh . . . pardon me?"

"He invited me down for a weekend. Said to bring a friend. How about it?"

Michael almost yelped. *"Me?* Are you serious? Lordy mercy, man! Me at _____ _____'s house? Is this for real?"

Ned nodded, beaming like a father who had just offered his eight-year-old a shot at Disneyland.

They rode back to the city in Ned's pickup, carrying six buddies and their bedrolls as cargo.

The illusion presented was almost redneck—except for the telltale chartreuse crinolines from last night's Andrews Sisters sketch. And, of course, the three identical auburn wigs on styrofoam stands.

At a stop sign near the K-Mart in Saratoga, Ned pulled alongside a bronze Barracuda that was draped in pink toilet paper and spray-painted with this legend: JUST MARRIED—SHE GOT HIM TODAY—HE'LL GET HER TONIGHT.

A whoop went up from the back of the truck.

The bridegroom, resplendent in a powder blue tuxedo with matching ruffled shirt, cast a nervous glance in their direction, frowned and turned back to his bride. Michael saw the word "fags" form on his lips.

Rolling the window down, he shouted across at the couple: "Hey!" They were moving again now, but Ned kept the truck even with the car.

"Yeah?" said the bridegroom.

"Congratulations!" yelled Michael.

"Thanks!" shouted the bride, still holding tight to her husband's free arm.

"What's your song?"

"Huh?"

"Your *song.* What is it?"

The bride beamed. " 'We've Only Just Begun.' "

Michael hollered to the guys in the back of the truck. "HIT IT, GIRLS!"

The Andrews Sisters were never lovelier.

Idol Chatter

ICHAEL WAITED UNTIL THE FAMILY WAS ASSEM-
bled for Mary Ann's birthday dinner before
breaking the news.

Mary Ann was the most flabbergasted.

"Now wait just a minute!"

Michael held up his hand. "Scout's honor, Babycakes. Ned invited me yesterday."

"I'm not questioning that," said Mary Ann, "but, you mean _____ _____ is *gay?*"

"As the proverbial goose," said Michael.

"Hell," said Brian, sawing off a chunk of pot roast. "Even I knew that. Remember that story about his gay wedding to _____ _____ back about . . . ?"

"Well, of course I *heard* that, but . . ." Mary Ann was almost sputtering; she hated it when her Cleveland naiveté popped up like an overnight zit. "Well, I always thought it was just some sort of . . . bad joke."

"It *was* a bad joke," said Michael. "A couple of tired queens in Hermosa Beach or some place sent out party invitations announcing a mock wedding and . . . the rumor just got started. _____ and _____ were never even lovers. Just

45

friends. They couldn't be seen in public together after that. It would only confirm the rumor."

"Do you always refer to him by his first name?" teased Mary Ann.

Michael grinned. "Just practicing."

Mrs. Madrigal heaped more carrots onto Michael's plate. "That's a rather sad story, isn't it?"

Michael nodded. "It must've been a bitch, staying closeted all these years."

"Yeah," said Brian, his mouth full of pot roast, "but two mil a movie must soften the blow."

Mary Ann giggled. "So to speak."

Michael's eyes widened in pseudo-horror. "Well, look who's getting smutty in her senior years." Mary Ann stuck her tongue out daintily.

Mrs. Madrigal stirred her coffee as she stared off into space. "_____ _____," she murmured, intoning the matinee idol's name as if it were one of Mona's mantras. "Well, it makes perfect sense. He's always been a stunning creature. Remember when he took off his shirt in _____?" The landlady heaved a prolonged sigh. "I was quite taken with him when I was a young . . . whatever."

Mrs. Madrigal's tenants laughed at this playful reference to her veiled past. Then Michael lifted his glass: "Well, here's to our birthday girl . . . who's about to become an *old* whatever like the rest of us."

Mary Ann leaned over and kissed him on the cheek. "Prick," she whispered.

Then she turned to her other side and kissed Brian lightly on the mouth.

Michael completed the circle by blowing a kiss to Brian.

Smiling contentedly, Mrs. Madrigal watched the ritual like a doting matchmaker, hands clasped under her chin. "You know," she said. "You three are my favorite couple."

After dinner, the landlady produced a Wedgwood plate of Barbara Stanwyck joints. Then came cake and ice cream and Mary Ann's presents: a bottle of "Opium" from Brian, a cat-shaped deco pin from Michael, an antique teapot from Mrs. Madrigal.

"And now," announced the landlady, "if you gentlemen will kindly excuse us, I would like to do a Tarot reading for Mary Ann."

Mary Ann's eyes danced. "I didn't know you knew how to do that!"

"I don't," replied Mrs. Madrigal, "but I make up *wonderful* things."

So Brian and Michael retired to the roof, where they watched the bay through the eyes of Miss Stanwyck.

"You know what?" said Brian.

"What?" said Michael.

"She's right. Mrs. Madrigal, I mean. The three of us do so much stuff together that we're kinda like a couple."

"Yeah. I guess so. That bother you?"

Brian thought for a moment. "Nah. You're my friend, Michael. And she's your friend, and . . . hell, I don't know."

Michael handed the joint back to Brian. "Lots of people do things in threes here. Check out the audience the next time we go to a play."

Brian laughed. "Trisexuals. Isn't that what you called them?"

"For want of a better term."

Brian laid his arm across Michael's shoulder. "You know what's bugging me, Michael?"

Michael waited.

"It just bugs the hell out of me that I'll never be everything she needs."

Michael smiled feebly. "I know that one."

"Yeah?"

"You betcha. I busted my butt trying to be everything to one person. Finally, I had to settle for being one thing to every person."

"What's the one thing?"

Michael hesitated. "Hell, I was hoping you could tell me."

Brian laughed and squeezed his shoulder. "You're crazy, man."

"Maybe *that's* it."

"I tell you what," said Brian, looking directly at his friend.

"I love you, Michael. I love you like my brother."

"No shit?"

"No shit."

There was a moment, a very brief moment, when their eyes met with unembarrassed affection. Then Michael retrieved the joint and took a hit. "Is your brother cute?" he asked.

Father Paddy

HAVING MADE UP HER MIND TO SEARCH THE PARK FOR her missing wolfhound, Prue Giroux spent the morning at Eddie Bauer choosing just the right safari jacket for the job. To her surprise, she encountered one of her Forum regulars in the camping supplies department.

"Father Paddy!"

Swinging sharply—so sharply, in fact, that his crucifix grazed Prue's chest—Father Paddy Starr turned to face his public, flashing the fluorescent grin that had endeared him to thousands of local late-night television viewers.

"Prue daaarrrllling!" He pecked her once on each cheek, then held her at arm's length as if to check the merchandise for damage. "What on earth are you doing in this he-man, roughneck place?"

"I'm looking for a safari jacket. What about you, Father? They don't make cassocks in khaki, do they?"

Father Paddy shrieked, then sighed dramatically. "And more's the pity, my child, more's the pity! Wouldn't that be divine? This tired old basic black . . . year in, year out. It's truly loathsome. I *long* for a new dress."

Prue tittered appreciatively. She loved the cute way Father Paddy joked about his "dress" and used the word "divine" in the civilian sense. It made him seem accessible somehow. Not like a priest at all, more like a . . . spiritual decorator.

"Actually," the cleric added breathlessly, "I'm desperate for a good, no-nonsense picnic basket. I promised Frannie Halcyon I'd take her to Santa Barbara to see the Shroud of Turin."

"Ah," said Prue cheerily. "Who's in that?"

Father Paddy seemed to ponder for a moment, then explained: "It's not actually an opera, my child. It's a . . . well, a shroud. The cloth that Christ was buried in. At least, that's what they *think* it is. Quite fascinating, really, and all the rage in ecclesiastical circles."

"How marvelous," said Prue.

Father Paddy leaned closer, as if to disclose confidential information. "Hotter than the Tut and Tiffany exhibits combined. You should write about it in your column."

Prue retrieved her Elsa Peretti pen from her Bottega bag and made a brief notation in a tiny Florentine notebook. "So," she chirped when everything was in place again, "I'd say you deserve a little vacation . . . after all that awful business with the . . . militants trying to sing at St. Ignatius."

Father Paddy nodded grimly. "The Gay Chorus. Yes. That was most unfortunate. Dreadful. The Archbishop, bless his heart, had his back against the wall. In a manner of speaking."

Prue shook her head sympathetically. "Some people just don't know where to stop, I'm afraid."

Another nod, even graver.

"They can hire a hall," Prue added.

"Of course they can. We're *liberals,* you and I. It isn't that we aren't in favor of . . . well, human rights and that sort of thing. We are. We *feel.* We care. We reach out and touch those in need of our caring. But a chorus of admitted homosexuals singing in a church? Well, *please* . . . I haven't lived this long not to know tacky when I see it!"

* * *

Prue's driver dropped her off at the conservatory in Golden Gate Park shortly before noon.

His instructions were to return in two hours.

If her efforts proved fruitless, they could mount the search from another corner of the park, systematically combing every acre of the terrain until the dog was found. Or not found. Prue was braced for the latter, but she knew she would never forgive herself if she didn't at least try.

She had lost Vuitton in the tree ferns, so that was where her search began, there amidst the lush and lacy extravagance of those otherworldly plants.

Momentarily moved by the beauty of her surroundings, she stopped and jotted a reminder in her notebook: "If *W* calls, ask to be shot in the tree ferns." She expected to be included in the magazine's summer spread. And why be photographed at home, looking stiff and matronly like the rest, when they could shoot her here, framed in exotica, wild and free as a white-plumed cockatiel?

She set off along an asphalt path that wound through the tree ferns then dramatically ascended to a densely wooded ridge lined with eucalyptus trees.

"Vuitton," she called. "Vuitton."

An aging hippie woman, dressed in Birkenstocks and a fringed poncho, passed Prue on the pathway and frowned at her.

But Prue was lost in the singlemindedness of her search. *"Vuitton . . . Vuiiiiitton . . ."*

Chain Reaction

I T WAS NOON WHEN EMMA BROUGHT IN THE MAI TAIS WITH the morning mail. Frannie Halcyon was still propped up in bed, her peach satin sleep mask askew across her forehead, like the goggles on an aviator who had died in a dogfight.

"Mornin', Miss Frannie."

"Set it on the dresser, please, Emma dear."

"Yes'm."

"Miss Singleton didn't call back, did she?"

"No'm."

"What about Miss Moonmeadow?"

Emma scowled. "No'm."

"You needn't look at me like that. I am fully aware of your feelings about Miss Moonmeadow."

Emma fluffed her mistress' quilt almost violently. "Mr. Edgar would turn over in his grave if he knew you was seeing that witch woman."

Frannie sighed wearily and removed the sleep mask. "Emma, she is a *psychic.* Please don't call her a witch woman. It distresses me so."

"She takin' yo' money. I know that."

"She keeps me in touch . . ."

"Oh Lord, Miss Frannie . . ."

"She keeps me in touch with my only child, Emma, and I don't want to hear another word about it. Is that understood, Emma?"

Emma pouted, unrepentant, then skulked to the window and jerked open the Roman shades. She kept her back turned to her mistress.

"Don't you see?" Frannie asked in a gentler tone. "Miss DeDe was all I had left. Miss Moonmeadow gives me hope that . . . that Miss DeDe is still alive."

Emma walked for the door, rigid as a poker. "It was them kinda folks that killed her."

The mail offered little in the way of refreshment: a bill from Magnin's, an invitation to Vita Keating's Italian Earthquake Relief concert, a thank-you note from that Giroux woman, and a chain letter from Dodie Rosekrans.

This is the Socialite Chain Letter. Break it and you invite risk to life, limb, and personal or inherited wealth. Chrissie Goulandris broke the chain, and a week later broke not one but two nails on the evening of Helene Rochas' Red Ball in Geneva. Ariel de Ravenel broke the chain, and broke a collarbone at Gstaad the same day. Betty Catroux broke the chain, and three weeks later her two-year-old Asti had to be quarantined in a tiny kennel in Managua for eight months without cohabitation privileges. DON'T LET THIS HAPPEN TO YOU!!!!

Mail six copies of this letter to friends whom you KNOW to be serious minded when it comes to fun. Add your name to the bottom of the list and place your return address on the envelope. In six weeks you will have 1,280 new addresses. Ideal for planning international get-togethers. P.S. Husbands who try to interfere with the chain will also be hit by bad luck. Paquita Paquin's husband threw her copy into the wastebasket

53

and a week later his foundation lost its tax exempt status in Argentina. THE FORTUNE YOU SAVE MAY BE YOUR OWN!!!!

D.D. Ryan
Marina Cicogna
Delfina Ratazzi
Dominique Schlumberger de Menil
Nan Kempner
Paloma Picasso
Loulou Klossowski
Marina Schiano
Apollonia von Ravenstein
Countess Carimati de Carimate
C.Z. Guest
Douchka Cizmek
Betsy Bloomingdale
Nancy Reagan
Jerry Zipkin
Adolfo
Dodie Rosekrans

It was cute of Dodie to send the chain letter, but Frannie knew she was beyond the cheering-up stage. That list of names, furthermore, depressed the matriarch more than all her other tribulations combined.

This desolation took tangible shape when she watched the afternoon movie on television: Susan Hayward in *Back Street*. Even Mary Ann Singleton's perky mid-movie commentary on homemade refrigerator magnets failed to revive her sagging spirits.

She seemed like such a nice girl, that Mary Ann.

Couldn't she at least have called back?

Or had she simply deduced the reason for Frannie's call and chosen to ignore it?

Emma, of course, had been dead right. *Dead right.* An uncannily accurate choice of words. *DeDe was dead.* The first person to receive that news had been the last to accept it as the truth.

Now she accepted it.

DeDe was dead and Edgar was dead and Beauchamp was dead and Faust was dead and Frances Alicia Ligon Halcyon was utterly and inexorably alone in the world.

It was time to join her family.

Où est Vuitton?

I T LOOKED, TO PRUE, LIKE A SCENE FROM A DINOSAUR movie.

She was standing on a U-shaped ridge, peering down into the dark green center of the U—a primeval lake-turned-swamp ringed with tree ferns so large that she half expected a sixty-foot Gila monster to come lumbering into view.

Her Maud Frizons were killing her.

Still, she pressed on, following the path that led her deeper and deeper into the unpopulated regions of the park. "Vuitton," she called. "Vuiiiitton." If the wolfhound was there, she would know; he had never failed to respond to his name.

The swamp, she decided, was a bad idea. Most of the terrain around it was too open to be able to conceal her beloved dog. She chose instead a westerly route—at least, she *thought* it was west—and skirted the Paleolithic bowl until the landscape fanned out around her to form the rhododendron dell.

The flowers were almost gone. They lay against their dusty green-black foliage like a thousand cast-off corsages on the morning after the prom. Prue thought about that for a moment: *Like a thousand cast-off corsages on the morning after the prom.*

That was really good. She dug her little notebook from her purse and made another notation. She was getting so much better at this writing business.

The asphalt eventually petered out. The path became whatever route she could weave for herself through the mammoth rhododendrons. Some of them were as big as small carousels. Hmm. *The rhododendrons were as big as small carousels as I continued my relentless search for my beloved . . .*

The notebook came out again.

Then Prue plunged onward. "Vuitton . . . Vuitton." Her ankle straps were almost more than she could take now, but she tried not to think about them. What a foolish mistake. She would just have to leave out the Maud Frizons when she wrote the story.

One of the rhododendrons repeated itself. Or maybe there were two rhododendrons with the same arrangement of dead blossoms. Wasn't she still heading west? Had she veered off her course after taking the last note?

She looked for the sun. The sun would be west. She remembered that much from Camp Fire Girls. *I struggled to remember the training I had received as a Camp Fire Girl in Grass Valley.* Did they still have Camp Fire Girls? It made her sound awfully old, she realized.

Anyway, the sun wasn't even visible; a thick summer fog had already settled over the park.

It was all too hopeless for words.

Vuitton had been missing for well over two weeks now. Even if he had managed to remain in the park, where would he have lived all that time? What would he have eaten? Where would he be safe from dognappers . . . or average citizens showing kindness to a lost dog . . . *or Cambodians?*

If only she could find a clue, some tiny shred of evidence affirming Vuitton's presence in this wilderness. She needed more than determination now: she needed a *sign.*

And then she stepped in it.

* * *

She knew from experience how difficult it was to clean wolf-hound poop off a pair of pumps. And *this* was wolfhound poop, pure and simple; this was Vuitton's poop. Her heart surged with joy.

Looking about her in the dell, she tried to whistle but failed. "Vuitton," she cried. "Mommy's here, darling!"

She heard the rustle of dry leaves, subtle as a zephyr in the underbrush. Twenty feet away a carousel of dead corsages quivered ominously, then parted. Something pale appeared. *Like a newborn chick pecking out of a painted shell.*

It was Vuitton!

"Vuitton, baby! Precious! Darling!"

But the wolfhound merely stood there, appraising her.

"Come on, sweetheart. Come to Mommy."

The dog withdrew into the dying blossoms; the carousel slammed shut.

What on earth . . . ?

Prue pushed her way into the shrub, ducking under its huge black branches until she emerged in a kind of clearing, bounded on the opposite side by a tangle of ivy and eucalyptus trees. Cream-colored fur flickered in the shadows.

"Vuitton, for God's sake!"

The terrain dropped sharply. Vuitton was shimmying clumsily down a steep, sandy slope which ended in a cul-de-sac on an ivy-strangled ledge. There on the ledge stood a curious-looking shack.

And next to the shack stood a man.

He smiled up at the society columnist for *Western Gentry* magazine. "Got time for coffee?" he asked.

Downers

FRANNIE HALCYON HEAVED A LONG SIGH OF SURRENDER and reached for the pills on her bedside table.

They had been a birthday present, oddly enough, a sixtieth birthday present from Helena Parrish, the elegant proprietress of Pinus, a resort in the hills of Sonoma County where Frannie had spent several languorous weeks making a graceful passage into her senior years.

"They're Vitamin Q," Helena had explained, "and they're good for what ails you."

Even now, Frannie managed a thin smile at the thought of her earlier innocence. Vitamin Q, indeed. They were Quaaludes, what the young people called "downers." She had taken maybe half-a-dozen of them during her days at Pinus, giving them up when she discovered they didn't mix well with Mai Tais.

Well, now it didn't matter.

She popped two of them into her mouth, washing them down with her Mai Tai. There were at least a dozen pills in the bottle, surely enough to put her out of her misery. She was about to swallow two more when she remembered an important detail.

"Emma!" she called.

She waited for the sound of the maid's footsteps.

Nothing.

"EMMA!"

Finally, there was a shuffling noise in the hallway. Emma appeared at the door, holding a dust mop. "Yes'm?"

"Have you seen my rosary beads, dear?"

"No'm. Not lately."

"I think they're in the desk in the library. Would you check for me, please?"

"Yes'm."

She was gone for several minutes, long enough for the matriarch to down two more Quaaludes and tidy up the bedclothes. Taking the beads from the old black woman, Frannie felt a great sadness sweep over her. She fought back the tears. "What would I do without you, Emma?"

And what would Emma do without her?

It was too late for that now, too late for turning back. Emma was handsomely provided for in Frannie's will. That would just have to do. Still . . .

"You feelin' poorly, Miss Frannie?"

Frannie refused to meet her companion's eyes. The rosary beads had betrayed her. No one knew better than Emma that Frannie's commitment to the church was minimal. "I'm fine, dear. Really. I just want to say a little prayer for Miss DeDe."

Emma didn't budge. "You sure?"

"Yes, dear. Now leave me alone for a while, will you?"

Emma looked around the room, as if searching for evidence to refute the matriarch's statement. (The Quaaludes were hidden under Frannie's pillow.) Then the maid sighed, shook her head, and trudged out of the room.

As Frannie reached for the pills, the phone rang.

She thought for a moment. If she didn't answer it, Emma would take the call and return to the bedroom with the message. So she reached for the phone, hoping to eliminate this final obstacle to her departure.

"Hello." Her voice sounded sluggish to her. She felt as if she were speaking in a dream.

"Who is this, please?" asked the voice on the other end.

"This is . . . who is *this?*"

"Mother? Oh God, Mother!"

"Wha . . . ?"

"It's DeDe, Mother! Thank God I got . . ."

"DeDe?" It *was* a dream . . . or a hallucination . . . or a wicked prank perpetrated by one of those sick minds that . . . but that voice, *that voice.* "DeDe, baby . . . is it you?"

She heard loud sobs on the other end. "Oh Mother, I'm sorry! Please forgive me! I'm safe! The children are safe! We're O.K., understand? We're coming home just as soon as we can!"

Now Frannie had begun to wail, so loudly in fact that Emma rushed into the room.

"Miss Frannie, what on earth . . . ?"

"It's Miss DeDe, Emma! Our baby's coming home. Precious baby's coming home! DeDe . . . *DeDe, are you there?*"

"I'm here, Mother."

"Thank God! But *where,* darling?"

"Uh . . . Arkansas."

"*Arkansas?* What on earth are you doing there?"

"They're holding me here. At Fort Chaffee. Can you mail me a credit card or something?"

"*Who's* holding you? Not . . . oh God, not those Jonestown people?"

"No, Mother. The government. The American government. I'm at the settlement camp for gay Cuban refugees."

"*What?*"

"It's a long story, Mother."

"Well, tell them to let you out, for heaven's sake! Tell them who you are! Tell them there's been a mistake, DeDe!"

A long pause, and then:

"You don't understand, Mother. I *am* a gay Cuban refugee."

The Breastworks

ICHAEL HAD SEEN IT A DOZEN TIMES, BUT THE sign on the pathway to Lands End never failed to give him a delicious shudder: CAUTION— CLIFF AND SURF AREA EXTREMELY DANGEROUS— *People have been swept from the rocks and drowned.*

"I love that thing," he told Mary Ann and Brian as the trio passed the signpost. "It's so . . . Daphne DuMaurier. 'People have been swept from the rocks and drowned.' It's almost lyrical. Where else but here could you find a government sign painter with poetry in his soul?"

Mary Ann studied the sign for a moment, then continued the trek down the railroad tie stairs. "I don't know why," she said, "but I agree with you."

"So do I," added Brian, "and I'm not as loaded as you guys."

"It's because we're all Jeanettes," explained Michael. "Jeanettes always notice that sort of thing."

Mary Ann shot him a wary glance. "I'm afraid to ask."

Michael grinned. "Just a new theory of mine. I've come to the conclusion that there are really only two types of people in San Francisco, regardless of race, creed, color or . . . what's the other one?"

"Sexual orientation," said Brian.

"Thank you," said Michael.

Mary Ann rolled her eyes. "So what are they?"

"Jeanettes," answered Michael, "and Tonys. Jeanettes are people who think that the city's theme song is 'San Francisco' as sung by Jeanette MacDonald. Tonys think it's Tony Bennett singing 'I Left My Heart in San Francisco.' Everyone falls into one camp or another . . . in a manner of speaking."

Brian's brow wrinkled in thought. "That makes sense, but it's always subject to change. Mary Ann used to be a Tony, for instance. Some people don't know . . ."

"I was *never* a Tony." Mary Ann was quietly indignant.

"Sure you were," said Brian breezily. "I remember. You had a Pet Rock, for God's sake."

"Brian, that was Connie Bradshaw and you know it."

"Well, it's the same thing. You lived with her. The Pet Rock was on your premises."

Mary Ann sought Michael's support. *"He's* the one who picked her up in a laundromat, and I get the lecture on taste." She turned back to Brian. "If I remember correctly, you were still calling women 'chicks' when I met you."

"You remember correctly," said Brian.

"Well?"

Brian shrugged. "Women still *were* chicks when you met me."

"Which reminds me," said Mary Ann, ignoring his deliberate piggery. "Would you watch it with the naked ladies this time?"

"Hey," Brian protested. "All I did was *talk* to them. How was I supposed to know they were dykes?"

"You weren't," said Mary Ann.

"Hell," added Brian. "It all evens out, anyway. Most of the guys down there must think I'm gay."

Michael smiled. "Or wish you were."

* * *

For San Francisco, it was a scorcher, a day when half the population called in sick to the other half. Some of them came here to recover, here to a secret, sun-drenched cove where they stripped off their clothes and offered up their cocoa buttered bodies to The Goddess.

The beach would have been an odd sight from the air. It was checkerboarded with dozens of tiny stone forts, makeshift windbreaks accommodating anywhere from two to ten sun-worshipers in varying stages of undress.

Michael called it The Breastworks.

Today, the three of them had a fort all to themselves. Mary Ann and Brian sunbathed bare-chested but with bottoms; Michael took off everything, having finally decided that tan lines went out with The Seventies.

The celebrants lay in silence for several minutes. Mary Ann was the first to speak.

"Maybe this would do."

"That's putting it mildly," said Brian.

"I mean, as a story. I need a really hot feature idea if I'm ever gonna get liberated from *Bargain Matinee.*"

"You need more than that," said Brian.

"Besides," added Michael, "nude beaches are old stuff. They've been done to death."

"You're right," sighed Mary Ann. "What about S & M?"

"Not right now," said Brian. "I just put the Coppertone on."

"That's even more tired," said Michael. "Whenever these local stations see their ratings flagging they do another exposé on S & M. It's like earthquake stories or Zodiac letters. Anything to keep the public spooked."

"The problem," remarked Mary Ann, "is that you can't really plan it. The really big San Francisco stories just drop out of nowhere without warning."

"Like Guyana," added Brian.

"Or Burke and those cannibals at Grace Cathedral." This interjection was Michael's, and he regretted it instantly. Mary Ann's old boyfriend, Burke Andrew, was now an associate editor at *New York* magazine. Brian appeared to be jealous of the long-dead relationship, so Mary Ann and Michael usually avoided mentioning it in his presence.

Mary Ann changed the subject by interrogating Michael. "So you're off to _____'s house on Memorial Day weekend?"

Michael nodded. "I'll never be tan enough."

"Maybe he'll come out," mused Mary Ann, "and offer me an exclusive on the story."

"Uh-huh," said Michael. "And maybe the sky will fall."

Luke

THE MAN ON THE LEDGE WAS STILL SMILING UP AT PRUE, waiting for an answer to his question.

"Uh . . . what?" she mumbled. Her right hand, meanwhile, burrowed deep into her bag until it closed around her tiny Tiffany rape whistle. If he made so much as a move, she would . . .

"I said . . . you got time for coffee?"

He gestured behind him towards the shack, a makeshift wooden structure straight out of Zane Grey. A thin curl of smoke rose from a rusty stovepipe that protruded from the building like an exclamation point.

There was coffee inside?

Prue cleared her throat. "That dog is mine," she said evenly. "The one that ran into your . . . into that place." Her face was crimson now; her throat was dry as chalk.

The man continued to smile, hands thrust deep into the pockets of his baggy woolen trousers. "That so?" he replied, using a tone that seemed to taunt more than inquire. "S'nice dog, ol' Whitey."

Whitey? Had this derelict tried to stake a claim on Vuitton by giving him a new name? His proper name and owner were

66

clearly engraved on his dog tags. Even his collar—a Christmas present from Father Paddy Starr—had been crafted out of Louis Vuitton vinyl.

"I was here several weeks ago," Prue exclaimed feebly. "He ran away from me down in the tree ferns. I'm so relieved that he's safe."

The man nodded, still smiling.

"If you've been . . . taking care of him," Prue continued, "I'll be happy to reimburse you for any expenses you might have incurred."

The man laughed. "But no coffee, huh?"

Prue's hand tightened on the whistle. "Really, I'm . . . that's awfully kind . . . but, um . . . my driver . . . that is, I have a friend waiting for me down at the conservatory. Thank you, though. That's very nice."

The man shrugged, then turned and entered the shack, closing the door behind him.

Prue waited.

And waited.

This was really *too* annoying. What did he think he was doing, anyway? It would be easy enough to prove ownership of the dog, to have this tramp arrested for holding Vuitton against his will.

Prue considered her options: She could walk back to the conservatory and wait for her driver to return; he was imposing enough to intimidate this man into releasing Vuitton. Or, of course, she could simply call the police.

On the other hand, why compound the nuisance by official intervention? Surely this was something she could handle on her own.

Clutching at shrubbery for support, she made her way down the sandy slope until she reached the ledge where the shack stood. It was amazing really, this secret cul-de-sac, virtually invisible to the casual passerby, yet still within hearing distance of the traffic down below on Kennedy Drive.

Prue strode purposefully towards the door of the shack—so purposefully, in fact, that she snagged a heel on a root and tumbled to the ground, scattering the contents of her purse. Mortified, she scooped up her belongings as quickly as possible and staggered to her feet.

She rapped on the door.

The first thing she heard was Vuitton's off-key bark. Then came the sound of wood scraping wood as a homemade latch was undone.

The door swung open, revealing the same smiling face, a face made almost handsome by high cheekbones, a strong jawline and unusual amber-colored skin. The stranger's longish dark hair was combed neatly into place. (Had it been before?) He appeared to be in his late forties.

"That's better," he said.

Prue tried to placate him. "I'm sorry if I offended you in some way. I've been so anxious about my dog. I'm sure you can understand."

Vuitton poked his long, pale muzzle through the crack in the door. Prue reached down to stroke him. "Baby," she cooed. "It's O.K., Mommy's here."

"You got proof?" asked the man.

"Look at him," said Prue. "He knows me. Don't you, baby? His name is Vuitton. It's on the collar. For that matter, *my* name is on the collar."

"What's your name?"

"Giroux. Prue Giroux."

The man extended his hand. "Mine's Luke. Come on in."

Inside

WHEN PRUE ENTERED THE SHACK, HER MIND raced back to Grass Valley . . . and to the tree house her brother Ben had built on the hill behind the barn.

Ben's tree house had been a holy place, a monk's cell for a thirteen-year-old that was incontestably off limits to his little sister and her friends.

One day, however, when Ben was at the picture show, Prudy Sue had climbed into the forbidden aerie and perused, with pounding heart, the secret icons of her brother's adolescence: dirty dime novels, joy buzzers, a Lucky Strikes magazine ad featuring Maureen O'Hara.

Today, forty years later, Prue couldn't help remembering the surprising *order* of Ben's lair. There had been something almost touching about the neat rows of Tom Swift books, the hand-sewn burlap curtains on the tiny windows, the quartz rocks displayed on orange crates as if they were diamonds in a vault. . . .

"I wasn't expecting company," said Luke. "You'll have to excuse this."

"This" was a single room, about six-by-ten-feet, furnished with wooden packing crates, an Army surplus cot, and a large chunk of foam rubber which appeared to function as a couch. A rock-lined pit in the packed earth floor was filled with graying embers. On the grate above the fire sat a blue enamel coffee pot.

The man picked up the pot and poured coffee into a styrofoam cup. "You take cream? I only have the fake stuff, I'm afraid."

"Uh . . . what? . . . oh, no thank you." Prue was still absorbing the room. How long had he been here, anyway? Did the park people know about this?

The man read her mind and winked. "You'll get used to it," he said. "Sweet 'n Low?"

"Yes, please."

He cracked open the pink packet like an egg, shook it into the coffee and handed her the cup. "I thought you might like to see where your dog's been living, that's all."

Vuitton, in fact, having greeted his mistress at the door, had returned to a bed of rags in a corner near the fire. He looked up and wagged his tail at her appeasingly, apologizing perhaps for such an effortless abandonment of his Nob Hill lifestyle.

Prue blew on her coffee, then looked about her. "This is . . . just fascinating," she said. She meant it, too.

The man chuckled. "Every kid loves a playhouse," he said.

Then he *is* like Ben, thought Prue.

A further examination of the room revealed additional touches of boyish whimsy. Ball fringe over the bed, forming a faux-canopy. A can of sharpened pencils on a shelf above the "sofa." A soot-streaked map of the city tacked to the wall above the fire.

Over the doorway hung a plywood plaque, its lettering laboriously crafted in bent twigs:

THOSE WHO DO NOT
REMEMBER THE PAST
ARE CONDEMNED
TO REPEAT IT

70

Prue smiled when she read it. "That's nice," she said.

"Santayana," replied the man. *Life of Reason.*"

"Excuse me?"

The man seemed to study her for a moment, then said quietly: "Why don't you take your dog now?"

"Oh . . . of course. I didn't mean to keep you."

The man went to the bed of rags and roused the wolf-hound. "C'mon, Whitey. Time to go, boy." Vuitton rose awkwardly to his feet and licked the man's hand excitedly. "He thinks we're going exploring," explained his keeper. "I made a leash for him, if you want it."

He opened a box next to Vuitton's bed. It contained canned dog food, a battered grooming brush, and a length of rope with a hand-made leather tag reading WHITEY. The top of the box said WHITEY in bent twigs.

Earlier, Prue had felt real resentment about this alien name; now, for some reason, she thought she might cry.

She fumbled in her bag. "Please . . . I insist on reimbursing you for your . . ."

"No," said the man sharply. Then, in a sober tone: "The pleasure was mine."

"Well . . ." She looked about her, suddenly at a loss for words. The man clipped the rope on Vuitton's collar and handed it to Prue.

"Thank you," she said as earnestly as possible. "Thank you so much . . . Luke, isn't it?"

The man nodded. "If you're ever back in these parts, I wouldn't mind a visit from him."

"Of course, of course . . ." She had nothing further to say as she led Vuitton away from the shack and up the steep, sandy slope. The wolfhound went willingly, barking his good-bye when they reached the top of the rise.

But the door of the shack was closed again.

Off to Hollywood

NED LOCKWOOD'S PICKUP WAS PARKED ON LEAVEN-worth when Mary Ann came down the rickety wooden stairway from Barbary Lane. He offered her a jaunty salute, cupping his huge hand against his forehead. His bald pate was tanned the color of saddle leather.

"He'll be down in a minute," she said. "He's trying to choose between fifteen different shades of Lacostes."

Ned grinned and threw up his hands, bringing them to rest on the steering wheel. "So where are you off to?"

Mary Ann mugged. "Work. Not all of us get to spend the weekend with a movie star." She held up a large Hefty Bag. "Care for a darling bow-wow?"

Ned looked into the bag. "Stuffed animals? What for?"

"My show. What else?"

"They're some sort of bargain, huh?"

"Factory seconds. God, it's so depressing, Ned. Get me out of here, will you? Abduct me or something. Hasn't _____ got an extra cabana he could hide me in?"

Ned smiled. "I'm afraid it's one of his all-boy weekends."

"How dumb," said Mary Ann.

"I think so, too. But he's sort of an old-world fag."

"Big deal. Couldn't I be an old-world fag hag?"

Ned threw back his head and laughed. "I wish he could be that comfortable about it."

Mary Ann managed a smile herself. "So you're leaving me to my misery, huh?"

"You're a star," said Ned. "Stars aren't supposed to be miserable."

"Who's a star?" A cheap ploy to fish for praise, but right now she'd take anything she could get.

The nurseryman shrugged. "My aunt in the East Bay says you're a star. She watches your show all the time."

"Harlequin glasses, right?"

Ned grinned.

"Not to mention Harlequin *books.* And a bedroom full of yarn poodles that she made on her doodle-loom. Am I right?"

"Actually," said Ned, "she makes braided rugs out of old neckties."

"Right," nodded Mary Ann.

Michael appeared at the top of the stairway, decked out in an apricot Polo shirt, white linen trousers and emerald green Topsiders. "Get him," said Ned. "Is that L.A. or what?"

Michael presented himself to Mary Ann for inspection.

"Very nice," she remarked, "but you'll be pitted out by the time you reach the pea soup place."

"Then I'll *change* at the pea soup place." He pecked her on the mouth and sprang into the truck. "If I'm not back in three days, send in the Mounties."

"Make him wear a bathing suit," Mary Ann instructed Ned.

"That's a tall order," said the nurseryman.

"I know," replied Mary Ann. "He almost burned his butt off last week at Lands End."

As usual, there wasn't a legal parking space within five blocks of the station. She finally settled on a commercial zone in an alley off Van Ness, leaving an outdated press pass on the dashboard of the car.

73

She hurried past the security guard, eating Cheetos at the front desk, and boarded the elevator where she stabbed the button for the third floor.

She checked her Casio. Two-thirty-eight. God, she was pushing it these days. Time was when she would show up two hours early for the three o'clock broadcast. Time was she had actually found this crap *exciting*.

Bambi Kanetaka was leaving the dressing room when Mary Ann arrived.

"Hi," said Mary Ann. "Why so early?"

"We're shooting on location," the anchorperson replied breathlessly. "Larry's found some woman who used to date the Trailside Killer. What's in the bag?"

It was almost uncanny, Mary Ann decided, how Bambi could find her way straight to the soft spot. "Just some seconds," she muttered.

"Awww," said Bambi, peeking into the bag. "They're *precious*. Honestly, you get to do the most fun things, Mary Ann. I get so tired of all the . . ." She sighed world-wearily. "You know, the heavy stuff."

The makeup man, who had just returned from his grandmother's funeral in Portland, was done up in gold chains and black Spandex—his idea of mourning garb.

". . . and so I went to the funeral home and I *insisted* . . . look up, would you, hon . . . good . . . I insisted that they open the casket . . . a little to the left now . . . so they opened it for me, and *what* do you think they had on Grandma's lips? TITTY PINK! I mean, *really* . . . head up, hon . . . so I said just let me handle this because *my* grandma is getting nothing less than Cocksucker Red when they put her in the ground. . . ."

Denny spied Mary Ann and stuck his head through the doorway. "There you are."

She hated "There you are" when it meant "Where have you been?"

"That woman's on the line again," said the associate producer.

"What woman?"

"The drunk. She spelled her name this time. It's *Halcyon,* not Harrison."

"God," said Mary Ann.

"Ring a bell?"

"I think I used to work for her husband." She checked the wall clock: six minutes to air time. "Tell her I'll call her back after the intro."

We Must Have Lunch

Mary Ann delivered her spiel on stuffed animals in less than three minutes, which meant that she had to spend the same amount of time getting gushy about *Say One for Me.*

It wasn't easy. She had never been able to buy Bing Crosby as a priest. Or Rosalind Russell as a Mother Superior. Or Helen Reddy as a nun. Hollywood had some pretty funny ideas about what Catholics were supposed to look like.

"Mary Ann, you were too yummy for words. I watched you on the monitor."

It was Father Paddy Starr, San Francisco's idea of a priest, hell-bent for Studio B as Mary Ann beat a hasty retreat.

"Thanks, Father. Break a leg." It sounded weird, saying that to a priest, but this one was in show business, after all. Father Paddy's late-night show, *Honest to God,* was taped every afternoon following Mary Ann's show.

*   *   *

Back at her cubbyhole, she checked to see if Denny had left a number for Mrs. Halcyon. He hadn't, of course, but she finally got it out of Directory Assistance after two overlapping recorded voices—one male, one female—chastised her for doing so.

She dialed the number.

"Halcyon Hill."

Mary Ann recognized the voice from her days at Halcyon Communications when she had spent a fair amount of time relaying messages between Edgar Halcyon and his wife. "Emma?"

"Yes'm?"

"This is Mary Ann Singleton. Remember me?"

" 'Course I remember you! It's mighty good to hear you, *mighty* good! Oh Lord, I could fairly bust, Mary Ann. Jesus looks out for his children, if we only just . . ." There was a scuffling noise in the background. "Give me that!" snapped a voice that Mary Ann recognized as Frannie Halcyon's.

"Mary Ann?" Now the voice had softened to a matronly purr.

"Yes, Mrs. Halcyon. What a nice surprise."

"Well . . . I'm just a *big* fan of yours."

"How sweet."

"I am. Truly. You're a very talented young lady."

"That's so nice. Thank you so much."

A long pause, and then: "I . . . uh . . . I called because I hoped you'd be able to have lunch with us . . . with me, that is, on Sunday. The weather's just lovely down here now and the pool is . . . well, you could bring your bathing suit if you like and . . ."

"I'd be delighted, Mrs. Halcyon." Mary Ann almost giggled. Michael's get-away to L.A. had made her yearn for escape, and she and Brian hadn't had a good, cheap mini-vacation in a long time. This was practically a Godsend. "Would it be O.K. if I brought a friend?"

"Oh . . . I . . . actually, I'd rather you didn't, Mary Ann."

"Of course . . ."

"I'm really not prepared to entertain more than one."

"Fine. I understand." She didn't, actually, but now her curiosity was aroused.

"Just a little . . . girl talk. You and I have got so much to catch up on."

Mary Ann was thrown. She and Frannie Halcyon had absolutely *nothing* to catch up on. Why was this sweet, but rummy, society dowager talking to her like an equal?

Well, she thought, the poor woman lost a daughter in Guyana. That was reason enough to be a little indulgent. Besides, she had a pool. That was an offer no San Franciscan could refuse.

"What time shall I be there?" asked Mary Ann.

Larry and Bambi were returning to the station when Mary Ann left the building. It was all they could do to keep their hands off one another, she observed.

"Great tie," said Mary Ann, breezing past them in the lobby. He was wearing the one with the Porsche emblem in a repetitive pattern.

"Hey," said Larry, "thanks."

The only fun thing about assholes, Mary Ann decided, was that they almost never noticed when you were calling them assholes. "How was the Trailside Killer's girlfriend?" she asked Bambi.

"Shaken," said the anchorperson.

"Mmm. I'd imagine."

Ever so subtly, Larry steered Bambi toward the elevator. "Stay out of this business," he told Mary Ann. "It ain't a bit pretty."

"Mmm."

"Really," he added. "You're better off out of it."

She cursed him all the way back to Barbary Lane.

Tinseltown

NED LOCKWOOD CHECKED THE CLOCK ON THE DASH-
board as his pickup rattled through the corridor
of palms flanking Hollywood High.

"Ten-twenty. We did O.K. Hail to thee, Alma
Mater."

"You went to Hollywood High?" asked Michael.

Ned's jaw squared off in a grin. "Didn't everybody?"

"Then you were *trained* to live with a movie star. It didn't
just come natural to you."

"I suppose you could say that," laughed Ned.

Michael shook his head in wonderment. "Hollywood
High," he murmured, as the pale building slid by in the
darkness. "I always wanted to go to school with Alan Ladd's
son when I was a little boy."

"Why?"

Michael shrugged. "The quickest way to Alan Ladd, I
guess. I had the biggest crush on him."

Ned laughed. "When you were *how* old?"

"Eight," said Michael defensively. "But a kid can dream."

"Horny little bugger."

"Well," retorted Michael, "if I remember correctly, you had some sort of a thing for Roy Rogers, didn't you?"

"I was at least ten," said Ned.

Michael laughed and looked out the window again. There weren't many libidos that hadn't been stirred, one way or another, by the kingdom which stretched out luxuriantly before him.

Like a lot of his friends, he made a ritual of bad-mouthing Los Angeles behind her back—her tacky sprawl, her clotted freeways, her wretched refuse yearning to breathe free. . . .

But at times like this, on nights like this, when everyone in town seemed to own a convertible and the warm, thick jasmine-scented air made itself felt like a hand creeping up his thigh, Michael could abandon the obvious and believe again.

"It's amazing," he said. "Every time I come here I feel like Lucy and Ricky hitting town. This place must get more second chances than any place on earth."

Suddenly, Ned swerved the truck, narrowly missing a bottle blond teenager on a skateboard. His 69 football jersey had been hacked off just below his nipples to reveal a foot of tanned midriff. Passing him, Ned exhaled with relief: "Nobody *walks* the streets anymore!"

Michael looked back to see the kid leaning into a silver Mercedes parked at the curb in front of the Famous Amos chocolate chip cookie headquarters. "Bingo," he said. "He's got one."

"A star is born," said Ned.

The truck turned off Sunset and climbed into Beverly Hills, a land of shadowy lawns and deathly silence.

The streets grew steeper and narrower. Most of them appeared to be named Something-crest, though it was next to impossible to tell where one left off and another began. Michael found it unimaginable that anyone who lived in this neighborhood could find his way home at night.

"Will he be there when we get there?" he asked Ned. "I must look like shit."

Ned reached over and squeezed his knee. "There's a roach in the ashtray. Why don't you smoke it?"

"If you think that'll relax me, you're crazy. I'll meet him and run screaming into the night."

"He may not be back from Palm Springs yet. Don't sweat it."

Michael looked out the window. The lights of the city were spread out beneath them like computer circuitry. "If he's not there," he asked, "who'll let us in?"

"The houseman, probably."

"Is he the whole staff?"

Ned shook his head. "There's a cook, most of the time. And a secretary and a gardener. Probably just the houseman to-night, though."

Michael tried to picture such an existence, falling silent for a moment. "You know what?" he said at last.

"What?"

"My mother thought _____ _____ was the hottest thing going. She'd shit a brick if she knew I was doing this."

Ned turned and smiled at him. "Take careful notes, then."

"Right . . . how big was his dick again?"

The nurseryman chuckled. "Big enough to make some people suspicious about his Oscar nomination."

"Bigger than a breadbox?" Michael laughed nervously at his own bad joke, then leaned over and kissed Ned on the neck. "I can't believe this is happening. Thanks, pal."

Ned shrugged it off. "I think you'll both enjoy each other. He's a real nice guy." He pulled the truck off the road, stopping in front of a huge metal gate. Then he pushed a button on a squawk box partially concealed in the bushes.

"Yes?" came a voice.

"It's Ned."

"Lions and tigers and bears," said Michael.

"That was the houseman. Relax."

There was nothing much to see from this vantage point. Just a bougainvillea-covered wall and an archway, apparently leading into a courtyard. "Ned?"

"Yeah, Bubba?"

"This isn't like a date, is it?"

"Why?"

"I don't know. Suddenly I feel like a mail-order bride or something."

"Just take it easy, Michael. There are no expectations, if that's what you mean." Ned turned and grinned slyly at his friend. "Not on *his* part, at least."

Prayers for the People

BACK IN THE CITY, FATHER PADDY STARR WAS DISCUS-sing the state of his flock over a late supper at L'Etoile. "Poor Bitsy," he sighed, nibbling on an asparagus tip, "I'm afraid she needs our prayers again."

Prue knew there was only one Bitsy: Bitsy Liggett, Society Kleptomaniac. Her infamy had been an embarrassment to the social set for almost a decade now.

"Oh, dear," said Prue, trying to sound prayerful in spite of the fact that she herself had lost a Lalique vase, several crystal dogs and an antique tortoise shell brush set to the pathologi-cal compulsion of the woman being prayed for.

"The problem is," the cleric lamented, "you can't *not* invite her, can you? It wouldn't do. The Liggetts are good stock. Bitsy's a charming woman. You just have to be ready for her, that's all."

"Who wasn't ready for her this time?"

The priest's mouth curled slightly. "Vita."

"No!"

"Bitsy's on her Italian Earthquake board. When she left

Vita's house after the meeting yesterday, a Fabergé box fell out of her pantyhose."

"No!"

"Right there in the foyer. Could you die?"

Prue pressed both hands against her mouth and giggled.

"Could you die?" repeated Father Paddy, arching an eyebrow for maximum comic effect. Then, suddenly, the lines of his face turned down, as if he were made of wax and melting. "Really, though, it's quite dreadful. It's a disease, like alcoholism. She needs our prayers, Prudy Sue."

Then he told her three more people who needed their prayers.

Prue got to *her* news over dessert.

"I've been meaning to tell you," she said. "I found Vuitton."

"Ah." Father Paddy reached across the table and fondled her hand. "I'm so happy, my child! Where was he? The poor thing must have been famished!"

Prue shook her head. "That's the amazing part. He was living with this man in the park."

"A park official, you mean?"

"No. A man in a funny little shack. Up on the ridge above the tree ferns. He had a bed and a fireplace and everything. Vuitton seemed to adore him, so I couldn't really get upset about it. Him keeping Vuitton, I mean."

"He didn't call you?"

"No. I found him. Or rather, I found Vuitton and Vuitton led me to him. He seemed a little sad when I took Vuitton away. He'd made a leash for him, and he had a grooming brush and everything."

Father Paddy poured cream on his raspberries. "How endearing."

"It was. I was truly *touched*, Father. He told me to bring Vuitton for a visit sometime. I think I may do it."

The priest's smile hovered, but his brow furrowed. "Well, I don't know about *that*, Prudy Sue."

"Why?"

"Well, you really have no way of knowing who he . . ."

"I'm trusting my instincts, Father. This man is a gentle spirit. Life hasn't treated him well, but he's still smiling back at it. He even has a quote from one of the saints on his wall."

"Really," smiled Father Paddy, "who?" Now they were back on *his* turf again.

Prue thought for a moment. "Santa somebody. I forget. It's something about remembering the past. He made it out of twigs." She took a bite of her trifle. "Besides, characters like him are a San Francisco tradition. Like Emperor Norton, and . . . remember Olin Cobb, that man who built the little lean-to on Telegraph Hill?"

Father Paddy grinned at her sideways. "You're going to write about this, aren't you?"

"Maybe," said Prue coyly.

"Uh-huh."

"Anyway, I *have* to go back at least one more time."

"Now, Prue . . ."

"I left my rape whistle there."

"Oh, *please.*"

"It's from Tiffany's," explained the columnist.

The priest corrected her. "Tiffany, darling. No apostrophe *s.*"

"Tiffany," repeated Prue. "Reg gave it to me. I'm sort of sentimental about it. I dropped my purse on the ridge. The whistle must've fallen out. Don't look at me like that, Father."

The priest simply shook his head, a gently chastising smile on his lips.

"You're so sweet," said Prue, picking up the check. "It's nice having somebody worry about me."

The Castle

THE SILENCE WAS SHATTERED BY THE SOUND OF YAPPING dogs. They seemed a motley group, judging by their barks—young and old, big and small. Michael smiled, remembering a hot summer night in Palm Springs when he and Ned had eaten mushrooms and tried to climb Liberace's fence.

"Oh no," he whispered, "does *he* have attack poodles, too?"

Ned chuckled, his teeth flashing like foxfire in the darkness. "These aren't guard dogs. These are family."

The big neo-Spanish door swung open. The houseman, a diminutive, jockey-like man in his mid sixties, held the door ajar with one arm and fended off the dogs with the other. "Hurry," he said, "before one of these retards makes a run for it."

Ned led the way, with Michael heavy on his heels. The dogs—an ancient, rheumy-eyed shepherd; a pair of hysterical Irish setters; a squat, three-legged mongrel—cavorted deliriously around the feet of the man who had once shared the house with them.

Ned knelt in their midst and greeted them individually.

86

"Honey, ol' Honey, how ya doin', girl? Yeah, Lance . . . *good* Lance! Heeey, Guinevere . . ."

Michael was impressed. It was one thing to know _____
_____. It was quite another to be on a first name basis with his dogs.

Ned cuddled the three-legged runt in his lap. "How's this one been doing?"

The houseman rolled his eyes. "He got out last week. The little pissant made it all the way down to Schuyler Road. Lucy found him, of all people. Called _____. He was practically in mourning by then, wouldn't eat, wouldn't take calls . . . well, you know."

Still kneeling, Ned held the dog up for Michael's inspection. "Noble beast. Named after yours truly."

Michael didn't get it at first. He was still wondering if it had been *the* Lucy who'd found the dog. "Uh . . . you mean his name is Ned?"

The mutt yipped asthmatically, confirming the claim. Ned let him down and stood up. "We go back a long ways, him and me. Guido, this is my friend, Michael Tolliver."

Michael shook hands with the houseman, who offered a half-smile, then turned back to Ned. "He's not back till tomorrow. You've got the place to yourself tonight. I left the heat on in the Jacuzzi."

Michael breathed a secret sigh of relief. At least there would be time to collect himself.

Guido led them down a tiled walkway under an arbor that framed the courtyard. Fuchsia blossoms the color of bruises bumped against their heads as they walked. Across the courtyard, floating above the rectilinear lights of Los Angeles, a swimming pool, gigantic and glowing, provided the only illumination. It might have been a landing strip for UFO's.

Guido opened another door—the *real* front door, Michael presumed. He caught a fleeting impression of oversized Spanish furniture, suits of armor, crimson carpets (Early Butch, Ned once had dubbed it) as they climbed the grand staircase to the second floor.

"I put you both in the trophy room tonight," said Guido drily, "if that's all right."

"Fine," said Ned.

"The red room's a mess. Two kids from Laguna stayed over last night. Lube on the sheets, poppers on the carpet. Honestly."

Ned and Michael exchanged grins. "We won't be nearly as much trouble," said Ned.

The trophy room was almost too much for Michael to absorb: a whole row of plaques from *Photoplay* magazine (mostly from the fifties); keys to a dozen cities; telegrams from Hitchcock, Billy Wilder, DeMille; silver-framed photos of _____ _____ with JFK, _____ _____ with Marilyn Monroe, _____ _____ with Ronald Reagan; a needlepoint pillow from Mary Tyler Moore.

After Guido had left, Michael just stood there, shaking his head. "Is this *his* room?"

"Across the hall," said Ned. "Wanna see it?"

"Should we?"

Ned smiled sleepily. "It used to be my room, too, remember?"

They passed through double doors, massive and oaken, into a space that looked like a set for a movie star's bedroom. The windows opened onto the pool and the world. The bed was enormous, exactly the sort of bed Michael expected _____ _____ to sleep in.

He approached it in earnest, like a pilgrim, and sat down tentatively on the edge. Smiling sheepishly at Ned, he admitted, "I feel like such a tourist."

"You'll get used to it soon enough."

"The *bed?*" laughed Michael.

"There's coffee in the morning if you want it."

Michael sprang to his feet, feverish with guilt. Guido stood in the doorway, eyeing them.

"Thanks," said Ned, apparently unruffled. "I'm just giving Michael the house tour."

Guido grunted. "Don't trip any alarms," he said as he left the room.

Michael listened until his footsteps had died out, then gave a nervous little whistle.

"He's just doing his job," Ned explained.

"Yeah," said Michael, "like Mrs. Danvers in *Rebecca.*"

Halcyon Hill

MEMORIAL DAY DAWNED BRIGHT AND CLEAR. MARY Ann left for Hillsborough just before noon, only to get caught in a traffic snarl at the intersection of DuBoce and Market. She puzzled over this turn of events until she saw the throng gathered on the pavement at the 76 station.

About five hundred people were cheering hysterically while a statuesque man in nurse drag—boobies, bouffant, the works—thrashed about violently on the back of a mechanical bull. In other words, thought Mary Ann, just another Memorial Day.

A battered Volvo pulled alongside the Le Car. "What the fuck *is* this?" asked a frizzy-haired woman with an infant child and a back seat full of No Nukes posters.

"The Great Tricycle Race," said Mary Ann. She had learned that much from Michael.

"What's that?" asked the woman.

"Uh, well . . . gay guys on tricycles. It's a benefit for the SPCA."

The woman beamed. "Wonderful!" she shouted, as the cars began to move again. "How goddamn wonderful!"

Curiously enough, Mary Ann knew exactly what she meant. How could anyone feel threatened by this kind of whimsy? If she ever had a child, she would want him to grow up in San Francisco, where Mardi Gras was celebrated at least five times a year.

She hadn't always felt that way, of course. Once she had harbored deep resentment at the sight of dozens of near-naked men gamboling in the streets, their cute little butts winking unavailably in the sunshine.

But some straight men, thank God, took care of their bodies as well as gay men did.

Besides, a cute butt was a cute butt, so what-the-hell?

She almost jumped the curb looking at one.

She was sorry that Brian wasn't with her. He had been such a sport about it when she told him of Mrs. Halcyon's luncheon invitation. "Go ahead," he had said. "She might do you some good. I'll catch some rays in the courtyard. We'll do a flick or something when you get back."

God, she did love him. He was so easy, so uncomplicated, so willing to understand, whatever the circumstances. They were friends now, she and Brian. Friends who had terrific sex together. If that wasn't love, what was?

By the time she hit the freeway, she was buzzing along merrily on one of Mrs. Madrigal's Barbara Stanwyck joints. She turned on the radio and sang along as Terri Gibbs sang "Somebody's Knockin'."

Once more, she couldn't help wondering about this summons to Hillsborough. She knew that some society people liked to court celebrities, but surely her own limited fame was far removed from Frannie Halcyon's league.

Was she just being nice, then?

Maybe.

But *why,* after all these years?

*　　*　　*

As a secretary, Mary Ann had worked for the Halcyon family for almost two years—first for Edgar Halcyon, the founder of Halcyon Communications; later, for Beauchamp Day, Mr. Halcyon's slimy son-in-law.

Today, however, was the first time she had ever laid eyes on the family estate.

Halcyon Hill was a mammoth mock-Tudor mansion, probably built in the twenties, set back from the road in a grove of towering oaks. A black Mercedes, with a license plate reading FRANNI, was parked in the circular driveway.

An old black woman, very thin, opened the door.

"You must be Emma," said the visitor. "I'm Mary Ann."

"Yes'm, I feel like I . . ." Before the maid could finish the sentence, Frannie Halcyon came scurrying into the foyer. "Mary Ann, I am delighted, just *delighted* you could come. Now, you brought your bathing suit, I hope?"

"Uh . . . in the car. I wasn't sure if . . ."

"Emma, get it for her, will you?"

"Really, I can . . ." Mary Ann abandoned the protest; the maid was already tottering towards the car.

"Now," said Mrs. Halcyon, "we'll have a nice lunch on the terrace . . . I hope you like salmon?"

"Yum," replied Mary Ann.

"And then we can chat."

"Fine."

The matriarch took her arm protectively. "You know, young lady, Edgar would be so *proud* of you."

Dames

HIGH ATOP BEVERLY HILLS, MICHAEL AND NED WERE lolling by _____ _____'s pool, breakfasting on the eggs Benedict that Guido had brought them. "He's O.K.," Michael commented, after the houseman had left. "He had me sorta spooked last night."

Ned popped a triangle of toast into his mouth. "He didn't know you last night. It's his job to be careful. The *National Enquirer* tries to scale the wall here about once a week. _____'s lucky to have Guido."

The three-legged mongrel named Ned hobbled up to Michael's chaise lounge and presented his muzzle for scratching. Michael obliged him. "These old dogs," he said. "You expect something sleek, like greyhounds or something. Or ferocious, maybe. It makes me feel so much better about him to know that he keeps these mangy mutts."

"That one's fourteen," said Ned. "We found him when he was a puppy, scrounging in a garbage can behind Tiny Naylor's. _____ adores him. He got hit by a car about five years ago, so the leg had to go." Ned smiled lovingly at his namesake. *"He's* the one who should write the book."

Guido appeared on the terrace with a tray of bullshots. "I thought you gentlemen could use a little refreshment before the twinkies invade."

"Thanks," said Ned, taking a drink. "What twinkies?"

Guido's pupils ascended. "_____ called a little while ago, still in P.S. Won't get here till two. Meanwhile, God help us, one of his buddies from West Hollywood decides to throw a little spur-of-the-moment Welcome Home. *Here,* thank you very much."

Michael looked at Ned, suddenly feeling anxious again. "Should we be getting dressed or something?"

"Forget it," Guido reassured him. "The last time this happened the party lasted two days. There were so many Speedos hung out to dry that the Danny Thomases called to ask why we were flying signal flags."

Guido's forecast proved uncannily accurate. One by one, the young men began arriving, long-limbed and Lacosted to near perfection.

"What is this?" asked Michael, hovering near the kitchen. "The summer spread of *GQ?*"

"They *wish,*" said Guido, frantically fluffing the parsley on a tray of deviled eggs. "They're anybody's spread, at this point . . . and honey, when you've been in this business as long as I have, you see them come and you see them go. Mostly come . . . ya know?"

"They're so gorgeous," said Michael. "Are they actors or what?"

"What, mostly. Starlets. Harry Cohn knew all about it, only he did it with girls. Same difference. Same dumb dames standing around the pool." The houseman wolfed down a deviled egg and scurried out the door with the tray.

Michael found Ned by the swimming pool.

"I need a joint," Michael whispered, surveying the crowd. "If I'm going to be paranoid, I want there to be a good reason for it."

"I wouldn't do it here," Ned warned him.

"Huh?"

"_____'s kind of old-fashioned."

"Right," said Michael, looking around him. "Gotcha."

* * *

The movie star's arrival was heralded by joyful barking at the
front gate. The dogs, in fact, provided the only official greeting that Michael could observe. While most of the men
around the pool exuded airs of easy familiarity with their
surroundings, none stepped forward to welcome the host.

They don't know him either, Michael realized.

The idol was grayer than he had expected—a little
paunchy, too—but he was truly magnificent, a lumbering
titan in this garden of younger, prettier men. When he knelt
and scooped the three-legged dog into his arms, he won
Michael's heart completely.

"C'mon," said Ned. "I'll introduce you."

"Couldn't we save it?"

"Why?"

"Well, won't he be swamped for a while?"

Ned smiled at him indulgently, rising from his chaise.
"Come on over when you feel like it, O.K.?"

Michael stayed by the pool, watching silently as the chatter
resumed.

"He must be on great drugs," said a voice behind him.

"Who?" said another.

"The Pope."

"Huh?"

"Well, they've had him on painkillers since the shooting,
right? And he's the Pope, right? He must be getting great
stuff."

"Yeah, I never thought of that. Did I tell you that Allan
Carr wants me for *Grease II?*"

Michael rose and headed for the buffet table, where Guido
was emptying ashtrays and grumbling. He was no longer Mrs.
Danvers at Manderley; he was Mammy at Tara, entertaining
the resident Yankees against her better instincts.

"Where's Ned?" asked Michael.

"In the screening room," said Guido, "with _____."

So Michael took a deep breath and went in to join them.

Buying Silence

AS PROMISED, MARY ANN ENJOYED A LUNCH OF COLD salmon and Grey Riesling on the flagstone terrace overlooking the swimming pool at Halcyon Hill.

Mrs. Halcyon was extraordinarily solicitous, oohing and aahing melodramatically over Mary Ann's brief, but snappy, repertoire of true-life TV horror stories.

"It certainly is," she agreed, when Mary Ann had finished. "It's *just* like the *Mary Tyler Moore Show.* They didn't exaggerate one bit, did they?"

"I love it, though," Mary Ann hastened to add. "I'll just love it more when they let me do some nighttime work." She smiled a little ruefully. "They will, sooner or later. They just don't know it yet."

"That's the spirit!" Mrs. Halcyon clamped her plump, bejeweled hands together, then appraised her guest, smiling. "Edgar always said you were ambitious. He told me that many times."

"He was a great boss," Mary Ann replied, returning a dead man's compliment. She felt increasingly uncomfortable under the matriarch's steady gaze.

"He also said you were tactful," continued Mrs. Halcyon, "and extremely discreet."

"Well, I always *tried* to be." *What the hell was going on here?*

"He trusted you, Mary Ann. And *I* trust you. You're a young woman with character." A kindly twinkle came into her eyes. "I wasn't trained for much in this life—outside of opera guilds and museum boards—but I'm a pretty good judge of character, Mary Ann, and I don't think you'll let me down."

Mary Ann hesitated. "Is there something . . . uh, specific you had . . ."

"I need a PR person. The Halcyon family needs a PR person. On a short-term basis, of course."

"Oh . . . I see." She didn't, of course.

"It shouldn't interfere with your job at the station. I need you as a consultant, more or less. I'm prepared to pay you a thousand dollars a week for a period of roughly four weeks."

Mary Ann made no attempt at playing it cool. "That's wonderfully generous, but I don't . . . well, I'm not *trained* at PR, Mrs. Halcyon. My duties at Halcyon Communications were strictly . . ."

"There's a story in this, Mary Ann. A big one. And it's yours when the right time comes. This will get you on nighttime television, young lady—I can promise you that."

Mary Ann shrugged helplessly. "Then . . . what do you want me to do?"

The matriarch rose and began pacing the terrace. When she clasped her hands behind her back, the pose was so suggestive of Patton briefing the troops that Mary Ann was forced to suppress a giggle.

"I want you to give me your utter allegiance for a month," said Frannie Halcyon. "After that, you are free to act as you see fit. The Halcyon family has a story to tell, but I want it told on our own terms."

She stopped dead in her tracks; her tiny fist clenched determinedly. "I will not . . . I will *not* be chewed up and spit out by the press the way the Hearsts were!"

She was obviously rolling now, so Mary Ann waited, reinforcing her hostess with sympathetic little nods. Mrs. Halcyon continued, shaking her head somberly as she stared at the light dancing on the surface of the swimming pool.

"Poor Catherine," she intoned softly. "Her family knew everything about journalism, but nothing about PR."

Mary Ann smiled in agreement. This dowager was no dummy.

Mrs. Halcyon continued: "The really *good* PR people, as my husband must have taught you, are the ones who keep people's names *out* of the newspapers. That's what I want from you, Mary Ann—for a month, anyway."

"Why a month?"

"That will be explained later. The point is this: if you take this job, I don't want Barbara Walters crawling through my shrubbery a week from now. I'm too old to take on the networks alone, Mary Ann."

"I can understand that," said Mary Ann. "It's just that I can't *guarantee* . . ."

"You don't have to guarantee anything . . . except your silence for a month."

"I see."

"That's four thousand dollars for your ability to keep a secret for a month. After that, we'll give you . . . an exclusive. That's the word, isn't it?"

Mary Ann smiled. "That's the word."

"It's agreed, then?"

Mary Ann didn't hesitate. "Agreed."

Mrs. Halcyon beamed.

"So what's the story?" asked Mary Ann.

The matriarch signaled Emma, who was standing just inside the double doors on the edge of the terrace. The maid scurried away, returning moments later with a young blond woman, very lean and tanned.

"That's the story," said Frannie Halcyon. "Mary Ann, may I present my daughter DeDe. I believe you two have already met."

The Bermuda Triangle

THE BARS WHERE MICHAEL HUNG OUT, WHEN HE DID
that sort of thing, often featured a big black Harley-
Davidson bike, reverentially pinspotted and suspended from the ceiling on shiny chrome chains.

Mary Ann, on the other hand, haunted a place
called Ciao, a white-tile, toilet-tech bistro on Jackson Street
where a pristine wall-mounted moped—a Vespa Ciao, of
course—reigned supreme as the house icon.

Today, Memorial Day, while Mary Ann was poolside in
Hillsborough and Michael was poolside in Hollywood, Brian
was worshiping the motorcycle of *his* choice, a glossy wine-
red Indian Warrior from the fifties, dangling overhead at the
Dartmouth Social Club, a watering hole on Fillmore Street
for the terminally collegiate.

Jennifer Rabinowitz had appeared out of nowhere.

"God, what are *you* doing back in The Bermuda Triangle?"

Brian smiled. Regulars to the Cow Hollow singles scene
often referred to the intersection of Fillmore and Greenwich
as The Bermuda Triangle. Nubile computer programmers
and other innocents had been known to pass through this
mystical nexus and never be heard from again.

It was stretching it, however, to regard Jennifer as nubile. Brian had been freshening her coffee at Perry's for over half a decade now. They were veterans of the bar wars, he and Jennifer, and Jennifer, like her incredible breasts, was still hanging in there.

"Gotta eat somewhere," grinned Brian, holding up his hot roast beef sandwich. "Grab a seat. Sit down."

She did just that, smiling ferociously. "You look great, Brian. Really."

"Thanks."

"You *went* to Dartmouth, didn't you? This must be like old home week or something." She pointed to a plate glass window emblazoned with a gold leaf Dartmouth Indian. Once upon a time, Brian realized with a twinge of nostalgia, he would have insisted on calling it the Dartmouth Native American.

"Yeah," he admitted, "but that's not it. I just like the sandwiches." He was damned if he'd let her peg him as an old preppie finding his roots.

"Yeah," she said, "they *are* primo." Her smile was relentless. *This is a pick-up,* he told himself. Why did the peaches always fall when you weren't shaking the tree?

"Look," she added, "do you have plans for the day or what?"

He shrugged. "Just this."

"I've got some great weed," she said. "My new place is just around the corner. What say? Old time's sake?"

He was already suffering for her. He liked this cheerful, good-hearted woman. He'd felt a curious kinship with her for five or six years now, ever since she'd barfed on him at the Tarr & Feathers sing-along. He knew what drove her, he thought—the same thing that had driven him before Mary Ann came into his life.

"I've got a better idea," he said. "How 'bout I buy you a drink?"

The smile wavered for a moment, then she salvaged it. "Sure. Whatever. No big deal."

He reached across the table and took her hand. "You look great yourself. Better than ever."

"Thanks." She smiled at him quite genuinely for a moment, then fumbled in her purse for a cigaret, lighting it herself. "I've watched your friend all week," she said.

"Who?"

"The afternoon movie girl. Isn't she your girlfriend now?"

Brian flushed. "Sort of," he said. "Not exactly."

"She's very good, I think. Natural. It's hard to find that on television."

"I'll tell her you said so."

"You do that." Jennifer took a long drag on her cigaret, appraising him with an air of faint amusement. "You've been domesticated, haven't you?"

"Jennifer, I . . ."

"It's all right if you have, Brian. It happens to the best of us. I'm still relentlessly single myself."

"Oh?"

Jennifer nodded very slowly. "Relentlessly."

"Whatever," said Brian.

"Exactly." She blinked at him for a moment, then chucked him affectionately under the chin. "Some guys don't recognize a friendly fuck when it's staring 'em right in the face."

Give a Little Whistle

VUITTON BOUNDED DOWN THE FAMILIAR SLOPE AND barked joyously at the door of the shack. Luke emerged almost immediately and greeted his former companion.

"Whitey, ol' boy . . . well, look who's back!"

He glanced up at Prue, who found herself vaguely embarrassed about invading the intimacy of this reunion. "I've missed this ol' boy," he said.

She smiled a little awkwardly. "It looks like he missed you, too."

"Happy Memorial Day," grinned Luke.

"Same to you."

"The coffee's on, if . . ."

"I'd be delighted," said Prue. Now, she realized, she felt almost *privileged* to be asked, like a little girl from a fairy tale who had earned the confidence of the troll who lived under the village bridge.

Luke was no troll, however. If you discounted his seedy clothes and his rustic surroundings, he was quite a striking man, really. His amber skin and high cheekbones suggested . . . what? . . . Indian blood?

She followed him into the shack and sat down on the big chunk of foam rubber. Vuitton remained outside, chasing small animals through the underbrush. When Prue called to him, Luke advised her: "He knows his way around. Don't worry about him. He'll be back when you want him." He handed the columnist a mug of steaming coffee, catching her eye as he did so. "He's home now."

Prue faltered for a moment, then looked down at her coffee. "This smells marvelous."

"Good. Glad you like it."

"By the way, Luke . . . uh, you haven't run across a little silver whistle, have you?"

Smiling, he opened a cigar box on the shelf above the fire. He handed her the Tiffany trinket.

Prue glowed. "Thank heavens. I'm so sentimental about this silly thing. My husband gave it to me when we were divorced."

"You dropped it on the ledge. I was saving it for you."

"I'm so glad. Thank you so much."

There was something gentle and boyish in his eyes when he looked at her. "It's good protection for a woman. I was worried about you not having it. There's a lot of crazy folks running around these days." He smiled, revealing teeth that were surprisingly even and white. "I guess a lot of people would take me for crazy, huh?"

"I wouldn't," said Prue.

"You did," Luke replied, without malice. "It's natural. People judge people by the houses they live in, the clothes they wear. It takes a little longer to look into the heart, doesn't it?"

"Yes," said Prue, "I guess it does." She looked down, then blew on her coffee, touched and embarrassed by such an accurate assessment of their first encounter.

"Do you know who trusts me?" asked Luke.

Prue flushed. "Luke, I'm sorry. I trust you. I was just . . ." She threw up her hands, unable to finish.

Luke's smile was forgiving. "Besides you, I mean?"

She shook her head.

"Watch," said Luke, sitting down on the edge of his bed. He drummed his fingers on the packed earth floor. "Chipper, Jack, Dusty . . ."

Right on cue, three chipmunks scampered from under the bed and climbed onto Luke's hand. He lifted them to his face and nuzzled them. "These fellows trust me. The buffalo down the road trust me. So do the raccoons over by Rainbow Falls." He let the tiny creatures down again. "I'm nice to humans, too, but I don't do so well with them. It's just a question of knowing where your talent lies, I guess."

Prue was captivated. She reached down to touch the chipmunks, but they scurried under the bed again. "I see what you mean," she said.

"I used to have a whole flock of humans," said Luke.

"What do you mean?"

"A congregation," smiled Luke.

"You were a preacher?"

Luke nodded. "People are the hardest way to find God, though. It's easier out here with the animals . . . and the beauty. Sometimes there's so much beauty it makes me want to cry." His white teeth shone at her again. "See what I mean? Crazy as all get-out."

"I don't think that's crazy," Prue replied. "What happened to your congregation?"

Luke shrugged. "They left me . . . lost the faith. No one wants to find God anymore."

Prue stared at him, tears in her eyes. "Luke . . . if I . . . would you mind if I . . . helped you tell your story?"

"Tell who?"

"The people . . . the public."

"You're a reporter?"

"No. Not exactly. Just a writer. You can trust me, Luke, I promise."

He looked at her for a long time, then lifted his big calloused finger and brushed the tear from her eye. "You are filled with God," he said.

Meeting ——

ICHAEL STOOD IN THE DOORWAY OF THE SCREEN-
ing room and studied the two giants kneeling
over film cans in the corner. They looked like
Vikings ransacking a wine cellar, but their
laughter was so intense and so intimate that an
outsider might have come to the erroneous conclusion that
they were still lovers.

—— held up a film can so Ned could read the label.
"What about this one?"

"I dunno," answered the nurseryman. "I kinda doubt it."

The movie star smiled ruefully. "Me too. I screened it for
some teenyboppers the other day and they were all in hyster-
ics by the time we got to the hayfork scene."

"You were great in the hayfork scene."

"My *lats* were great in the hayfork scene."

"Fuckin' A! And they'll appreciate that. Play to your audience, man!" Ned rapped ——'s chest with the back of his
hand.

"Well," said ——, "maybe it'll keep 'em outa the bushes.
Mr. Shigeda will have my ass if his begonias get crushed.
Where did they come from anyway?"

Ned shrugged. "Santa Monica Boulevard, for all I know. Guido said that Charles told him that Les thought it would be a hot idea."

"And God knows," laughed _____, "Les can round 'em up quicker than Selective Service."

Ned laughed with him. "My friend Michael is out there somewhere."

Michael saw an entrance and raised his hand. "Uh . . . present and accounted for."

Two heads turned instantly in Michael's direction. Both of them smiled at him. Michael stepped forward hastily and extended his hand. "I'm Michael Tolliver," he said. "This is a great party."

"Yeah?"

"Well, I don't know anybody, of course, but . . ."

"Here's a handy guideline," grinned _____. "The blonds are all named Scott. The brunettes are all named Grant. Now you know everybody. Except me. I'm _____."

Michael nodded. "The suspense wasn't killing me."

_____ looked at Ned. "You two aren't married, huh?"

"No way," said the nurseryman, winking at Michael.

"He needs a lover," _____ told Michael. "Find a lover for him, will you?"

"He turns them away every week," said Michael.

"Is that right?" asked _____.

Ned shrugged. "I like being single. Lots of people like being single. *Michael* likes being single." He looked to his friend for confirmation of this fact.

"He likes being a slut," said Michael.

_____ roared, then crooked his arm around Ned's head and kissed his naked scalp. "I love this slut," he said. "Hey . . . how 'bout a house tour, you guys?"

"I think I'll pass," said Ned.

"Hot date?" asked _____.

Ned nodded, smiling. "Somebody named Scott."

The matinee idol turned to Michael. "What about you?"

"Sure," said Michael. "I'm game."

* * *

The house tour included an extensive film library, the pool and cabanas, a terraced garden under the deck off the pool, and the upstairs bedrooms. In *the* bedroom, _____ flung open the French windows overlooking the guests. "The movie should start in a minute. That'll quiet things down."

"What's the movie?" asked Michael.

The actor made a face. "_____. Pure crapola, if you ask me."

"I've never seen it," Michael admitted.

"There's a reason for that," grinned _____.

Michael looked at him directly for the first time. "I think you put yourself down too much. Those guys must be down there for something."

"Who?"

"All those . . . Scotts and Grants. That must tell you something. If you're fooling people about your talent, at least you're fooling a lot of them." Michael smiled suddenly, embarrassed by his own audacity. "If you ask me, that is."

The movie star appraised him jovially. "You work with Ned at the nursery, huh?"

"Right."

"And you guys sing together in some sort of group?"

"Uh-huh." Michael couldn't hide his pride. "The Gay Men's Chorus. We're touring nine cities beginning next week."

The movie star frowned. "I'm afraid I don't understand that."

"What?"

"Why some people make such a big deal out of being gay."

Michael hesitated. He'd heard this line countless times before, usually from older gay men like _____ who had suffered silently for years while *other* people made a big deal out of their homosexuality. "We just want to make it easier for people," he said at last. "Easier for straight people to like us. Easier for gay people to be proud of their heritage."

_____ chuckled ruefully. "Their heritage, huh?"

Michael felt himself bristling. "That's a good enough word, I think." He looked at the movie star and smiled. "You're part of it, incidentally."

DeDe

THE WOMAN WHO STOOD THERE WAS ALMOST A STRAN-
ger, not at all the marshmallow-plump post-
debutante that Mary Ann remembered from days
gone by.

This woman was wiry and brown, with long, sun-
bleached hair that flowed down her back in a ponytail.
Dressed up in one of her old shirtwaists—vintage 1975 or
so—she seemed as awkward as a desert island castaway attempting to walk in shoes again.

Mary Ann was speechless. She stared at DeDe, then turned
back to Mrs. Halcyon, slackmouthed. "I can't . . . I never
dreamed . . ."

Mrs. Halcyon beamed, obviously delighted with the impact
she had made. "You two need to get acquainted again. I'll
leave you alone for a while. If you need anything, Emma can
help you." The matriarch squeezed her daughter's arm,
pecked her on the cheek, and entered the house through the
double doors on the terrace.

Mary Ann fumbled for words again, advancing clumsily to
embrace the apparition that confronted her. "I'm so glad,"

she murmured, almost on the verge of tears. "I'm so glad, DeDe."

She was glad mostly that *someone* could have a happy ending to the Jonestown tragedy. She had never known DeDe very well; she had simply been the boss's daughter. And Beauchamp's wife. The two women, in fact, had seen each other last at Beauchamp's funeral, where neither had made a particularly visible display of grief.

Mary Ann let go of DeDe, suddenly remembering: "Oh . . . the twins?"

DeDe smiled. "Upstairs. Sleeping."

"Thank God."

"Yes."

"And . . . D'orothea?"

"She's in Havana," said DeDe.

They sipped wine by the pool while DeDe told her story.

"D'orothea and I joined the Temple in Guyana in 1977. The twins were just babies, but I wanted them to grow up in a place without prejudice. Their father was Chinese. I suppose you know that."

Mary Ann nodded. The whole town knew it.

"I don't expect you to believe this, but I actually felt a sense of purpose in Jonestown that I had never felt before. For a while, anyway. On my third day there Jones held a catharsis session and made me stand up and explain . . ."

"A catharsis session?"

"That was his term. They were nights when he called us together and made us confess our sins. When I stood up, he said: 'O.K., Miss Rich Bitch, what is it that you think *you* can do for the revolution?' I knew I couldn't lie to him, so I told him I had no skills, and he said: 'You buy things, don't you?' So that's what I ended up doing. I became a kind of procurement officer for Jonestown."

"What was your schedule like?"

"Well, twice a week I took the *Cudjoe,* this little shrimp boat that belonged to the Temple. I caught it in Port Kaituma . . ."

"I'm afraid I don't know . . ."

"The nearest village. On the Barima River. The airstrip is there. Where they killed the congressman."

Mary Ann nodded gravely.

"It was six hours from Port Kaituma to Kumaka, where I did most of my shopping. I supervised the loading of the *Cudjoe,* foodstuffs mostly. That took about three hours, and we always headed back the same day. The captain was a man named William Duke, who didn't work for the Temple but was . . . uh, sympathetic. He was a Communist, the PPP representative in Port Kaituma, and he liked me and adored the twins. Several days before . . . it happened, Captain Duke took me into his cabin and told me about the hundred-pound drum he had on the fantail. It was full of potassium cyanide."

Mary Ann winced. "Jesus."

"Thank God for that little guy," said DeDe. "Thank God for that crummy job. I never would've known otherwise." A hunted look came into her eyes.

"Well," said Mary Ann, trying to help, "it's over now. You're home and you're safe."

DeDe finished off the last of the wine, then set the bottle down with a frown that suggested anything but safe at home. "I'm sorry," she said. "I need some more of this before we continue."

Meanwhile...

JENNIFER RABINOWITZ SAT UP IN BED AND PUT HER BRA back on. "Was that great weed or what?"

"Mmm."

"My friend Scooter gets it directly from Jamaica. He says Bob Marley used to smoke the stuff. It's like . . . official reggae grass or something."

"Rastafarian grass."

"Right. That's the word. I think I could get into that, couldn't you?" She was on her hands and knees now, feeling under the covers for her pantyhose.

"What? The religion?"

"Yeah. I mean, it's a pretty terrific religion. They smoke enormous joints and dance their asses off and support equal opportunity and all that."

"They also think Haile Selassie was God. *Is* God."

"Yeah. I know. I'd have a problem with that, I guess." She considered the issue as she wriggled into her pantyhose. "Still . . . it might be worth it for the grass. Do you see my skirt on your side?"

He shook his head slowly. "The other room."

"Riiight. I am such a space case." She bounded out of bed,

110

stopping suddenly when she reached the door. "Look," she said earnestly, cocking her head, "if it looks like I'm tossing you out, I guess I am. I've got Dancercise at four, and this wasn't exactly an official date."

"No problem," he said.

"You're a great guy. I've had a swell time." She was hopping on one foot now, pulling on a pump. "And I know how whory this looks, believe me."

He laughed. "I've had a great time, too."

"Can I drop you off somewhere?"

"No thanks. I live in the neighborhood."

"What's your last name, by the way?"

"Smith."

"John Smith. For real?"

He nodded rather dolefully. "I'm afraid so."

"That's a riot. We should check into a hotel sometime."

He let her joke slide by. "Maybe we'll bump into each other again at the Balboa."

"Sure," she said cheerfully. "Maybe so. It's been great. Really. I was feeling kind of bummed out when you met me."

The Saga Continues

A ROBIN WAS TRILLING IN A TREETOP AT HALCYON Hill—an odd accompaniment, indeed, for a story as grisly as this one.

"Wait a minute," said Mary Ann. "How could you be sure that the cyanide was intended for . . . for what he used it for?"

"I knew," DeDe replied grimly. "If you were there, you knew. Captain Duke was even more certain than I was. He also knew about Dad's fixation with the twins, and he knew that . . ."

"Your *father* was . . . ?"

"My father?"

"You said Dad."

DeDe grimaced. "I meant *him*. Jones. We called him Dad, some of us." She shuddered, sitting there in the sunshine, then smiled wanly at Mary Ann. "If that doesn't give you the creeps, nothing will."

The flesh on Mary Ann's arm had already pebbled. She held it up so DeDe could see.

DeDe continued: "The point is . . . Jones was obsessed with my children. He called them his little third world wonders.

He saw them as the hope of the future, the living embodiment of the revolution. Sometimes he would single them out at the day-care center and sing little songs to them. I knew he wouldn't leave without taking them." She looked directly into Mary Ann's eyes. "I knew he wouldn't kill himself without killing them."

Mary Ann nodded, mesmerized.

"So I discussed it with D'orothea and we planned the escape . . . with Captain Duke's help. We left on a regular morning run to Kumaka. Sometimes D'orothea would go along with me, so nobody was particularly suspicious. The twins, of course, had to be sneaked on board when nobody was looking. When we got to Kumaka we took on supplies, then we just kept on going down the river to a village called Morawhanna, where Captain Duke bribed the captain of the *Pomeroon,* a freighter that made regular trips between Morawhanna and Georgetown . . . usually with fish on board."

"Uh . . . dead fish, you mean?"

DeDe shook her head. "Tropical fish. It's a big export item in Guyana. They had these big tin drums on board for the fish, and some of them were empty, so we hid out in two of them until we reached Georgetown. Twenty-four hours later."

"Jesus," said Mary Ann.

"I fed a sedative to the children. That helped some. But most of the trip was at sea. Ghastly. The worst experience of my life. It was a little easier when we reached Georgetown. Captain Duke arranged for us to be met by another PPP official . . ."

"You mentioned that before. What's PPP?"

"People's Progressive Party. Jungle Communists. They had us on a flight to Havana within twenty-four hours. D'orothea and I were already working in a cannery when the news of the slaughter broke."

"How long did you live in Havana, then?"

"Two-and-a-half years. Up until last month."

"They wouldn't let you come home?"

"If you mean, here, I didn't *want* to go home. D'orothea and I were happy. The children were happy. There were principles involved, things that mattered to us." DeDe smiled

113

forlornly. "Mattered. Past tense. One of our beloved comrades found out."

"Found out?"

"That D'orothea and I were lovers."

Mary Ann flushed, in spite of herself. "So they . . . uh . . . deported you?"

DeDe nodded. "They gave us a choice, sort of. D'orothea decided to stay. She felt that being a socialist was more important than being a lesbian." She smiled almost demurely. "I didn't agree with that, so I ended up at Fort Chaffee, Arkansas, where I did what I always do when the shit gets this deep."

"What?"

"I called Mother," grinned DeDe.

Later, they tiptoed into an upstairs bedroom where DeDe's four-year-olds lay sleeping. Seeing them there, sprawled blissfully against the bedclothes, Mary Ann was reminded of the little silk dolls sold on the street in Chinatown.

"Beautiful," she whispered.

DeDe beamed. "Edgar and Anna."

"Named for your father and . . . who?"

"I don't know," said DeDe. "Daddy just liked the name. He asked me to name her that on the night he died."

"What they've seen," said Mary Ann, looking down at the children. "They don't remember anything, do they?"

"Not from Guyana, if that's what you mean."

"Thank God."

After a moment of silence, Mary Ann said: "I can't help telling you . . . this is just the most . . . amazing story, DeDe. I'm so flattered you chose me for this."

DeDe smiled. "I hope it'll do you some good."

"There's one thing I don't understand, though."

"Yeah?"

"Why do you want to wait before releasing the story? It ought to be told now, it seems to me. You'll only have to hide out, and sooner or later someone will . . ."

"There are things I have to do," DeDe said sternly.

"Like . . . what?"

"I can't tell you yet," DeDe replied.

When she leaned down to kiss her children, there was something indefinable in her eyes.

Wishing Upon a Star

_____ _____ SAT UP IN BED AND LIT A CIGARET. "MAYBE WE'D better take a break, huh?"

"Yeah?" said Michael, "I'm sorry." *God, was he sorry.*

"It's O.K., pal."

"Maybe with you."

"Nah. It's fine. Happens all the time."

"It does?" Michael sat up, so that now they were both propped against the regal headboard.

The movie star gave his thigh a friendly shake. "Sure. All the time."

"That must be kind of a drag," said Michael.

The same sleepy, half-lidded smile that seemed to work so well on _____ _____'s leading ladies flickered across the actor's face. "I'm just another guy like you, you know."

Michael smiled back at him. "Not yet, you aren't."

"No sweat," said _____, taking another drag on his cigaret. "We're not in any hurry. I'm not, anyway."

"Won't the movie be over soon?"

The movie star shrugged. "You didn't miss anything. I can promise you that."

"Not *down*stairs, maybe."

"Hey, ease up, pal . . . if I don't turn you on, there's no harm done."

"Are you kidding? You've turned me on since I was eleven."

"Hey," grinned _____, "thanks a helluva lot."

Michael laughed apologetically. "I'm not doing very well, am I?"

_____ looked at him with affection, then tousled his hair. "All right. Pretty damn all right."

"It's such a waste," Michael lamented. "Your dick is so beautiful."

The actor nodded his thanks.

"I can't believe what a fuck-up I am. I mean, Jesus God . . . how many cracks do you get at _____ _____?"

"Two or three," said the movie star, tweaking Michael's nipple. "And possibly lasagna. Guido's dishing it out to the hordes downstairs. Why don't I bring us a plate?"

Fifteen minutes later, when _____ came back with the food, Michael had some good news for him: "I found the popper case. It was wedged between the mattress and the headboard."

"Great," said _____, easing into bed holding two forks and a plate of lasagna.

Michael examined the black leather pouch. "Jees. Your initials and everything. And *real* poppers inside. Lord, it's so grand here at the Harmonia Gardens."

_____ speared a chunk of lasagna and handed the fork to his guest. "That was a present from Ned. Christmas before last. He knows how to buy for me."

Michael took a healthy bite out of the lasagna. "That was what did it, you know. Those goddamn initials on that little leather case. All I could think of was: 'Hey, that's right. That must make me _____ _____.'"

"She's a little tougher than you," said the actor, "but I like your body better."

Michael smiled with a mouthful of lasagna. "Something tells me you've said that before."

_____ spoke to the tip of his fork. "Well, you're not exactly the first guy to say he feels like _____ _____."

"Good point."

"It'll pass. It just takes a while sometimes."

"I think it already has."

"Huh?"

"Do you mind if we ditch the lasagna and have another go at it?"

"You're on," grinned _____.

Somewhere in Arizona, Michael is hitchhiking on a stretch of desert highway. The trucker who picks him up is older than he is—gray and a little grizzled—but his body is massive and hard. Without a word, he lays a thick-veined hand on Michael's thigh and takes him to a sleazy motel on the edge of the desert. It is there that it finally happens, there that Michael tastes diesel fuel on a sunburned neck and commits himself totally to the appetites of a stranger.

"Uh . . . Michael?"

"Mmm?"

"You O.K.?"

"Does Nancy have a red dress?"

"What?"

"Sorry. Just a little post-coital campy."

"Oh."

"I'm great. How are you?"

"Great. All things are possible, huh?"

"Uh-huh," said Michael dreamily, wondering if somewhere in Arizona a lonely hitchhiker was sleeping with a truck driver, but fantasizing about _____ _____.

It seemed only fair.

Womb for One More

THE SAMADHI CENTER ON VAN NESS WAS ACROSS THE street from a Midas muffler shop and next door to Hippo Hamburgers. Brian pointed this out to Mary Ann, adding wickedly: "It kinda makes me feel mystical already."

Rolling her eyes, Mary Ann pushed the button for the third floor. "This isn't like *Altered States,* you know. It isn't a psychedelic number. It's whatever you want it to be. Brian, promise me you won't be a wiseass with the attendant. They take this place seriously."

"Right." Brian assumed an appropriately sober expression. "Are you actually a member here now?"

"I signed up for ten floats," said Mary Ann. "I can take them anytime."

"How much was that?"

"A hundred and twenty-five dollars."

Brian whistled.

"That's not so much," said Mary Ann. "Not for what it does for me. Besides, it's close to work and I . . ."

"Where are you getting this kind of money?"

"What kind of money?"

"We've been living like lords for the past *week,* Mary Ann. Ever since you got back from Hillsborough."

"We may have splurged a bit now and then."

"Yeah." Brian counted on his fingers. "Dinner at L'Orangerie. Uh . . . scalper's tickets to Liza Minnelli. That big motherfucker floral horseshoe you sent Michael when he left on the tour. Have I left anything out?"

Mary Ann wouldn't look at him.

"It's that old lady," persisted Brian. "She's giving you money, isn't she?"

"Brian . . ."

"Just tell me that much, O.K.?"

"All right!" said Mary Ann. "She's giving me money. Are you satisfied now?"

"I knew it! She's buying hot consumer tips from you!"

The elevator door opened. "Very funny," said Mary Ann, striding briskly across gray industrial carpeting. "Will you behave yourself now?"

The room assigned to Brian contained a Samadhi tank and a private shower. The tank stood chest high, roughly as long and wide as a twin bed. According to the attendant, it contained ten inches of water in which 800 pounds of Epsom salts had been dissolved.

"Is it dark in there?" asked Brian.

The attendant nodded. "Completely. We also have earplugs, if you like."

"How do I know when my hour is up?"

"They play music," said Mary Ann.

"In the tank?"

The attendant smiled euphorically. "Pachelbel."

"My favorite," said Brian.

Mary Ann shot daggers at him. "I'll be in the tank across the hall."

Brian winked at her. "Last one to Nirvana is a rotten egg."

* * *

It took him several minutes to get used to it, to accept the fact that he could relax, even sleep, lying flat on his back in the pitch darkness, suspended like a fetus in this vat of warm, viscous water.

The earplugs, furthermore, obliterated everything but the sound of his own breathing.

It was not what he wanted.

He crawled out of the tank, showered off the salty slime, and stole across the hallway to Mary Ann's room. Still naked, he knocked on the door of her tank.

The vinyl-covered hatch opened slowly, revealing the whites of her eyes.

"Brian! You scared me to death!"

"Sorry," he said.

"Did they see you come over here?"

Brian shook his head. "Cohabitation is against the rules?"

"It's supposed to be a *womb,* Brian."

"And I should go back to mine, huh?"

Finally she smiled at him. "You're just the worst."

"Anyway," said Brian, "we can tell them we're twins."

They were floating in space, fingertips touching.

"I'll make a deal with you," whispered Brian.

"What?"

"If you'll tell me about your secret mission to Hillsborough, I'll tell you about Jennifer Rabinowitz."

"No deal."

"I'll tell you, anyway."

"I figured you would," said Mary Ann. "Who is she?"

"Just a Good Time Charlene I used to know."

"And?"

"And . . . I didn't fuck her while you were in Hillsborough."

Mary Ann laughed. "Terrific."

"I *could* have. Easy as pie. She knew about you and didn't mind . . ."

"Brian, *I* don't mind."

"I knew *that,* too. She didn't mind and you didn't mind, and she *knew* that I knew that you didn't mind. I had the whole goddamn world's permission to fuck Jennifer Rabinowitz, and I didn't do it."

She squeezed his hand affectionately. "I don't think there's a medal for that, sport."

"I don't want a medal," he murmured. "I want you to know what it means."

"I know what it means," she said softly.

A Man Like Saint Francis

BEHIND THE WHEEL OF HIS RED 1957 CADILLAC EL Dorado Biarritz, Father Paddy took on a disturbingly secular aspect. Prue could see why the car was a continuing embarrassment to the archdiocese, but she also felt that a bona fide television personality should be entitled to a few idiosyncrasies.

"Well," said Father Paddy, grinning at the society columnist, "what's the latest on Nature Boy?"

Prue chastised him with a little frown. "He's a very good man, Father."

"Did I imply otherwise?"

"He used to be a man of the cloth, in fact."

The cleric's eyebrow arched. "A Catholic?"

"No . . . some sort of Protestant, I think. He was an investment broker before that."

"*What?*"

"I have no reason to doubt him," she said defensively. "He doesn't talk much, but he's quite literate when he does. He's amazing, Father. He's done everything. He even taught English once at a private school in Rio. He's done it all, and now he's . . . doing this."

"Doing *what?*"

"Living. Being. Existing with God."

"Has he hit you up for cash yet?"

Prue was shocked. "No! As a matter of fact, I *offered* to help him out and he turned me down."

"I see."

"He's been living there for almost a year-and-a-half, he says. The park police know about him, but they let him stay because he respects the environment. He's marvelous with animals, in fact. He has three little chipmunks that live under the bed."

Father Paddy frowned. "This is all very charming, my child. But how does he *eat?*"

"I don't know. He scrounges, I guess." Prue turned and looked out the window as the Biarritz climbed into Pacific Heights. "Your skepticism distresses me, Father. He's no different from Saint Francis, really."

The priest smiled indulgently. "I'm only concerned for your safety, darling."

She took his hand appreciatively. "I know that. But it's *such* a marvelous story, isn't it?"

"How many times have you been there, anyway?"

"Uh . . . I'm not sure."

"Give us a guess."

She searched in her bag for her lipstick. "Maybe five or six times."

Father Paddy's eyes flickered mischievously. "My, my . . . such a *long* story, too."

That Word

FOR ALMOST A WEEK NOW, FRANNIE HALCYON HAD BEEN giddy as a schoolgirl. She believed in life again, in children, in sunshine, in motherhood, in miracles. And she longed, more than ever, to share her joy with the world.

"Viola called today," she announced at lunch. "It was all I could do to keep from blabbing."

DeDe frowned. "Don't even joke about that, Mother."

"I know, I know."

"I need time, Mother. Viola would be on the phone to the *Chronicle* in two seconds flat. Please help me out on this, O.K.?"

"I got Mary Ann for you, didn't I?"

"I know, Mother, and I appreciate . . ."

"I just don't understand why you need a whole month, DeDe. Surely a week or so would . . ."

"Mother!"

"Never mind, then." Frannie looked down at her spinach salad. "Have you talked to her today?"

"Who?"

"Mary Ann."

DeDe nodded. "She's coming by tomorrow."

"She's such a sweet girl," said Frannie.

"She wants to tape me," said DeDe.

"Oh . . . I see." The matriarch contemplated her salad again. "About . . . your experiences, I suppose?"

DeDe looked faintly annoyed. "That *was* our arrangement, Mother."

"Of course."

"She's promised not to release anything until the month's up. I trust her."

"So do I. Uh . . . DeDe?"

"Yeah?"

"You won't be talking about the . . . business with D'orothea, will you?"

DeDe's fork stopped in mid-air. She looked up, smoldering. "Mother, the *whole* business was with D'orothea. I lived with her for four years, remember?"

"You know what I mean," said Frannie.

"Yes," DeDe replied flatly. "I know what you mean." She dug into her salad as if she were trying to kill something in it. "You've made your feelings quite clear about that."

Frannie hesitated, dabbing the corners of her mouth with her napkin. "DeDe . . . I think I've been a lot more . . . accepting than most mothers might have been. I accepted those precious children long ago, didn't I? I don't quite . . . *understand* your friendship with D'orothea, but I would never presume to pass judgment on you for it. I just don't think it's something that warrants public discussion."

"Why?" asked DeDe. She didn't look up.

"It's in poor taste, darling."

DeDe set her fork down and looked at her mother for a long time before speaking. "So," she said at last, her lip curling slightly, "I should restrict my reminiscences to *tasteful* things like cyanide and public torture. Super, Mother. Thanks for the advice."

"You needn't be snide, DeDe."

"D'orothea Wilson helped save your grandchildren's lives. You owe her a *lot,* Mother."

"I know that. And I'm grateful."

"Besides, I ended up with the gay Cuban refugees. I'm a

126

dyke on *paper*, Mother. It's a matter of public record, for God's sake!"

"Don't use that word around me, DeDe!" Frannie fumbled for her napkin. "Anyway, the refugee people could have made a mistake, a clerical error or something."

"I loved her," DeDe said coolly. "That was no clerical error."

There was harmony again after supper when Frannie, DeDe, Emma and the twins romped together on the lawn. Frannie took new delight in her grandchildren, these precious almond-eyed sprites who called her "Gangie" and frolicked on American soil as if it had always been theirs.

When DeDe and the children had retired, Frannie repaired to her bed with a Barbara Cartland novel.

Shortly after midnight, she heard a moan from DeDe's room.

The matriarch clambered out of bed, made her way down the hall, and listened outside her daughter's door.

"No, Dad. PLEASE, DAD . . . NO, PLEASE DON'T . . . OH, GOD HELP ME! DAD! DAD!"

Frannie flung open the door and rushed to DeDe's bedside. "Darling, it's all right. Mother's here, Mother's here." She rocked her daughter in her arms.

DeDe woke up and whimpered pathetically.

In the next room, the twins were sobbing in unison.

Letter from the Road

DEAR MARY ANN AND BRIAN,

Greetings from Motown! The tour is going great so far, though I have failed to meet anyone even remotely resembling _____ _____. Yesterday morning, on the flight from Lincoln, we had a whole 737 to ourselves, so all hell broke loose. Mark Hermes, a fellow baritone, put on a wig, scarf and apron—and two teacups for earrings—and impersonated the stewardess while she did her oxygen mask instructions. She loved it. The flight people have all been fabulous, as a matter of fact—especially the two hot Northwest stewards we had (not literally, alas) on the flight between Chicago and Minneapolis. One was gay, the other questionable. Naturally, I fell for the questionable one.

Lincoln, believe it or not, has been the high point so far. The local homos threw a lovely little potluck brunch for us in Antelope Park. (In fact, I've been to so many potluck functions that I'm beginning to feel like a lesbian.) The main gay bar in Lincoln is called—is this discreet enough?—The Alternative. It is the scene of much bad drag. White boys impersonating Aretha Franklin, etc. Most of us opted for the alternative to The Alternative—a joint called the Office Lounge. It was stifling in there, so we took off our shirts after we'd been boogying for a while. A major no-no. Apparently there's a law that says you can't take your shirt off in Nebraska.

The chamber singers were supposed to appear on Channel 10 in Lincoln, but the station manager canceled at the last minute because he didn't want to "rub people's faces in it"—whatever "it" is. By and large, though, people have been pretty wonderful. The audience at First Plymouth Church was about fifty percent old ladies. Old ladies can always tell "nice young men" when they see them.

The audience was skimpy in Dallas—possibly because the Dallas morning *News* refused to print our ads. Our consolation was a private swim party thrown at the fashionable Highland Park home of a gay doctor named—I'm not making this up—Ben Casey. Some of the boys did an impressive nude water ballet to the music of "Tea for Two."

We stayed at the Ramada Inn in Mesquite, Texas—the town that gave hairspray to the world—and we were a smash hit at the Denny's there, where a waitress named Loyette (pronounced Low-ette) thinks we're the biggest thing since the death of Elvis. Oh yes—we ran out of hot water at the Ramada Inn. One-hundred-and-thirty-five faggots without hot water. Not a pretty scene. As luck would have it, the friendliest place in town was the steam room at the First Baptist Church—an enormous complex that covers about four square blocks of downtown Dallas. A lot of organists hang out there, if you catch my drift.

After the Minneapolis concert, a bunch of us went to a bar called The Gay Nineties. Apparently it's been called that for years, even when it was the city's oldest strip joint. It has three separate rooms—one for leather types, one for disco queens, one for preppies. I wandered around aimlessly, having my usual identity crisis. Ned, of course, sauntered into the leather section and racked up so many phone numbers that he looked like the bathroom wall at the Greyhound station.

David Norton, one of our tenors, had twenty members of his family show up for the concert in Minneapolis. That's been happening a lot, all over. Lots of hugs and boo-hoos backstage. Also in Minneapolis, I met an old couple—both in their eighties—who came up and thanked me in the lobby after the concert. They were brother and sister, both gay, and they'd driven all the way from their farm in Wisconsin to hear us sing. They had thick white hair and incredible blue eyes and all I could think of was the "eccentric old bachelor and his spinster sister" who used to live down the road from us in Orlando. We talked for about fifteen minutes, and we hugged when we said goodbye as if we had known each other forever. The old lady said: "You know, when we were your age, we didn't know there was a word for what we were."

As the song says—"Other places only make me love you best." Next comes New York, Boston, Washington and Seattle. A big hug for Mrs. M. Tell her the brownies were perfect.

In haste,
MICHAEL

P.S. I have it on the best authority that the chorus will be returning to the city in the vicinity of 18th and Castro at 5 P.M. on Father's Day. If you can make it, I'd love to see your shining faces in the crowd. Make Brian wear something tight.
P.P.S. Dallas men wear their muscles like feather boas.

Her Wilderness Like Eden

LUKE'S FAVORITE BIBLICAL QUOTATION CAME FROM Isaiah:

For the Lord will comfort you; he will comfort you; he will comfort all her waste places, and make her wilderness like Eden, her desert like the garden of the Lord.

Prue entered the passage in her notebook, then read it aloud again. "That makes such perfect sense, now that I think of it."

"What?" asked Luke, looking up from his cot. He was stroking one of the chipmunks with his forefinger.

"That quote. This place. You've made this spot your garden of the Lord. You've made this wilderness like Eden." True, the rhododendron dell wasn't exactly a wilderness by most people's standards, but the metaphor worked for Prue.

Luke smiled benignly. "You could do it, too."

"Do what?"

"Change your wilderness into a garden."

Prue's brow furrowed. "Do you think I'm living in a wilderness?"

He let the chipmunk down and laid his hands to rest on his knees. "That's for you to decide, Prue."

The sound of her own name stunned her. She was sure he had never used it before. "You don't know that much about me," she said quietly, trying not to sound defensive. Why did she suddenly feel like a butterfly on the end of a pin?

"I know things," he said. "More than you know about me. I've read your column, Prue. I know about the thing you call a life."

She didn't know whether to feel flattered or indignant. *"Where?"* she exclaimed. "How in the world did you . . . ?"

"How in the world did a hermit get a copy of *Western Gentry* magazine?"

"I didn't mean it like that, Luke."

He seemed amused by her disclaimer. "Yes you did. You can't help it. You're a woman who worships material things. I don't mind, Prue. Jesus found room in his heart for people like that. There's no reason why I can't, too."

She reddened horribly. "Luke, I'm sorry if . . ."

"Sit down," he said, patting a place on the cot next to him. Prue obeyed, responding instantly to a tone of voice that conjured up images of her father back in Grass Valley.

"It hurts me to see people in need," said Luke.

Prue thought this was just plain unfair. Her Forum discussions often focused on the needy. "Luke, just because I have money doesn't mean I don't feel compassion for the poor."

"I'm not talking about the poor. I'm talking about you."

Silence.

"I've never seen such need, Prue."

"Luke . . ."

"You need someone who doesn't see the fancy dresses and the house on Nob Hill. Someone who refuses to be distracted by the myth you've spent such a long time creating. . . ."

"Now, wait a minute!"

"Someone who *really* sees Prudy Sue Blalock, not the party girl, not the pathetic creature who spends her time bragging about how far she's come. Someone who would have loved her if she had never left Grass Valley at all."

"Luke, I appreciate your . . ."

"You don't appreciate a damn thing yet, but you will. I'll teach you to love God again, to love yourself as God made you, to love the little girl who's deep down inside of you, aching to cast off those stupid, goddamn Alice-in-Wonderland clothes and tell the world what's really in her heart. Look at me, Prue. Don't you see it? *Don't you see it in my eyes?"*

When she finally looked at him, all she felt was an uncanny familiarity, as if she had known this man all her life—or in a past life. She *knew* these features: the extraordinary cheekbones, the amber skin, the full lips, the strong hands that now cradled one of hers as though it were a wounded bird.

Tears spilled out of Prue's eyes. "Please don't do this," she said.

"You can change," he offered gently. "It doesn't have to stay this way."

"But . . . *how?"* Her heart was pounding wildly. Through the teary blur, she could see the chipmunks gamboling on the dirt floor. She felt as if she were in a Disney cartoon.

"You can start by trusting me," he said. "You can trust me to love you unconditionally. On your terms. At your pleasure. As often or as little as you want. Forever."

She knew in her heart that he meant it.

So she took his hand and put it where she needed him.

Adam and Eve

P<small>RUE</small>?"
    "Mmm?"
    "You like some coffee?"
    "Huh-uh. Don't get up yet. I'm fine."
    "You look fine. Beautiful."
"Thank you."
"What about your driver?"
"What about him?"
"You've been gone three hours. Won't he worry about you?"
"He's used to waiting. That's what he's paid for."
"But . . . if he calls the police . . ."
"He won't call the police. Why should he call the police?"
"No reason. It's getting dark, that's all. I thought he might worry about you."
"It's dark already?"
"Uh-huh."
"If you want me to leave, I . . ."
"I don't want you to leave."
"Good."
"If I had my way, you would never leave. We would lock

ourselves away from that madness out there and . . . Jesus, that feels good."

"Mmm."

"Your hair is so soft. Like a baby's."

"Mmm."

"I meant what I said, Prue."

"Mmm."

"Will you come back?"

"Mmm."

"You wouldn't lie to me?"

"No."

"Good. Do that some more."

"Mmm."

"I know you can't be seen with me. I know that."

"Luke . . ."

"No. Listen to me. I know you. I know this isn't easy for you. Just promise me you won't torture yourself later."

"Torture myself?"

"Feeling guilty. Punishing yourself for loving a man who could never fit into your world."

Silence.

"That's the truth, isn't it? You know it, and I know it. What we have can only happen here. And never often enough. I know all that, Prue, and I accept it. I want you to do the same."

"Luke, I would never . . ."

"Forget about never. Forget about forever. All I want, Prue, is a little now from time to time. Promise me that, and I'll be happy."

"I promise."

"I can show you wonderful things."

"You already have."

"I think you should go now."

"All right."

"Don't be afraid, Prue. Please."

"Of what?"

"Us."

"I'll never be afraid of that."

"Don't be so sure."

135

"I don't understand."

"Just come back, O.K.?"

"Soon."

"I'll be here."

D'or

MARY ANN'S LE CAR BARRELED ALONG SKYLINE Drive on a June evening at sunset.

"God," said DeDe, glimpsing the sea. "It's so infernally beautiful, isn't it?"

"It sure is," said Mary Ann.

"It never goes away, you know."

"What?"

"That. Or the memory of that. Even in the jungle . . . even in *that* jungle, there were things about California that never left me. Even when I wanted them to."

Mary Ann hesitated, then asked: "Why would you want them to?"

"You didn't grow up here," said DeDe. "Almost anything can be oppressive given the right circumstances." She smiled almost wistfully. "And salvation comes when you least expect it."

Mary Ann turned and looked at her. "Surely you don't consider Guyana your salvation?"

DeDe shook her head. "I was talking about D'orothea."

"Oh."

"I'd like to now, if you don't mind. Does it make you uncomfortable?"

"Not at all," said Mary Ann, lying only slightly.

"It makes Mother climb the walls."

"Different generation," said Mary Ann.

"Did you know her at Daddy's agency?"

"Who?" asked Mary Ann.

"D'orothea."

"Oh . . . not very well, actually. She just came in and out sometimes. She was our biggest client's top model. Frankly, she intimidated the hell out of me."

DeDe smiled. "She had a way with her. Has, that is."

"She used to be friends with a friend of mine. A copywriter named Mona Ramsey."

"They were lovers," said DeDe.

"Yeah." Mary Ann grinned sheepishly. "That's what I meant, actually. Sometimes the Cleveland in me takes over."

DeDe chuckled, eyes glued to the sunset. "You're doing better than I ever did. I never learned about a goddamn thing until it actually happened to me."

Mary Ann pondered that for a moment. "Yeah," she said drily, "but what hasn't happened to you?"

DeDe shot her a wry glance. "Good point," she said.

"It's a journalist's dream," observed Mary Ann, adding hastily: "I hope that doesn't sound callous."

"No. I'm aware of its potential."

"There's a book in it for sure. Maybe even a movie-for-TV."

DeDe laughed ironically at the prospect. "Won't Mother love the hell out of that? 'Starring Sally Struthers as the Society Lesbo.' Jesus."

Mary Ann giggled. "We should be able to do better than that."

"Maybe . . . but I'm prepared for the worst."

Mary Ann looked earnestly at her passenger. "I'll do everything I can to help."

"I know," said DeDe. "I believe that. But not until the month is out, O.K.?"

Mary Ann nodded. "I wish I understood why."

"If I tell you, will you promise me that Mother won't hear about it?"

"Of course."

"She thinks I need the time to rest up, to get my bearings before the publicity begins. That's true enough, but not the whole truth. The whole truth has always been a bit too much for Mother."

Mary Ann smiled. "I've noticed that."

"I need to talk to some people. People who might know . . . what I need to know."

"Who? Can you say?"

"Temple members," answered DeDe. "And people who knew him."

"Jones?"

DeDe nodded.

"You could start with the governor," said Mary Ann. "And half the politicians in town. He was quite a popular fellow around here."

DeDe smiled faintly. "I know. At any rate, I'm stalling right now, because I haven't got all the facts. And I certainly don't relish the thought of being branded as a nut case."

"That would never happen."

"In two weeks," said DeDe, "you may have changed your mind."

They parked to watch the sun go down in flames.

"I guess I changed the subject," said Mary Ann.

"When?"

"You wanted to talk about D'orothea."

"Yeah, well . . . there wasn't much to say, really. Just that she cared for me. And made me laugh a lot. And the twins worshiped her. And she made love like an angel. And I wish she'd get her silly socialist ass out of Cuba and come home to me and the children. The usual stuff. Not much."

"Until you lose it," said Mary Ann.

"Until you lose it," said DeDe. She watched the sea in silence for a moment, then turned to her companion. "I'm glad you're here. You're a generous listener. You take things in stride."

Mary Ann smiled. "Billie Jean King helped."

"Huh?"

"I guess you haven't heard about that."

"She's a dyke, too?"

"Well," said Mary Ann. "She had an affair with a woman. Does that make her a dyke?"

"It does if she did it right," DeDe replied.

Gaying Out

THE WEATHER HAD BEEN RELENTLESSLY SUNNY FOR AL-
most a week, so Michael and Ned had their hands
full at God's Green Earth. Business was so brisk at
the nursery that it was three o'clock before they sat
down amidst the other living things requiring par-
tial shade and contemplated their Yoplait.

"What do you think I should do?" asked Michael.

"About what?"

"The parade."

Ned shrugged. "You're going, aren't you?"

"Sure. But what do I *wear*? There's a big demand for the
All-American look, and I pull that off pretty well. On the
other hand, the Sisters of Perpetual Indulgence have asked
me to be a nun this year."

Ned spooned yogurt into his mouth. "Go for the nun," he
said.

Michael thought for a moment. "Have you ever tried getting laid when you're dressed as a nun?"

"Why not? There must be nuns who have."

"Climb every mountain, huh?"

Ned laughed. "I suppose you could be an All-American nun."

"What's that? A denim habit?"

"Denim *under* your habit," smiled Ned.

"Right. So I can swing into action at a moment's notice. Like Superman. I like it, Ned—style *and* content. You got an answer for everything."

The nurseryman gave him a once-over, then smiled. "Sister Mary Mouse, huh?"

They remained there in the dappled light, finishing their lunches in silence.

Then Michael said: "Do you ever get tired of all this?"

"The nursery, you mean?"

"No. Being gay."

Ned smiled. "What do you think?"

"I don't mean being homosexual," said Michael. "I wouldn't change that for anything. I love men."

"I've noticed."

"I guess I'm talking about the culture," Michael continued. "The Galleria parties. The T-shirts with the come-fuck-me slogans. The fourteen different shades of jockstraps and those goddamn mirrored sunglasses that toss your own face back at you when you walk into a bar. Phony soldiers and phony policemen and phony jocks. Hot this, hot that. I'm sick of it, Ned. There's gotta be another way to be queer."

Ned grinned, tossing his yogurt cup into the trash. "You could become a lesbian."

"I might," Michael replied. "They do a lot of things that I'd like to do. They *date,* for Christ's sake. They write each other bad poetry. Look . . . we give them so much grief about trying to be butch, but what the hell are *we* doing, anyway? When I was a teenager, I used to walk down the street in Orlando and worry about whether or not I looked like . . . well, less than a man. Now I walk down Castro Street and worry about the same thing. What's the difference?"

Ned shrugged. "They don't beat you up for it here."

"Good point."

"And nobody's *making* you go to the gym, Mouse. Nobody's making you act butch. If you wanna be an effete poet and pine away in a garret or something, you're free to do it."

"Those are my choices, huh?"

"Those are everybody's choices," said Ned.

"Then why aren't they exercising them?"

"They?" asked Ned.

"Well, I meant . . ."

"You meant 'they.' You meant everybody else but you. You're the only sensitive one, right, the only full-fledged human being."

Michael scowled. "That isn't fair."

"Look," said Ned, sliding his arm across Michael's shoulders, "don't shut yourself off like that. There are two hundred thousand faggots in this town. If you generalize about them, you're no better than the Moral Majority."

Michael looked at him. "Yeah, but I know you know what I mean."

"Yeah. I know."

"It's just so fucking packaged," said Michael. "A kid comes here from Sioux Falls or wherever, and he buys his uniform at All-American Boy, and he teaches himself how to stand just so in a dark corner at Badlands, and his life is all posturing and attitude and fast-food sex. It's too easy. The mystery is gone."

"Is it gone for you?"

Michael smiled. "Never."

"Then maybe it isn't for that kid. Maybe it's just what he needs to get Sioux Falls out of his system."

A long silence, and then: "I'm sounding awfully old, aren't I?"

Ned shook his head. "You're just a little gayed out after the tour. I feel that way sometimes. Everybody does. Nobody ever said it would be easy, Michael." He tightened his grip on his friend's shoulders. "You want me to help you make your habit?"

Michael's eyes widened. "You sew?"

"Sure," said Ned, "when I'm not standing in a dark corner at Badlands."

Unoriginal Sin

PRUE RUMMAGED FURIOUSLY FOR THE RIGHT WORDS. "He's just . . . different, Father. He's different from any man I've ever known."

"Somehow," replied the priest, "I have no trouble believing that."

"He's decent and he's kind and intuitive . . . and he has such respect for nature, and he understands God better than anyone I've ever known."

"And he's a helluva lot of fun in the sack."

"Father!"

"Well, let's get the cards on the table, girl. This isn't the dressing room at Saks, you know."

Prue didn't answer for a moment. She sat there rigidly in the darkness, hearing the scuffle of feet outside the confessional. "Father," she said at last, "I think somebody's waiting."

A sigh came through the hole in the wall. "Somebody's *always* waiting," bemoaned the cleric. "It's just that time of the month. Can't this wait till lunch on Tuesday?"

"No. It can't."

"Very well."

"You're so sweet to . . ."

"Get on with it, darling."

"All right . . ." Prue hesitated, then began again. "We *have* slept together."

"Go on."

"And . . . it was good."

The priest cleared his throat. "Is he . . . clean?"

Stony silence.

"You do understand me, don't you, my child? I'm talking hygiene, not morals. I mean, you don't know where he's been, do you?"

Prue lowered her voice to an angry whisper. "He's perfectly clean!"

"Good. You can't be too careful."

"I don't need you to tell me how . . . different he is, Father. I know that better than anyone. I also know that I need him in my life very badly. I can't eat . . . I can't write . . . I can't go back and make things the way they were before I met him. I can't, Father. Do you understand what I'm saying?"

"Of course, my child." His voice was much gentler this time. "How are his teeth, by the way?"

"For God's sake!"

"Prue, lower your voice. Mrs. Greeley is out there, remember?"

A long silence, and then: "How can I share this with you, if you won't be serious with me."

"I'm being *deadly* serious, darling. I asked about his teeth for a reason. It would help to know how . . . uh, presentable he is. Does he look O.K., aside from his clothes? I mean, would we have to fix him up?"

"I cannot believe this!"

"Just answer the question, my child."

"He's . . . magnificent," Prue sputtered. "He's a handsome middle-aged man with nice skin, nice teeth. His vocabulary is better than mine."

"So all he needs is Wilkes?"

"For *what?*"

"To pass. What else? The man needs a new suit, darling. We all had to pass at one point or another. Henry Higgins did it for Eliza; you can do it for Luke. Simple, *n'est-ce pas?*"

Prue was horrified. "Luke will not be . . . fixed up, Father."

"Have you asked him?"

"I wouldn't dream of that. He's such a proud man."

"Ask him."

"I couldn't."

The cleric sighed. "Very well."

"Anyway, where would I do it?"

"Do what?"

"This . . . makeover. He won't come to my place, I know that. What would I do? Make him hide in the closet when my secretary's there? It's perfectly ridiculous."

Father Paddy seemed to ponder for a moment. "Let me work on it, darling. I have an idea."

"What?"

"It'll take a bit of arranging. I'll get back to you. Run along now. Father knows best."

So Prue collected her things and left the confessional.

Glowering, Mrs. Greeley watched her walk out of the cathedral.

White Night

I T HAD BEEN FIVE DAYS SINCE THEIR LAST TAPING.

"It's wonderful to see you," said DeDe. "I was going a little stir crazy at home."

They were eating dinner at a seafood place in Half Moon Bay. DeDe was wearing a Hermès scarf on her head and oversized sunglasses. Mary Ann was reminded of Jackie O's old shopping get-up for Greece.

"I'd think you'd be used to it by now," said Mary Ann.

"What?"

"Being confined. First Jonestown, then the gay Cuban refugee center."

"You'll never know true confinement," mugged DeDe, "until you've lived with a hundred Latin drag queens."

Mary Ann grinned. "Grim, huh?"

"*Noisy.* Castanets day and night. Aye-yi-yi till it's coming out your ass."

Mary Ann laughed, then concentrated on her scallops. Was this the time to ask? Could she ease into the subject delicately? "Uh . . . DeDe?"

"Yeah?"

"Are you doing all right? I mean . . . is something the matter?"

DeDe set her fork down. "Why do you ask?"

"Well . . . your mother says you've been having nightmares."

Silence.

"If I'm prying, tell me. I thought it might help you to talk about it."

DeDe looked down at the Sony Micro Cassette-Corder that Mary Ann had bought with her first paycheck from Mrs. Halcyon. "It wouldn't make bad copy, either."

Mary Ann was devastated. She turned off the machine instantly. "DeDe, I would never . . ."

"Please. I didn't mean that. I'm sorry." DeDe's hand rose shakily to her brow. "Turn it back on. Please."

Mary Ann did so.

"I'm edgy," said DeDe, massaging her temples. "I'm sorry . . . I shouldn't take it out on you . . . of all people. Yeah, I'm having nightmares."

"About . . . him?"

DeDe nodded.

"How well did you know him, anyway?"

DeDe hesitated. "I wasn't in the inner circle, if that's what you mean."

"Who was?"

"Well . . . mostly the ones who slept with him. He had a sort of coterie of young white women who were always getting screwed for the revolution. Sometimes he had sex as often as ten or twelve times a day. He used to brag about it. It was how he took control."

"But he never . . . ?"

"He knew about me and D'orothea, and he hated it. Not because we were lesbians, because he couldn't have us."

"It was that important to him?"

DeDe shrugged. "His track record's available. He took two wives from Larry Layton, and he fathered a child by one of them. He fucked anything he could get his hands on, including some of the men."

"I see."

"He was . . . with me only once. At Jane Pittman Gardens."

Mary Ann looked puzzled.

"Our dorm," explained DeDe. "A lot of them were named after famous black women. I was sick that night, with a fever. D'orothea and most of the others were at a white night. . . ."

"Uh . . . ?"

"Suicide practice. Somebody else must've run the show, because Jones came to the dorm and climbed into bed with me."

"Jesus."

"He told me quite calmly that he thought it was about time the twins saw who their father was."

Mary Ann shook her head in disbelief.

"And then . . . he raped me. The twins were in the crib next to us, screaming through the whole thing. When he finally left, he leaned over and kissed both of them rather sweetly and said: 'Now you're mine forever.' "

"Awful."

"He means it, too."

Mary Ann reached across the table and took her hand. "Meant," she said quietly.

DeDe looked away from her. "Let's go get a drink somewhere."

Man and Walkman

I T WAS LATE AFTERNOON, THE TIME OF DAY WHEN SUNSHINE
streamed through the green celluloid shades at the
Twin Peaks and made the patrons look like fish in an
overpopulated aquarium.

Michael sat on a window seat, against the glass—like
the snail in the aquarium, he decided, passive, voyeuristic,
moving at his own pace. He was still wearing his God's Green
Earth overalls.

The man next to him was wearing a Walkman. When he
saw Michael watching him, he took off the tiny earphones and
held them out to him. "Wanna listen?"

Michael smiled appreciatively. "Who is it?"

"Abba."

Abba? This guy was built like a brick shithouse, with an
elephantine mustache and smoldering brown eyes. What was
he doing hooked up to *that* sort of smarmy Euro-pop? On the
other hand, he was also wearing a Qiana shirt. Maybe he just
didn't know any better.

Michael avoided the confrontation. "Actually," he said,
"I'm not big on Walkmans. They make me kind of claustro-
phobic. I like to be able to get away from my music."

"I use them at work mostly," said the man, "when there's a lot of paperwork. I smoke a doobie at lunch, come back, put these babies on and go with the flow."

"Yeah. I can see how that might help."

The man laid the Walkman on the table. "You're in the chorus, aren't you?"

"Uh-huh."

"I came to your welcome home," said the man. "What a scene!"

"Wasn't it great?" grinned Michael. Five days later, he was still tingling with the exhilaration of that moment. Several thousand people had mobbed their buses at the corner of 18th and Castro.

"I saw you kiss the ground," said the man.

Michael shrugged sheepishly. "I like it here, I guess."

"Yeah . . . me too." He fiddled with the Walkman, obviously searching for something to say. "You don't like Abba, huh?"

Michael shook his head. "Sorry," he replied, as pleasantly as possible.

"What sort of stuff do you like?"

"Well . . . lately I've been getting into country-western." Michael laughed. "I don't know what came over me."

"Redneck music," said the man.

"I know. I used to hate the crap when I was a kid in Orlando. Maybe it's just the old bit about gay people imitating their oppressors. Like those guys who spend their days fighting police brutality and their nights dressing up like cops."

The man smiled faintly. "Never done that, huh?"

"Never," said Michael. "Was that strike two?"

The man shook his head. "I've never done it either."

"Well, then . . . see how much we have in common?" Michael extended his hand. "I'm Michael Tolliver."

"Bill Rivera." *Latin,* thought Michael. This was getting better all the time.

"I have a friend," Michael continued, "who used to go to The Trench on uniform night, because he loved having sex with people who looked like cops or Nazis or soldiers. One night he went home with a guy in cop drag, and the guy had this incredible loft south of Market, with neon tubing over the bed and high-tech everything . . . to die, right? Only my friend didn't say a word, because he was supposed to be a prisoner, and the other guy was supposed to be a cop, and a prisoner doesn't say 'What a fabulous apartment' to a cop. He said he could hardly wait for the sex to be over so he could ask the guy where he got his pin spots from. I don't have that kind of self-discipline, I suppose. I wanna be able to say 'What a fabulous apartment' first thing. Is that too much to ask?"

The big mustache bristled as he smiled. "It is at *my* house."

Michael laughed. "It doesn't have to be fabulous."

"Good."

"It doesn't even have to be *your* apartment. Mine's available."

"Where do you live?"

"Russian Hill."

"C'mon," said the man, downing his drink, "mine's closer."

He lived on 17th Street in the Mission. His tiny studio was blandly furnished, with occasional endearing lapses into kitsch (a Mike Mentzer poster, a Lava Lite, a plastic cable car planter containing a half-dead philodendron).

Michael was enormously relieved. Bill Rivera wasn't tasteless—he was taste free. Gay men with *no* taste were often the hottest ones of all. Besides, thought Michael, if we ever kept house together, he'd probably let me do the decorating.

Then he spotted the handcuffs on the dresser.

"Uh . . . pardon me?"

Bill looked up. He was sitting on the edge of the bed, removing his Hush Puppies. "Yeah?"

Michael held out the handcuffs, as if presenting Exhibit A. "Aren't into this, huh?"

Bill shook his head. "It's just a living."

"Uh . . . ?"

"I'm a cop. Does that mean you wanna leave?"

"Now wait a minute . . ." Michael was dumbfounded.

Bill stood up and removed something from a dresser drawer, holding it out to his accuser.

"My badge, O.K.?"

Michael looked at it, then back at Bill, then back at the badge again.

"O.K.?" asked Bill.

"O.K.," said Michael.

Almost numb, he sat down on the bed next to the policeman and began unlacing his shoes. "What a fabulous apartment," he said.

The Pygmalion Plot

P RUE HAD ALREADY RIPPED THREE SHEETS OF PAPER from her typewriter when her secretary stepped into the study.

"It's Father Paddy," she said. "He says it won't take long."

Prue groaned softly and picked up the phone. "Yes, Father?"

"I know you're on deadline, darling, but I need you to answer a few questions."

"Shoot."

"How does your schedule look? The next three weeks or so."

Prue hesitated. "What are you up to?"

"Tut-tut. Aren't we snippy this morning. Just answer the question, my child."

Prue checked her appointment book. "O.K.," she said. "Fairly slow, actually."

"Good. Keep it that way."

"Father . . ."

"And tell your Mountain Man not to fill up his dance card either. I've plans for the two of you."

"What?"

"Never you mind. In good time, my child, in good time."

"Father, I don't know what you're cooking up, but you might as well know that Luke is not . . . well, he's not the sort of man who'll take orders from other people."

"Even you?"

"Of course not!"

"But, surely, if he *really* cares about you, Prue . . . if he wants to be part of your life, then he should be willing to meet you on some . . . middle ground."

"We've already talked about that. There is no middle ground."

"Ah, but I think there is! Something that will appeal to his love of nature and to your sense of propriety. For God's sake, girl . . . are you happy?"

A long silence, and then: "No."

"No," repeated Father Paddy. "You are not. And *why* are you not happy? Because you're in love with that creature, and you want to be with him night and day." The cleric paused dramatically, then lowered his voice for emphasis. "I'm going to give you that, darling. I'm going to give you exactly what you want."

Prue sighed audibly. "If you won't tell me what it is, how in the world can I . . ."

"All right, all right . . ."

So he told her.

Countdown

THE LINE FOR *RAIDERS OF THE LOST ARK* WAS SO HOPE-lessly serpentine that Mary Ann and Brian decided to forego their movie plans and watch television together at home.

"I like this better, anyway," said Mary Ann, lifting her McChicken sandwich from its styrofoam coffin. "I haven't had a good TV-and-junk-food pig-out in ages."

Brian swallowed a mouthful of Big Mac, then mopped up with the back of his hand. "It fits the budget, anyway." He cast an impish glance at Mary Ann. "But you don't have to worry about that now, do you?"

Mary Ann frowned. "Why do you keep riding me about that?"

Brian shrugged. "Why do you have to be so secretive about it? Who am I gonna tell, huh? Some gin-soaked old society dame puts you on her payroll, and you run around acting like I need a National Security Clearance just to talk to you."

"C'mon, Brian. You're the one who keeps bringing it up."

"Gimme a hint, then, and I'll shut up."

Mary Ann hesitated. "If I tell you . . ."

Brian beamed triumphantly.

"*If* I tell you, Brian, you've got to promise me it won't go any further than this. I mean it, Brian. This is deadly serious."

Brian made a poker face and held up his hand. "My solemn oath. A lovers' pact."

"I haven't even told Michael."

Brian bowed. "I'm deeply honored."

"DeDe Day is back in town," said Mary Ann.

"Wait a minute . . ."

Mary Ann nodded. "Mrs. Halcyon's daughter. The one who disappeared from Guyana."

Brian whistled. "Holy shit."

"She's been living in Cuba for the past two-and-a-half years."

"What about . . . whatshername . . . Mona's old girlfriend?"

"D'orothea. They were living together . . . along with the twins that DeDe had by the delivery boy at Jiffy's. D'orothea's still in Cuba. DeDe's hiding out in Hillsborough now. Her mother hired me to handle the press when DeDe breaks the story."

Brian's brow furrowed. "*When* she breaks it? You went to Hillsborough weeks ago. Why hasn't she broken it already? What's she hiding out for?"

"That's the part I'm fuzzy on. She claims she wants to talk to some Temple members about something. She won't tell me what it is yet."

Brian smiled sardonically. "She's probably looking for a good publisher. Half of those Jonestown people are writing books."

Mary Ann shook her head. "It's much more serious than that. Besides, *I'm* writing the book when the time comes."

"Good."

"I just don't know *what* I'll be writing."

"Not so good."

"You're telling me! Something big is missing, Brian . . . something she lives with night and day. I can almost feel it in the room with us when we're talking."

"Like what?"

"I don't know." Mary Ann shivered suddenly. "God, it gives me the creeps. I agreed to keep quiet about everything until next week. Then I'm free to negotiate with the station. She's promised to fill me in as soon as she finds out . . . whatever she's trying to find out."

"It sounds like she's afraid of recriminations."

"I've thought of that," said Mary Ann, "but it doesn't really make any sense. If the other survivors are working the talk show circuit, as you pointed out, what has *DeDe* got to be afraid of?"

"She could be just plain wacko."

"I don't think so," said Mary Ann. "She's a pretty solid person."

"That airhead debutante . . . ?"

"She's changed a lot, Brian. I guess the children did it. She *lives* for them now. She may be a little paranoid about their safety, but that seems perfectly normal after what she's been through."

"I think you're the one who should be paranoid," said Brian.

"Why?"

"What's to stop another reporter from stumbling on this one before you break it?"

Mary Ann winced. "I know, but she's being as careful as possible. She hides in the guest wing whenever visitors come. And she doesn't leave the house that much."

"Just to visit Temple members, huh?"

She saw his point all too well.

They were in bed watching Tom Snyder when the phone rang.

Mary Ann answered it. "Hello."

"Mary Ann . . . it's DeDe." Her voice sounded small and terrified. Mary Ann glanced at the digital clock on the dresser. It said 1:23.

"Hi," said Mary Ann. "Are you O.K.?" She assumed that DeDe was having those bad dreams again.

"I need to see you," said DeDe.

"Sure. Of course. When?"

"Tomorrow morning?"

"Could we make it the afternoon? Brian and I had planned on . . ."

"*Please.*" The word reverberated like a scream in a tomb. It was all Mary Ann needed to hear.

"Where?" she asked.

"Here. Halcyon Hill. I don't want to leave the house."

"DeDe, what on earth has . . . ?"

"Just come, O.K.? Bring your tape recorder. We can eat breakfast here. I'm really sorry about this. I'll explain everything in the morning."

When Mary Ann set the receiver down, Brian smiled at her sweetly. "Scratch the roller-skating, huh?"

"I'm afraid so," she said.

"What's up?"

"I wish I knew," said Mary Ann.

Nothing to Lose

I T TOOK PRUE GIROUX EXACTLY TWELVE HOURS TO SUC-
cumb completely to the wild romanticism of Father
Paddy's scheme. The following morning she hurried out
to the park and made her own pitch, snuggled cozily in
Luke's arms.

He gazed at the ceiling in stony silence.

"Well?" asked Prue.

"You would do that?" he said finally.

"I would if I thought it would bring us closer together."

"Is that what you think?"

"It might."

Another long silence.

"Besides, if it doesn't work out, what harm has been done?
We've got nothing to lose, Luke."

"I hate the bourgeoisie," he replied sternly. "I've spent
most of my life subverting it . . . or running from it."

The columnist bristled. "Am *I* the bourgeoisie? Is that
what you're telling me?"

He leaned down and kissed her forehead. "Unlike a lot of
good things, you're best when taken out of context."

"But . . . this *would* be out of context. Just us, if that's the way we want it. Two weeks that belong to *us,* Luke."

"And then what?"

"I don't know. Does it matter? Aren't you the one who said to forget about forever?"

She had him there. He smiled at her in concession, then shook his head slowly. "Prue, I have no clothes for that sort of thing, none of the . . ."

"I can take care of that."

"I don't want your charity."

"It's a loan, then. It all reverts to me after two weeks. For God's sake, you're not selling your *soul,* Luke."

"That remains to be seen."

"Look," she snapped, "you keep telling me that I'd be ashamed to be seen with you. Well then . . . *prove* it, if you can!"

"Prue . . ."

"The truth is . . . you're ashamed to be seen with *me.* You're such a snob, Luke. You're the biggest snob I ever met!"

"If it helps you to think that, then go ahead."

"What have you got to lose, Luke?"

He rolled away from her.

"Do you remember what you said that first night? You said you would love me unconditionally, at my pleasure . . . as little or as much as I wanted. Well . . . this is what I want. Do this for me, Luke."

"I meant *here,*" he said quietly, speaking to the wall.

But she knew she had won.

DeDe's Tale

MARY ANN TURNED ON THE SONY. "I'M AFRAID I'M a little muddled. I'm not exactly sure where to begin."

"It isn't your fault," said DeDe. "I haven't let you play with a full deck." The flesh around her eyes was so dark, Mary Ann observed, that she could have been recovering from a nose job. *What on earth had happened?*

"Where are the children?" asked Mary Ann.

"Upstairs with Mother and Emma. I don't want them here while this is happening. Any of them."

"I see."

"Frankly, I don't know *what* you think of me at this point. I suppose you have every reason to regard me as a certified nut case."

"No way."

DeDe smiled feebly. "Well, it doesn't get better, I can promise you. I suppose you already know that Jim Jones wasn't a healthy man?"

"To put it mildly."

"I mean physically, as well. He had diabetes and hypertension. One of the women who slept with him told me he was supposed to have seventeen hundred calories a day, but he was hooked on soda pop and sweet rolls. He also had a chronic coughing condition."

"I've read about that," said Mary Ann.

"He coughed all the time. A lot of Temple members thought he was just taking on their diseases."

"I don't understand."

"Well, he cured people, you know. Or he went through the motions, anyway. A lot of people looked on him as a healer. He would hold healing sessions where he'd pray for somebody who had, say, cancer . . . and he'd leave the room and come back a few minutes later with a handful of chicken gizzards which he said was the cancer."

"You mean . . ."

"He had yanked the cancer right out of their body."

"They believed that?"

"Some of them did. Others humored him, because they approved of his goals."

"Like a lot of people here."

"Yes. And a lot of those poor souls believed that he took on their disease as soon as he cured them of it. It was his way of going to Calvary. His illness was all the more pitiful—we were told—because it was really *our* illness, and he was bearing it for us."

"How awful."

DeDe shrugged. "You have no idea how noble it made him look at the time."

"You weren't buying it, were you?"

"The point is," said DeDe, almost irritably, "the man was sick. Anybody could see that. It's easy to look back *now* and see that a lot of it may have been psychosomatic or something . . . but it looked pretty damn real at the time. So did the arthritis. The swelling in his wrists and hands was quite noticeable. I was shocked the first time I saw it. I came into the nursery one day and found him with the twins . . ."

"There was a nursery?"

DeDe thought for a moment. "The Cuffy Memorial Baby Nursery, to be precise."

"Cuffy," repeated Mary Ann. "That's sort of sweet, actually."

"He was a black liberation leader in Guyana."

"Right."

"At any rate, Dad was . . . Jones was standing there in the nursery, holding little Edgar, singing something to him . . . with those huge swollen hands. It was pathetic and horrible all at the same time. I should've felt complete revulsion, I guess, but all I could feel was an odd sort of pity . . . and panic, of course. I moved closer to hear what he was singing, but it wasn't his usual revolutionary anthem; it was 'Bye Baby Bunting.' "

Mary Ann almost said "Aww," but caught herself in the nick of time. "There must have been *something* decent about him or you wouldn't have stayed so long. You didn't even plan your escape, did you, until you heard about the cyanide?"

DeDe nodded. "Partly because of his illness, I guess. It made him seem less threatening, more vulnerable. And partly because I was . . . used to things. It was a shitty little world, but at least I knew how it worked. You know what I mean?"

Mary Ann nodded, flashing instantly on Halcyon Communications.

"The truth is," DeDe continued, "I was an idiot. I actually cried when he called us together and announced that he had cancer."

"When was that?"

"August, I guess. Early August. Later in the month, a doctor named Goodlett came in from San Francisco. He examined Jones and said he couldn't find any cancer. He said it was probably some sort of fungus eating at his lungs. Anyway, he tried to get Jones to leave the jungle for proper tests to diagnose his illness, but Jones was terrified of leaving Jonestown even for a day. Charles Garry made special arrangements for him to have a medical examination in Georgetown—without getting arrested, that is—but Jones was afraid of a rebellion in his absence."

"So he was still *thinking* clearly."

"Always," said DeDe, "when it came to keeping control. Of course, later that summer the addiction started. Quaaludes mixed with cognac, Elavil, Placidyl . . . Valium, Nembutal, you name it. Marceline saw him falling apart before her very eyes and realized that something had to be done."

"Who was Marceline?"

"His wife."

"Right," said Mary Ann hastily, feeling stupider by the minute. "I'd almost forgotten he was married."

Chums

BRIAN AND MICHAEL SPENT SATURDAY MORNING roller-skating in Golden Gate Park—a precarious undertaking at best, despite the sleek, professional-looking skates Mrs. Madrigal had given them the previous Christmas.

"You've been practicing," Brian shouted accusingly as they wobbled past the de Young Museum. "That's against the rules, you know?"

"Says who?"

"Mary Ann said you went skating on Tuesday. With your cop friend."

"That was *indoors*. That doesn't count."

"Where'd you go?"

"The rink in El Sobrante. It's loaded with Farrah Fawcett minors, blow-dried for days. . . ."

"*Girls?*"

"You wish. Twinkies. It's an amazing sight. I should take you and Mary Ann sometime. We can take the bus."

"There's a special bus?"

Michael nodded. "It makes the rounds of half-a-dozen gay bars, then drops everybody off at the rink. It's a lot of fun.

You get to make out on the bus on the way home."

Brian smiled nostalgically. "I remember that."

"So do I. Only I never did it in high school. I never did it at all until last Tuesday. I remember, though . . . all those kids listening to Bread and making out in the dark in the back of the bus on the way home from out-of-town ball games."

Brian held out his hand to stop Michael at the intersection. "Watch it," he said. "Don't get lost in your memories. This place is lethal on weekends."

"Think of that, though. I was thirty-one before I ever kissed anybody on public transportation. I consider it a major milestone."

"It was more than that," teased Brian. "Some people *never* get around to kissing a cop, much less doing it on a bus. It *was* the cop, wasn't it?"

Michael feigned indignation. "Of course!"

"Hey . . . what does a breeder know?"

Michael grinned. "Where did you learn that word?"

The light changed. They proceeded with graceless caution across the pebbly asphalt. "One of the guys at Perry's," replied Brian. "He said that's what the faggots call us."

"Not this faggot," said Michael.

"I know." Brian turned to look at him, almost losing his balance.

Michael grabbed his arm. "Easy . . . easy. . . ."

"Anyway," said Brian, regaining his composure, "it's not even applicable to me. I'm thirty-six years old and I've never bred so much as a goldfish."

When they reached the other side, Michael aimed for a bench and sat down. Brian collapsed beside him, expelling air noisily.

"Do you want to?" asked Michael.

"What?"

"Have children."

Brian shrugged. "Sure. But Mary Ann doesn't. Not right now, anyway. She's got a career going." He smiled benignly. "In case you haven't noticed."

Michael began unlacing his skates. "Where is she today, anyway?"

"Having lunch. On the peninsula."

"What on earth for?"

"Just . . . business."

They sat together in silence for several minutes, watching the passing scene in their bare feet. Finally, Michael said: "I think you two should get married."

"You do, huh?"

"Uh-huh."

"Have you told her that?"

"Not in so many words," replied Michael.

Brian grinned. "Neither have I."

"Why not?"

Brian reached down and yanked up a handful of grass. "Oh . . . because I think I know what the answer would be . . . and I don't need to hear that right now. Besides, there are lots of advantages to living alone."

"Name one."

Brian thought for a moment. "You can pee in the sink."

Michael laughed. "You do that, too, huh?" Suddenly, he clamped his hand on Brian's leg and exclaimed: "Well, get a load of *that,* would you?"

"What?"

"Over there . . . by the conservatory. That overdressed blonde climbing into the limo."

"Yeah?"

"That's Prue Giroux."

"Who?"

"You know . . . the dizzy socialite who writes for *Western Gentry* magazine."

"Never heard of her."

"She's grinning like a Cheshire cat," said Michael. "Where do you suppose she's going?"

The Trouble with Dad

A NYWAY," DEDE CONTINUED, "MARCELINE *KNEW* how sick he was. She was worried about it all the time."

"You knew her?"

DeDe nodded. "We were friends, of sorts. She was a pretty savvy woman."

"Yet she didn't . . . ?"

"Hang on, O.K.? I wanna get through this. A Russian doctor named . . . Fedorovsky, I think . . . I'll have to check my diary . . . this doctor came to Jonestown in the fall and said that Jones had emphysema. Marceline made a special trip to San Francisco to tell Dr. Goodlett that Jones' fever was getting worse. He told her he couldn't be responsible for treating him, if Jones wouldn't leave the jungle for proper treatment. He washed his hands of it, in other words.

"At this point, apparently, Marceline decided to approach a former Temple member who lived in San Francisco. This man was one of Jones' most devoted disciples, but he was also a serious mental case . . . so serious, in fact, that Jones had refused him permission to participate in Jonestown."

"What was his name?" asked Mary Ann.

"I don't know. Marceline never told me. The point is . . . this guy bore a really freaky resemblance to Jones . . . the same body type and coloration, the same angularity to his face. He even capitalized on it by wearing sideburns and mirrored sunglasses."

"But . . . why?"

DeDe shrugged. "All of the others wanted to follow Jones. This one wanted to *be* him."

"Did Marceline tell you this?"

"Uh-huh. I also saw it with my own eyes."

"In Jonestown?"

DeDe nodded. "I saw them meeting together one night. Jones and this guy. I could barely tell them apart. The plan—according to Marceline—was for the imposter to run the operation until Jones could get to Moscow for medical treatment. A week at the most, she said. He would do most of his work on the loudspeaker system, with occasional walk-throughs to keep people in line. The man was briefed on *everything*, including the suicide drills. Jones was so sick, of course, that no one expected him to sound like himself . . . or even to actively participate in the day-to-day life of the camp. He just had to *be* there, a figurehead to prevent an insurrection."

"Then . . . this happened? *Jones left?*"

"I don't know. Two days after the imposter arrived in camp, Captain Duke told me about the cyanide. I didn't stick around to find out. For once in my life, I missed out on the action and was damn glad of it."

"So you left . . . when?"

"Two days before the congressman and the others were murdered at the airstrip."

"Meaning that this man . . . the imposter . . . may have been the one who ordered the mass suicide?"

"Yes."

"And may have been the one who . . . ."

When Mary Ann faltered, DeDe finished the sentence. "The one who died."

"My God!"

DeDe simply blinked at her.

"That's . . . DeDe, that's *grotesque.*"

"Isn't it, though?"

"But . . . surely . . . the government must've checked those bodies at the time. Somebody must've . . . I don't know . . . what do they do? A blood test or something?"

DeDe smiled patiently. "There were nine hundred bodies, remember?"

"I know, but . . ."

"One of those bodies was lying in front of the throne with its head on a pillow. Bloated as it was, it *looked* like Jones . . . and it was probably carrying his identification. Do you think they stopped to check his fingerprints?"

"Wasn't there an autopsy?"

"There was," said DeDe, "and I've been trying like hell to find the report. That's why I needed *time,* don't you see? If someone could prove to me conclusively that he was really dead . . ."

"What about those Temple members?"

DeDe grimaced. "They were useless. They wanted no part of it. They treated me like I was crazy or something."

Mary Ann said nothing.

"Mary Ann . . . please . . . don't write me off just yet." DeDe looked at her imploringly as her eyes filled with tears. "I haven't even gotten to the crazy part."

Mary Ann took her hand. "Go ahead," she said. "I'm listening."

"I don't know what to do," sobbed DeDe. "I'm so damn tired of running . . ."

"DeDe, please don't. It can't be as bad as you . . ."

"I've *seen* him, Mary Ann!"

"*What?*"

"Yesterday. At Steinhart Aquarium. Mother was driving me crazy, so I drove to the city . . . just to walk around. I went to a concert in the park . . . and later I went to the aquarium . . . and I saw him there in the crowd."

"You saw . . . Jones?" Mary Ann was thunderstruck.

DeDe nodded, her face contorted with fear.

"What was he doing?"

"Looking . . ." She was almost incoherent now. Feeling her own lip begin to quiver, Mary Ann squeezed DeDe's hand even tighter.

"Looking?" she asked guardedly.

DeDe nodded, wiping her eyes with her free hand. "At the fish. The same as me."

"It's awfully dark in there. Are you sure you . . . ?"

"*Yes!* He was thinner looking, and much healthier, but it was him. I knew the minute I looked into his eyes."

"He *saw* you?"

"He smiled at me. It was awful."

"What did you do?"

"I ran all the way back to the car and drove home. I haven't left the house since. I know how this sounds, believe me. You have every right to . . ."

"I believe you."

"You do?"

"I believe it's real to you. That's enough for me."

DeDe's sobs stopped. She glared at Mary Ann for a moment, then jerked her hand away angrily. "You think I'm hysterical, don't you?"

"DeDe, I think you've been incredibly brave . . ."

"*Brave?* Look at me, goddamnit! I am scared shitless! Do you think I don't know what the police would say about this . . . what the whole goddamn world would say about that poor little rich girl who went off the deep end in Jonestown? Look how *you're* acting, and you're supposed to be my friend!"

"I am your friend," Mary Ann said feebly.

"Then what am I gonna do? *What am I gonna do about my goddamn children?*"

Gangie

LITTLE EDGAR AND HIS SISTER ANNA RAN ACROSS THE brown lawn at Halcyon Hill and accosted their grandmother on the terrace, each tugging joyfully at a leg.

"Gangie, Gangie . . . look!"

Frannie set her teacup down on the glass-topped table and smiled at the four-year-olds. "What is it, darlings? What do you want to show Gangie?"

Little Anna thrust out her tiny fist and uncurled it. A small gray toad, pulsing like a heart, was offered for examination. Frannie's nose wrinkled, but she did her best to sound appreciative. "Well, now . . . just look at him, would you? Do you know what that is, Edgar?"

Edgar shook his head.

"It's a fwog," said Anna, somewhat smugly.

Edgar cast a disdainful look at his twin. "I found it," he declared defiantly, as if to compensate for his vocabulary failure.

"Well, it's just wonderful," said Frannie sweetly, "but I think you should take it back where you found it."

"Why?" they asked together.

"Well . . . because it's one of God's little creatures, and it looks like a baby to me. It probably misses its mommy. You wouldn't like it if someone took you away from *your* mommy, now would you?"

Four almond eyes grew larger; two little heads shook simultaneously.

"Well, then . . . you run along and put him right back where you found him, and Gangie will have a big surprise for you when you get back."

Frannie watched as they scurried back to the edge of the rose garden, delighting in the classic simplicity of the scenario. She was sure she had spoken the same words—in the same place, moreover—when DeDe had been that age.

"Could I have a word with you, Mother?"

The matriarch turned around to confront the grown-up DeDe, looking lean and beautiful and unusually . . . purposeful. "Hello, darling. Will Mary Ann join us for tea?"

"She just left," said DeDe.

Frannie pecked her daughter on the cheek, then glanced lovingly in the direction of the twins. "They're such a joy. I can't tell you."

DeDe's smile was weary. "They seem to have taken to you, all right. Mother . . . could we talk for a moment?"

"Of course, darling. Is something the matter?"

DeDe shook her head. "I think you'll like it. I *hope* you'll like it."

Emma kept the children amused with ice cream in the kitchen, while DeDe sat with her mother on the sunporch and explained what was on her mind.

"Mary Ann is going to release the story," she said. "Not yet, though . . . maybe a week or so from now. We haven't quite worked that part out yet. The point is . . . I think you and the twins should be out of town when it happens."

"*What?*"

"Think about it, Mother. The publicity will be excruciating no matter what we do. I just don't want you or the children subjected to that kind of pressure."

"That's very sweet, darling, but sooner or later that's bound to happen, isn't it?"

DeDe nodded. "To some extent . . . but things will have cooled down somewhat, and I think you'll be better equipped to handle it." DeDe handed her mother a page from the travel section of the *Chronicle*. "I think this looks marvelous myself. They say it's the most spacious ship afloat, and it sails for . . ."

"DeDe, what on earth . . . ?"

"Hear me out, Mother. It sails for Alaska next week for a two-week cruise. You see the glaciers and lovely old Russian buildings in Sitka . . ."

"DeDe, I'm touched by your thoughtfulness, but . . . well, I like it here, darling. And I really don't think the publicity will be too much for me to . . ."

"Mother, I want the children out of town!"

Frannie was taken aback by the ferocity of DeDe's declaration. "Darling, I'll do anything you want. I just don't understand why it's so . . . well, so *important* to you."

DeDe composed herself. "Just help me on this, Mother. Please. It's a marvelous trip. The twins will adore it, and you'll get to know them so much better. It's perfect, really." She looked at Frannie almost plaintively. "Don't you think?"

The matriarch hesitated, then gave her daughter a hug. "I think it sounds lovely," she said.

A Starr Is Born

THE CLOTHES FROM WILKES BASHFORD ARRIVED AT Prue's house about half-an-hour before Father Paddy did.

"What do you think?" the cleric asked breathlessly. "Daniel Detorie helped me pick them out. I *know* I went overboard on the Polo shirts, but the colors were so yummy I couldn't resist."

"They're fine," Prue replied, almost blandly. She was in shock, she realized, for now she *knew* it was going to happen. *It was really going to happen.* She conjured up a smile for the priest. "I can't believe how sweet you're being."

"Pish," said Father Paddy. "The pleasure was all mine, darling. I've never been turned loose in Wilkes before." He lifted a blue blazer from its box. "This is Brioni," he said. "I debated getting the Polo blazer, which was four hundred, but not nearly so *shaped* as the Brioni. And since we're going for effect here, eight hundred seemed reasonable enough. Has he gotten a haircut yet?"

"I don't think so," said Prue.

Father Paddy rolled his eyes. "He can't get on the ship looking like the Wild Man of Borneo, darling!"

"I know," said Prue, "but if we slick his hair back . . ."

"Forget that. I'll send over a hairdresser with the manicurist on Sunday." He sighed exuberantly. "God, this is fun, isn't it?"

"I'm still so nervous," said Prue.

"Well, don't be. It's a piece of cake." The priest removed a packet from his breast pocket. "Now, here are the tickets, my child. You'll board between three o'clock and four-thirty on Sunday. Luke's stateroom is two doors down from yours on the same deck. You can board half-an-hour apart, if you like, so nobody'll be the wiser. Now . . . is he spending the night here on Saturday, I hope?"

Prue nodded. "I've given my secretary the weekend off."

"Good. Smart girl."

Prue perused the tickets, her brow wrinkling. "Wait a minute . . . this ticket says Sean P. Starr."

"Right," grinned Father Paddy. "Yours truly."

"But . . . Luke can't impersonate you, Father."

"Why not?"

"Well, it's just too risky. What if he needs to show an ID or something?"

The priest shrugged. "He'll show mine. That's included in the tour package, my child."

"That's very sweet, but . . . well, Luke just wouldn't do that, I know it."

"Do what?"

"Pretend to be a priest."

Father Paddy held out the ID card for her examination. "Show me where it says priest. He'll just be Sean Starr, *bon vivant* and world traveler, a charming middle-aged bachelor who just happens to meet a certain charming middle-aged society columnist on a cruise to Alaska. What could be more natural? Or more *romantic,* for that matter? Your readers will eat it up with a spoon!"

Prue laughed for the first time all day. "You're absolutely insidious, Father."

The cleric accepted the compliment with a demure little bow. "The rest is up to you, my child. The church can only go so far in secular matters. If I were you, though, I'd lean very heavily on his investment broker background. Didn't you say he used to do that?"

Prue nodded. "A long time ago. Before he was a preacher."

"Marvelous. Then it's the truth. That's always handy." He leaned over and pecked Prue impetuously on the cheek. "Oh, Prue . . . you've got such an adventure ahead of you, *such* an adventure."

The columnist heard herself giggle. "I do, don't I?"

"And you're giving that poor man a new start in life. That's something to be proud of . . . *and,* incidentally, something to write home about. I want *vivid* details, darling. That's my fee for this service. By the way, do you love him?"

"Oh, yes!"

"Then, he'll see that for two solid weeks, darling. He'll see it, and he'll never go back to what he was before. Some people *are* made for each other, my child, and when that happens, almost anything is possible. *Now* . . . what sort of hairdresser would you like?"

In Hillsborough, it was DeDe who gave the last-minute briefing.

"Just relax, Mother, that's the main thing. Relax and enjoy your grandchildren . . . but for God's sake don't tell people that's who they are or you'll defeat our whole purpose."

"Then, what exactly am I supposed to tell them?"

"Simple. They're your *foster* grandchildren. Vietnamese orphans in your charge for the summer."

The matriarch was indignant. "No one will believe that!"

"Why not? It makes more sense than the truth, doesn't it?"

Silence.

"I know it'll be tempting to brag, Mother. But you mustn't. Not to anyone. There'll be time enough to celebrate with your friends after we break the story."

"What if I see someone I know?"

"You won't, probably. Cruise ships have been middle class for years. But if you do, the story's still the same. Say 'foster' every time you say 'grandchild' and you've got it licked. O.K.?"

Frannie nodded begrudgingly. "It seems awfully silly, somehow."

"Mother." DeDe's voice was all business now. "It may seem silly to you, but it's of vital importance. Do you understand me? The most well-meaning person could leak the story to the press before we know what hit us. Remember what Daddy used to say: 'Loose lips sink ships.' "

Frannie wrinkled her nose at her daughter. "I can do without the leaking and the sinking, thank you."

DeDe laughed nervously. "Bad choice. Sorry. Oh Mother, I hope you have the time of your life!"

"I will," smiled Frannie. "We will."

Now, Voyagers

THE GANGPLANK TO THE *SAGAFJORD* WAS ASWARM WITH passengers, but Prue could see only one. "Look at him," she purred. "Have you ever beheld anything more beautiful?"

Father Paddy crossed himself, an altogether suitable reply considering the object of their scrutiny. For the creature in the Brioni blazer *was* beautiful, a sleek, chiseled racehorse of a man who might easily be mistaken for a diplomat or an international financier.

"I want to run up there and hug him," said Prue.

"Easy," muttered the cleric. "Clothes might make the man, but *you* can't do it until the ship's under way."

Prue giggled nervously. "You're terrible, Father."

"Does Luke have his ticket?"

Prue nodded. "I gave him the Olaf Trygvasson Suite. I wanted the Henrik Ibsen for myself. It seemed more literary."

"Entirely appropriate," said Father Paddy. "Do you want me to come on board, by the way?"

"That's sweet. I'll be able to manage, I think."

The priest arched an eyebrow. "I should certainly hope so."

"*Stop* it, Father."

Father Paddy chuckled and hugged his friend. "Have a wonderful time, darling. I hope you meet someone *marvelous* on board."

"Something tells me I will," smiled Prue.

"But *don't* meet him until the proper occasion arises."

Prue nodded. "I understand."

"And remember to call him Sean when other people are around."

"I will."

"And, for God's sake, don't fret over the fact that Frannie Halcyon is on board."

"*What?*"

"I just spotted her on the pier. She may be seeing someone off, of course. At any rate, you have a perfect right to any romance that may happen to . . . come up, once you're on board. Luke is certainly *more* than presentable at this point, and I doubt if Frannie . . ."

"Where is she?" asked Prue. "God, that makes me nervous!"

"Oh, Prue . . . lighten up. This is a vacation, remember?"

Prue smiled gamely. "I'll try to."

"God bless," said Father Paddy.

"Ta-ta," said Prue.

Down on the pier, three women clustered around two small children and made uneasy chatter.

"Now promise me," said DeDe, squatting to confront the twins, "you'll do everything that Gangie says."

Little Anna attached herself to DeDe's neck like a koala bear. "Why don't you come, Mommy?"

"I can't, sweetheart. Mommy's got some things to do. But I'll be right here to meet you when you get back. I promise."

"Will D'orothea be here then?"

"She might, sweetheart. Mommy doesn't know yet."

Mary Ann knelt next to DeDe and addressed the children: "It's going to be so much fun. They have movies on the ship, you know. And you'll see wonderful animals up in Alaska."

"What kind?" asked little Edgar.

Mary Ann's face went blank. "What kind?" she murmured to DeDe.

"Uh . . . moose, I guess. Mooses?"

"*Big* animals," explained Mary Ann. "With big horns." Then she saw the look on the little girl's face, and added hastily: "But they're very sweet . . . like a big ol' dog or something."

DeDe rose to her feet and embraced her mother. "Thank you for doing this. I love you dearly. I hope that much is clear, at least."

"It is," said Frannie, beginning to weep. "It always was, darling."

DeDe found a Kleenex in her purse and blotted the matriarch's eyes. "It's better this way," she said. "I know they'll be safe with their Gangie."

"But what could be safer than home?"

"Now, now . . . you know the publicity would . . ."

"It isn't just the publicity, is it?" Frannie fixed her daughter with a gaze that demanded the truth.

DeDe turned away, discarding the Kleenex.

"Is it?" Frannie persisted.

A bone-rattling blast from the *Sagafjord* announced its impending departure.

"There we go," said DeDe, a trifle too cheerily.

"DeDe, I want you to . . ."

DeDe silenced her with another hug. "Everything will be fine, Mother . . . just fine."

Keeping Up with the Joneses

LARRY KENAN DIDN'T LAUGH—HE *BRAYED*—WHEN MARY Ann made her request. "That's rich, lady! That is really rich!"

"Well, I'm sorry if it . . ."

"*Reserve* air time?"

"You don't have to repeat it, Larry. I get the message."

"Air time is not something you reserve, like a room at the Hilton or something . . ."

"Right. Gotcha."

"Air time is something you *create* . . . and we have to know what we're creating, right?"

"Right." Mary Ann rose and headed for the door.

The news director kept his face tilted heavenward towards Bo Derek. "Hold it," he said.

Mary Ann stopped at the door. "Yeah?"

"If you've got a story, you should let us know about it. You have a *responsibility* to let us know about it. As a journalist."

"I'm not a journalist," said Mary Ann crisply. "You just said so yourself."

"I said you were not a journalist *yet*. And, even if you were, I couldn't sign you up for free air time without knowing what the fuck you're gonna talk about!"

"I already told you," said Mary Ann calmly. "I can talk about it a week from today."

"Then why don't you do that, huh?"

"Fine."

"Only don't expect to talk about it on the air."

"Larry . . ."

"Do you read me, lady? We have professionals we pay for that. That's not what we pay you for. I think we could work out a credit line on the crawl. *Maybe.* I don't know what rabbit you've got treed, but don't expect it to turn you into Bambi Kanetaka overnight."

She squelched a "God forbid" and walked out the door. So much for Plan A.

Plan B, she expected, would be a lot more fun.

DeDe seemed amenable to the idea. "I don't care how we do it," she said. "I'm more concerned about when."

"Would Tuesday be O.K.?" asked Mary Ann.

"A week from today?"

Mary Ann nodded. "That'll give us a week to mop things up before your mother and the children get back. The trip was a good idea, really . . . if only for logistical purposes."

DeDe's face clouded over. "But you think I'm a little paranoid, just the same."

"I think you're being conscientious."

"Don't mince words, Mary Ann."

"DeDe, I . . ."

"Jim Jones is dead, right? He must be. You saw it on the goddamn news!"

The outburst miffed Mary Ann. "All I care about," she said firmly, "is that you get a fair chance to tell your story . . . in as safe a fashion as possible. This is a mind-boggling scoop, DeDe. Period. My opinion doesn't make a good goddamn at this point. The point is . . . to raise the questions. The answers will sort themselves out later."

"You're right," said DeDe resignedly.

"It won't be easy. I know that. If you like, you can confine your remarks to a written statement, and I'll handle the questions from the press. Then you and the twins can disappear, take another vacation, start life afresh."

DeDe's smile was rueful. "It'll be anything but that."

"I know it'll be tough for a while, but . . ."

"It'll be tough until I know for sure. I saw that guy, Mary Ann. I've never been so sure about something."

Mary Ann appraised her for a moment. "All right, then . . . let's say that you did."

DeDe waited.

"Let's say that he made it to Moscow, and his double died in his place. The whole world thinks he's dead, but he's really alive and well and living in Moscow. Why on earth, then, would he come back to San Francisco and be seen wandering around Steinhart Aquarium?"

Silence.

Mary Ann was gentle. "These are the things they're going to ask you, DeDe. I want you to be ready."

"I'll never be ready," she said grimly.

Mary Ann rose and moved to DeDe's side, hugging her clumsily. "I'm so sorry. God, I . . . look, we can leave out the stuff about the double, if you want. We can just announce that you're back and leave out the rest . . ."

"No!" DeDe's head shook adamantly. "I want to nail that asshole. I want this over once and for all. I don't want to creep around the rest of my life, wondering if he's waiting for me . . . wondering if . . . if the children . . ."

"What if it was the double you saw?"

Another decisive shake of DeDe's head. "It wasn't."

"How can you be so sure?"

"I just am, that's all."

"He hasn't changed at all? Surely people would recognize him."

"Would you?" asked DeDe. "Who the hell expects to bump into *him* on the street?"

"Yeah. I see your point."

"Besides . . . there *was* something different about him. His nose, maybe . . . I don't know. They could've given him plastic surgery in Moscow. God, I wish you believed me! I remember the past, Mary Ann. I *won't* be condemned to repeat it!" DeDe

185

flinched as if she'd been slapped. *"Jesus!"*

"What's the matter?" asked Mary Ann.

"Nothing," said DeDe. "I'm still spouting his jargon, that's all."

"What jargon?"

DeDe shrugged it off. "Just a stupid quotation he hung over his throne."

Taste Test

SORRY I'M LATE," SAID BILL RIVERA, JOINING MICHAEL AT a table in Welcome Home. "My ex-lover's brother's lover just left town."

"Hang on. Your . . . ?"

The policeman smiled. "Ex-lover's brother's lover. He came out about a week ago."

"Out here, or out of the closet?"

"*Both,* more or less . . . and the sonofabitch picked my apartment to do it in. He showed up on my doorstep with fourteen different fantasy costumes."

"Like . . . leather?"

"Leather, cowboy stuff, bandannas out the ass, tit clamps, three-piece suits . . . you name it."

Michael smiled. "And guess who's supposed to show him around."

Bill shook his head. "I hardly saw the guy. He'd stop by long enough to crash or change costumes or swipe my poppers, and then he'd take off again. He trashed his way from Alta Plaza to Badlands to The Caldron and back again, while I stayed home and watched TV. This morning, when he left, he got real serious all of a sudden and said: 'You know, Bill.

This place is just too decadent. I could never live here.' I felt like strangling the prick with his harness."

Michael laughed and handed Bill a menu. "The people from L.A. are the worst."

"This guy's from Milwaukee. Even the faggots there think we've gone too far."

Michael smiled suddenly, remembering something. "Did you hear about the fire in the Castro Muni Metro station last week?"

The policeman shook his head.

"It wasn't much of one," Michael continued. "But a whole hook-and-ladder showed up, complete with half-a-dozen hot firemen. They parked across from the Castro Theatre, but couldn't get into the Metro station without passing through a hoedown being held by The Foggy City Squares."

"Translate," said Bill.

"A gay square dance group. They were doing this big do-si-do number in front of the Bank of America. Clapping and yee-hawing and singing 'The Trail of the Lonesome Pine.' All men. It was great. What struck me about it, actually, was the look on the firemen's faces: blasé as all get-out. They nodded to everybody kind of pleasantly and went right about their work . . . as if they *always* passed through a crowd of square dancing men before putting out a fire. That wouldn't happen anywhere else on earth. That's why I live here, I guess. That and the fact that some of the cops are a little funny."

Bill grinned. "More than a little."

"Just enough," said Michael. "You're not real big on country-western, are you?" He'd deduced as much from Bill's reaction to his square dancing yarn.

The cop made a noncommittal grunt.

"I ask because . . . well, I was wondering if you'd like to go to the rodeo with me."

Bill looked up from the menu. "The gay one."

Michael nodded.

Bill frowned. "More faggots pretending to be cowboys, huh?"

"Not all of them," Michael replied. "Some are pretending to be Tammy Wynette."

*   *   *

Mary Ann didn't hide her surprise when Michael showed up on her doorstep just before midnight. "I thought you were seeing your Boy in Blue tonight."

"I was. I did."

"I see."

"He doesn't like to sleep with people," said Michael. "All night, that is."

Mary Ann made a face. "He sounds like a lot of fun."

Michael shrugged. "I think we're both in it for the sex. It's just as well. He has sleepsleepsleep sheets."

"He has *what?*"

"You know . . . those sheets that say sleepsleepsleep. They go with the towels that say drydrydry. It's awful, Babycakes. His taste is not to be believed."

"Wait a minute! *I* had some of those sheets."

"You did?"

"Yes, I did! What's wrong with those sheets?"

"That isn't the point," said Michael. "The point is . . . we have very little in common."

"Except sex."

Michael nodded. "Except *great* sex. And that has a curious way of canceling out the tacky sheets. Not to mention a belt buckle that says BILL and a shower curtain with a naked man on it."

"I think you're an awful snob," frowned Mary Ann.

"Maybe so," said Michael, "but at least it keeps me from overreacting to the great sex. If he had any style at all, I'd probably be in love with him by now."

"And you don't want that?"

"No."

"Why not?"

Michael thought for a moment. "It's like this sweater. Have you seen this sweater, by the way?"

"It's nice," said Mary Ann. "The color's good on you. Is it cashmere?"

Michael nodded. "Fifteen bucks at the Town School's second hand shop."

189

"A steal!" She fingered a sleeve. "It's almost new, Mouse."

"Not so fast." Michael lifted his arm to reveal a dime-sized hole in the sweater's elbow.

"You could patch it," Mary Ann suggested.

"Not on your life. That's what I'm talking about. I *like* that hole, Babycakes. It keeps me from worrying about my new cashmere sweater. I can have the style, the feel, the luxury of cashmere without any fussing and fretting. It's *already* flawed, see, so I can relax and enjoy it. That's exactly the way I feel about Bill."

"And how does he feel about you?"

"He thinks of me as a fuck buddy. Period."

"How romantic."

"Exactly. So I take refuge in his atrocious taste and tell myself that it would never work out, anyway. Even if he *wasn't* so crushingly unsentimental. Even if he *didn't* keep *Meat* on top of his toilet tank."

"I don't think I'll ask about that," said Mary Ann.

"It's a book," said Michael.

"Thank God. Tell me something sweet. What have you heard from Jon lately?"

Michael managed a look of faint irritation. "You can squeeze him into any conversation, can't you?"

"I don't care," said Mary Ann. "He was my friend, too. He was generous and gorgeous and . . . he thought you were the greatest thing going. He was cashmere without the hole, Mouse. That wasn't so terrible, was it?"

Michael sighed wearily. "I don't hear from Jon, O.K.?"

"O.K. Sorry."

He didn't bother to hide the wistfulness in his eyes. "You haven't, have you?"

North to Alaska

PRUE GIROUX WAS WEARING HEELS, FRANNIE NOTED. *Stiletto* heels on which she tottered precariously as she made her way along the rain-slick Promenade Deck of the *Sagafjord*. Her gown, as usual, was totally inappropriate, flouncy and cream-colored and dreadful.

Her escort, on the other hand, was as debonair as the Duke of Windsor in his elegant blue blazer, crisp white collar and gray silk tie. Good heavens, thought Frannie, how does she manage to do it?

Prue seemed to waver for a moment when she caught sight of Frannie in the deck chair. Then she smiled a little too extravagantly and clamped a hand on her companion's arm, as if he were a trophy she was about to present.

"Isn't this marvelous?" she cooed, meaning the scenery.

"Mmm," replied Frannie. "Magical."

"Wasn't Alert Bay the most precious place? One's reminded of those little ceramic villages one buys at Shreve's at Christmastime!"

And sometimes, thought Frannie, one is much too common to get away with using "one" all the time.

"Have you met Mr. Starr?" asked the columnist.

The matriarch smiled as regally as possible and extended her hand, still recumbent and blanket-swathed. "How do you do?" she said.

"Mr. Starr is a stockbroker from London," beamed Prue.

The woman is impossible, thought Frannie. Who else would volunteer her consort's credentials so eagerly. "I adore London," she said vaguely.

The poor man seemed horribly uncomfortable. "I'm not a . . ."

"He's not British," Prue interrupted, squeezing the man's arm even tighter. "I mean . . . he's not a native. He's an American working in London."

"I see," said Frannie.

The man nodded to confirm Prue's statement, clearly humiliated by her incorrigible pushiness. Well, thought Frannie, here's one shipboard romance that won't last the duration of the cruise.

"Where are those precious little orphans?" asked Prue.

Frannie did her best not to scowl. This "orphan" business, like melancholia and mild seasickness, was part of her vacation package. "They're in the movie theatre," she said casually, "watching Bugs Bunny."

The warmest smile imaginable stole across Mr. Starr's aristocratic features. "They are beautiful children," he said. "You must be very proud of them."

"Oh, *yes,*" exclaimed Frannie, adding quickly: "They aren't really *mine,* of course . . . but I'm alone in the world, and they're such splendid company, and . . . well, what else am I going to do with my time?"

Mr. Starr's response was almost intimate, as if he had known Frannie for years. "I think that's extraordinarily generous of you," he said.

The matriarch flushed. "Well, I . . . thank you, but . . . well, I get a lot of satisfaction out of it . . ." Her voice trailed off ineffectually. Mr. Starr was all but caressing her with his eyes. Already, Frannie sensed a rapport with him that she was certain he didn't share with Prue Giroux.

"We should chat about that sometime," said Prue.

"Uh . . . what?" Frannie was still mesmerized by Mr. Starr's extraordinary gaze.

"The foster grandparent program," said Prue. "I'm sure my readers would love to hear your comments on that."

"Oh, yes," Frannie murmured absently. "That might be . . . very nice."

"I can tell you love them," Mr. Starr said to Frannie, all but ignoring Prue's presence. "It shows in your face. And where there is love . . . there is a bond, regardless of blood."

Prue grimaced. "Blood?"

Frannie smiled indulgently. *What an idiot.* "I think Mr. Starr is referring to kinship, Prue." She turned back to her new admirer. "I love them as if they were my own, Mr. Starr."

He winked almost imperceptibly. "I know," he said. What a sweet thing to say, thought Frannie, trying to discern what it was that seemed so *familiar* about this stranger's face.

"Do you, by any chance, know a Father Paddy Starr in San Francisco?" asked Frannie.

"I asked him that already," blurted Prue. "I wondered the same thing myself."

Frannie smiled. "The name is the same. I just thought . . . there might be . . ."

"No," said Mr. Starr. "There are lots of us, I guess."

"Mmm," said Frannie.

"By the way," added Mr. Starr, "if you ever need help with the babysitting, I'd be glad to oblige."

"How kind," beamed Frannie. "I think I can manage, though."

"I'm good with children," he said.

Frannie nodded. She was sure he was.

Aurora Borealis

THAT EVENING, WHILE MOST OF THE PASSENGERS CONgregated in the ballroom for the rhumba contest, Prue and Luke snuggled under wooly Norwegian blankets on the Lido Deck and watched the miracle of the northern lights.

"My Daddy was right," said Prue, her eyes riveted on the baby blue ribbon that trimmed the black velvet sky along the horizon. "Now I know exactly what he meant."

"About what?" asked Luke.

"Oh . . . beauty, I guess. He told me never to get bored with life, because there are some types of beauty you won't even understand until you see them for yourself. I've heard about the northern lights all my life, but I never really . . . believed in them . . . until now."

Luke answered by tightening his grip on her shoulder.

"I guess," Prue added, "I never really believed in *us* until now. I wanted to, God knows, but I never allowed myself to surrender completely. It seemed too unreal, too much of a pipe dream somehow."

Luke cupped her face in his hands. "It's real, Prue. Every bit of it." His smile flashed like whitecaps against a dark sea.

"Except maybe these damn clothes."

"You look *magnificent,*" Prue gushed. "I'm so proud of you, Luke. Have you *seen* the way those old biddies look at you when we walk into the dining room? They're eating you alive! I'd get a little nervous, if I didn't know better."

Luke almost snapped at her. "Can't you forget about appearances for once?"

Prue was hurt. "Luke . . . I'm telling you what's in my heart."

"I know, I know." His tone was placating.

"I'm *happy,* Luke. That's a little miracle in itself. I didn't even know what the word meant until I met you. Now . . . I feel like singing at the top of my lungs." She smiled at her own impetuousness. "I've always gone to a lot of trouble to make people think of me as madcap. For the first time in my life, Luke, I *feel* madcap. I want this to go on forever."

He turned and looked at the lights again. "Two weeks isn't forever."

Prue's brow furrowed. "Luke . . ."

"Don't plan things, Prue. Or you'll lose the moment."

"What if I want more than the moment?"

"You can't. We can't."

"Why? There's no reason in the world why this can't keep going when we get back to San . . ."

"There are lots of reasons."

"What? Why can't we just . . . ?"

"Hush, darling . . . hush." He drew her closer, stroking her hair as if she were a child. "You want so much, my love . . . so much."

She pulled away from him, suddenly disoriented, flailing for absolutes. "Is it too much to want to build on what we have? My God, Luke . . . have I been reading this wrong? Haven't I seen love in your eyes?"

"Yes," he nodded, "yes, you have."

"Then what is it?"

He regarded her for a moment, then shook his head slowly. "Who are we kidding, Prue? Your friends will never buy this act."

"Luke . . . you would *charm* my friends."

"Like that old bat with the Vietnamese orphans? No, thank

195

you. I'm not interested in charming the bourgeoisie . . . and they'd *see* that in about ten minutes."

Prue didn't hide her pique. "If it really matters to you, that old bat—as you call her—lost a daughter and two grandchildren in Guyana. Those orphans are obviously her means of compensating for the loss of . . ."

"What's her name?"

The ferocity of his query startled her. "Frannie Halcyon. I introduced you, didn't I?"

"No. The daughter's name."

"Oh. DeDe Day. DeDe Halcyon Day. The papers made a big fuss about it at the time. You must've read . . . Luke, is something the matter?"

He was standing there, ramrod-straight, his hands clamped on the railing. A vein was throbbing in his neck, and his breathing seemed curiously erratic.

Prue struggled to undo the damage. "Luke, I know you're not insensitive. I didn't mean to accuse you of . . ."

He wheeled around to face her. "It's all right . . . it's all right. I'm sorry I yelled at you. Forgive me, will you? Will you do that?"

"Oh, Luke!" She scooped him into her arms and wept against his shoulder. "I love you, darling. I'd forgive you for anything."

"I pray you don't have to," he said.

Telepathy

T HESE DAYS, MARY ANN DID HER BANKING AT THE CO-
lumbus Avenue branch of the Bank of America. She
frequented this graceful old North Beach landmark
because (a) it had starred in a Woody Allen movie
(*Take the Money and Run*) and (b) its tellers were
cheerful, Italian and gossipy.

Today's was no exception.

"My husband and I have never fit in," announced a particularly aggressive teller in her late thirties. She delivered this
information so earnestly that it almost seemed as if Mary Ann
had requested it.

"Really?" said Mary Ann.

"Never. *Never.* Years ago when nice girls didn't live with
nice boys without benefit of matrimony, Joe and I were
shacked up big as life. Then suddenly *everybody* was shacking
up. What do we do? We get married. O.K., so along comes
ZPG, and *nobody's* having babies, right? Wrong. Joe and I had
babies like crazy. Now suddenly it's terribly fashionable to
have babies again, so a lot of people my age are experiencing
motherhood and mid-life crisis at the same time. Joe and me,
our children are teenagers now, fairly independent. We've

got the leisure to *plan* our mid-life crisis. He's decided to buy a Porsche and have an affair with a nineteen-year-old. My plans are roughly the same. I tell you . . . you can't help but gloat a little."

This charming chronology (and the check from Frannie Halcyon she had just deposited) kept Mary Ann smiling all the way home from the bank.

Then she stopped to consider her own options:

Of course, she would have children. She had always planned on that. But when? She was thirty now. *When?* After her career had taken hold? When would that be? Did babies mean marriage? She wasn't *that* modern, was she? What about Brian? Would marriage merely heighten his insecurities about her upward career mobility? Did he even *want* to get married at this point? Was it fair to ask him to wait? Would he wait?

Who should be the first to ask?

They slept at her place that night, teaspoon nestled in tablespoon. Just before dawn, she felt him slip away from her. She rolled over, slept some more, and awoke half-an-hour later to find him sitting naked in the wingback chair facing the bed.

"Let's do it," he said quietly.

She rubbed her eyes. "What?"

"Get married."

She blinked several times, then smiled sleepily. "Telepathy," she said.

"Yeah?"

"I've been thinking about it all day. I figured it was just Taurus meets Venus. What's your excuse?"

He shrugged. "I thought I'd better make an offer *before* you're on the cover of *People.*"

She grinned. "Take your time."

"No. I'm proud of you. I want you to know that. Great things are about to happen to you, Mary Ann, and you deserve every bit of it. I think you're an amazing person."

She looked at him lovingly for a long time, then patted the empty spot next to her. "Why aren't you in bed?"

"Don't change the subject. I can adore you just as well from over here."

"As you wish, sire." It was true, anyway; she could almost feel it.

"When is the press conference?" he asked.

"Tuesday."

Brian whistled. "Close."

"It's not actually a press conference. The station won't give me air time without knowing what I want it for, and I'm not about to tell them at this point."

"Then how will you do it?"

"I've got my own show, remember?"

When the light dawned, Brian shook his head in wonderment. "Jesus, that's brilliant!"

Mary Ann accepted the compliment with a gracious nod. "How many escapees from Jonestown get to resurface on the afternoon movie show? I figure we can drop the bomb, then wait for somebody *else* to organize the press conference."

"What sort of bomb is it?"

"What do you mean?"

"I mean . . . give us a preview."

"Well . . ." Mary Ann pondered the request for a moment. She didn't want to talk about DeDe's double theory yet. It was still too shaky in her own mind. "For one thing, she escaped down the river in a tin drum that was intended for tropical fish. And Jones raped her one time when she was bedridden."

"Jesus," murmured Brian. "I guess that oughta hold 'em."

"It's a story, all right."

"Do you think you can tell it all in five minutes?"

Mary Ann shook her head. "We won't even try. We'll sketch out the basics and give the rest to the highest bidder. I like doing things on my own terms. Speaking of which, come to bed."

"You still haven't answered my question."

"I know."

"You don't have to answer it, actually. I just wanted to ask you before the commotion began. I wanted you to know."

"I'm glad to know." She smiled at him tenderly. "You'll never know how glad."

Claire

WHERE, GANGIE, *WHERE?*"

Little Edgar was leaping ecstatically, trying to spot the whales that had been sighted off the starboard side of the *Sagafjord.* His sister, Anna, stood calmly at his side, somewhat less impressed.

Frannie knelt beside the four-year-olds and pointed. "See? Over there . . . that big spout of water. That's the whale. He's blowing all that water through a hole in his back."

Edgar frowned. "Did somebody shoot him?"

"No, darling . . . why would . . . ? Oh, the hole. Well, you see . . . all whales have a hole like that, so they can . . . so they can blow water through it." Frannie moaned softly and cast an imploring glance at Claire McAllister. "Get me out of this."

Claire chuckled throatily. "Why does a whale have a hole? That's a dangerous question to ask *me,* honey!"

Frannie giggled. Claire was an ex-chorine of indeterminate age, with a chronic weakness for *double entendres* and racy jokes. Her very-red lips and very-black hair were oddly suggestive of Ann Miller, though Claire had long ago bid farewell to show business. She was currently married to the third richest man in Oklahoma.

"All right," smiled Frannie. "Forget I asked."

Claire smiled expansively at the twins. "They're just cute as a button, Frannie. What's that name they call you?"

Frannie reddened. "Uh . . . Gangie. It's just a pet name. Frannie's a little too personal . . . and Mrs. Halcyon seemed too . . . formal."

"Gangie," repeated Claire, her dark eyes twinkling with a hint of playfulness. "Sounds an awful lot like Grannie to me."

Frannie fidgeted with a wisp of hair over her ear. "Well . . . I . . . uh . . . wouldn't mind that one bit. They *seem* like my own grandchildren."

"Uh-huh," said Claire. The twinkle remained.

"Well," exclaimed Frannie, turning to confront the twins again, "we've seen the whales, so it's about time for a little nappie, don't you think?"

The children groaned in protest.

As Frannie took their hands and led them away, Claire winked at her conspiratorially. "Meet you in The Garden, honey."

"The Garden" was the Garden Lounge, an elegant bar on the Veranda Deck that featured chamber music by a group called the San José Trio. Frannie and Claire retreated there daily to bask in lovely, old-fashioned renditions of tunes like "Over the Rainbow" and "Londonderry Air."

"Where's Jimbo?" asked Frannie, as soon as the Mai Tais arrived. Claire's husband was almost always with them. His loving attentiveness to Claire made Frannie quite lonesome sometimes.

Claire's eyelids fluttered histrionically. "In the goddamn casino, wouldn't ya know it? I figured the bug would bite him sooner or later. I told him to go right ahead and gamble to his heart's content . . . I'd just find myself a nice gigolo."

Frannie smiled. "They don't actually have . . . ?"

"Of course they do, honey! They don't call them that, of course, but those boys on the cruise staff are all . . . shall we say *expected* to dance with the old ladies . . . and the last time I checked I *qualified,* goddamnit!"

Frannie laughed. "But that's where it stops, isn't it?"

"You want more?" roared Claire. "Forget it, honey. Most of 'em are gay. The boy that does the exercise class is shacked up with the tap dancer, and that magician only has eyes for the cute wine steward. And that's just the staff! Don't get me started on the passengers, honey. That Mrs. Clinton, for instance . . . the one with diabetes who has to travel with a companion to make sure she doesn't eat too much sugar? Hah! Companion, my ass. Oh, I tell you, it is *rich.* The gossip on this tub is almost better than the food. I love it! I'm addicted to cruise ships. It's not like it used to be in the old days, though. Some of the glamor is gone. The truly rich don't ride these babies anymore. But there's nothing like being at sea, honey . . . nothing! Lord, look at the mist on that mountain!"

Frannie, in fact, was already looking. Edgar would have loved this, she thought. He was always such a grump on tropical vacations—and such a lovable creature when the air was brisk and the sky was gray.

Frannie set her Mai Tai down and smiled apologetically. "I'm sorry, Claire. As usual, my timing is dreadful."

"Honey, is something the . . . ?"

The matriarch laid her hand delicately on her waist. "Just a little . . . queasiness."

"Lord, you *do* look a little green. And me running off my goddamn mouth like that." Claire checked her watch. "You're in luck. The doctor's still in. You should stock up on Dramamine, honey. He's down on B-Deck near the elevator."

Frannie rose and thanked her. "Do you know his name?"

"Fielding," replied Claire. "You can't miss him. He's one gorgeous hunk of man."

I See by Your Outfit...

I
F RENO WAS ANY INDICATION, THE NUMBER 6 HAD FINALLY become synonymous with cheap motel. Besides the original Motel 6 (which actually *had* charged six dollars a night, long ago), Michael and Bill could choose from the Western 6 Motel (attached to a Denny's) and the 6 Gun Motel (near the Nevada State Fairgrounds).

They settled on the 6 Gun, because Michael felt that the weekend's cowboy motif should be carried out to the fullest. He wasn't disappointed. The motel's nightstands featured an upturned pistol surmounted by a lampshade. There was also an enormous foam rubber ten-gallon hat on the wall in the lobby.

"Ah, the West!" exclaimed Michael, as he flung open the curtains to let in the sunshine.

Bill continued unpacking. "You live in the West."

"Yeah," said Michael, "but sometimes you have to go east to be Western."

"How's the view?"

"Awe inspiring. The Exxon station and the hills beyond."

Bill chuckled. "Great."

"There are also seven—count 'em—seven homosexuals

sunning on the ten square feet of grass between us and the Exxon station. God, is this town ready?"

Bill shrugged. "Slot machines can't tell the difference between queer money and the other kind."

"I don't know," said Michael. "According to the papers, the lieutenant-governor didn't seem any too thrilled. Besides, after that *Examiner* headline, they must be a little nervous about fags coming to Nevada."

"What *Examiner* headline?"

"You know . . . the MGM Grand story: GAY SEX ACT SPARKS HOTEL FIRE."

"Oh, yeah."

"Think of it," said Michael. "The whole damn town could go up in flames tonight."

A back-lighted plastic sign proclaimed the event to passersby on the highway: RENO NATIONAL GAY RODEO. As Bill swung his Trans Am into the dusty parking lot, Michael began to speculate out loud.

"Now, how many of these dudes do you think are real cowboys?" He related to this issue personally. His week-old Danner boots felt leaden on his feet; his teal-and-cream cowboy shirt seemed as fraudulent as a sport shirt worn by a sailor on leave.

"For starters," said Bill, "that one isn't." He pointed to a wiry brunette wearing a T-shirt that said: MUSTACHE RIDES—5¢.

There were similar signs of clone encroachment, Michael noted. Too many sherbet-colored tank tops. Too many straw hats that looked suspiciously like the ones at All-American Boy. Too many Nautilus-shaped bodies poured into too many T-shirts brazenly announcing: IF YOU CAN ROPE ME, YOU CAN RIDE ME.

One obvious city slicker, in deference to the occasion, had traded his nipple ring for a tiny silver spur, but Michael found the gesture unconvincing.

"God almighty!" he gasped, catching sight of the heroic pectorals on display at the entrance to the rodeo arena.

"Where do they all come from?"

"It ain't the ranch," said Bill. "Real cowboys have big bellies."

"Don't be so jaded. One of them's got to be real."

"Sure," replied Bill, "there's a real waiter from The Neon Chicken."

Bill's defective imaginative powers were beginning to get on Michael's nerves. Inside the arena, he concentrated on the event itself—a raucous display of calf-roping, bull-riding and "wild cow-milking." The latter competition involved a cooperative effort between a lesbian, a drag queen and a "macho man"—an impressive achievement in itself.

By mid-afternoon, most of the shirts had come off, turning the stands to a rich shade of mahogany. The beer flowed so freely that almost no one could resist the urge to clap along with The Texas Mustangs, billed as "the only gay country-western band in the Lone Star State."

"I like this," Michael told Bill. "Everybody's off guard. It's harder to give attitude."

"Yeah," said Bill, "but wait till tonight."

"The dance, you mean?"

Bill nodded a little too smugly. "As soon as this dust gets washed off, all the little disco bunnies will emerge. Just watch."

Michael didn't want to agree with him.

Physician, Heal Thyself

FRANNIE'S UTTER DISBELIEF WAS REFLECTED IN THE face of the handsome, blond doctor who awaited her in his office on the *Sagafjord's* B-Deck.

"Mrs. Halcyon! My God!"

Frannie smiled and extended her hand. "Dr. Fielding."

"How wonderful to see you," said the doctor. "I had no idea you were on board. I didn't check the passenger manifest this time, and . . . well, it's been a long time, hasn't it?"

Frannie nodded, already sensing the extreme awkwardness of the situation. This, after all, was the man who had brought the twins into the world. Would she be forced to lie to *him* about the "orphans" in her care? And would he believe her?

"I feel so silly about this," said Frannie feebly.

The doctor's smile was as white and crisp as his uniform. "About what?" he asked.

Frannie touched her mid-section. "Tummy problems. Mature women aren't supposed to get seasick, are they?"

The doctor shrugged. "I'm afraid it strikes indiscriminately. I'm not exactly immune myself, and I've been sailing for a year now. How far topside are you?"

"Excuse me?"

"Your stateroom. Are you in one of the suites?"

Frannie nodded. "On the Terrace Sun Deck."

"I thought so," grinned the doctor.

"Why?"

"Well . . . the motion's more noticeable up there. Usually it doesn't matter, but when the sea gets a little choppy, the luxury suites are the first to feel it." He winked at her winningly. "We peasants down here in the bilges have it a little easier."

Frannie felt greener by the minute. "There's not much I can do, I suppose?"

The doctor opened a white metal cabinet. "We'll get you prone with a little Dramamine." He handed Frannie a pill and a paper cup full of water. "Can you keep me company for a while? It's a slow day. We'll have the place to ourselves, probably."

Frannie accepted readily. No wonder DeDe had adored this man.

He sat in a chair near the bed, while she stretched out. After days at sea with the twins, it was nice to have someone fussing over *her*.

They shared a long moment of silence, and then he said: "I'm sorry about DeDe and the children, Mrs. Halcyon. I didn't hear about it until . . . somewhat after the fact."

She thought her heart would break. She longed to share her good news with this gentle, compassionate man. Instead, she replied: "Thank you, Dr. Fielding. DeDe was terribly fond of you."

After another pause, he said: "I was working in Santa Fe when I read about it."

"Oh, yes?" She jumped at the chance to talk about something else.

"I had a gynecological practice there for a while, before I went back to general practice and landed this job. My life got a little . . . confusing . . . and this was as close as I could get to joining the merchant marines."

"You must've seen the world by now," said Frannie. "I envy you that."

"It's . . . not bad," replied the doctor. There was something bittersweet in his tone that puzzled Frannie.

"Alaska's extraordinary," she offered. "There's so *much* of it . . . and those fjords! They're like something out of Wagner . . . so grand, so heartbreaking. I'm just sorry . . ." She cut herself off.

"Sorry about what?"

Frannie smiled dimly, staring at the overhead. "I forgot you never knew him."

"Who?"

"My husband, Edgar. I miss having him with me. When you're a widow, doctor, the main thing that hurts is that you've lost your playmate. You've lost someone who can look at a mountain with you and know what you're thinking . . . someone to share the silences with. It takes a long time to build that . . . and it's hard to give it up."

"I know," he replied.

"You aren't married, are you?"

"No."

"Have you ever had anybody who . . . ?"

"Once," he answered. "Once I had that."

"Then you know."

"Yes."

Frannie hesitated, suddenly wary of becoming too personal. Then she asked: "How did you . . . lose her?"

Silence.

"I'm sorry," said the matriarch. "I didn't mean to . . ."

"It's O.K.," said the doctor. "I know exactly what you mean about those mountains. They don't look the same anymore."

The Hoedown

A FIVE-FOOT MIRROR BOOT, COMPLETE WITH SPURS, spun slowly over the dance floor at the Nevada State Fairgrounds, casting its glittery benediction on the assembled multitudes. The event was called "Stand By Your Man" and most of the dancers were doing just that.

Michael looked up at the shimmering icon and sighed. "Isn't that inspired?" he asked Bill.

The cop regarded the boot for a split second, then frowned. "Goddamnit!"

"What's the matter?" asked Michael.

"I forgot to get poppers."

Michael smiled. "This is country music, remember? Not disco."

"No," said Bill. "I mean . . . for later."

"Oh."

"Maybe they sell them at The Chute."

"It doesn't really . . ."

"Somebody there will know how to get them."

"I don't need them," said Michael. "If you'd like some, then . . ."

"I don't *need* them," barked Bill. "I'd like some, that's all."

Michael didn't want an argument. "Fine," he said evenly. "What shall we do?"

"I'll drive into town," answered Bill, sounding less hostile now. "You can hold down the fort here. I shouldn't be long, O.K.?"

Michael nodded, soothed by his friend's inadvertent rusticism. *Drive into town. Hold down the fort.* They might have been hitching up the buckboard for a trip into Dodge City. "O.K.," he smiled. "I'll be here."

Bill nuzzled him for a moment, whispering "Hot man" in his ear, then disappeared into the crowd.

It was an escape of sorts, Michael realized. Bill detested this music. He had managed to endure the rodeo with the aid of his Walkman and an Air Supply cassette. He was clearly not prepared to commit himself to an entire evening of country songs by Ed Bruce and Stella Parton and Sharon McNight.

Michael was relieved. He felt fragile and sentimental tonight—achingly romantic—and he knew that those sensations could not long coexist with Bill's horrifying literalness. It wasn't poppers *per se* that had put Michael off—he got off on them himself—it was the soul-deadening way they sometimes reduced sex to a track event, requiring timing, agility and far too much advance planning.

How many man-hours had been wasted, he wondered, searching for that stupid brown bottle amid the bedclothes?

It wasn't Bill's fault, really. He *enjoyed* sex with Michael. He enjoyed it the way he enjoyed movies with Michael or bull sessions with Michael or late-night pizza pig-outs with Michael. He had never, apparently, felt the need to embellish it with romance. That wasn't Bill's problem; it was Michael's.

Michael moved to the edge of the dance floor and watched couples shuffling along shoulder to shoulder as they did the Cotton-Eyed Joe. There was genuine joy in this room, he realized—an exhilaration born of the unexpected. Queers doing cowboy dancing. Who would've thunk it? Kids who grew up in Galveston and Tucson and Modesto, performing the folk dances of their homeland finally, *finally* with the partner of their choice.

It didn't matter, somehow, that teenagers out on the highway were screaming "faggot" at the new arrivals. Here inside, there was easily enough brotherhood to ward off the devil.

Ed Bruce shambled onto the stage. He was a big, fortyish Marlboro Man type who spoke of golf and the Little Woman as if he were singing to a VFW convention in Oklahoma City. His big hit, "Mamas, Don't Let Your Babies Grow Up to Be Cowboys," took on a delectable irony in this unlikely setting.

Twenty years ago, thought Michael, gay men were content to shriek for Judy at Carnegie Hall. Now they could dance in each other's arms, while a Nashville cowboy serenaded them. He couldn't help smiling at the thought.

Like magic, across the crowded dance hall, someone smiled back. He was big and bear-like with a grin that seemed disarmingly shy for a man his size. He raised his beer can in a genial salute to Michael.

Michael returned the gesture, heart in throat.

The man moved towards him.

"Pretty nice, huh?" He meant the music.

"Wonderful," said Michael.

"Do you slow dance?" asked the man.

"Sure," lied Michael.

Learning to Follow

AT FIVE-NINE, MICHAEL WAS DWARFED BY THE MAN who had asked him to dance.

To complicate matters further, this lumbering hunk clearly expected him to *follow*—a concept that hadn't crossed Michael's mind since the 1968 Senior Prom at Orlando High. And then, of course, Betsy Ann Phifer had done the following.

There was a secret to this, he remembered. Ned had learned it at Trinity Place's Thursday evening hoedowns: *Extend your right arm slightly and straddle his right leg—tastefully, of course—so that you can pick up on the motion of his body.*

Check. So far, so good.

It felt a little funny doing things backwards like this, but it felt sort of wonderful, too. Michael laid his head on the great brown doormat of his partner's chest and fell into the music.

Ed Bruce was still on stage. The song was "Everything's a Waltz."

The man stepped on Michael's foot. "I'm sorry," he said.

"That's O.K.," said Michael.

"I'm kind of new at this."

"Who isn't?" grinned Michael.

Not so long ago, he realized, men *had* slow danced in San Francisco. He recalled the tail-end of that era, circa 1973. The very sight of it had revolted him: grown men cheek to cheek, sweaty palm to sweaty palm, while Streisand agonized over "People" at The Rendezvous.

Then came disco, a decade of simulated humping, faceless bodies writhing in a mystic tribal rite that had simultaneously delighted and intimidated Michael. What that epoch had lacked some people were now finding in country music. The word was romance.

"Where are you from?" asked Michael.

"Arizona," replied the man.

"Any place I know?"

"I doubt it. A place called Salome. Five hundred people."

So he *was* a real cowboy. That explained the hands. They felt like elephant hide. Bill could just go fuck himself. "Salome," repeated Michael, copying the man's pronunciation (Sa-loam). "As in Oscar Wilde?"

"Who?"

Michael's heart beat faster. *He's never heard of Oscar Wilde.* Dear God, was this the real thing? "Nobody important," he explained. "It doesn't really matter."

It really didn't. He felt so profoundly *comfortable* in this man's arms. Even his gracelessness was endearing. It wasn't the man, he reminded himself, but the circumstances. Two prevailing cultures—one very straight, one very gay—had successively denied him this simple pleasure. He felt like crying for joy.

"Did you . . . uh . . . ride in the rodeo?" he asked.

" 'Fraid not. I'm just a construction worker."

Just a construction worker! Jesus God, had he died and gone to heaven? Why hadn't someone told him there was a place he could go to slow dance with a construction worker?

"What do you do for . . . this . . . in Salome?" Michael asked.

The man pulled away from him just enough for his smile to show. "I go to Phoenix." He leaned down and kissed Michael clumsily on the edge of his mouth. "You're a nice guy," he said.

"You too," said Michael.

They danced for another minute in silence. Then the man

spoke huskily into Michael's ear. "Look . . . would you like to make love tonight?"

Make love. Not have sex. Not get it on. Michael's voice caught in his throat. "I'm actually . . . here with a friend. He's just . . . off right now."

"Oh." The disappointment in his voice warmed Michael to the marrow.

"I could give you my phone number. Maybe, if you're ever in San Francisco . . ."

"That's O.K."

"Never go there, huh?"

"Not yet," said the man.

"I think you'd like it. I could show you around."

"I don't travel much," said the man.

Michael decided against suggesting a trip to Salome. "Look," he said, "would you believe me if I told you that this is better than all the sex I've had this year?"

The man grinned. "Yeah?"

"Infinitely," said Michael.

"I'm stepping all over your . . ."

"I don't care. I love it."

The man's chest rumbled as he laughed.

"You're doin' just great," said Michael. "Just keep holding me, O.K.?"

"Sure."

So Michael settled in again, lost in a sweet stranger's arms until Bill came back with the poppers.

Over the Glacier

WHEN THE *SAGAFJORD* REACHED JUNEAU, PRUE and Luke went ashore with the other passengers and explored the tiny frontier town—a place heralded by the local chamber of commerce as "America's largest capital city."

"It must be a joke," said Prue, puzzling over the brochure in her hands.

Luke shook his head. "They mean land mass."

"But how . . . ?"

"It covers more square miles than any other capital city. Everything's out of whack up here. It's further from here to the Aleutians, at the other end of the state, than it is from San Francisco to New York."

Prue thought for a moment. "That's a little scary, somehow."

"Why?"

"I don't know. It makes you seem so much smaller, I guess. Like the landscape could . . . swallow you up. You could just disappear without a trace."

Luke smiled at her. "People do. That's the point."

Prue shivered. "Not to me, it isn't."

"Wait till you see the glacier."

"What glacier?"

Luke slipped his arm around her waist. "I thought we'd rent a float plane and fly over the ice fields. They say it's as close to God as you'll ever get."

Prue looked troubled. "Can't He just come to us?"

Luke touched the tip of her nose. "What's the matter, my love?"

"Nothing . . . I just . . . well, those tiny planes and my tummy don't always get along."

"It's just forty-five minutes."

He pulled her closer until Prue relented. In many ways, she realized, he had already become her talisman against harm.

The float plane skimmed the surface of the water like a low-flying dragonfly, then lifted them into the slate-gray sky above Juneau. Besides Prue and Luke, there were four other passengers: a youngish couple from Buenos Aires and two lady librarians, traveling together.

Luke sat directly behind the pilot and conversed with him inaudibly, while Prue watched the alien world beneath her turn from dark blue to dark green to white. No, *gray*. A pale gray plateau as far as the eye could see—a living entity, sinuous as lava at the edges, brutal and beautiful and unexplainably terrifying.

It relieved her somewhat to see that the glacier had boundaries. Splintering and hissing, it tumbled into a dark sea where the water crackled like electricity. As the float plane dipped lower, Prue peered into fissures so brilliantly blue that they seemed unnatural, blue as the lethal heart of a nuclear power plant.

"Look, Luke . . . that color!"

But her lover was deep in conversation with the pilot, their voices drowned out by the engine sounds.

Prue leaned closer. "Luke . . ."

He didn't hear her. He continued to interrogate the pilot, a rapt expression on his face. Prue could make out only two words. Oddly enough, the pilot repeated them.

She fell back into her seat, frowning. This moment should have been theirs: hers and Luke's. This buddy-buddy business with the cockpit was inexcusably selfish, thoughtless. When Luke finally sat back and squeezed her hand, she let him know she was pouting.

"You O.K.?" he asked.

She waited a beat. "Well, what was all *that* about?"

"All what?"

"My God! You haven't stopped talking."

He pumped her hand again. "Sorry. Just . . . plane talk. I guess I got carried away."

"What was that about dire needs?"

Luke blinked at her. "Huh?"

"You said something about dire needs."

"No, I didn't." His face was resolute.

"Luke, I heard you. You said something, something . . . dire needs. And the pilot said it back. Just a minute ago."

He studied her for a moment, then smiled and shook his head. "You misunderstood me, darling. We were talking about geography." He held up his hand like a Boy Scout. "Honest injun. You didn't miss a thing."

Prue let it drop. For one thing, the other passengers had begun to take an interest in her vexation. For another, she wanted this moment to be special, free from earthbound anxieties. Luke did, too, it seemed. He gave her his undivided attention for the rest of the tour, turning away only long enough to make a brief notation on the inside of a matchbook.

"What was that?" she smiled. "A reminder?"

Luke looked up, distracted.

"I do that myself," she added, not wanting to appear nosey. "My mind's like a sieve."

He smiled faintly and returned the matchbook to his breast pocket.

"Let's go dancing tonight," he said.

The First to Know

BACK AT WORK AT GOD'S GREEN EARTH, MICHAEL UN-loaded his rodeo experiences on an ever-indulgent Ned. The saga suffered in the retelling. Michael's brief interlude with the slow-dancing construction worker emerged somehow as a hackneyed mastur-batory fantasy, no longer the rare and wonderful thing it had seemed at the time.

That night, he tried invoking the spirit of the weekend by listening to country music on KSAN, but Willie Nelson took on an oddly hollow note in a room full of bamboo furniture and deco kitsch. Cowboys didn't collect Fiesta Ware.

So he wandered downstairs and smoked a roach on the bench in the courtyard. The dope and the silence and the tiny sliver of a moon hanging in the trees all conspired to make him more contemplative than usual.

Contemplative, hell—he was simply depressed.

Nothing grand, of course. This was a garden-variety de-pression, born of boredom and loneliness and a pervasive sense of the immense triviality of life. It would pass, he knew. He would make it pass.

But what would he put in its place?

The clock said 3:47 when the phone woke him.

He stumbled out of bed and lunged for the receiver. "This better be good," he told the caller.

"It is," came the reply. Mary Ann's giggle was unmistakable. Michael settled himself in a chair. "What's up, Babycakes?"

"Brian and I are getting married!"

"Now?"

Another giggle. "Next month. You aren't pissed, are you?"

"Pissed?"

"About waking you up. We wanted to make it official. Calling you was the only thing we could think of."

Michael was so touched he wanted to cry. What followed, though, was total silence.

"Mouse? Are you there? You *are* pissed, aren't you? Look, we'll talk to you in the . . ."

"Are you kidding? This is *fabulous,* Babycakes!"

"Isn't it, though?"

"It's about time," said Michael. "Are you pregnant?"

Mary Ann roared. "No! Can you believe it?"

"Is Brian?"

He heard her speak to Brian. They were obviously in bed. "He wants to know if you're pregnant."

Brian came on the line. "The bitch knocked me up."

Michael laughed. "Somebody had to do it."

"Are you alone?" asked Brian.

"Hell, no," answered Michael. "Say hello to Raoul."

"Hey, that's O.K. . . . ."

"Calm down," laughed Michael. "I made that up."

"You shithead."

"I know. Sorry."

"I was picturing some French Canadian with five o'clock shadow."

"That's funny," said Michael. "So was I. God, Brian . . . this is so damn wonderful."

"Yeah . . . well, we just wanted you to be the first to know."

"Goddamn right," said Michael.

"We love you, man. Here's Mary Ann again. She's got some more news for you."

"Mouse?"

"Yeah?"

"Have you got a TV set at work?"

Michael thought for a moment. "Ned's got a portable that he brings from home sometimes."

"Good. Get him to bring it on Tuesday. I want you to watch the show."

"*Bargain Matinee?*"

"Is there any other? You don't need to watch the movie . . . just my little halftime bit. I think you'll be mildly amused."

"Don't tell me. You've found a new use for empty Clorox bottles."

"Just watch the show, smartass."

"Roger."

"And get some sleep. We love you."

"I know that," said Michael.

But he slept much better knowing it.

That Nice Man

CLAIRE MCALLISTER'S HUSBAND WAS IN THE CASINO again, so the raven-haired ex-chorine sought out Frannie's company on the Promenade Deck of the *Sagafjord*. Frannie was thrilled to see her.

"Pull up a chair," she smiled, laying down her Danielle Steel novel. "I haven't talked to a grown-up in ages."

Claire mugged amiably. "Who you callin' a grown-up?"

"You'll do," said Frannie. "Believe me."

Claire lowered her formidable frame into an aluminum deck chair and sighed dramatically. "So where *are* the little darlings?"

Frannie shushed her with a forefinger to the lips. "Don't even mention it, Claire. It's almost too good to be true."

"What?"

Frannie made a sweeping gesture with her arm. "This. Solitude. Blessed relief. I *adore* the children, as you know, but . . ."

"You've found a baby-sitter!"

The matriarch nodded triumphantly. "It was his idea, poor man. I hope he hasn't bitten off more than he can chew."

"Do I know him?" asked Claire, pulling a blanket across her lap.

"I think so," said Frannie. "Mr. Starr."

Claire drew a blank.

"You know," added Frannie. "That American stockbroker from London."

"That good-looking thing traveling with the hoity-toity blonde?"

Frannie smiled demurely. "They aren't exactly traveling together."

"Horseshit."

"They met on the ship," the matriarch explained, her face burning from the profanity. "I know her . . . somewhat remotely. She's a gossip columnist in San Francisco. I'm afraid she's a little common."

Claire snorted. "You'd think she was the Queen of Sheba. She puts on airs something fierce. What the hell does that elegant man see in her?"

Frannie shrugged. "She's rather pretty, don't you think? I understand she listens well, too. At any rate, I can't complain; she introduced me to *him.* I think I'm relaxed for the first time since we left San Francisco."

"Did the children take to him?"

"Like a house on fire! He's full of wonderful stories and jokes." Frannie thought for a moment. "You know, he's rather moody around adults . . . not sullen or rude, really . . . just introspective. Around the children, though, he's a bundle of energy! He never stops trying to impress them. He's like a child competing for a grown-up's attention, instead of the other way around."

"He sounds perfect," said Claire.

Frannie nodded. "I think it's important for the children to have a masculine presence." She didn't elaborate on this thesis, but it gave her pleasure to articulate it to a woman as sensible and down-to-earth as Claire. The twins had never had a father, after all . . . only that woman who had kept DeDe company in Guyana and Cuba. It wasn't natural, Frannie reminded herself. Thank God for Mr. Starr!

"Say," said Claire, after an interlude of silence, "Jimbo has a little business to do when we dock this afternoon. Howsabout you and me exploring Sitka together? There's a darling little Russian church and some marvelous scrimshaw shops. A couple of girls on the town . . . whatdya say?"

Frannie hesitated. "Well . . . I . . ."

"I *know* it's a thrilling offer, honey, but try not to bust a gut!"

Frannie smiled apologetically. "I was just thinking . . . well, the children."

"Can't your Mr. Starr take them off your hands for a while?"

Frannie's brow wrinkled. "He *did* offer, as a matter of fact."

"Wonderful! Then, it's settled!"

"It seems such an imposition, though."

"Look, honey, if that man is cuckoo for kids, that's *his* problem, not yours. You've gotta learn to recognize a gift from God when you see one!"

Frannie conceded with a grin. "You're right. This *is* supposed to be a vacation."

"Exactly," said Claire.

Half-an-hour later, when Frannie went to pick up the twins, she found them giggling under a "fort" that Mr. Starr had constructed from two deck chairs and a blanket. Edgar had done that often—for DeDe—long, long ago.

Without announcing herself, Frannie stood outside the woolen shelter and reveled in the mirthful music of her grandchildren's voices.

Then Mr. Starr began to sing to them:

"Bye baby bunting, Daddy's gone a-hunting, gone to get a rabbit skin to wrap the baby bunting in . . ."

The sheer familiarity of that ancient nursery rhyme was all the reassurance the matriarch needed.

It was comforting to know that some things never changed.

The Uncut Version

MRS. MADRIGAL'S ANGULAR FACE SEEMED EVEN more radiant than usual as she reached for the heavy iron skillet that meant breakfast at 28 Barbary Lane.

"I still can't take it in," she said. "Two eggs or three, dear?"

"Three," said Michael. "Neither can I. I've been promoting it for months, but I didn't think either one of them could handle the commitment right now. Mary Ann more so than Brian, I guess."

Mrs. Madrigal cracked three eggs into the skillet, discarded the shells, and wiped her long fingers on her paisley apron. "I was the one who introduced them. Did you know that?"

"No."

"I did," beamed the landlady. "Just after Mary Ann moved in. I had a little dinner one night, and Mary Ann told me she was afraid there weren't enough straight men in San Francisco." Mrs. Madrigal smiled nostalgically. "That was before she knew about me, of course. If she *had,* I suppose we would've lost her to Cleveland for good."

Michael smiled. "So you introduced her to Brian?"

"Not exactly. I told Brian she needed help moving the furniture. I let them take care of the rest. Wheat toast or rye, dear?"

"Wheat, please."

"It was an unmitigated disaster, of course. Brian was a shameless womanizer, and Mary Ann was madly in love with Beauchamp Day at the time—God help her." The landlady shook her head with rueful amusement. "*Then* she started dating the detective that Mona's mother hired to check up on me."

Michael nodded soberly.

"I was always rather glad he disappeared, weren't you?" Her grin was as mischievous as it could get. "I do wonder what happened to him, though."

Michael felt himself squirming. He avoided this subject as much as possible. Mary Ann alone had witnessed the detective's fall from a cliff at Lands End, and she had shared that secret with no one but Michael. There were some things that even Mrs. Madrigal should never be allowed to know.

"Then came Burke Andrew," said Michael, moving right along, "and those cannibals at Grace Cathedral."

Mrs. Madrigal's Wedgwood eyes rolled extravagantly. "She knows how to pick 'em, doesn't she?"

"Yep. But I think she's finally got it right."

"So do I," said the landlady. "I'm a little surprised, frankly."

"Why?"

"I don't know, exactly. I just have this gut feeling she's up to something. She seems so preoccupied lately. I would have guessed marriage to be the last thing on her mind."

"So," asked the landlady as they sat down to eat, "what has our wandering boy been up to lately?"

Michael pretended to be engrossed in the marmalade jar. "Oh . . . nothing much." He knew she was inquiring into his love life, and he didn't feel like talking about it. "I'm having a celibacy attack, I think. I stay home and watch TV a lot."

"How *is* that?"

"How is what?"

The landlady flicked a crumb off the corner of her mouth. "TV."

Michael laughed. "My favorite thing this week was a special report on circumcision."

"Indeed?" Mrs. Madrigal buttered another piece of toast.

"It was a hoot," said Michael. "They interviewed a circumcision expert named Don Wong."

"No!"

Michael crossed his heart. "Swear to God."

"And what did he have to say?"

Michael shrugged. "Just that there's no valid reason anymore for mutilating little boys at birth. Jesus. How long does it take people to figure things out? My mother isn't exactly a modern thinker, but she knew *that* thirty years ago."

Mrs. Madrigal smiled. "You should write her a thank you note."

"The funny thing is . . . I hated it when I was a kid. I was always the only kid in the shower room who wasn't circumcised, and it bugged the hell out of me. Mama said: 'You just keep yourself clean, Mikey, and you'll thank me for this later. There's not a thing wrong with what God gave you.' "

"Smart lady," said Mrs. Madrigal.

Michael nodded enthusiastically. "I was invited to an orgy this week."

The landlady set her teacup down.

"It was for uncut guys only."

She blinked at him twice.

"It's O.K.," said Michael. "It was a benefit."

"Oh, really?"

"For the chorus."

"Ah." Mrs. Madrigal's deadpan was ruthless. "A foreskin festival. Do they check you at the door or what?"

Michael laughed. "I know. It's pretty silly. Still . . . I'm glad that attitudes have changed. There's no reason in the world to be snipping at your genitalia."

The landlady looked down at her teacup, suppressing a

smile until Michael added hastily: "Unless, of course, you're prepared to go all the way."

Mrs. Madrigal looked up again and winked.

"More coffee, dear?"

Daddy's Gone

A VIGOROUS FUR-TRADING MONOPOLY IN THE LAST century had given Sitka a distinctively Russian cast: a Russian blockhouse, Russian grave markers everywhere, Cossack dancers performing for tourists, even a pretty Russian Orthodox cathedral in the center of town.

Prue adored every inch of it.

"Isn't it incredible, Luke? To think that this is America!"

Luke, however, was occupied with the orphans. He was kneeling next to them on the street, adjusting the miniature fur-trimmed parkas he had bought for them half-an-hour earlier. With the hoods up, the children looked like little Eskimos, almost too adorable to be true.

"Isn't it a little warm for that?" asked Prue. "The weather's practically like San Francisco."

He looked up distractedly. "Be with you in a second."

He hadn't even heard her. Ordinarily, she might have been annoyed, or faintly jealous. Prue resented people—like Frannie Halcyon and her friend Claire, for instance—who demanded so much attention from Luke that they diminished her share of his love.

But the children were different. Seeing them with Luke, Prue remembered what it was that had captivated her about the scruffy, ill-dressed phantom who had cared for her wolf-hound in Golden Gate Park. Luke related to children the way he related to animals—as a peer who respected their feelings.

The little girl knew that already. "Mr. Starr," she chirped, tugging on his arm. "Take us on a flying boat, *please.* Take us on a flying boat."

Prue smiled. "You told them about our float plane trip."

Luke didn't look up. "They pick up on things fast."

"They speak English so well," Prue observed. "For Vietnamese, I mean."

Luke zipped up the little boy's parka. "They're refugees. They may have been raised by Americans . . . I don't know." There was a slightly caustic edge to his voice, implying that Prue should mind her own business. Suddenly, she felt as if she had walked in on a private conversation.

The little boy took up the cry. "Flying boat! Yeah! Take us on a flying boat!"

Luke confronted him sternly. "Edgar . . . not now!"

A tiny lower lip pushed out. "You promised."

"His name is Edgar?" asked Prue.

Luke ignored her.

"Edgar was Frannie's husband's name. Do you think she named him?"

"Prue, would you shut up, please! I'm having enough trouble with *these* children!" The vehemence of the attack stunned her momentarily, until she realized that the children *were* genuinely upset. They were sniffling softly, not in a bratty way, but as if a trust had been violated.

"Luke," she said warily, "if you promised them a float plane trip, I wouldn't mind doing it again. Really."

Luke stood up. He was rigid with anger. The big vein in his neck had begun to throb. "I didn't promise them anything," he muttered. "C'mon, we haven't eaten since breakfast."

Prue assumed a placatory tone of voice. "A little food would do us all some good." She smiled down at the orphans. "I'll bet they have yummy ice cream in Alaska. Shall we go see?"

They peered up at her wet-eyed—sad, round faces encircled in fur—then reached out for her hands.

Luke walked ahead of them, sulking.

His mood had improved considerably by the time they reached the restaurant, a knotty-pine-and-Formica greasy spoon near the cathedral.

"The meatloaf isn't bad," he said. "How's your salad?" A feeble attempt at apologizing, but an effort nonetheless.

She decided to smile at him. "Awful. It serves me right for ordering a salad in Alaska." She turned to the children. "Those hot dogs went down awfully fast."

The orphans flashed mustardy grins at her. She marveled at how soon children could forget a hurtful situation. Then she reached across the table and stroked Luke's hand. "Do I dare risk the little girls' room?"

"Go ahead," he winked. "The experience will do you good."

The bathroom proved to be pungent with disinfectant, but surprisingly clean. She was there for five minutes, taking care of business and thanking the powers-that-be that her first significant conflict with Luke had fizzled out before it exploded.

When she returned to the dining room, their table was empty. Luke and the orphans were gone.

"Excuse me," she asked the man behind the counter. "My friend and the children, did they . . ."

"They paid up and left," said the man.

"*What?* Left? Where did they go? Did they say?"

The man shrugged. "I figured you'd know."

Panic in Sitka

THE MAN BEHIND THE COUNTER SAW THE CONFUSION IN Prue's face and managed a kindly smile. "Maybe he just expects you to . . . catch up with him."

"He didn't say *anything?*"

"No ma'am. Just paid the bill and took off."

Prue stared at him, mortified, then glanced at the empty table again. Luke had left a tip, she noticed. What in God's name was happening? Was this his way of punishing her? That little tussle over the float plane trip certainly didn't justify this kind of childish stunt.

And what right had he to involve the orphans in this . . . this . . . whatever it was? Prue was livid now, scarlet with humiliation. There had better be a damn good explanation.

She left the restaurant and looked both ways down the street. They were nowhere in sight. To her right, the little gray-and-white frame Russian cathedral offered refuge to a steady stream of tourists. Maybe *that* was it. Maybe the children had grown restless while she was in the rest room, and Luke had taken them to the next logical stop on their tour of Sitka.

Maybe he had expected her to know that.

She entered the cathedral, paid a two-dollar donation, and stood in the back, scanning the room. She recognized several people from the *Sagafjord,* including the loud brunette who hung out with Frannie Halcyon, but Luke and the orphans were not there.

Out in the sunlight again, she considered her alternatives. If Luke was, in fact, trying to teach her some sort of lesson, then he could just go to hell. She could see the town on her own, if need be. On the other hand, what if some unforeseen emergency had arisen which had *demanded* that Luke leave the restaurant?

But what could have happened in five minutes?

She strode back to the restaurant, surveying it once more through a grease-streaked window.

Nothing.

Keep calm, she ordered herself. *There's an explanation for this.* If he had planned on upsetting her, he had succeeded completely. She would never let him know that, though. She would not let him see her cry.

Reversing her course, she walked in the direction of the ship, casting anxious sideways glances down the cross streets. When she was three blocks from the cathedral, she passed a narrow alleyway where a small furry figure caught her eye.

It was one of the orphans. The little girl.

She was standing at the end of the alleyway, framed prettily against a weathered wooden building.

"Hey!" shouted Prue.

The little girl remained immobile for a moment, looking confused, then waved tentatively.

Her name, thought Prue. *What was it?*

Remembering, she yelled again. "Anna! It's me! Is Mr. Starr down there?"

Her answer came in the form of a looming shadow . . . and then Luke himself, lunging in from the left to snatch up the startled child.

"Luke! For God's sake, what are you doing?"

His head pivoted jerkily, like the head of a robot, as he turned to look into her terrified face. The alien rage in his eyes made her blood run cold. Who was this man? *Who in the world was he?*

She ran towards him, screaming: "What have I done, Luke? Just tell me what I've done!"

But he was gone again, sprinting down another alleyway with Anna under his arm.

Prue kept running, her heart pounding savagely in her chest. She watched Luke cross a vacant lot, then disappear into a thicket of weeds and wildflowers. Where was the other orphan, anyway? *What had he done with Edgar?*

When she tried to follow, her heel caught on a rusty bedspring, wrenching her violently to the ground. She lay there, disbelieving, choking on her sobs while blood gushed from her ankle.

"LUKE," she screamed. "PLEASE LUKE, I'M BLEEDING . . . PLEASE . . . PLEASE. . . ."

But there wasn't a sound.

Still on her stomach, Prue jerked an oily rag from beneath a discarded refrigerator and clamped it frantically against her ankle, scattering the flies that had already begun to gather.

She eased herself into a sitting position, leaning against the refrigerator as her eyes glazed over with the full horror of the thing that had happened:

A man with no last name, a man she had loved, a man carrying the identification of Father Paddy Starr, had kidnapped the foster grandchildren of Frannie Halcyon in a small town in Southeast Alaska. And the *Sagafjord* would sail in less than two hours.

It was time to pay the piper.

Atrocity

REMEMBERING AN ANCIENT TEACHING OF THE CAMP Fire Girls, Prue made a tourniquet from another oily rag and applied it hastily to her ankle.

Three minutes later, she loosened the device enough to see that the bleeding had stopped, then raised herself cautiously to her feet. A pearl-sized drop of blood, dark as a ruby, bubbled to the surface as soon as she placed weight on the ankle. She blotted it warily, whimpering as she did so, until she felt secure enough to walk.

Then she set off in the direction of the ship.

As she left the litter-strewn lot, an angry voice called out to her. "Hey, lady!"

She flinched at the sound, turning to see a heavy-set, red-headed man in his late forties. He was wearing overalls and carrying a hoe upright, like a spear.

"Was that son of a bitch with you?"

Prue struggled to find her voice. "I . . . if you mean . . . uh . . ."

"Look, lady . . . I'll kill the bastard if I have to! I'll find out who he is and I'll . . ." He stopped, seeing the blood on Prue's

ankle. "What's that?" he asked, using a tone that was only slightly less hysterical.

"I fell," she said feebly. "I cut myself on that bedspring. Please don't yell at me." She began to sniffle. "I can't take it anymore. *I can't.*"

The man dropped his hoe and walked toward her. "Did he do this to you?"

"A man in a blue blazer?"

"Yep. You know him?"

Prue nodded defeatedly. "I was . . . chasing him. Did you see which way he went?"

"Through there," said the man, pointing to a dilapidated wooden fence with two missing planks. "Through my goddamn garden, the son of a bitch!"

For about five seconds, Prue considered pursuing him, but her spirit was broken now, and she knew that Luke and the orphans would be long gone. She thanked the man and resumed walking, adding lamely: "I'm sorry if he damaged your garden."

The man exploded. "Garden, hell!" He seized her wrist and pulled her toward the hole in the fence. "You're gonna see this, lady!"

See *what,* for God's sake? What on earth had Luke done?

Passing through the opening, they came into a small backyard—virtually indistinguishable from the junk-scattered lot it adjoined. A row of tractor tires, painted white and planted with petunias, was the sole concession to aesthetics. Along the back fence stood a shed of some sort, compartmentalized for . . . what? . . . cages?

The man led her to the shed.

"All right now, you tell me what the hell that means!"

What she saw made her scream, then gag, then vomit in the weeds behind the shed.

The man stood by awkwardly, finally offering her his handkerchief.

"Your friend is crazy, lady. What else can I say?"

*   *   *

Half-an-hour later, Frannie Halcyon was nervously pacing the Promenade Deck of the *Sagafjord*. Since two other cruise liners were already docked in Sitka, the ship was moored in the harbor, with launches making shuttle runs to the pier. The matriarch's eyes were glued on those launches.

"If something's happened, I'll never forgive . . ."

"Nothing's happened," said Claire. "Relax, honey. You're worse than a new mother."

"But we sail in an *hour.*"

"They know that," said Claire.

"And I know that Giroux woman. She's nothing if not flighty. She's probably dragged that man off to a shop somewhere, with total disregard for . . ."

"Look!" cried Claire, pointing to the dock, "there's another launch heading this way!"

Frannie's tension eased instantly. "Thank God!"

Claire scolded her with a grin. "You're the *worst* worrywart!"

"What deck's the gangplank on?"

"A-Deck, I think."

"I'm going to meet them," said Frannie.

"Want company?"

Frannie smiled. "I know you think I'm silly. I get these feelings sometimes. There's no rational explanation for them."

Her fears disintegrated as soon as she saw the gossip columnist's blonde tresses emerge from the launch.

"You see?" said Claire.

But then they saw that Prue was alone.

DeDe Day's D-Day

MRS. MADRIGAL WAS TRIMMING THE IVY IN THE courtyard when Mary Ann left for work.

"Off to the station, dear?"

Mary Ann nodded. "A big day. A *big* day."

The landlady set down her shears and stood up. "Your little surprise, you mean?"

"You know about it?"

Mrs. Madrigal smiled. "Michael told me. He didn't say what, actually . . . just when. I can't imagine what it is."

"It's a wonderful surprise, actually. Not to mention a great story, if I do say so myself."

"A marriage proposal *and* a great story. How many milestones can you squeeze into one week?" The landlady grasped Mary Ann's shoulders, planting a kiss firmly on her cheek. "Congratulations, in advance, dear. I always knew you could do it."

Mary Ann beamed. "Thanks."

"And I want to plan a little do for you. For you and Brian."

"As a matter of fact," said Mary Ann, "I was hoping you'd plan the wedding."

The landlady's face lit up. "I'd be *thrilled.* Here, you mean?"

Mary Ann nodded.

Mrs. Madrigal looked about her in the courtyard. "Let's see. You can say your vows under the lych gate. A coat of paint will fix it up just fine. And we can bring in a cellist, maybe . . . or a harpist . . . a harpist would be heavenly." She clapped her hands together almost girlishly. "This is so wonderful . . . my little family . . . God's been so grand to us, Mary Ann."

"I know," she replied.

And she meant it, too, for the first time in years.

Her revenge, she had just begun to realize, would be sweeter than she had ever dared to dream. Larry Kenan saw to that by being an even bigger bastard than usual.

"Well, how's our little fighting journalist today?"

Mary Ann didn't look up from her desk. She was organizing her note cards on DeDe, pruning and reshuffling to keep within her five minute format. It wasn't easy.

The news director remained in the doorway, thumbs hooked in his Gentlemen's Jeans. She could feel his smirk burning into the top of her head. "Look," he said, "Denny needs to see your props for today's show."

"Right," muttered Mary Ann, continuing to shuffle.

"Now, lady."

Mary Ann gazed up at him, steely-eyed. "It's just a goddamn sea sponge, Larry."

He snorted noisily. "For *what?"*

Mary Ann looked down again. "An alternative to tampons."

There was silence for a moment, then Larry began chortling like an idiot.

Mary Ann picked up a pencil and made a meaningless note on her calendar. "Toxic shock your idea of a big yuck, Larry?"

"Not at all," said the news director, turning to leave. "Just glad to hear you're doing a little *in depth* reporting. Break a leg, O.K.?"

The movie for today's show was *Move Over, Darling* and the irony wasn't lost on Mary Ann. Doris Day has been marooned on a desert island for seven years and comes home unexpectedly to find her husband, James Garner, on the verge of marrying Polly Bergen. Meanwhile, DeDe Day shows up at intermission. It was too delicious for words.

Mary Ann's phone rang at 2:15.

"Mary Ann Singleton."

"It's DeDe, Mary Ann. Listen to me carefully: Have you told them anything yet?"

"Where are you? I need you here before the . . ."

"Have you told them anything?"

Mary Ann was thrown by the urgency in DeDe's voice. "Of course not," she replied. "We won't say anything until we're on the air."

"I can't do that, Mary Ann. We can't."

"Now wait just a minute!"

"Mother just called! The children have been kidnapped!"

"What? *In Alaska?*"

"He's got them, Mary Ann. I'm almost positive."

"Jesus . . . are you . . . ? How is that possible?"

"There isn't time to talk. I'm flying to Sitka in an hour. Will you come with me?"

"DeDe, I . . ."

"I'll pay for everything."

"It isn't that. I'm supposed to be on the air in . . ."

"I need you, Mary Ann. *Please.*"

"O.K. Of course. Where shall we meet?"

"At the airport—catch a cab. And don't say a word to anyone, Mary Ann . . . *not a word!*"

A Sucker for Romance

THERE WAS A RUMOR RAMPANT THAT THE HOTTEST BOD-
ies from the City Athletic Club had graduated to the
Muscle System farther down Market Street, but Michael found it hard to believe.

Today, for instance, the club was wall-to-wall
horse flesh—sleek, river-tanned torsos straining heroically
against the high-tech tyranny of the Nautilus machines. All in
all, a profoundly discouraging sight.

For Michael's own body needed work. Badly.

After forty-five minutes of torturous leg lifts, decline
presses, overhead presses, and super tricep exercises, he repaired to the Hollywood-size Jacuzzi where Ned was lan-
guishing like an aging gladiator.

Michael eased himself into the bubbling water. "It's practically an unwritten law," he said.

"What?" asked Ned.

"If I'm in shape, I'm not in love. If I'm in love, I'm not in
shape."

Ned laughed and squeezed the back of his neck. "Who's the
lucky guy?"

"Thanks a lot," said Michael.

"Well, I assume you meant . . ."

"I know, I know. And there is no lucky guy, either. I'm just ready for . . . something nice."

Ned extended his legs and floated on his back. "What about your cop friend? I thought he was making the earth move."

Michael shook his head. "It was only the bed."

The nurseryman laughed.

"Besides," added Michael, "I've had it with falling in love with love. I'm a lot more cautious than I used to be."

"Right." Still on his back, Ned turned his head and smirked at him.

"I *am,*" Michael insisted. "You have to be cautious. Some guys have given up on love altogether, settling for a list of ten people they can have terrific sex with. You can think you're falling in love, when really you're just auditioning for the list. Does that make any sense?"

"Did you make his Top Ten?" grinned Ned.

"I didn't mean Bill specifically," said Michael.

"Oh."

"Anyway, I think I'm more of a Golden Oldie now. It doesn't matter. I'm kind of a washout at buddy sex. Why am I telling *you* this, anyway? You've got your own list."

Ned let his legs drop and sat up again. "It beats cruising the bars and fast-food sex. There's a lot to be said for sex with friends, Michael."

"Maybe. But a little romance would be nice. A little sentiment."

"Fine. Go get it, Bubba."

Michael smiled. "I'm trying, God knows."

"Is that what you were doing at The Glory Holes last week?"

"In my own way. Hell, I don't know. I run in cycles, I guess. Sometimes I think I'm the horniest guy alive . . . and I don't need a damn thing in the world but some hot stranger tweaking my tits and call me "buddy" in the dark. I mean . . . some anonymous sex is so wonderful that it almost seems to prove the existence of God."

Ned splashed water on him. "That's because you're on your *knees,* kiddo."

241

Michael laughed. "But that's just part of the time. As soon as the moon changes or something, I want to be married again. I want to sit in a bathrobe and watch *Masterpiece Theatre* with my boyfriend. I want to *plan* things—trips to the mountains, dinners in Chinatown, season tickets to whatever. I want order and dependability and somebody to bring me NyQuil when I feel like shit.

"And yet . . . I know that'll pass too. At least, for a while. I *know* there'll be times when I want to prowl again. I'm too much in love with adventure. I panic at the thought of being with only one person for the rest of my life. So what the hell is the answer?"

Ned shrugged. "You find somebody who understands all that. And loves you for it."

Michael looked at his friend for a moment, then ducked beneath the surface of the water. When he reemerged, he said: "Why am I getting heavy in the Jacuzzi? It must be that damn wedding."

"Mary Ann and Brian's?"

Michael shook his head. "Chuck and Di's."

"Is that today?"

"Tomorrow morning. At three o'clock our time."

"I think I'll miss that," said Ned.

"Not me. I think she's great. He's kind of a nerd, I guess, but she's a doll. And I'm such a sucker for romance."

Ned regarded Michael affectionately, then gave his knee a playful shake. "God save the Queen," he said.

"C'mon," grinned Michael, climbing out of the water, "it's almost time for Mary Ann's show."

The Search Begins

THE AIR ALASKA FLIGHT TO SEATTLE TOOK ALMOST TWO hours—the one to Sitka, about three, with a brief stopover in Ketchikan, just inside the Alaskan border. By the time they reached Sitka, Mary Ann was drained.

DeDe, however, showed amazing resilience.

"How do you do it?" asked Mary Ann, as the duo boarded a cab at Sitka Airport.

DeDe smiled wearily. "Do what?"

"Well . . . I'd have fallen apart by now. Just thinking about it."

DeDe searched for a mint in her tote bag. "I did my falling apart earlier. I screamed for five solid minutes after Mother called. No more . . . that's it." She popped a mint into her mouth. "It would only get in the way of what I have to do."

The faintly John Wayne-ish undertone of this remark unsettled Mary Ann. "Are you sure we shouldn't notify someone. I mean . . . if not the police, then someone who'll at least know . . ."

"No. No one. If it's him, then media coverage is the last

243

thing we need. The man doesn't take to being cornered. We would only freak him out."

"But surely some sort of protection would be . . ."

"When we find him," said DeDe. "When we know we can nail him without harming the children . . . and not before."

When, observed Mary Ann, not *if.* They had no proof whatsoever that the twins were still in Sitka, but DeDe kept the faith. It was hard to imagine a more courageous display of positive thinking.

The cab driver asked: "Where to in town?"

"The Potlatch House." DeDe turned to Mary Ann. "The ship left this afternoon, I gather. Mother and Prue Giroux took rooms at this place." She smiled sardonically. "If there was ever an odd couple . . ."

"What did they tell the ship people?"

"Nothing," said DeDe, "at my instruction. They just disembarked, saying they had decided to spend some time in Sitka. Pretty flimsy-sounding, I guess, but we had no choice. *Any* report of the kidnapping would be deadly at this point."

Mary Ann felt her flesh pebbling. She had never heard "deadly" used quite so literally. "I'm surprised your mother didn't call the police."

"So am I," said DeDe. "Fortunately, she called me first. I'm sure that Prue encouraged it. He was *her* boyfriend, after all. The last thing she wanted was to tangle with the police. It's not really the sort of thing she can use in her column."

"She met him on the ship, though. We can't exactly hold her responsible for . . ."

"She *says* she met him on the ship."

Mary Ann frowned. "I'm sorry. You're losing me again."

"I think she knows more than she's telling Mother," explained DeDe. "And I think Mother knows more than she's telling us."

"About what?"

DeDe sighed. "I don't know . . . just . . . well, something about her beloved Mr. Starr finally convinced her he was off the deep end."

"I would certainly think so," said Mary Ann.

"Something besides the kidnapping."

"Oh."

"She started to tell me, and then just shut up. I guess she's protecting me. We'll find out soon enough, won't we?" DeDe's smile was ironic and heartbreakingly brave.

Mary Ann took her hand to ward off her own tears. "Don't make it any worse than it is," she said.

"Is that possible?" asked DeDe.

The cab crossed a streamlined white bridge, while the driver drew their attention to an extinct volcano that presided majestically over an archipelago of tiny islands. The town lay ahead of them, clean and compact as Disneyland. As a setting for indescribable menace, it was not very convincing.

Mary Ann checked her watch. It was 9:13. Twilight.

DeDe peered out at Sitka harbor. "It's kind of pretty, isn't it?"

"Yeah . . . I suppose."

"I'm scared shitless," said DeDe.

"So am I," said Mary Ann.

The Interrogation

AT MARY ANN'S SUGGESTION, DEDE'S INITIAL MEET-
ing with her mother was private. Mary Ann spent
the time catnapping in her room at the Potlatch
House, secretly relieved that she had escaped
the anguish of the confrontation.

An hour later, DeDe returned to the room and collapsed
into a chair next to Mary Ann's bed.

Mary Ann rubbed her eyes as she sat up. "Rough, huh?"

DeDe nodded.

"Is she O.K.?"

"Better," sighed DeDe. "I gave her a Quaalude."

"Poor thing," said Mary Ann.

DeDe rubbed her forehead with her fingertips. "She knows
less than we do. I can't believe how out of it she is sometimes."

"What about Prue?"

DeDe picked distractedly at the arm of the chair. "She's
next. I didn't want to question her with Mother around. I
figured she'd be intimidated. It's gonna be hard enough as it
is to get the truth."

"How well do you know her?" asked Mary Ann.

"Not very." DeDe laughed bitterly. "I made a confession to her once, but that's about it."

"What do you mean?"

"She has these luncheons," explained DeDe. "She calls it The Forum—very grand. Everyone sits around with a visiting celebrity and bares their souls. Consciousness-raising for social climbers. Pretentious and awful. I went to the one she did on rape. 'A rap about rape,' she called it." DeDe shook her head in disgust. "Jesus."

"But . . . you said you confessed."

"I told her I'd been raped."

"When was this?"

"Oh . . . five years ago."

"I didn't know you'd been raped *before* Jonestown."

"I hadn't been," said DeDe. "I just told her that."

"Why?"

DeDe shrugged. "Social pressure, I guess. I'd also just been to bed with Lionel, and I needed somebody to blame it on. Pretty revolting, huh?"

"Was Lionel . . . ?"

"You got it. The twins' father."

"The grocery boy," said Mary Ann.

"Not anymore. He *owns* the store now, according to Mother. In the meantime, I got raped for real in Guyana by Prue Giroux's goddamn boyfriend."

"We don't know that for sure," said Mary Ann. She had already decided that somebody had to play devil's advocate in this crisis.

"C'mon," said DeDe, "I need your help on this one."

They found out less than they had hoped.

"I told you," insisted Prue, "all he said was that he was an American stockbroker living in London. We were on a cruise, for heaven's sake. You don't really ask much more than that."

"Sean Starr," repeated DeDe.

The columnist nodded but avoided DeDe's eyes. "He appeared to be crazy about the children, and *everyone* liked him, and I think it was perfectly natural for your mother to entrust

the children to him. He was quite polished . . . good-looking
. . . an *elegant* man." She shook her head woefully, her eyes
still red from crying. "It just doesn't make any sense."

Mary Ann sat down next to Prue. "Look," she said gently,
"it isn't that we don't believe you." (Not entirely true, of
course; DeDe appeared extremely distrusting.) "It's just that
it would help us a lot if you could remember details . . . *any*
details."

"Well . . . he was in his late forties, I guess. He dressed
nicely."

"How nicely?" asked DeDe.

"You know. Blazers, silk ties . . . that sort of thing. Under-
stated."

"Do you have any pictures of him?" asked Mary Ann.

"The ship's photographer took one or two."

Mary Ann glanced excitedly at DeDe, then turned back to
Prue. "Can we see them?"

"I didn't buy any," said Prue. "They're on the ship."

DeDe looked as if she might slap the columnist at any
moment. "And you noticed nothing unusual in his behavior?
Nothing at all?"

Prue shook her head. "He didn't start acting funny, really,
until we reached Juneau."

"Funny how?"

"I don't know . . . moody, distracted. We took a float plane
trip over the glaciers, and he didn't talk to me once. He spent
the whole time mumbling to the pilot."

"About what?" asked DeDe, almost ferociously.

"He kept saying dire needs," said Prue.

Mary Ann's eyes widened. "Maybe they left by plane!"

"Dire needs," repeated DeDe, ignoring her colleague's
brainstorm. "Plural?"

Prue frowned. "What?"

"He said dire needs, not dire *need*? That's the usual expression. In dire need."

Prue looked confused. "I think so. I heard the pilot repeat
it. There was lots of plane noise, though."

"And that was it?" asked DeDe.

"What?"

"Nothing else peculiar?"

"Not until Sitka," said Prue, her face contorting to a look of naked terror. "Not until . . . he took them . . . and . . ." She clamped her hand against her mouth, choking on her sobs.

"And *what?*" demanded DeDe.

"The . . . rabbits."

DeDe exploded. *"The rabbits?"*

"Your mother didn't tell you?" Prue stared at her aghast.

"No."

"Oh, God," said the columnist.

A Delicate Matter

WHAT RABBITS?" ASKED DEDE.

Prue looked away, her lower lip trembling violently. "When he took the children we were in a restaurant not far from here. I went to the little girls' room and . . . when I came out, he was gone."

DeDe nodded impatiently. "Mother told us that already."

"Anyway," continued the columnist, "I looked up and down the street . . ."

"And you found Anna in an alleyway." This was Mary Ann, trying to move the story along. DeDe's annoyance with Prue was obviously escalating.

Prue nodded funereally. "After I saw him drag her off, I sat down in this vacant lot . . ."

"What?" thundered DeDe.

"I was *hurt*. I ran after him, but I cut my ankle." She lifted her foot as evidence. "This man came along and started yelling at me, because he thought I was with Lu . . . Mr. Starr. I told him I . . ."

"Wait just a goddamn minute! What did you just say?"

Prue blinked at her balefully. "Nothing."

"Yes you did, goddamnit! You started to call him some-thing else!"

Mary Ann caught DeDe's eye and said quietly: "Why don't we let her finish?"

Prue took that as her cue to continue. "So he dragged me over to his backyard . . ."

"Who?"

"This man . . . the one who . . ."

"O.K., O.K."

"He had these rabbit cages . . . hutches . . . and there was blood all over the place . . . and he made me . . ." Something seemed to catch in her throat. She pressed her hand against her mouth and closed her eyes. When she opened them again, she was almost whimpering. "He made me look at these two little rabbits that had been . . . skinned."

"Jesus," murmured Mary Ann.

DeDe remained cool. "Your friend did that?"

Prue nodded, fighting back the tears. "It's so awful. I've never known anyone who could . . ."

"Were the skins still there?" asked DeDe. Mary Ann shud-dered. What on earth was she getting at?"

Prue thought for a moment. "I don't think so. There was so much blood that I . . ."

"And you know nothing about this *elegant* man, as you call him, except that he was an American stockbroker living in London? What was he doing on *that* cruise, anyway?"

"I don't understand," said Prue.

"Doesn't it strike you as just a teensy bit out of his way?"

The columnist shook her head slowly. "No. I mean . . . he seemed to have enough money to . . ."

"Was he your lover?"

Prue's mouth dropped open.

"Was he?"

"I don't see what business that is of . . ."

"I have a reason for asking. Did you ever see him with his clothes off?"

Prue's indignation was monumental. "Look here, I'm sorry about your children, but you have no right to . . ."

"You'll be even sorrier when we talk to the police. Not to mention the press."

Prue began sniffling. "I had no way of knowing he would do a thing like that . . ."

"I know." DeDe's tone was kinder now. She reached over and took the columnist's hand. "No one ever does."

Prue continued to weep until DeDe's message sank in. "You *know* him?" she asked dumbfoundedly.

"I think so," said DeDe softly. She turned to Mary Ann. "This is kind of delicate. Would you excuse us for a moment?"

Mary Ann shot to her feet. "Of course . . . I . . . what time shall we . . . ?"

"I'll meet you in our room," said DeDe. "Half-an-hour?"

"Fine," said Mary Ann.

It was more like an hour.

When DeDe appeared, she looked thoroughly exhausted. "Think we could get a drink somewhere?"

"Sure. Are you O.K.?"

"Sure."

"Could you find out if . . ."

"It's him," said DeDe.

"How do you know?"

DeDe moved to the window and stared out at the blackness. "Does it matter?"

Mary Ann hesitated. "Sooner or later it will."

"Then . . . could we make it later?"

An awkward silence followed. Then Mary Ann said: "I've been thinking about those rabbits."

"Yeah?"

"That nursery rhyme he used to sing. 'Bye baby bunting, Daddy's gone a-hunting . . .'"

DeDe finished it. "'Gone to get a rabbit skin to wrap the baby bunting in.'"

"You thought of that," said Mary Ann.

"Yeah," DeDe replied listlessly. "I thought of it."

On the Home Front

MARY ANN'S PHONE WAS RINGING OFF THE HOOK. Brian stood on the landing outside her doorway and debated his responsibility. She hadn't *asked* him to tend to her affairs in her absence. What's more, she hadn't even told him where she was going, and he resented that more than he would admit to anyone.

The caller, however, was persistent.

So it was curiosity, more than anything, that sent him up the stairs to his tiny studio, where he conducted a frantic search for his keys to Mary Ann's apartment.

Finding them, he bounded downstairs again, opened the door and lunged for the wall phone in Mary Ann's kitchen.

"Yeah, yeah."

"Who is this?" asked a male voice.

"This is Sid Vicious. Who is *this?*" It really pissed him off when people didn't identify themselves on the telephone.

A long silence and then: "Is this Mary Ann Singleton's apartment?" The guy was annoyed, Brian noted with some degree of pleasure.

"She's out of town right now. I suggest you try again in a few days."

"Do you know where she went?"

That did it. "Look . . . who the hell is this?"

"Larry Kenan," replied the caller. "Ms. Singleton's boss." His voice was dripping with sarcasm.

"Oh . . . I see. Mary Ann's mentioned you. The news director, right?"

"Right."

"This is Brian Hawkins. Her fiancé." It was the first time he had ever used that word to describe himself. It had a curiously old-fashioned sound, but he enjoyed the hell out of it. Things were official now, he realized.

"Good," said the news director. "Then you can tell her she's in deep shit."

"What's the problem?" asked Brian, trying to change his tone to one of responsible concern.

"The problem," snapped Larry, "is that she skipped out on us yesterday—twenty minutes before the show. That's the problem, Mr. Hawkins."

Brian thought fast. "She didn't tell you?"

"What?"

"Her grandmother died. Unexpectedly. In Cleveland." Brian winced at this hackneyed alibi. There was practically nothing that hadn't been blamed on a dead grandmother.

"Well . . . I'm sorry about that . . . but she didn't say a word to anybody . . . not a goddamn word. There's such a thing as professionalism, after all. We were stuck. We had to get Father Paddy to announce the movie."

"I saw that," said Brian. "I thought he was rather good."

"Well, you tell your friend that she'd better report to me on Friday or she's out on her ass. Got that?"

Brian longed to tell him to shove it. Instead, he said: "I'm sure she'll be back by then. She should be checking in with me, so I'll be glad to tell her. I'm sorry. I know she wouldn't intentionally . . ."

"Friday," said Larry Kenan. "After that, *finito.*"

*   *   *

254

Brian's face was hot with rage when he hung up. While most of his anger was directed towards the news director, he was also upset with Mary Ann for not giving him enough information to cover for her properly.

What could have prompted such an abrupt exit, anyway? He presumed it involved her story about DeDe Day's return from Guyana. That could even mean she was still in town—in Hillsborough, perhaps, putting the finishing touches on the piece.

"I'm going away," was all she had told him. "I'll probably be gone a few days, so please don't worry about me. I'll call as soon as I get a chance. I'm so glad we're getting married."

Swell. But where was she?

He found her address book and looked up the number of the Halcyon residence in Hillsborough. When he dialed it, he reached a maid who was straight out of *Gone With the Wind.* There was no one there, she said.

As soon as he had hung up, the phone rang again. He answered it, trying to sound a little nicer this time.

"Is Mary Ann there?" came a woman's voice that sounded strangely familiar.

"She's in Cleveland," he replied, opting for consistency. "She should be back by Friday."

"Will you give her a message for me?"

"Sure."

"Tell her I found the notes she left behind at the station. It's vitally important that I talk to her."

"Right. Who is this, please?"

"Bambi Kanetaka. Shall I spell it?"

"No," said Brian. "I know it. You're the anchorperson, right? You're famous."

"Tell her I can't sit on this."

Brian suppressed a laugh. To hear Mary Ann tell it, this must be the *only* thing that Bambi Kanetaka couldn't sit on.

"Tell her that I won't tell Larry until she calls me . . . but she *must* call me as soon as possible. From Cleveland, if necessary. Do you understand?"

"I think so," said Brian.

Now what? he thought. *Now what?*

Dire Needs

MARY ANN SLEPT FITFULLY AT THE POTLATCH House. Twice during the night she awoke to DeDe's screams, only to fall victim to her own nightmares when she plunged into sleep again. Morning came as a reprieve at 7:30.

DeDe was already up, studying a map as she sipped a cup of black coffee. When she realized that Mary Ann's eyes were opened, she smiled apologetically and said: "*Night of the Living Dead,* huh?"

Mary Ann smiled back at her. "We can handle it."

"Want some coffee?"

"I think I'll wait," said Mary Ann. "I'm wired enough as it is."

DeDe looked down at the map again. "We're having breakfast with Prue, if that's O.K. with you. I want her to take us to the man with the rabbits. Later, I thought we could check the car rental agencies and airplane people."

A long silence followed while Mary Ann wrestled with the monstrous futility of their search. Then she said: "DeDe . . . don't you think . . . ?" She cut herself off, suddenly wary of seeming disloyal to the undertaking.

"What?" said DeDe. "Say it."

"Well . . . it just seems to me that we're losing time by doing this ourselves. If we told the police, they could be issuing all-points bulletins, or whatever it is that they do."

"Issuing press releases is more like it."

"But we don't have to tell them who we think he is . . . just that he took the children." From Mary Ann's standpoint, that was all that mattered, anyway: *someone* had kidnapped the twins.

DeDe poured herself more coffee. "The point is not what the police know, but what *he* knows."

"But surely he can't expect us to . . . ?"

"I *know* this man, Mary Ann. You keep forgetting that."

"But how can you be so sure he won't . . . Surely, those rabbits were proof enough of his . . ."

"Those rabbits were a little bit of bad symbolism and nothing more. He has a weakness for grand gestures. That was just his way of . . . being Daddy."

"But what makes you think he won't harm the children?"

DeDe shrugged. "Because he loves them."

"You can't be serious!"

"Well, that's the way *he* sees it. What happened in Jonestown, anyway? When did the killing start? When the outside world invaded his private fantasy of peace and love. I missed the massacre, Mary Ann, and I'm not going to let it happen again. If I want my children back alive, I've got to find them before the media find out about Jones. It's as simple as that."

Breakfast was a harrowing affair. Prue was a wreck, and Mrs. Halcyon was a worse wreck. DeDe, to her credit, stayed calm throughout, absolving her mother and the columnist of all guilt in exchange for their absolute silence on the subject. Prue had no trouble consenting to this condition; Mrs. Halcyon did so with great reluctance.

DeDe, of course, gave no indication that she knew who the kidnapper was.

On the way to the airport, Prue pointed out the house of the man with the rabbits. Mary Ann made a quick note of the

257

address, feeling weirder by the minute. Half-an-hour later, Prue and Mrs. Halcyon were airborne, bound for San Francisco, while Mary Ann and DeDe conferred with the last known witness of the abduction.

"I was in the kitchen when it happened," said the rabbit fancier. "He was out here with the kids at the hutches. I couldn't tell what was happening until I got out here, and then it was too late."

Mary Ann looked contrite. "We're awfully sorry about the . . ."

"He didn't say anything?" interrupted DeDe. "Nothing at all?"

"Hell, no. He hightailed it. I found a book of matches out here later in the day. He must've dropped it, I guess. They were from the Red Dog Saloon in Juneau. That help you any?"

"Do you still have them?" asked DeDe.

"Hang on," said the man. He went into the house, returning seconds later with the matchbook. DeDe turned it over in her hand, then opened it. Written in felt-tip pen on the inside was this word: DIOMEDES.

" 'Diomedes,' " said DeDe, turning to the man. "Do you know what that means?"

The man shook his head. "Sorry."

DeDe frowned, discarding the matchbook. "It probably doesn't mean a damn thing."

"Wait," blurted Mary Ann.

"Yeah?"

"Diomedes. *That's* what Prue heard. Not dire needs—Diomedes!"

Definitions

DIOMEDES.

It had a vaguely scientific sound to it, chemical perhaps. It also suggested a classical figure, like Diogenes and Archimedes. Mary Ann, however, deduced that its roots were geographical, since Mr. Starr had been heard using the word in conversation with a pilot.

"You're probably right," said DeDe, pocketing the matchbook. "It's not like him, though, to be so careless about leaving a clue behind. I think it's best to check our logical sources first."

Their first stop, via cab, was a car rental agency near the waterfront. There, sounding remarkably nonchalant, DeDe confronted a fastidiously groomed young woman in a two-tone green uniform.

"A friend of ours may have rented a car here yesterday. We were wondering if you'd mind checking . . . if it's no trouble."

The young woman's smile fell. "We don't normally give out that kind of information."

"Why the hell not?"

Mary Ann stepped forward, touching the small of DeDe's

back. "Uh . . . it's kind of stupid, really. He told us to be sure to use the same rental agency he used, and we forgot to ask him the name. Dumb, huh?"

The woman refused to thaw. "Customer records are confidential. If I gave out that kind of information, I'm afraid it would be an invasion of privacy. If you'd like to rent a car, I'd be glad . . ."

"This isn't a fucking missile station, you know!" DeDe was edgier than ever.

This time Mary Ann gripped her elbow. "We don't need you to check the computer, actually. They'd be easy to recognize."

"I thought it was one person."

"One adult," amended Mary Ann, before DeDe could speak. "A nice-looking man about fifty and four-year-old twins, a boy and a girl."

"Eurasian," added DeDe.

"I'm *what?*" snapped the woman.

DeDe groaned. Before she could retaliate, Mary Ann said: "The children are part Chinese. They were wearing fur-lined parkas. I think you would've remembered them if . . ." The woman had become an obelisk; it was futile to continue. Mary Ann addressed DeDe, who was smoldering. "I think we'd better go."

DeDe shot daggers at her adversary until she was out of sight.

At the next agency, DeDe did all the talking, while Mary Ann looked for a dictionary at a neighboring motel. The desk clerk produced a battered volume which Mary Ann consulted while standing in the lobby.

She found this:

Diomedes n. Class. Myth. 1. the son of Tydeus, next in prowess to Achilles at the siege of Troy. 2. a Thracian king who fed his wild mares on human flesh and was himself fed to them by Hercules.

When DeDe emerged from the rental agency, Mary Ann was waiting for her on the street.

"Any luck?" asked DeDe.

"Afraid not."

"They didn't have a dictionary?"

"They had one. Diomedes wasn't in it."

"There's a book store over there. Maybe they would know."

Mary Ann shook her head. "I think we're beating a dead horse." Clever girl, she told herself. You have a cliché for every occasion.

DeDe persisted. "The sign says: 'Specializing in Alaska Lore.' If anybody would know, they would. It's worth a try, at any rate. C'mon."

Hundreds of musty volumes were stacked everywhere in the tiny book store: on shelves, on tables, on the floor. But there wasn't a person in sight.

"Hello," hollered DeDe.

No answer.

"I think we should check the float plane places," said Mary Ann, inching towards the door.

"Hold it . . . I hear somebody."

The proprietor, an Ichabod Crane look-alike, emerged from the back room. "Yes, ladies. May I help you?"

"I hope so," said DeDe. "We need some information. Do you know what the word 'Diomedes' means?"

The man smiled instantly, unveiling the sizable gap between his front teeth. "You mean, *The* Diomedes." He might have been talking about old friends, like The Martins or The Browns. "What would you like to know about 'em?"

"For starters," said DeDe, "what are they?"

"Islands," replied the bookseller.

"Thank God!" said Mary Ann.

DeDe turned and scrutinized her. "Why thank God?"

Mary Ann reddened. "I . . . well, I'm just glad somebody knows."

"Where are they?" asked DeDe, addressing the proprietor again.

"Way north of here. In the Bering Strait. Cute little buggers. Little Diomede and Big Diomede. The little one's about four square miles. The other's . . . oh, twenty or so. No trees. Lots of rocks and Eskimos. The two of 'em are just a few miles apart."

"Is anything . . . special there?" asked Mary Ann.

The man grinned like a jack o'lantern. "It's not *what* they are, but *where.*"

"How so?" asked DeDe.

"Well," said the man. "Little Diomede's in the United States and Big Diomede's in Russia."

Revising the Itinerary

THAT SON OF A BITCH," MUTTERED DEDE, BACK IN THEIR room at the Potlatch House, "that two-bit Bolshevik son of a bitch. Jesus H. Christ . . . Russia!"

Mary Ann felt more ineffectual than ever. "I'd forgotten how close we were," she said.

"He probably *lives* there," added DeDe. "He's got what he wanted and he's heading home."

"But the trip was *our* idea, DeDe. How could he have known we were doing it? How could he . . . ?"

"Maybe he just lucked into it. How the hell do I know? What does it matter, this speculation? He could be back in Moscow by now!"

"Not really," said Mary Ann, perusing DeDe's map of Alaska. "Not unless they made terrific airlines connections. The closest big city to the Diomedes is Nome and that's over eleven hundred miles from here. Then he'd have to get a smaller plane to take them to the Diomedes. Plus, there must be some sort of restriction on travel between Little Diomede and Big Diomede. It's a pretty complicated scheme."

"If anybody could do it, he could."

"It would take money," countered Mary Ann.

"Prue said he had lots of it. He had lots of it in Jonestown—trunks of it—enough to last him the rest of his life. He could bribe his way from here to Timbuktu if he wanted to."

Mary Ann rummaged for a word of consolation. "In one way, you know, this helps us. I mean . . . it narrows the focus of our search. The man at the book store said Little Diomede is only four square miles. Any airplane trying to land there would be noticed immediately . . . if he's trying to make a jump into Russia."

"Yeah," said DeDe dourly. "I suppose so."

"So, if we call the authorities in Nome, they could relay . . ."

"No. No police!"

"We wouldn't have to tell them . . ."

"No. I told you how I feel about that." DeDe grabbed her tote bag and headed for the door. "There's a travel agent two blocks away. I'll check on the flights to Nome. Be back in twenty minutes."

"DeDe . . ."

"All we've got to do is beat him there. We can hire people, if we have to. Once he lands on that island, we've got him cornered. Jesus, we've gotta hurry!" DeDe stopped when she reached the door. "Oh . . . I'm assuming you're going with me?"

Mary Ann hesitated, then smiled as confidently as possible. "You assumed right," she said.

As soon as DeDe had gone, Mary Ann called Brian at Perry's.

"It's me," she said, perhaps a little too blithely. "Alive and well."

"And living where?" He was understandably miffed.

"I'm sorry, Brian. I didn't count on this."

A long pause and then: "I've heard of brides-to-be getting cold feet, but this is ridiculous."

She laughed uneasily. "You know it isn't that."

"Is it . . . the Jonestown business?"

"Yeah."

264

"Christ! You aren't *in* Jonestown, are you?"

Another laugh. "God, no. I'm fine. DeDe's with me, and we should be back in a few days. I'm sorry to be so mysterious about all this, but I gave DeDe my word I wouldn't talk for a while."

"I miss the hell out of you."

"I miss you, too." For a moment, she thought she might cry. Instead, she said brightly: "It's gonna be wonderful being Mrs. Hawkins!"

"Yeah?"

"You bet."

"You don't have to take my name, you know."

"Fuck that," she said. "I'm from Cleveland, remember?"

Finally, he laughed. "Get home, hear?"

"I will. Soon. How's everybody?"

"O.K., I guess. Michael says he's not getting laid these days. But who is? Jesus . . . I almost forgot. That asshole from the station called. He says you're . . . let me get this right . . . 'out on your ass' if you're not back at work on Friday."

"Larry Kenan?"

"Uh-huh. And I think he meant it."

"Breaks my heart."

"I thought you might say that. Also, Bambi Kanetaka called to say that you left some notes at the station. She says she'll give them to Larry if you don't call her right away. What's that all about?"

It took a moment for the catastrophe to sink in. "Oh, *no,*" groaned Mary Ann. "Those were my notes on DeDe and the whole . . . oh God, this is awful, Brian. Look, I have to call her right away. I'll call you soon, O.K.?"

"Sure, but . . ."

"I love you. Bye-bye."

Rough Treatment

I T WAS SUCH A STUPID MISTAKE—SUCH A STUPID, CONVENtional, deadly mistake. Even in her panic and excitement, how could she have rushed off to Alaska, leaving those incriminating notes behind at the station?

At least Larry hadn't found them. That was some consolation. Bambi was bad enough, of course, but there was some hope that her simplemindedness and/or vanity might be activated to prevent her from leaking the story to the world at large.

She pondered the problem for a minute or so, then looked up Bambi's number in her address book and dialed her direct.

"Hello." Bambi's voice, vapid and breezy as ever, was accompanied by the sound of Andy Gibb's falsetto.

"Bambi, it's Mary Ann."

"Aha! You still in Cleveland?"

Cleveland? Is that what Brian told her? "Uh . . . yeah . . . what's up?"

"Didn't your boyfriend tell you?"

"Well . . . he said something about some notes, but I wasn't exactly sure what he meant."

"Does Jonestown ring a bell?"

Mary Ann counted. One . . . two . . . three . . . four. "Oh," she exclaimed, "my treatment. How embarrassing! I hope you didn't *read* it. It's hopelessly corny at this point."

"Treatment?"

"For a movie. I had this dumb idea for a thriller, and a friend of mine who knows this agent in Hollywood said I should work up some notes before making a formal presentation."

"Oh."

"It's kind of moonlighting, I guess. I'd appreciate it if you wouldn't mention it to . . ."

"You *made up* a story about Jim Jones?"

"Why not?" said Mary Ann. "Lots of writers make up stories about . . . say, Jack the Ripper. He was the boogeyman of his time; Jones is ours."

"And that stuff about him having a double . . . ?"

"Pretty dumb, huh?"

Silence.

"Oh well," sighed Mary Ann. "This is my first crack at it. I guess I'll get better as . . ."

"I like your casting," said Bambi.

"Huh?"

"DeDe Day as the one who escapes from Guyana with her twins in tow. It's ingenious, really, using a real-life person like that. It's so outlandish that it could almost be true, couldn't it?"

Silence.

"Couldn't it, Mary Ann?"

The jig was obviously up. "Bambi, look . . ."

"No, *you* look. I have an obligation to give those notes to Larry, Mary Ann. I wanted you to know that. Frankly, I'm surprised you would sit on a story of this magnitude without seeking some sort of professional journalistic guidance."

Meaning *her,* of course. "I had planned on consulting the news department," said Mary Ann. "In fact, I thought you would be the ideal person to . . ." The lie caught in her throat like a bad oyster. "The story is yours, Bambi. I promise you that. Only we have to wait . . . just a little while."

"Forget it. News doesn't wait. Larry Layton's trial is going full tilt right now. Don't you think this might have *some* bearing on the case?"

"Not really," replied Mary Ann. "He's charged with murdering the congressman at the airstrip. DeDe left before any of that even happened."

"Ah . . . this treatment gets better all the time."

Desperate, Mary Ann threw caution to the winds. "Bambi . . . DeDe's children are in great danger. *Any* public notice of this . . . situation could result in their death. I wish I could give you the details, but I can't. I'm begging you . . . please give me a week to . . ."

The newswoman laughed derisively.

"Three days, then."

"Mary Ann . . . you have *got* to learn a little detachment, if you ever want to be a practicing newsperson. If those kids are in some sort of trouble, it's a crying shame, but the public has a right to know about it. You can't just pick and choose when it comes to news."

This was a load of crap, and Mary Ann knew it. The journalists she dealt with were picking and choosing all the time. "Can we at least talk before you tell Larry about it?"

"We're talking now."

"I mean, in person."

"Terrific. But you're in Cleveland."

"My plane gets in tomorrow afternoon," said Mary Ann. "I could meet you at my apartment at . . . say, three o'clock. This would help *you*, actually. I could clarify the things you're not clear on before you present it to Larry."

"All right. But I'm definitely telling him about it on Friday."

"Fine. I really appreciate it, Bambi. Got a pencil handy?"

"Go ahead."

"I'm at 28 Barbary Lane, apartment 3. If my plane should be a little late or something, my friend Brian will let you in. Please don't say a word till then, O.K.?"

"O.K.," said Bambi.

After hanging up, Mary Ann placed another call to Brian. "Hi," she said grimly, "I've got a big favor to ask you."

Clerical Error

As SOON AS HE RECOGNIZED PRUE'S VOICE, FATHER Paddy tittered through the grille in the confessional: "Really, darling, we can't go on meeting like this!"

Prue answered him soberly. "I want this to be . . . official, Father."

"Meaning, zip the old lip, huh?"

"It *must* be confidential," whispered Prue. "I promised Frannie Halcyon I wouldn't tell anybody. Apparently, it's a matter of life and death."

"My God, girl! What happened on that ship? I *thought* you were back a little early. Don't tell me that you and Luke had some sort of . . . ?"

"Luke is gone, Father!"

"What!"

The cleric stirred audibly in the confessional.

"What are you doing?" asked Prue.

"Getting a cigaret," he replied. "Bear with me, darling." There was more moving about, then Prue heard the cat-like hiss of Father Paddy's lighter. "All right," he said finally, expelling smoke. "Take it from the top, darling."

*　　*　　*

It took her ten minutes to outline the disaster for him. When she had finished, Father Paddy uttered a faint moan of disbelief.

"Well?" said Prue.

"Does he still have my ID?" inquired the priest.

"I'm afraid so. I'm sorry, Father . . . I . . ."

"Don't apologize, darling. It was my stupid idea in the first place. What about Frannie Halcyon? Did she make any connection between *that* Sean Starr and me?"

"None, as far as I know," said Prue. "I doubt if she realizes your first name is Sean. She was too upset about the children to be functioning in a rational . . ."

"Mary Ann might figure it out, though."

"You *know* her?" asked Prue.

"We work at the same station. I tape my *Honest to God* show just before she does the afternoon movie. I had to stand in for her on Tuesday when she didn't show up. No one had any idea where she was, and I certainly had no idea she was . . . Lord, this is getting sticky!"

"The thing that upsets me," said Prue, "is that DeDe appears to have . . . known Luke." The very thought of this made her eyes well up with tears again.

Father Paddy must have heard her sniffling. "Darling . . . you don't mean . . . biblically?"

"Yes!" sobbed the columnist.

"Oh my," said the priest. "She *told* you they had been lovers?"

"Not exactly. But she knew something about him that she couldn't possibly have known if she hadn't been . . . intimate with him."

The priest sucked air in noisily. *"What?"*

Prue hesitated. "I don't see how that matters. She just *did,* that's all."

A long silence. "Very well, then . . . I guess it's time for my next customer."

"But, Father . . . what should I *do?"*

"You've already done it, my child. You told them what you know."

"I didn't tell them about the shack in the park . . . or the fake ID. I didn't tell them I had known Luke before the cruise."

"Purely extraneous, darling. It's obvious you've stumbled on some private romantic squabble between DeDe and Luke. I know it must be painful to accept that, but you can't let your emotions drive you into doing something rash. If I were you, I'd lay low for a . . ."

"Father, he took her children, for God's sake!"

"Well, of course, that's dreadful . . . and she deserves our prayers . . . but your little interlude with Luke is hardly pertinent to her dilemma. Where did she know him, anyway? I thought you said she'd been hiding out at Frannie's place since her return from Cuba."

"I don't know for sure. I guess she could have . . . you don't think she knew him in Guyana, do you?"

"I was wondering when you'd get to that."

"You mean . . . a Temple member?"

"It's certainly possible," said the cleric. "Now, is that really the sort of thing you want to get mixed up in, darling?"

"But I *am* mixed up in it, Father. If they find him and he's carrying your ID . . ."

"I'll tell them the truth."

"But . . ."

"I'll tell them that I lost my wallet in the park about a month ago. And you'll confirm it, because you were with me at the time. And that will be the end of that. Do you read me, darling?"

"I think so," said Prue.

"Good. Now run along and be a good girl. This will all come out in the wash . . . I promise you."

"But . . . what if he tells them about me?"

"Then, they'll just have to choose between the word of a reputable columnist and the word of a kidnapper. That shouldn't be too tough. Scoot, now! I've got customers waiting. And, Prue . . . put this all behind you, darling."

"All right."

"That means: *stay away from that shack.*"

"O.K.," said Prue defeatedly.

"God bless," said Father Paddy.

Tea

S HE ARRIVED RIGHT ON THE DOT, AS BRIAN HAD EXpected.

"You're Bambi," he said as cordially as possible, extending his hand. "I'm Brian, Mary Ann's friend. I watch you on TV all the time."

She barely returned his handshake. "She's not here, huh?" She scanned the room as she spoke, as if she might spot Mary Ann peering out from under a tablecloth or crouching behind a curtain. "I haven't got a lot of time, you know."

"She just called from the airport," said Brian. "Apparently, she had a little trouble making a connection in Denver—the traffic controllers' strike. Here, let me take your coat. I'm sure she won't be long."

Bambi slid out of her bronze metallic windbreaker but retained control of the matching shoulder bag. Hanging the jacket on a chair, Brian grinned with calculated boyishness and said: "You look even better in person."

"Thanks," said Bambi.

Another grin, this time ducking his head. "I guess you hear that a lot?"

The newswoman shrugged. "It's nice to hear it, anyway."

Brian sprawled on the sofa, letting his denimed legs fall open carelessly. "I liked your stuff on the gas leak, by the way. Very cool-headed and thorough."

"You saw that?"

Brian nodded. "On three channels, as a matter of fact. Yours was the only one that made sense. Sit down. You might as well get comfortable."

Bambi pulled up a Breuer chair and sat down, keeping the handbag in her lap. "They almost didn't send me on that story," she said.

"Really?"

The newswoman nodded. "You'd be surprised what prejudice there is against letting women do any of the really hard-hitting disaster stuff. I just keep pushing, though." She smiled valiantly.

"Good for you!" said Brian. "Look . . . I'm gonna have a cup of tea. Will you join me?"

Bambi shook her head. "I can't handle the caffeine."

"It's herbal," said Brian. "Our landlady makes it. Incredibly soothing. You should try a cup."

"Oh . . . all right."

He was back in five minutes, his hand shaking slightly as he handed her the cup. She sipped it tentatively, then unleashed her best six o'clock smile. "It's *marvelous!* What's in it?"

"Uh . . . hibiscus flowers, orange peels . . . stuff like that."

"Does she have a name for it?"

"Oh . . . Alaskan Twilight, I think."

Bambi took another sip. "Mmmm . . ."

Brian kept up the idle chatter for another five minutes until the newscaster's speech began to slur. For one terrifying moment, she seemed to realize what had happened, staring at him in confusion and anger. Then her eyelids drooped shut, and she slumped forward in the chair.

"Jesus," murmured Brian. He rose and checked the body; she was out cold but still breathing. When he tilted the head back, a pearl of saliva rolled from the corner of the newscaster's mouth.

"O.K.," he said out loud.

The door to the hallway swung open. Michael's head appeared first, then Mrs. Madrigal's. The landlady's brow was creased with concern. "Are you sure she's . . . ?"

"She's all right," Brian assured her. "What's in that stuff, anyway?"

"Never mind," said Mrs. Madrigal. "It's organic."

"And it lasts fifteen minutes?"

"More or less," replied the landlady. "I wouldn't push it. Michael dear, if you'll grab the feet, Brian can take her arms. I'll make sure the coast is clear."

Michael knelt by the body and grasped the newscaster's ankles. "We *could* just finish her off."

"Michael!" Mrs. Madrigal was in no mood for joking.

Hoisting their quarry until she was waist high, Brian and Michael staggered into the hallway.

"Alaskan Twilight," grinned Michael. "Gimme a break!"

The New Boarder

NIGHT HAD FALLEN BY THE TIME MRS. MADRIGAL rejoined her "boys" on the roof of 28 Barbary Lane.

"Well," she said, slipping between them and squeezing their waists, "her temper's as foul as ever, but her appetite's improved considerably."

Brian looked relieved. "For a while there, I was sure she was going for a hunger strike."

"Has she stopped yelling?" asked Michael.

The landlady nodded. "I think I convinced her the basement is soundproof. We don't need to worry about the neighbors, really. Even when she's making noise, you can't hear her beyond the foyer. Visitors are another story."

Michael gazed out at the lights on the bay. "It's like *The Collector*," he said.

"She has all the amenities," insisted the landlady. "A comfy bed, a space heater, all my Agatha Christies. I even gave her Mona's old TV set." She turned to Michael. "What did you do with her car?"

"I parked it down on Leavenworth. Five or six blocks away."

Brian frowned. "That doesn't exactly cover our tracks."

"Well," shrugged Michael, "if you know of a swamp near-by . . ."

"Leavenworth is fine," said Mrs. Madrigal. "I don't expect we'll be keeping her longer than two or three days. I hope not, anyway. She says she's due at the station on Friday afternoon. Somebody's bound to start getting suspicious."

"Mary Ann took care of that," said Brian.

"How?" asked Michael.

"She called the station and said that she and Bambi are on the trail of a big story and that they won't be back until the weekend. The news director was plenty pissed, but he bought it. He didn't have much choice."

"So no one else knows that DeDe and the kids are alive?"

"No one except the kidnapper," said Brian.

"And they've got no idea whatsoever who he is?"

Brian shook his head. "Just some guy Mrs. Halcyon met on the ship. Mary Ann is convinced that any media attention at all would seriously jeopardize their chances of getting the kids back alive."

"That's quite enough for me," said Mrs. Madrigal.

"She wouldn't have asked us to do this," added Brian, "if the situation wasn't desperate." He turned to the landlady. "Did you get Mary Ann's notes, by the way?"

Mrs. Madrigal nodded. "I locked them in my safe."

"Good. We'll come out of this O.K. I mean . . . it isn't like we're torturing her or holding her for ransom or something."

"You're right," Michael deadpanned. "Maybe we're not thinking big enough."

"Michael, dear." Mrs. Madrigal remonstrated with her eyes.

Brian addressed the landlady: "I think you're great to be doing this. Mary Ann says she'll take full responsibility when she gets back."

Mrs. Madrigal's smile was understandably weary. "It's not just for her, you know."

"What do you mean?"

"Those children," explained the landlady. "I wept for a week when I read about their disappearance in Guyana."

"You *knew* them?" asked Michael.

Mrs. Madrigal smiled wanly and shook her head. "I knew their grandfather."

"Mary Ann's old boss?"

Another nod.

"You mean you . . . ?"

"We had a rather friendly little affair just before he died. Nothing earth-shattering, but . . . nice."

Both men stared at her in amazement.

The landlady took ladylike delight in their confusion. "If I'm not mistaken, one of the twins was named after me. The little girl, I presume."

"That's right," laughed Brian. "Her name is Anna. Mary Ann told me. Jesus, you're a trip!"

"The little boy is Edgar," added Mrs. Madrigal. "Edgar and Anna. Isn't that lovely symbolism? Our affair was memorialized by those children. They're coming home safe and sound if I have to *strangle* that ridiculous woman in the basement."

Michael regarded her with admiration. "What a fabulous ulterior motive!"

The landlady gave both of her boys a jaunty shake. "How about some brownies for my partners in crime?"

"When did you have time for *that?*" asked Michael.

"Well . . . I made a batch for our houseguest, and there are plenty of leftovers."

"You got *her* loaded?"

Mrs. Madrigal's face was resolute. "I want her to be comfortable."

"This woman knows how to take prisoners," said Brian.

The Diomedes

AFTER SEVERAL HOURS OF SEARCHING IN NOME, Mary Ann and DeDe found an Eskimo bush pilot who filled their requirements exactly. His name was Willie Omiak, and his cousin Andy had served for the past four years as a National Guardsman on Little Diomede.

"He can have it," declared Willie, shouting over the engine noise. "Nome's small enough for me. I tried living in Wales for a while and even that drove me crazy."

"You mean . . . the British Isles?" Mary Ann couldn't picture this round-faced, brown-skinned youth living among Welshmen.

The Eskimo grinned. "Wales, Alaska. The nearest mainland town to the Diomedes. We'll be stopping there to refuel and check weather conditions. You sure you want to stay overnight on Little Diomede?"

"We may," said DeDe. "It depends."

"They don't have a Holiday Inn," smiled Willie.

"We'll manage."

"Sure," said the pilot. "Maybe Andy's family can put you up." He winked, apparently sensing the first question that occurred to Mary Ann. "Don't sweat it. They've never lived in igloos—mostly sod huts propped up on stilts. The Bureau of Indian Affairs built 'em some new houses about six or seven years ago. Polyurethane walls . . . much warmer."

"I'll bet," said Mary Ann, privately saddened that even the Eskimos had been reduced to using plastics.

"What about defenses?" asked DeDe, as the tiny, single-engine Cessna skirted the coastline northwest of Nome.

"What about 'em?"

"Well, I mean . . . with Russia only two-and-a-half miles away?"

"According to Andy," said Willie Omiak, "they've got three M-14 rifles, one grenade launcher and one grenade. It isn't exactly a full-time job, being a scout."

"A scout?"

"Eskimo Scouts," explained the pilot. "That's the official name for Alaska National Guardsmen. They do most of their work in the winter, I guess, when you can walk right across the ice. Most people know better these days. Back in '47, the Russians held Andy's dad for almost two months when he crossed the strait to visit relatives. Hell, it was just family. Nobody even knew about the Cold War."

"Do the Russians have forces on Big Diomede?" asked Mary Ann.

Willie Omiak grinned. "About as scary as ours. A guy in a little shack on the highest part of the island."

"What does he do?"

"Watches," answered the pilot. "While our guy watches back. Nobody has much reason to visit Big Diomede anymore. Most of our cousins were shipped to the Siberian mainland back in the fifties. For that matter, nobody goes to Little Diomede either. What got *you* interested?"

"We're looking for someone," said DeDe.

"An Eskimo?"

"No," DeDe replied. "An American."

Willie Omiak looked at his passenger, then turned and winked at Mary Ann. "We'll forget she said that, won't we?"

*   *   *

They appeared out of nowhere it seemed—two granite crags united by their isolation, but divided by politics. On the smaller one, a village was visible, a cluster of clapboard and tarpaper houses snuggled against the base of a sixteen-hundred-foot cliff.

"That's Ingaluk," said Willie Omiak, making a low pass between the islands. "It's Thursday down there. Over there on Big Diomede it's Friday already."

Mary Ann peered down. "You mean . . . ?"

"We're flying directly over the International Date Line." He grinned at her over his shoulder. "This place confusing enough for you?"

It was eerie, all right. Two continents, two ideologies, two nations—neatly bisected by today and tomorrow. What better place to search for two frightened little children teetering perilously between two fates?

As the Cessna swooped lower, Mary Ann could make out a schoolhouse and a church. Then the airstrip materialized: a rectangle of asphalt near the shore, delineated by oil drums and half-a-dozen people awaiting their arrival.

"There's Andy," yelled Willie Omiak, as the plane bumped the runway.

"He looks awfully glad to see you," said Mary Ann.

The pilot patted the leather satchel on the seat next to him. "I've got the new *Playboy,*" he grinned.

Mary Ann's giggling stopped when she saw the naked dread in DeDe's eyes. They had chased their quarry to the end of the world. What if it was too late?

Deadline

PRUE SAT AT HER CORONAMATIC AND WEPT SOFTLY TO herself. Her maid, her secretary and her chauffeur were all in the house, so a visible (or audible) display of grief was completely out of the question.

She slipped a piece of paper into the typewriter. It hung there listlessly, like a surrender flag, a horrid metaphor for the emptiness she felt now that Luke was gone. What was there to write about, really? What was there to live for?

She yanked the paper out again, just as the phone rang. "Yes?"

"All right, Prudy Sue, let's have it."

"Have what?" Getting right to the point was Victoria Lynch's annoying device for flaunting her intuitive powers. Prue refused to play along.

"You know. True confessions. What the hell's been going on? You've been in the most morbid funk ever since you got back from Alaska."

Silence.

"You looked like holy hell last night at the placenta party."

Prue almost bit her head off. "I don't *like* placenta parties, all right?"

(The party had been held in the spacious Pacific Heights garden of John and Eugenia Stonecypher. In keeping with a hallowed family tradition, the couple had planted Eugenia's most recent afterbirth in the same hole as a flowering plum sapling, a ritual intended to insure long life and happiness for the Stonecyphers' baby girl. Prue had almost thrown up.)

"It isn't my idea of a fun time," she added.

"You haven't even called me," countered her friend.

"I'm a little blue," said Prue. "What can I say?"

"You can say you'll call me. You can lean on your pal, Prudy Sue. Look, I've got the most marvelous news. I've found a place that sells Rioco!"

"What's that?"

"You remember. That Brazilian cola Binky told us about last spring."

"She didn't tell *me.*"

"Well, it's full of jungle speed or something. Half of Rio is buzzed on it. Guarana. It sounds like bat shit, but it's fabulous stuff. They've got it at the Twin Peaks Grocery. What say we dash out there?"

"I'm on deadline, Vickie."

"We could go this afternoon."

"Vickie . . ."

"All right, *be* in your funk, then."

"You're sweet to think of me."

"I'm not trying to be sweet, Prudy Sue. I want my friend back."

A long pause, then a sigh from the columnist. "I'm trying, Vickie. Give me a little time, O.K.?"

"You got it. Just don't mope, Prudy Sue. Get out and get some air, at least. Take Vuitton for a walk."

That was what did it: a little sisterly advice from an old friend.

Despite repeated warnings from Father Paddy, she had known that this moment would come. How could she have avoided it? How could she not return, however briefly, to the scene of her happiest moments on earth?

Besides, she might find a clue there—something to aid

DeDe in her search for Luke and the twins. She wouldn't have to tell DeDe everything—just enough to point her in the right direction. That couldn't hurt, could it?

She also wanted some answers herself. Maybe the truth, however painful, would free her from this crippling melancholy. It was worth a try, anyway.

And Vuitton needed the walk.

Ingaluk

THE FIRST THING MARY ANN NOTICED ABOUT LITTLE DI-omede was the row of crude wooden boxes perched on the rocks above the village. She asked Andy Omiak about them.

"Coffins," he replied amiably. "Most of the year the ground's frozen solid. We have to bury people above ground." Seeing Mary Ann's grimace, he added: "It's not as bad as it sounds. It's so dry here that the boxes last longer than . . . their contents. The dogs scatter whatever's left."

The dogs were the next thing she noticed. Dozens of them—thick-coated and yellow-eyed—roaming the island in ominous packs. "We're glad to have 'em," insisted Andy Omiak. "They function as our radar. If anybody comes over from the other island the dogs will let us know."

DeDe, who had been silent during the trek from the airfield, turned to the Eskimo Scout. "What about the other way around?"

Andy Omiak frowned at her. "You mean . . .?"

"If somebody tried to cross over to the Russian island, would you have any way of knowing it?"

"Oh . . . well . . . there it is. It wouldn't be too hard to *see* anybody who might try to cross over. This time of year it never gets dark, so . . . why do you ask, anyway?"

DeDe maintained her stride, looking straight ahead. "We think somebody may be trying to cross over. He may have already, in fact."

"From the mainland?"

DeDe nodded. "A man about fifty and two four-year-olds, a boy and a girl. They were Eurasian and dressed in parkas, so they might have been mistaken for Eskimos."

Andy Omiak smiled. "Not around here. Everybody knows everybody. We'd see that for sure."

Mary Ann asked: "If they came from the mainland, would they have to arrive by airplane?"

The Eskimo Scout shrugged. "Probably. That's the usual way. I guess he could come in by boat . . . from Wales or something. There wouldn't be much point in stopping here, though. Why wouldn't he go straight to Big Diomede?"

It was a good question—one that cast a shadow on the validity of their search. In light of the roving dogs and Eskimo Scouts, a stopover on Little Diomede would be almost fool-hardy. Why not go directly to Big Diomede, if you were going to go at all?

Willie Omiak, Andy's pilot cousin, parted company with them as soon as they reached Andy's house, a sturdy wood-and-tarpaper structure near the waterfront. "I'll be back at the airstrip," he said. "Give a holler if you need me."

"Thanks," said DeDe, looking genuinely grateful. "You've been very kind."

"No sweat. You leaving tomorrow, by the way?"

"I think so," said DeDe. "Can I let you know later?"

"Sure. Nana will take good care of you."

Nana was his grandmother, a rotund and wrinkled crone who reminded Mary Ann of the dried apple dolls sold at the Renaissance Pleasure Faire. Having little command of Eng-lish, she simply smiled at them toothlessly when she arrived with mugs of steaming cocoa.

Mary Ann made an exaggerated bow to show her appreciation. "How lovely," she said, addressing Andy Omiak.

"We don't get much company," he grinned. He turned to his grandmother, speaking to her in their common language. The old lady looked at Mary Ann, giggled, and scurried out of the room.

"So," said Andy Omiak, "maybe you'd better tell me what this is all about."

An awkward silence followed. Then DeDe said: "Someone has kidnapped my children."

The Eskimo Scout frowned. "Someone you know?"

"Yes."

"But . . . why?"

"He wants them for himself," she replied. "He's crazy. We think he plans to take them to Russia."

"Have you notified the mainland police?"

"No," said DeDe. "No one."

"Why not?"

"It's complicated," DeDe replied. "If he knows we're involved with the police, he might hurt the children."

"You must be very worried," said Andy Omiak.

"I'm desperate."

"And you want to find out if he's taken them to Big Diomede?"

"Yes."

The Eskimo started to speak, then stopped, looking away from DeDe. "I could get into a lot of trouble," he said at last.

"I'm afraid I don't . . ."

"If I help you . . . you can't tell *anybody.*"

"I promise you," said DeDe.

Andy Omiak leaned closer, speaking in a furtive tone. "I can take you," he said.

"To . . . ?"

He nodded. "I've done it before."

Mary Ann looked up from her cocoa. "Wait a minute. You don't mean . . . ?"

"It's all right," said the Eskimo. "It can be done."

"Without being shot at?"

Andy Omiak grinned. "It's possible."

Anna and Bambi

MRS. MADRIGAL WAS PREPARING BAMBI KANETAKA'S tray when Michael bounced into the kitchen.

"What's for din-din?" he asked, lifting the lid on a covered dish. "Mmmm . . . parakeet . . . my favorite!"

The landlady snapped at him. "It's five-spice chicken, Michael! And I'll thank you not to be so flip!"

Michael ducked his head repentantly. "Hey . . . sorry."

Mrs. Madrigal placed a pink rose in the bud vase on the tray. "I'm worried about her," she said. "She seems to be getting . . . desperate. I've told her time and again that we mean her no harm, but she just won't relax."

"I'm surprised your brownies didn't do the trick."

"She wants out," said the landlady. "Period. She even promised she'd keep quiet about DeDe if I'd set her free."

"You don't believe that, do you?"

"I can't afford to," replied Mrs. Madrigal, "not if there's the slightest chance of endangering those children. Besides, if I release her before there's *some* resolution, we'll only be in worse trouble. We need proof that we had a good reason to . . . detain her."

"Good point," said Michael.

Mrs. Madrigal lifted the tray. "I suppose things will work themselves out. They always do. I can't help worrying, though."

Michael looked at her earnestly. "We're in this together, you know. Brian and I have talked about it. If they haul you off to jail, then they're taking us, too. And we'll insist on the same cell."

The landlady smiled back at him, then pecked him on the cheek. "I'm sorry I barked at you, dear. This is all a bit new to me. I feel like such an *outlaw.*"

Michael winked at her. "But you *are,* Blanche . . . you *are.*"

Somewhat more at peace with herself, Mrs. Madrigal descended the stairs to the basement.

She listened for a moment outside the door, then set the tray down on the floor and undid the padlock. Bambi was sitting in the rumpsprung armchair that the landlady had retired when Mona moved to Seattle.

"Suppertime," chimed Mrs. Madrigal, trying to sound cheerful without patronizing her. She placed the tray on an ancient laundry hamper that Burke Andrew had left behind.

Bambi didn't stir.

"I checked the TV listings," said the landlady. *"The Barretts of Wimpole Street* is on tonight. I thought you might enjoy watching it."

A low growl from the newscaster.

"I know it isn't easy," continued Mrs. Madrigal, "but it won't be long now. We're all terribly sorry that it had to come to this, but . . ."

In a single lightning-swift movement, Bambi sprang to her feet and lunged at her captor, knocking the landlady backwards until she was pinned against the board where the house keys were hung. Mrs. Madrigal screamed in agony as the nails in the key board pressed into her back.

Crumpling to her knees, she looked up to see the news-caster's triumphant sneer as Bambi kicked her once . . . twice . . . three times in the stomach. On the third kick, Mrs. Madrigal seized Bambi's ankle and twisted it sharply, eliciting a scream of Samurai intensity. Bambi toppled to the concrete floor, then raised herself to her hands and knees and began crawling for the door.

Wheezing in pain, Mrs. Madrigal reached for a loop of garden hose and hoisted herself to a near-standing position. Something warm and wet—presumably blood—was trickling down her spine, pasting her kimono to her back. Her fingers found the handle of a shovel, which she wielded like a mace, bringing it down squarely on Bambi's backside.

For a moment, and only a moment, the newscaster was splayed against the floor like a swastika. Then she lurched to her feet and made her way through the doorway and up the steps.

Mrs. Madrigal staggered after her, still brandishing the shovel. When Bambi reached the top of the stairs, the land-lady swung wildly, clipping her adversary in the back of her knees. Bambi fell forward ingloriously, then slid back down the steps until her ankles were once more within the land-lady's grasp.

Mrs. Madrigal dragged the newscaster back into the base-ment, wrapped her ankles hastily with a length of electrical cord, and hurried out the door, locking it behind her.

Gasping for breath, she leaned against the door for almost a minute. Inside, Bambi was screaming bloody murder. Up-stairs, someone was ringing the door buzzer.

She made her way slowly up the stairs, hoping to God that the visitor hadn't heard the ruckus.

When she saw the man at the door, she wanted to weep in his arms.

It was Jon Fielding.

House Call

THE DOCTOR KNELT NEXT TO HIS PATIENT, WHO WAS lying face down on the red velvet sofa in her parlor. "O.K. now . . . bite the bullet, Mrs. M. This'll sting a little."

Her body tensed as he daubed gently at the puncture in her back. "Good girl," he said. "It's not nearly as bad as it looked. How did you do this, anyway?"

"It was silly," replied Mrs. Madrigal. "I slipped and fell against a nail."

"Where?"

"Uh . . . in the basement. Does it need stitches?"

"Not really. A Band-Aid will fix you up just fine. Got any?"

"In the bathroom cabinet," said the landlady. "Why don't I just . . . ?"

"Sit tight. You're indisposed."

He was back moments later, smoothing the bandage into place. "There," he said, rising to his feet. "I think you'll pull through just fine."

Mrs. Madrigal adjusted the bloodied kimono as she shifted to a sitting position and retied the silken cord around her waist. "Well," she said, smiling lovingly at Jon, "what did we ever do without a doctor in the house?"

Jon shrugged. "I was kind of hoping you'd tell me."

Mrs. Madrigal studied him for a moment, reassessing the Arrow Collar blond who had lived with Michael for almost three years. He seemed thinner now, a little haggard even, but his classically Nordic face was more beautiful than ever. "How old are you now?" she asked.

He replied with a smile. "Thirty-three."

"It suits you," she said.

"Thanks. You look pretty good yourself. Aside from the wound, that is."

She bowed graciously. "It's good to see you, Jon. It really is. Michael's upstairs, if you want to see him." She patted her hair to regain some sense of order. "I'm sure you didn't plan this detour."

"Actually," said Jon, "I did. It was your buzzer I rang, remember?"

"Then, I'm honored."

"I was hoping you could tell me the lay of the land."

"Oh . . . I see." She fussed with a wisp of hair over her ear.

"I haven't talked to Michael for a long time, and I'm not sure if . . ." He stopped talking and jerked his head sharply, like an animal picking up a scent. "What was that?" he asked.

"What was what?"

"I'm not sure . . . somebody yelling, I think. You didn't hear it?"

"It could be the children," said Mrs. Madrigal.

"Children?"

"Down on Leavenworth . . . skateboarding. It's quite bloodcurdling sometimes."

"It sounded closer than that."

"Look, dear . . . if you want to have a little chat, why don't we just stroll down to North Beach. It's such a balmy evening, and we could have a lovely little dinner somewhere."

"All right," said Jon, "but on me, O.K.?"

"You've got a date," said Mrs. Madrigal.

* * *

After changing clothes, she hurried him through the foyer, chattering as noisily as possible. Bambi's outburst seemed to have subsided, but Mrs. Madrigal breathed a secret sigh of relief when they were finally out of earshot on the lane.

They dined in a window seat at the Washington Square Bar and Grill.

"So how is he?" asked Jon, after they had placed their orders.

Mrs. Madrigal pursed her lips in thought. "A little restless, I suppose."

"How so?"

"Well, he makes a lot of fuss about his independence, but I don't think he really enjoys it very much."

"But he has friends," said the doctor.

"Plenty," said the landlady.

"That's good."

"Friends," smiled the landlady, "but no capital F Friend. That's what you wanted to know, isn't it?"

The doctor reddened. "I guess it was."

"Good."

"It's been a long time, though . . . almost two years."

"And you think you can pick up where you left off."

"No," said Jon, "I just . . ."

"It's all right, dear. I think you can, too."

He smiled at her almost timidly. "I'm not sure either one of us could handle it at this point."

"Why not?"

The doctor shrugged. "Things change."

"Do they now? Do you know what I think?"

"What?"

"I think you should stop beating around the bush, because you came here to get him back."

"You do, huh?"

"Uh-huh. And I think I'm going to help you." Her big blue eyes flowed into his.

Embarrassed, the doctor looked down.

"I'm a cranky old hen," said Mrs. Madrigal. "I like all my eggs in one basket."

To Russia with DeDe

ANDY OMIAK'S PROPOSAL STRUCK MARY ANN AS EX-ceptionally foolhardy, and she told DeDe so as soon as they were alone.

"What choice do we have?" countered DeDe.

"Well . . . we could notify the mainland police, and *they* could conduct the search."

"And go charging in there with guns and bullhorns, loaded for bear. If we tell them who he is, my children will be the last thing they'll worry about."

"Then we won't tell them. We'll just say . . . well, we could tell them the truth."

"Which is?"

"That a man from the ship kidnapped your children in Sitka . . . and we think he brought them up here."

"Do you seriously believe *he'll* think that's what we told them? Look . . . there's no reason for you to go with me, really. Andy'll be there, with a gun and all. It isn't fair to ask you . . ."

"Forget that," said Mary Ann. "I'm going."

"I'd feel awful if . . ."

"Don't. This is my decision."

DeDe squeezed her hand. "Thanks."

"Besides," added Mary Ann. "I've never been to Russia."

They napped for several hours, after which Andy returned.

"Have you had a chance to think it over?" he asked.

"We're game," said DeDe. Mary Ann nodded her agreement.

"O.K.," said Andy. "We should leave about an hour from now."

Mary Ann made a face. "In broad daylight?"

The Eskimo grinned. "We don't have much else."

"Oh . . . right."

"Anyway," continued Andy, "this'll be almost as safe as darkness. Between eight and ten o'clock the whole town's at the schoolhouse."

"*Everybody?*" asked DeDe.

"All eighty-two of 'em," smiled Andy.

"For classes or what?"

The Eskimo shook his head. "We get a movie from the mainland once a week."

"Oh."

"Tonight they're showing *Superman II.* I think we're safe."

"At least as far as Ingaluk is concerned."

"What do you mean?" asked Andy.

"The *Russians,*" said DeDe. "Don't tell me they're watching a movie, too?"

"Oh," said Andy drily. "Don't worry about *them.*"

As predicted, Ingaluk looked like a ghost town when the trio left the dock in Andy's fifteen-foot motor launch. Mary Ann stared up in awe at the dark cliffs above the village, the sun-bleached coffins flecking the rocks like seagull droppings. Then she turned her attention to the Russian island, only two miles away.

"What about that sentry shack?" she asked the Eskimo. "Won't he see us cross the strait?"

"He usually does," said Andy. "Every week at this time."

"I don't understand."

Andy smiled. "Neither would my C.O. That's why I'd appreciate it if you kept this under your hat."

"Of course."

"A friend of mine lives on Big Diomede."

"I see."

"My girlfriend, actually."

DeDe and Mary Ann cast quick glances at each other. It was Mary Ann who sought further details. "You mean she . . . ?"

"She's a radar technician. The guy in the lookout shack is her brother-in-law. We're kind of a family operation out here. If your kidnapper made it to Big Diomede, Jane will know about it."

Half-an-hour later, Andy docked the boat on the far side of the big island, out of sight of Little Diomede.

"Wait here," he told the women. "You'll be O.K. If there's any news, you can come ashore with me later." He leaped out of the boat and bolted down the dock to the shore.

Presently, a female figure appeared on the rocky ridge above the harbor, jumping from boulder to boulder until she reached the sand. Then Andy and Jane were in each other's arms, spinning like a couple in a corny commercial.

Mary Ann felt a curious kinship with them, seeing herself suddenly as Deborah Kerr in *The King and I.*

Cling very close to each other tonight—I've had a love of my own, like yours . . .

As usual, Brian was there when she needed him, nestled cozily in her heart.

The Eskimo lovers talked for several minutes, well out of earshot of DeDe and Mary Ann. When Andy returned, his face conveyed the news. "I'm sorry," he told DeDe.

"Nothing?"

"I'm afraid not," he replied. "They just haven't been here."

"Could she let us know if . . ."

"Of course. She'll keep an eye out."

There was a long agonizing silence. Then Mary Ann turned to DeDe. "What do you want to do?" she asked.

A single tear rolled down DeDe's face. "I want to go home," she said.

"We will, then," said Mary Ann. She searched in her windbreaker for a Kleenex, handing it to her friend. "We won't give up on this, DeDe. I promise you we'll find them."

As Andy shoved off from the dock, Mary Ann cast a final glance at the shores of the Soviet Union.

Jane was still standing there. Seeing Mary Ann, she smiled shyly, then lifted her hand and waved.

Mary Ann, of course, waved back.

Eden Revisited

A THICK SUMMER FOG HAD SETTLED OVER GOLDEN Gate Park by the time Prue arrived at the tree ferns. Shuddering slightly at the eerie familiarity of it all, she turned up the collar of her Montodoro trench coat and plunged into the wilderness.

Vuitton ran ahead of her up the path, chasing a squirrel to the edge of the U-shaped ridge. When she called to him, he made a rapid decision to ignore her altogether.

"Vuitton!" she called. "Come back here this second!" She was terrified of being left alone.

The wolfhound turned, wagged a cursory greeting to her, and bounded into the green-black depths of the rhododendron dell.

She ran after him, yelling. "Vuitton! COME BACK, GOD-DAMNIT!"

It was pointless, of course. Vuitton knew where he wanted to go. He even knew where *she* wanted to go. He would simply get there before she did. Why should that strike such fear in her heart?

She found the familiar path through the rhododendron

dell and maintained a brisk pace, catching occasional glimpses of Vuitton's champagne-colored fur amid the foliage. As she searched for the bush that marked the entrance to Luke's secret enclave, a foghorn bleated mournfully in the distance.

Vuitton, as usual, led the way. Barking deliriously, the wolfhound doubled back, burst through the gateway shrub and danced in circles around his mistress.

"Stay here!" she ordered him. "Heel, Vuitton, heel!"

But he was off again, scampering down the crumbly slope that led to the shack. When Prue caught sight of the dwelling, she had second thoughts about the search she had planned to conduct. She was reminded of a summer years ago in Grass Valley when she had explored her father's bedside table and found a package of Trojans there. Some mysteries were better left alone.

Vuitton, however, was outside the door of the shack, yapping his silly head off.

When no one responded to his bark, Prue stumbled down the slope and listened outside the door. Trying the latch, she found that the door wasn't locked.

Inside, it seemed that nothing had been touched. The big chunk of foam rubber was still there. Likewise, the army cot, the map of the city, and Luke's beloved motto hanging on the wall.

There weren't that many places to search, she realized. Her first choice was the handmade wooden box where Luke had stored his gear for Vuitton. Only now it wasn't on the floor; it was on the shelf above the foam rubber.

When Prue reached for it, her hand touched something cold and slimy. She screamed hysterically and dropped the box, thereby crushing a large banana slug that had affixed itself to the box's backside.

She stood there shaking, wiping her fingers frantically against her coat. Vuitton crouched at her feet and whimpered in sympathy. "It's O.K., baby," murmured Prue. "We're gonna leave in a minute."

"I think that's a good idea."

Prue's eyes shot to the door of the shack, where she was confronted by a uniformed policeman, staring down at her from the back of a large chestnut stallion.

"Oh . . . officer," she said. "I . . . uh . . . my dog ran in here, and I . . ."

The policeman smiled at her. "Pretty dog."

"Oh . . . well, thank you. He's such a nuisance sometimes."

The officer leaned forward in the saddle, peering into the shack. "Some place, huh?"

Prue nodded wordlessly. How long had he been watching her?

"It used to be a tool shed for the park, until a bum moved in about a year ago. I sort of keep an eye on things for him."

Prue sidled out of the shack with Vuitton by her side. If Prue was intimidated by the policeman, the wolfhound was more intimidated by the horse.

"I apologize, officer," said the columnist. "It's just so . . . fascinating."

The policeman smiled. "Isn't it?" He seemed much less foreboding now that Prue could see that he was young and darkly handsome, Latino probably.

And he was wearing a Walkman.

A Man Called Mark

H E'S QUITE A CHARACTER," SAID THE MOUNTED PO-
liceman.

Prue drew a momentary blank, still flushed
with guilt over being caught in the act of searching Luke's shack. "Uh . . . I'm sorry. What did
you say?"

The officer smiled forgivingly. "The guy who lives here.
He's something else. One of those characters you find only
in San Francisco."

"I suppose so," she said.

"You know him?"

"No," she replied hastily. "I mean . . . I *assume* he's a
character . . . judging by this place. It's so . . . quaint. And he
seems to keep it fairly neat."

"I'm surprised it hasn't been vandalized," said the policeman.

"Oh?"

"He's been gone for a couple of weeks . . . the longest time
yet. I guess he's coming back, though; he left his stuff here.
He was weird, but domestic, if you know what I mean."

"I think so," said Prue.

301

"Maybe I'd better take a look." The officer dismounted, tethering his horse to a tree. As the stallion shifted, Vuitton whimpered nervously to his mistress. The policeman reached down and petted the wolfhound. "What's his name?"

"Vuitton," answered Prue.

"Uh . . . French?"

"Uh-huh."

"What does it mean?"

Prue saw no point in explaining it. "It's just a proper name."

"He looks a lot like a dog that used to hang out with Mark."

"Who's Mark?" asked Prue.

"The guy who lives here. I don't know his last name." He smiled at the columnist. "For all I know, *he* doesn't know his last name."

Prue tried not to show her confusion. "You don't know very much about him, I take it?"

The officer shrugged. "What's to know? He's a drifter. Decent enough guy. Says he used to live in Hawaii. Ate mangoes on the beach, scrounged a lot. Same as here."

"Really?"

"Sure. There are lots of guys like that in San Francisco. Sleeping in packing crates, bumming free food when the restaurants close. It's been going on since Emperor Norton."

Prue frowned. "But this man . . . well, he seems to be sort of intelligent."

"How can you tell?"

"Well . . . that motto on his wall, for one thing . . . and those pencils and the map."

The policeman grinned. "He's probably trying to take over the world or something."

"You think he's crazy?"

The officer shrugged. "Maybe we're the crazy ones."

"Yeah," Prue replied vaguely. "Maybe so."

"He's educated, I know that. He studied at Harvard before he moved to Australia."

"*Australia?*"

The policeman enjoyed her amazement. "That came before Hawaii. He was foreman of a sheep ranch. Then he moved to Sydney and opened a travel agency. He hasn't had

302

a bad life, I guess . . . all things considered."

"No," said Prue, "I guess not."

The officer made a quick inventory of the shack's contents. "Most of his stuff seems O.K. I guess I'd better finish my rounds. It was nice talking to you, Miss Giroux."

Prue was flabbergasted. "How did you know my name?"

"C'mon," smiled the policeman. "You're a star. I saw you on TV once."

"Oh," said Prue feebly.

The officer mounted his horse, then leaned down and offered her his hand. "I'm Bill Rivera, by the way. Have a nice day."

Then the stallion and his rider were gone.

Prue stood there for a moment in mild shock.

When the silence had engulfed her again, she reentered the shack for a final appraisal of its contents. She had come this far, she decided, so she might as well play out the drama to the end.

The slug-smeared box lay on its side on the earthen floor. To avoid touching it, Prue poked it with her toe, but the latch was firmly secured. So she knelt beside it and prodded it with one of Luke's pencils until the lid creaked open.

Inside were two lumps of grayish fur.

Two little rabbit skins.

Behind, oblivious to this discovery, Vuitton spotted an old friend approaching through the underbrush and ran out into the fog to greet him.

Catching Up

WHEN JON AND MRS. MADRIGAL RETURNED TO Barbary Lane, they sat on the bench on the courtyard and smoked a joint.

"Just like old times," said the doctor.

The landlady gave him a drowsy smile. "Almost."

He smiled back, knowing what she meant.

"His light's still on," she said.

"Yeah. I see."

The joint was so resinous that it went out. Mrs. Madrigal relit it and handed it to Jon. "Am I pushing too much?" she asked.

"A little," he said.

"Sorry."

"I'll bet," he grinned.

She tugged his earlobe affectionately. "I want what's best for my children."

A long pause, and then: "I didn't know I was still part of the family."

The landlady chuckled. "Listen, dear . . . when you get this old lady, you get her for life."

"That's good to know," said the doctor.

"Funny thing," added Mrs. Madrigal, nodding towards the lighted window. "That one's the same way."

Jon turned and looked at her in silence.

"He is," she said softly. "I'm sure of it. He just has to be reminded of it sometimes . . . by the people who love him. If you catch my drift."

"If I didn't," smiled Jon, "you'd rent a sound truck and broadcast it." He rose, pecking her on the cheek. "Are you sure he doesn't have company?"

"I'm sure," said the landlady.

"You don't miss a trick, do you?"

She shook her head, smiling. "Not one. And I'm sure you didn't mean it that way."

Michael stood in the doorway, dumbfounded. "Jon . . . my God . . . I didn't even hear you ring."

"I didn't. Mrs. Madrigal let me in. We just had dinner together."

"Oh . . . great."

"Can I come in?"

"Sure . . . of course. It's great to see you."

"Thanks. Same to you."

"Great . . . great."

"I think we've agreed on that," smiled Jon. He stepped across the threshold and embraced Michael clumsily. "It's rotten notice. I'm sorry."

"No problem. It's great to see you." Michael winced and slapped his own face. "I promise the patter will improve."

Jon laughed and looked around the room. "I like this color."

"Can I get you a drink or something? Or a Diet Pepsi? I'm out of grass, but I'm sure I could bum one off . . ."

"I just did," grinned Jon. "I'm ripped to the tits."

"No wonder you like this color."

Another laugh, more nervous than the first. "No . . . really."

"You'll hate the bedroom," said Michael. "I got rid of the eggplant."

Jon made a mock-fierce expression. "What color is it now?"

"Crayfish."

"What color is that?"

"Sort of . . . cream."

"Crayfish are cream-colored?"

Michael laughed and pointed to a chair. "Sit down. God, where do we start?"

"Well . . . I know about Mary Ann and Brian. Mrs. M. told me. She invited me to the wedding, in fact."

"Great."

"Are you sure? This isn't exactly . . . my territory anymore. I don't want you to be uncomfortable, Michael."

Michael rolled his eyes. "Do I *look* uncomfortable?"

"It's a family thing, though . . ."

"You *are* family, Jon. Mary Ann would be crushed if you were in town and didn't come to the wedding. How long are you here for?"

"A week or ten days."

"Great. Which hotel?"

The doctor pointed out the window to the bay. "You can see it from here, actually."

"You're on the water?" asked Michael.

"*In* it," said Jon. "I'm a ship's doctor now."

"You mean like . . . in the Navy?"

"God, no. A cruise ship . . . Norwegian."

Michael's mouth fell open. "Which one?"

"The *Sagafjord*."

"I don't believe this!" Michael spun around and peered down at the great white ship. "That's it? It's back. This is really unbelievable!"

"It's a job," said Jon, obviously unsettled by Michael's reaction.

"Does Mrs. Madrigal know this?"

"Should she?" asked Jon.

"Yeah," said Michael. "I think she should."

Shipmates

MICHAEL LEFT JON IN HIS APARTMENT AND HURried downstairs to Mrs. Madrigal's under the pretext of bumming a joint.

"Look," he said. "How much did you tell him, anyway?"

"About what?"

"For starters, that media geisha we've got locked in the basement."

"We didn't discuss any of that," said the landlady.

"Does he know where Mary Ann is? Does he know about DeDe and the twins? He was on the *Sagafjord*, Mrs. Madrigal! He's the ship's doctor!"

"*What?*"

"I can't believe it either. Jesus . . . what are we gonna do?"

Mrs. Madrigal studied him for a moment. "That's up to you, dear."

"*Me?*"

"Well . . . if he's no longer a member of the family, I don't think it's fair to implicate him in our shenanigans. I think you should ask him to leave as soon as possible."

Silence.

"Unless, of course, you want him to stay."

Michael glowered at her. "He says you invited him to the wedding."

"I did. I think Mary Ann and Brian would like that. Where is Brian, anyway? Has Jon talked to him?"

"He's working," said Michael.

"I could put Jon in Burke's old room," offered Mrs. Madrigal. "If you don't mind, that is?"

"What makes you think he'd *want* to stay in a house with a kidnapped anchorwoman in the basement?"

"We could ask and find out."

Michael sighed resignedly. "Do what you want, O.K.?"

"Well," said the landlady, "I think we owe him an explanation. He brought those children into the world, remember?"

The explanation was a monumental task. When Michael had finished, Jon's confusion was obvious.

"Now, wait a minute! This makes no sense at all."

"Tell *me*," said Michael.

"You mean . . . those four-year-olds were DeDe's *children?*"

Michael and the landlady nodded in unison.

"But . . . I thought they were Mrs. Halcyon's foster grandchildren . . . Vietnamese orphans."

"That's what DeDe told her to say," said Michael. "They were trying to avoid publicity until Mary Ann could release the story properly."

"But they weren't *kidnapped*," said Jon.

Mrs. Madrigal blinked at him. "What on earth are you talking about, Jon?"

"They weren't kidnapped," the doctor repeated. "I watched a movie with them yesterday."

"Where?" asked Michael.

"On the ship. And Sean Starr was with them. They were getting along famously, too."

Mrs. Madrigal leaned closer to the doctor. "Jon, dear . . . are you sure we're talking about the same children?"

"We must be. I didn't even see them on the trip up . . . I suppose Mrs. Halcyon didn't want me to . . . but I saw them several times on the trip back. There can't be that many Oriental four-year-olds on a cruise ship. Besides, Sean *told* me they were Mrs. Halcyon's foster grandchildren."

"Jesus," murmured Michael.

"What do you mean?"

"Well . . . didn't you think it was strange that Mrs. Halcyon wasn't there?"

"A little," said Jon, "but Sean said that she and Prue Giroux had decided to spend more time in Sitka. He also said he was an old friend of the family, so I figured . . . well, I figured he *was*. He was a nice enough guy."

"Did he say where he was taking the children?" asked Michael.

Jon shook his head. "I assumed he was delivering them to Halcyon Hill."

Michael shook his head, groaning softly. Mrs. Madrigal looked deathly ill. "Are you thinking what I'm thinking?" asked Michael.

The landlady nodded. "Bambi."

"Who's Bambi?" asked Jon.

Michael regarded him for a moment, then turned to Mrs. Madrigal. "Your turn," he said.

Family Man

PRUE WAS SO HORRIFIED BY THE SIGHT OF THE RABBIT skins that she didn't look up until Vuitton's yelping disturbed her.

"Hush, Vuitton. We're going soon . . . I promise."

"I hope you don't," said a voice just outside the door.

The columnist's heart caught in her throat. She spun around to see Luke crouched in the doorway, stroking the wolfhound's muzzle. He looked up and gave her the sunniest smile. "Welcome home, my love."

"Luke, I . . ."

"Don't say a word, O.K.? I don't care where you've been, I'm just glad you're back."

Disbelieving silence.

"I knew you'd be back," Luke continued, rising to his feet. "I knew you'd come here to find me, if I waited long enough." He extended his arms in a posture of crucifixion. "Doesn't Dad get a hug?"

Some nameless instinct told her to do it.

"You're shivering," he said, holding her in his arms. "That fog's pretty bad, huh?"

She nodded against his chest.

"How did you do it?" he asked.

"What?"

"Miss the ship."

She pulled away from him. "Luke . . . what on earth are you talking about? This is . . . crazy. I've practically had a nervous breakdown this week. I can't take this anymore, Luke . . . I can't. Where are those children?"

"They're here," he smiled. "They're fine."

"Where?"

"Huh-uh. You answer my question first."

"Luke . . . uh, what question?"

He traced her eyebrow with his beefy forefinger. "I waited for you," he said quietly. "Two hours, at least. I was mighty worried, Prue."

"When? Where?"

"Back in Sitka. After we had our . . . little tiff at the café, I took the children back to the ship and waited for you in my room." His finger slid down the side of her face, stopping at her chin. "But no Prue. The ship sailed without you."

"You mean . . . *you were on it?*"

"You deserted me, Prue. No one's ever done that before. I hope you realize that."

"I deserted *you?* Listen to me, Luke . . . you dragged those children off under your arm! I saw you do it!"

Luke shrugged. "I was angry. I didn't want them to be around you . . . no, not you, your principles . . . all the bourgeois babble. Your world doesn't *work,* Prue. I realized that in Sitka. There's a reason I live the way I do. Surely you can see that now."

She jerked away from him and snatched up one of the rabbit skins. "I see *this,* Luke! I saw what you did to those poor little things!"

He took the skin from her and stroked its fur gently. "Didn't your brother ever skin rabbits back in Grass Valley?"

"Don't be ridiculous!"

"Well, didn't he?"

Prue looked away. "Why on earth would you . . . ? Those rabbits weren't yours, Luke. You had no right to. . . . This is insane! What am I even discussing this for?"

311

His hand moved down the long curve of her neck and came to rest on her shoulder blade. "You still haven't told me why you didn't come back to the ship."

"But I *did*. I spent half-an-hour searching for you in Sitka, and then I came back to tell Frannie Halcyon that . . . you and the children were missing."

"You didn't check my room?"

"Twice. It was locked both times."

"I must've been off with the children. I was still a little angry, hardly in a mood to seek you out. It simply never occurred to me that you might not be on board when the ship sailed. When I realized you weren't on board, I couldn't even ask for help, Prue . . . or report you missing. I was traveling with a phony ID. Anyway, why didn't *you* put out a missing persons notice?"

"We were going to," blurted Prue, "but Frannie called DeDe when we realized that the ship was about to sail . . . and DeDe said to get off the ship immediately and not to say a . . ."

"Wait a minute. She called who?"

"DeDe. Her daughter."

"I thought you said she died in Guyana."

"No . . . lost. I said she was lost. She's home now. Oh, Luke . . . we really thought you were ashore. I never dreamed you'd come back to the ship after . . ." She cut herself off.

"After what?"

"It doesn't matter. Really."

He leaned down and kissed her softly on the mouth. "What matters, my precious one . . . is that we're together again."

"Luke, I don't . . ."

"We're together in body *and* spirit. A unity."

Silence.

"This time it'll work, Prue. I know it. Everything is so much easier when you have a family."

Four on the Phone

M OTHER?"
     "DeDe! Thank God! Where are you?"
     "Nome. Listen, Mother . . ."
     "Did you find them?"
     "No. Not yet. I'm coming home, Mother. I just wanted you to know . . ."

"This is awful! Oh God, this is *awful,* DeDe. I thought you said you could . . ."

"I *tried,* Mother. I was sure we could. . . ."

"You're insane! I'm calling the police right now. We can't go on handling this thing on our own. I don't *care* about the publicity anymore. I don't . . ."

"It isn't the publicity, Mother. It's Mr. Starr. We can't afford to have him hear about this from the media."

"So you just let him run off with your children? I've never heard such madness! You've lost all sense of judgment, DeDe. Anyone who distrusts the police so much that . . ."

"I don't distrust the police. I just know your Mr. Starr."

"You've never met him!"

Silence.

"DeDe?"

"I think I *have* met him, Mother."

"What on earth are you talking about? DeDe . . . please, darling . . . you're scaring me to death!"

"I'm sorry, Mother. I've tried to protect you, but I need your help now. I want you to be brave. Can you do that for me?"

"Of course I can. What are you talking about?"

"Is Emma there?"

"Of course. She's always here."

"You've got company, then. Are any of those Quaaludes left?"

"DeDe . . ."

"I want you to take one after we hang up."

"DeDe, I'm calling the police after we hang up. You're not responsible for your actions anymore. That's become perfectly clear, and I *won't* be . . ."

"Sit down, Mother!"

"I *am* sitting down."

"Good. Now listen to me . . . Mother, please don't cry."

"I can't help it."

"I'll be back tomorrow morning, Mother. We'll talk about the police then."

Silence.

"In the meantime, I want you to know about Mr. Starr, so we can discuss this rationally when I get home tomorrow. You've won, Mother. I'll do whatever you want. Only hear me out. There isn't time to waste."

"Mouse, it's Mary Ann."

"Thank God! Where are you?"

"Nome. We didn't find them. The whole damn thing has been a wild goose chase."

"They're *here,* Babycakes! Somewhere."

"What!"

"Jon saw them come back on the ship. Jon Fielding. He's the doctor on the *Sagafjord!*"

"You're making this up!"

"I wish I were! Didn't somebody *check* to see if they were

314

on the ship? I mean . . . this doesn't sound like a kidnapping at all. Meanwhile, we've got a fairly pissed-off lady living in the basement."

"I know. I'll take care of that. Is Jon *sure?*"

"He's sure."

Silence.

"What now, my love?"

"God!"

"That isn't an answer, I'm afraid."

"Listen, Mouse . . . did Jon know where they were going?"

"He assumed they were being delivered to Halcyon Hill."

"Forget that."

"Jon said he was a friend of the family."

"Well, he's *not,* Mouse. He's lying. The man went berserk. He kidnapped those children!"

"And then cruised leisurely back to San Francisco."

"Mouse . . . I know it sounds crazy . . . but that's because *he's* crazy. Something's not right here."

"You'll get no argument from me."

"At least the kids are O.K."

"Mmm. Bambi will be relieved to know that, too."

"Jesus, Mouse . . . I'm really sorry."

"Do you let her out, then?"

"Well . . . no. I mean, the kids are still missing and . . . God, I can't think straight anymore. You might as well keep her until I get back tomorrow. I'd rather do my explaining there. Please tell Mrs. Madrigal not to worry . . . and tell Brian I love him. I tried to reach him, but the line was busy at Perry's."

"I'll tell him you called. Take care, Babycakes."

"You too. I miss you."

"Same here," said Michael.

"By the way, ask Jon . . ."

"He's staying for the wedding," said Michael.

"Fabulous."

"In Burke's room."

"Less than fabulous."

"Don't *you* start," said Michael.

When the Children Are Asleep

"YOU ASKED ABOUT THE CHILDREN," SAID LUKE, STILL holding Prue tight against his chest.

"Yes."

He studied her at arm's length for a moment, then beamed like a doting father. "Come along. It's getting dark. We should fetch them."

He led her up the slope into the rhododendron dell, grasping her arm as he steered her through the labyrinthine thicket.

Emerging from the dell, they followed the U-shaped ridge until the swamp below was visible through a clearing in the underbrush. There, frolicking along the water's edge, two tiny figures were visible.

"Edgar!" called Luke. "Anna! Come along, children. Time for bed."

The twins looked up and squealed in protest.

"No arguments!" shouted Luke. "It's almost dark."

So the children scampered up the steep path to the ridge. When they caught sight of Prue, they shouted her name gleefully. She knelt next to them and accepted their hugs, feeling curiously maternal.

"They look fine," she said to Luke. It was true.

"They can't stay out of the dirt," he said, tousling Edgar's hair. "Isn't that right, roughneck?"

Prue picked a twig out of Anna's sweater. "They'll be so relieved," she said.

"Who?" asked Luke.

"Frannie and DeDe."

Silence.

"We can call a cab from that phone booth outside the de Young," said Prue. "We can get them home in an hour. Oh, Luke . . . this is like a great weight being lifted off . . ."

"I don't want you talking that way in front of the children!"

That quicksilver rage had come back into his eyes.

"I didn't . . ."

"They *are* home, Prue! I thought you, of all people, would understand that!"

"Luke . . ."

"Shut up, Prue! We'll talk about it later. After the K-I-D-S are A-S-L-E-E-P. Understand?"

Back at the shack, she watched as the twins curled up on pallets on the floor. Luke tucked them in, giving each a rabbit pelt to hold. Then he tiptoed out into the fog, taking Prue with him.

"We're going away," he whispered.

"We can't just leave them . . ."

"No. The four of us, I mean. The family. We're complete now. We have everything we need. We'll move to South America and start a new life, Prue. God almighty! I'm so happy!"

"Luke . . . those children don't belong to us."

"And who do they belong to? That old society vulture? They aren't her flesh and blood. She got them at an agency, Prue. She told you so herself."

"I know, but . . ."

"Haven't you always wanted children?"

Silence.

"Haven't you?"

317

"Luke, that has nothing to . . ."

"It's too late to have them yourself. Well . . . now you have them! And a lover who adores you more than life itself. Don't you see how right this is? We're getting exactly what we deserve, Prue! Look into my eyes and behold your destiny!"

She looked into his eyes and beheld madness.

After a moment's hesitation, she said: "All right."

"All right what?"

"I'll go with you. It sounds wonderful, Luke."

He almost crushed her with his embrace. "Thank God . . . thank God!"

"We can leave in the morning," she said. "I'll need to pick up a few things . . . and some credit cards. We can charter a jet. We'll manage."

He sniffed back the tears. "It'll be paradise. You'll see."

Prue inched towards the ledge. "Wonderful. Then I'll meet you back here in the . . ."

"No. I want you to stay here with the children. I'm going out for a few hours."

"Oh."

"I shouldn't be long. I'll tuck you in with the children. I have a few . . . loose ends to tie up."

"I see." Prue's skin grew prickly with anticipation. Was this her chance for escape? Or would he simply lock the door when he left?

"Children can be so insistent," said Luke, caressing Prue's neck in the darkness.

"How's that?"

A low chuckle. "He wants his fire engine."

"The little boy?"

"Uh-huh. It's in the garden at the old lady's house. He's been missing it since Sitka. I promised him I'd get it for him. I guess that's the least his Dad can do."

Silence.

"Do you think that's foolish?"

"No. Not at all. I think it's sweet."

"I found the address on his luggage. I hope it's the right one."

"In Hillsborough?"

"Uh-huh. Do you think the old lady will be there?"

"I don't know."

"What about . . . whatshername . . . DeDe?"

"It's hard to say."

"I'll be careful, then."

"Do you have a way?" asked Prue. "Do you need cab fare? It's some distance."

He touched her cheek gently. "I can manage."

Then he led her back into the shack, tucked her into bed, and kissed her tenderly on the eyelids.

"Soon," he whispered.

When he left, closing the door behind him, she listened carefully for a click of the padlock.

It never came.

She felt, already, as if she had betrayed him.

Escape

PRUE CROUCHED THERE IN THE BLACKNESS, THE SOUND of her own breathing roaring in her ears like a hurricane.

The twins were already fast asleep, snuggled in the corner with their rabbit skins.

Luke's footsteps receded into the night.

Prue counted slowly to sixty, then pressed her ear to the door of the shack.

Nothing.

She eased the door open several inches and peered out into the darkness. She could see very little, only the fresh footprints in the sandy slope that marked Luke's exodus. Overhead, in the eucalyptus trees, the wind made a sound like tissue paper being crumpled.

She tugged the door shut again, wincing as it creaked, then knelt by the children and shook them gently. "Anna . . . Edgar . . . wake up, darlings."

The little girl stirred first. "What's the matter?" she asked loudly.

"Shhh," said Prue. "We've got to whisper."

Edgar sat up, rubbing his eyes. "Where's Dad?" he asked.

"Uh . . . he's out for a while." She found the little boy's jacket and helped him into it. "We're going for a little ride. Won't that be fun?"

"Where?" asked Anna.

"To my house," said Prue. "You've never seen my house."

Edgar began whining. "I don't want to! I'm sleepy!"

Prue felt around in the shadows for Anna's coat, her dread mounting every moment. Short of gagging the children, there was not much she could do about the noise. "We've got to be quiet, darling. Can you do that for Prue?"

Edgar persisted. "Why do we have to go?"

"Well . . . it's a surprise . . . for Dad."

"What kind of surprise?"

"You'll see," whispered Prue.

The whimpering continued.

"Don't you want to see your mommy?" asked Prue.

Edgar fell silent.

"Don't you?"

"Is she at your house?" asked Anna.

"She will be," whispered Prue. "Very soon. C'mon now . . . let's see how quiet we can be."

She guided them up the slope into the dell, jumping at the sound of every twig that cracked underfoot. Once they entered the thicket of rhododendrons the darkness was so total that she was forced to find the way from memory.

"I'm scared," said Anna, clutching at Prue's hand.

"It's all right, darling. It'll only be dark for a little bit."

The child began to cry noisily.

"Anna . . . please, darling . . . everything's O.K. Edgar, tell your sister not to be scared."

Silence.

"Edgar?"

No answer.

"*Edgar!* My God . . . Edgar, where are you?"

Anna broke into a full wail. Prue knelt and scooped her into her arms, stroking her hair. "Shhh . . . it's O.K., darling . . . it's O.K. We've just got to find Edgar, that's all." She rose, holding the child against her chest, and retraced her steps along the invisible path.

"Edgar!" she called, shouting in a whisper.

"Where are you?" came a tiny voice.

"Over here," she said. Not the most useful piece of information, she realized.

"Where?" cried the child.

"Walk towards my voice, darling."

She was relieved to hear something moving through the underbrush, until she noticed the speed with which it was approaching. A branch cracked, then slapped her brutally across the face. She and little Anna shrieked together as an unseen form lunged through the bushes, knocked her to the ground and thrust a huge wet tongue in her ear.

"Vuitton!"

The wolfhound barked excitedly, grateful to be reunited with his mistress. In her consternation over Luke, Prue had completely forgotten about him.

"It's just my puppy," she told Anna. "Are you all right, darling?"

"I wanna go back," sobbed the child.

"It's gonna be all right . . . I promise. Edgar . . . is that you?"

A tiny hand was clutching at her leg.

"Is that your dog?" asked Edgar.

"Yes, darling. He's a nice dog." She staggered to her feet, holding the children's hands. "We're gonna be just fine now."

Where was the nearest telephone, anyway?

The de Young Museum?

If Luke was on his way to Halcyon Hill, somebody should warn Frannie Halcyon.

Crazy Talk

IT WAS ALMOST NINE P.M. WHEN EMMA TOOK STOCK OF HER mistress and realized that something was wrong.

"Miss Frannie?"

The matriarch looked up with heavy-lidded eyes—a symptom that Emma had long ago learned to recognize. "Yes . . . Emma, dear?"

"I brought you some hot milk," scowled the maid. "I thought you might need some help gettin' to sleep."

"Oh . . . no, thank you, Emma."

The maid set the tray down on the dresser and moved closer to the bed. "You been takin' them pills again?"

Silence.

Emma's lower lip plumped angrily. "You answer me that, Miss Frannie!"

The matriarch looked away. "Miss DeDe told me to!"

"Where is it?"

"Where's what?"

"The bottle. How many you take?"

"Only three . . . like aspirin."

"That ain't aspirin, Miss Frannie! You gimme that bottle, hear?"

The matriarch made a fluttery gesture towards the bedside table. "That was the last of 'em. I'm all right . . . really. Don't you worry, dear." Her pathetic little smile was belied by the tear that rolled down her face.

Emma blinked at her for several seconds, then sat down on the edge of the bed and took her mistress' hand. "What's the matter?" she asked sweetly.

"Emma . . . I can't . . ."

"Yes you can. You can talk to Emma 'bout it. If you don't know that, you don't know nothin'."

The matriarch's lips parted in a silent sob. Then she pressed her palms to her face and rocked slowly back and forth, never making a sound. It was only when the maid leaned forward and hugged her that a low animal moan escaped from somewhere deep inside Frannie Halcyon.

"You go right ahead," said Emma. "You just go right ahead and cry."

So Frannie wept for several minutes, cradled in the old woman's arms.

Then she said: "DeDe thinks Jim Jones has got them."

Emma pulled away and stared at her mistress. "What you talkin' 'bout?"

"Jim Jones," repeated Frannie. "From Guyana."

"That's crazy talk, Miss Frannie! Jim Jones is dead!"

Frannie shook her head lethargically. "Miss DeDe . . . she thinks . . . she says he didn't die . . . she says . . ."

"You hush now. You get some sleep."

"No . . . you should know this, Emma. Somebody else died in Guyana. Mr. Starr . . . *he's* Jim Jones. He . . ."

"Shhh."

"Those poor little babies! I gave them away to Jim Jones, Emma. I just gave them . . ."

"Now you listen to me, Miss Frannie! You *saw* Mr. Starr, didn't you? He didn't look like no Jim Jones, did he? Any fool could recognize Jim Jones in a minute! Jim Jones is *dead,* Miss Frannie!"

"No . . . he had plastic . . ."

"Hush, now."

". . . plastic surgery . . . he had . . . Emma . . ."

And then the matriarch passed out.

*   *   *

Twenty minutes later, the phone rang.

Emma picked it up in the kitchen. "Halcyon Hill."

"Oh . . . is this Edna?"

"Emma."

"This is Ms. Giroux, Emma. It's urgent that I speak to Mrs. Halcyon."

"I'm sorry, Miz Giroux. She's asleep."

"Emma, I must speak . . ."

"I'll give her the message, Miz Giroux. She's dead to the world."

"Emma . . . please . . . you must wake her up . . . *immediately!* Tell her that the children are at my place and they're safe . . ."

"Praise the Lord!" exclaimed Emma.

"But she's got to leave the house immediately. Mr. Starr is heading that way."

"Here?"

"Any minute, Edna! He's crazy . . . he's lost his mind completely. I'm so afraid he'll . . . just get out of there, please. Does Mrs. Halcyon have her car there?"

"Yes'm, but I don't think . . ."

"Tell her not to get dressed or anything. Just *leave . . . get out of that house!* Do you understand me, Edna?"

"Yes'm."

She understood only too well.

The Way They Were

WHEN JON AND MICHAEL RETURNED TO MI-
chael's apartment shortly after ten o'clock,
Michael was considerably more relaxed.

"Frankly," he said, dropping onto the
sofa, "I was surprised you took it so well."

"What?" asked Jon, choosing the armchair.

"You know . . . Bambi-in-the-basement."

The doctor shrugged. "I lived here, remember?"

Michael smiled. "Nothing's changed, huh?"

"Not much. I was prepared for almost anything."

"That's sound thinking."

A long silence.

"So," said Jon, "the nursery's working out O.K.?"

"Great . . . terrific, in fact."

"It's been . . . how long?"

Michael thought for a moment. "Over three years . . . three
years at the same place. God . . . is it time to call the Guinness
Book?"

The doctor smiled. "I'm glad you like it. That's important."

Michael nodded. "It's the only way. Doing *anything* over

and over again is boring enough as it is."

The doctor regarded him for a moment. "Or any*one*, huh?"

"Hey . . ."

"Sorry. That was low."

"I'll say." Michael was stinging worse than he might have expected.

"Is Ned still running the nursery?" asked Jon, obviously attempting a retreat to the impersonal.

Michael nodded. "He's been talking about making me a full partner."

"Good. That's good to hear. You should be putting some money away."

"I know," said Michael. "Don't nag."

Jon smiled beseechingly. "Did it sound like that?"

Michael shook his head, smiling back. "It's just . . . you know . . . a tender spot."

"It always was," said Jon.

Michael drummed his fingers on the arm of the sofa. "Well . . . that's not something you have to worry about anymore, is it?"

Jon said nothing for a moment, then shook his head slowly in amazement. "It's still so damned convincing, you know."

"What?"

"You and that brave-waif-in-the-storm routine. Little Michael against the world. You've even got Mrs. Madrigal buffaloed. She thinks *I'm* the one who left you."

Michael stiffened. "I never told her that."

"You didn't have to," said the doctor. "You just ducked your eyes and looked pitiful, as usual. Someday he'll come along tra la. I've got news for you, Michael: he *did* come along and you tossed him out on his butt, because you didn't have the balls to get past your fantasy."

"*What* fantasy?" Michael was almost speechless.

"You tell me. Young Dr. Kildare, maybe? I don't know . . . whatever it was, I couldn't live up to it anymore . . . and you couldn't stand the thought of being loved by just another guy like yourself. You're tough, Michael—despite all that sad young man bullshit—but you're not tough enough to handle that one!"

Michael stared at him, stupefied. "You're so wrong it's not even . . ."

"Am I? How's the cop working out, by the way?"

Michael's mouth fell open. "What *didn't* Mrs. Madrigal tell you?"

"She told me about the cop," said Jon. "And the movie star. And the construction worker. You're not having a life, Michael—you're fucking the Village People, one at a time."

"Now wait a minute!"

"It's the truth," said Jon.

"What business is it of . . . ?"

"It *isn't* my business. You're right about that. It hasn't been my business for a long time . . . and I shouldn't have said anything. Except that Mrs. M. asked me to . . . and I wanted to . . . and I'm tired of hearing this crap about how nobody wants you. Somebody wants you, Michael . . . as if you didn't know it. And he knows the very worst there is to know about you."

"Jon . . . I'm sorry if . . ."

The doctor rose. "There isn't anything to apologize for."

Michael sat in silence as he headed for the door.

"I'll stay through the wedding," said Jon. "There won't be any scenes, I promise you."

"Do you . . . ? Is Burke's room O.K.? Do you need clean sheets or anything?"

"Thanks. Mrs. M. took care of that.

"I love you," said Michael.

"I know," said the doctor. "Isn't that the hell of it?"

Dead to the World

HARDLY BELIEVING HER EARS, EMMA SET THE RE-
ceiver down, then hurried back upstairs to her
mistress' bedroom. Frannie Halcyon was out
cold and snoring, one arm dangling inelegantly
off the edge of the four-poster.

"Miss Frannie," whispered the maid, bending over the matriarch. "Wake up, Miss Frannie!"

No response.

"Law', Miss Frannie, *you wake up now!*" Emma grasped her
mistress by the shoulders and shook gently. "He's comin',
Miss Frannie . . . Jim Jones is comin'!"

Still no response.

"Sweet Jesus!" murmured Emma. Those unholy pills, she
realized, had done their job but good.

She fetched a glass of water from the bathroom and tossed
half of it onto the matriarch's face. Frannie Halcyon's features
contorted momentarily. Then she uttered a half-hearted
groan and rolled over on her stomach.

"Please . . . oh Lord, *please,* Miss Frannie . . . you gotta wake
up! Jim Jones is comin'!"

Ripping off the bedclothes, Emma rolled the matriarch

over again and pulled her feet off the bed. Then she hoisted
her into a sitting position.

The matriarch's head hung slack. She mumbled something
unintelligible into her own cleavage.

"Do you hear me?" asked Emma.

"Grdlarmarelup."

"You just sit there," panted Emma. "I'll get you out of
here."

She dashed to the closet and conducted a frantic search for
her mistress' floor-length black mink. Finding it, she rushed
back to the bed and began pulling it onto the matriarch's
arms.

"C'mon now . . . c'mon, Miss Frannie . . . we gotta walk.
Can you do that for Emma now? C'mon . . ." Facing her
mistress, she slid her hands under the mink-sheathed arms
and lifted with all her might.

"Herpledarnover."

"Help me, Miss Frannie . . . you can do it. Stand on them
feet for me. . . ."

For a moment, the matriarch seemed to be doing just that.

"Good," said Emma. "That's real good. Now just start
walkin'. It's O.K. Emma's got you."

Seconds later, Frannie toppled like a felled bear, pinning
Emma painfully against the Chinese carpet. The maid somehow managed to dislodge herself, gasping for breath.

"Miss Frannie," she wept. "God help us both." She stared
at her mistress in despair before taking a pillow from the bed
and sliding it under Frannie Halcyon's head. The matriarch
snorted noisily, rolled over and fell asleep.

Emma went directly to the bathroom and removed the
bottle of rum that her mistress kept hidden in the toilet tank.
She took two burning swigs, then returned it to its hiding
place.

She had never done that before, but she knew what would
soon be required of her.

The matriarch kept her pistol in the bottom drawer of the
bedside table. It was a recent acquisition, Emma knew—pur-

chased only days after Mrs. Reagan announced her own reliance on a "tiny little gun."

The maid lifted it gingerly by the butt and crept out of the room, closing the door behind her.

Then she moved from room to room downstairs, turning off the lights as she went.

She checked the lock on the front door.

Then the one in the kitchen.

Then the one on the sunporch.

As she crossed the sunporch, heading for the living room, she heard a noise in the garden.

She ducked behind a big wicker chair, peering over the edge long enough to see a man push his way through the shrubbery and cross the lawn.

He stood in the middle of the lawn, assessing the house, looking from left to right.

Emma made a dash for the kitchen, then let herself out into the garage. The garage door was still open, so she slipped into the darkness, ran across the front lawn, and crept through the arbor in the side yard until the intruder was once again in view.

This time she was behind him.

The man moved closer to the house.

Then he tried to open the door to the sunporch.

"You!" shouted Emma. *"Jim Jones!"*

The intruder spun on his heels, locking eyes with the rail-thin old woman who stood on the lawn with a pistol in her hand. He raised his arms in a gesture of supplication and uttered his last word in a surprisingly placid tone of voice.

"Sister," he said.

Then Emma shot him between the eyes.

Not Gay

ONLY MINUTES AFTER JON LEFT MICHAEL'S APART-
ment, Brian showed up on the doorstep.

"How's the media widow?" asked Michael.

"Rotten," replied Brian. "You feel like a walk?"

"Sure," said Michael, "but only if misery loves company."

"Oh, no . . . what is it this time?"

Michael rolled his eyes. "What is it every time?"

"Uh . . . Jon?"

"You win the cigar."

"I saw him upstairs," said Brian. "Is he back for good?"

Michael shook his head. "Just the wedding . . . as far as I know."

"Do you want him to stay?"

Michael sighed wearily. "You aren't, by any chance, a spy for Mrs. Madrigal?"

"I just thought things might get complicated."

"More complicated?"

"I mean . . . with Bambi and all."

"Oh God," said Michael, suddenly remembering. "Things

have already gotten more complicated. You haven't heard the latest!"

As they walked to the Marina Green, Michael told Brian about Jon's sighting of the "kidnapped" twins.

"Does Mary Ann know this?" asked Brian.

Michael nodded. "She called while you were at work. She's coming home in the morning, by the way."

"Thank God. What the hell are we gonna do about Bambi."

"You got me. Jon says she's already had a knock-down-drag-out fight with Mrs. Madrigal."

"When?"

"Tonight."

"Christ." Brian shook his head. "That place is a madhouse."

Michael smiled. "Jon said the same thing."

A period of silence followed. Then Brian said: "Is he here to get you back?"

"Yeah," said Michael. "I guess he is."

"Is that what you want?"

Michael turned and looked at his friend. "Can I pass on that one right now?"

Brian laid his arm on Michael's shoulder. "You bet. I wouldn't rule it out, though . . . just because he needs you a little bit more than you need him."

Silence.

"That's it, isn't it? It's that way with me and Mary Ann . . . and *she* didn't rule it out, thank God."

"Brian . . . she loves you very much."

Brian gave his shoulder a brotherly shake. "Needing and loving are two different things."

Another period of silence ensued as they skirted the dark rectangle of the newly-named Moscone Playground. A large car passed them, screeched to a halt, and backed up until it was even with them.

A man in the passenger seat rapped his hand noisily against

the side of the car. "Hey faggots! You a couple of cocksuckers?"

Brian kept his arm on Michael's shoulder. "What's it to you, fella?"

"Hey," Michael whispered, "you're supposed to say 'yes, thank you' and smile."

The man leaned out the window as the car kept pace with them. *What did you say to me, cocksucker?*"

"Just keep walking," muttered Michael.

"Huh, faggot . . . *huh?* Would you like to suck my cock, cocksucker? Is that what you want?"

Michael noted that this witticism provoked raucous laughter from the back seat. There were at least four people in the car; one of them was a woman.

"Hey," said Michael. "I think it's time to run for it."

"Fuck that," said Brian.

"What did you say, faggot?"

Brian wheeled around and raised his middle finger to the heckler. "I said fuck you, buddy. Piss off!"

The car lurched to a stop. People spilled out of it like circus clowns from a fire engine. The first one went straight for Michael, kicking him squarely in the groin. He toppled backwards, his head striking the sidewalk with an audible thud.

He opened his eyes to see someone's hands moving in on his throat. The man raised him from the sidewalk almost gently . . . then slammed his head back down against the pavement. The noise this time was muffled, liquid.

"Hey," someone shouted, "over here!"

The man released Michael's throat and ran to join the other two. One of them was straddling Brian's chest; the other was holding his ankles. "O.K.," said the man who had jumped Michael, "you ready to die, faggot?"

When Michael saw the sudden flash of steel, he screamed in disbelief. "Please . . . please don't . . . he's not gay! *He's not gay!*"

But the knife came down again and again.

Home Again

WHEN MARY ANN SPOTTED HER LE CAR IN THE long-term parking lot at San Francisco International, she felt an unexplainable surge of optimism.

"You know," she said, taking DeDe's arm, "somehow I think the worst part is over."

DeDe's expression was hollow, devoid of hope. "Please don't try to make things better," she said. "You've done enough already. Really."

"I'm not trying to make things better. I really feel that way. If he came back with them on the ship . . . in full view of everybody . . . then, he must not have intended to kidnap them. Not in the usual sense, anyway. I mean . . . he may be crazy, but it doesn't sound like he's dangerous."

"Sure," said DeDe. "That's what they said back in '78."

Mary Ann proceeded cautiously. "But . . . we don't really know for sure if this Starr guy was really . . ."

"Stop saying that. *I* know. I know he is. He acted out that nursery rhyme, didn't he? And Prue's description seems perfectly compatible with . . ." She stopped in mid-sentence.

"With what?" asked Mary Ann.

"With . . . the way he looked."

"What did she tell you, anyway?"

"Who?"

"Prue. When you talked to her alone."

DeDe looked away. "This isn't the time for that."

Mary Ann unlocked the door of the car, climbed in and unlocked DeDe's door.

DeDe got in, saying nothing.

"When *will* it be?" asked Mary Ann.

Hesitating, DeDe looked directly at her friend. "Later . . . all right?"

"All right," said Mary Ann.

It was simple fatigue that prompted the long silence on the drive to Hillsborough. They needed time for healing, Mary Ann realized—time to be free from the crisis at hand . . . and each other. When they pulled into the circular drive at Halcyon Hill, Mary Ann approached the subject directly.

"I think we need a break," she said, "and some sleep. Why don't you let your mother pamper you for a while? I'll call in the morning and we'll talk."

DeDe leaned over and hugged her. "You've been great. I can't imagine anyone doing what you've done."

"That's O.K.," said Mary Ann.

"I hope they aren't mad at you."

"Who?"

"The station. For missing your show."

"Oh." She hadn't told DeDe about Bambi Kanetaka, and this was no time to start. "I think I can patch things up."

"I hope so." DeDe climbed out of the car and closed the door. "Sleep tight. I'll talk to you tomorrow."

"DeDe?"

"Yeah?"

"I think it's time to call the police."

DeDe remained surprisingly calm. "Yeah. So do I."

"Thank God."

"Well . . . it's come to that, I guess. We'll map it out tomorrow."

336

Mary Ann peered up at the house. "You're sure your mother is here?"

"Her car's here," said DeDe.

"Shall I wait for you to see?"

"No. I'm fine. Go home, Mary Ann. Climb in bed with Brian."

Mary Ann checked her watch. 7:57 A.M. "It might not be too late," she smiled.

DeDe winked at her. "It's never too late for that."

Pulling away from the house, Mary Ann watched DeDe in the rear-view mirror until she saw Emma appear at the front door. With that question resolved, she settled herself behind the wheel and began composing her explanation to Bambi.

This was the anchorwoman's third day of captivity, she realized.

Unless, of course, Mrs. Madrigal had been unable—or unwilling—to hold her that long.

She hadn't checked the newspapers at the airport. It was entirely possible that Bambi had *already* released the story. And what if Bambi had brought criminal action against Mrs. Madrigal and the others . . . ?

She had almost reached the gates to Halcyon Hill when she heard the commotion behind her. She looked in the mirror again to see DeDe running down the driveway, screaming at the top of her lungs.

"STOP! COME BACK, MARY ANN! COME BACK! . . ."

Corpus Delicti

THE MAID SAT IN A STRAIGHT-BACK CHAIR, HER HANDS folded regally in her lap, while DeDe and Mary Ann encircled her frantically.

"Where is he?" asked DeDe.

"Out back," answered Emma. "I drug him behind the garage." Seeing Mary Ann frown, she added: "He creeped right up in the dark, Miss DeDe. Miz Giroux . . . she called and said he was on the way, and your mama, she already tol' me he was Jim Jones . . . and I couldn't wake her up for nothin'."

"The children weren't . . . ?"

"Miz Giroux has 'em."

"They're . . . ?"

"He didn't harm a hair, Miss DeDe!"

DeDe closed her eyes and swallowed. She reached out and took Mary Ann's hand, sharing the moment with her. Emma looked at both of them with tears in her eyes. "The Lord looks out for us," she said.

DeDe rushed forward and knelt next to the old woman, embracing her vigorously. "It wasn't the Lord, Emma; it was *you.* God bless you, Emma. God bless my wonderful Emma!"

The maid pressed her hand against DeDe's cheek. "He was messin' with my family," she said.

DeDe laughed and hugged her again. "Is Mother all right?"

Emma shrugged. "She ain't woke up yet."

"You mean . . . she doesn't know?"

"Not a blessed thing," said Emma. "She took three more o' them pills last night."

"Jesus," muttered DeDe. "I told her to take one."

"I tried to wake her," said Emma. "When Miz Giroux called, I . . ."

"Does *she* know?"

Emma shook her head. "She never called back."

"And you didn't call the police?"

"No'm. I knew you was comin' back. I reckoned you'd want to call 'em yourself . . . after you knew the babies was safe."

"Exactly right." DeDe turned to Mary Ann. "I'm going out to the garage. Why don't you stay here and keep Emma company?"

Mary Ann was relieved, but she felt a nominal protest was in order. "You don't want me to go with you?"

"Actually," replied DeDe, "I'd rather you didn't."

She was gone for ten minutes. When she returned, her face was virtually expressionless. "Can I talk to you?" she asked quietly.

They conferred in the library, leaving Emma in the living room.

"I have to know something," said DeDe.

Mary Ann felt horribly uneasy. "Yeah?"

"What do you plan to do with this?"

"You mean . . . the story?"

DeDe nodded.

"Well . . . I hadn't really . . . DeDe, is it *him?*"

"Put that aside for a minute. We've got some fast decisions to make. She shot him in cold blood, Mary Ann—he wasn't even in the house, and he was unarmed. There's bound to be a murder trial, and that old woman is gonna go through hell all over again. . . ."

"But surely . . . if he's who you think he is . . ."

"Then Emma and Mother and the children . . . all of us
. . . will be subjected to the most hideous kind of public
scrutiny. I've had it, Mary Ann. I'm tired of torturing my
family. This is as close as I've ever gotten to a happy ending.
I'll do anything I can to hang onto it."

"DeDe . . . what are you saying? What do you want?"

"I want you to tell only part of the story. You can say all
you want about my escape . . . and the Cuban stuff. I just don't
want you to mention anything after that. You offered to do
that once. I need to know if the offer still holds."

"DeDe . . . you know I would, but . . ."

"But what?"

"Well . . . there are other people who know about it."

"Just Mother, really. And she slept through the bad stuff."

"And Prue," added Mary Ann.

"Are you kidding? She was sleeping with him, Mary Ann!
She'd like nothing better than to forget it ever happened. She
didn't even call back after she warned Emma. Forget about
that bitch."

"DeDe . . . we can't just forget a body in the backyard. We
can't just pretend it never happened."

DeDe looked at her long and hard. "Why not?" she asked.

"You mean . . . ?"

DeDe nodded. "If we hurry, we can do it before Mother
wakes up."

A Tangled Web

MARY ANN NOTICED, WITH SOME DISMAY, THAT there were still traces of mud on her shoes when she and DeDe arrived at Prue Giroux's townhouse on Nob Hill.

"God," she said, frowning down at them, "I thought I'd cleaned all that off."

DeDe rang Prue's door bell. "She won't notice. What's a little mud, anyway? It could happen to anybody. How's your back, by the way?"

"Better," said Mary Ann.

"Good."

"I'm not used to that kind of exercise."

DeDe's smile was sardonic. "I'm glad to hear that."

At this point, Mary Ann could only smile back. "What did you tell her?" she asked.

"Who?"

"Prue."

DeDe shrugged. "Just that we were coming over to pick up the kids." Then, hearing the door open, she squeezed Mary Ann's arm and whispered: "Don't worry. Let me do the talking."

There was little talking, however, when DeDe caught sight of her children. She fell to her knees and scooped them into her arms, weeping copiously.

Mary Ann and Prue watched in silence, also crying.

Only the children were free from tears, accepting the reunion as a matter of joyful inevitability. Released from their mother's embrace, they gamboled about her ecstatically, attempting to recount their adventures in DeDe's absence.

"Now, now," said Prue. "Your mommy's tired right now, so why don't you . . . ?"

"It's all right," beamed DeDe. "Let them yammer all they want." She reached out for Edgar again and hugged him. "It's sheer music." Looking up at Prue, she asked; "How . . . how did it happen?"

Prue flushed noticeably. "He . . . well, it's silly, but he came back on the ship."

"We know," said DeDe, standing up again.

Prue was obviously thrown. *"How?"* she asked.

"A friend of Mary Ann's saw him."

"Oh . . . then you . . . ?"

"How did he get *here?"* asked DeDe. "That's what I meant."

"Oh . . . well, he just brought them by the house."

DeDe frowned. *"When?"*

"Uh . . . last night. I called your mother's house immediately. That's when Emma took the message."

DeDe's brow furrowed. "But the ship got in yesterday."

"It did?"

"Yes," said DeDe darkly. "It did."

Silence.

DeDe studied the columnist's face. "He didn't suggest to you where he might have been for a day?"

"No," replied Prue. "Nothing."

"Why did you tell Emma he had lost his mind?"

Prue looked away. "I don't think I phrased it exactly that way. He was *upset,* of course . . . mostly because he'd been stuck with the kids for the rest of the trip. He waited for us back on the ship that day. When we didn't show up, he was angry. And worried."

"But it didn't occur to him to tell anybody? The ship's officials, for instance?"

Silence.

"Prue . . . why did you tell Emma that Mr. Starr had lost his mind?"

"I told you . . . I . . ."

"You told them to leave the house immediately!"

"Well . . . he was extremely upset. I'm sorry if I gave her the impression that . . ."

"Why didn't he bring the children directly to Halcyon Hill?"

"Uh . . . well, he didn't know the address. He knew *mine*, so he brought them here . . ."

"And then *you* called Halcyon Hill and told Emma to get my mother out of the house immediately. What sense does that make, Prue?"

"Well . . . he was furious at your mother, and I didn't want her to be subjected to . . ."

DeDe rolled her eyes impatiently. "If he was coming to Halcyon Hill anyway, why didn't he bring the children with him?"

Prue's eyes welled with tears again. "DeDe . . . please . . . I don't know. . . . He wasn't making any sense. I thought you'd be grateful to have your children back."

DeDe employed a more lenient tone. "I'm just trying to get at the truth. You can understand that."

Prue nodded, wiping her eyes. "He was acting funny. That's all I can say. It was just an instinct I had. If your mother had stayed at Halcyon Hill, she would have *seen* that!"

DeDe heaved a long sigh. "She did stay, Prue."

"What?"

"She was sound asleep," said DeDe.

"Then, maybe Emma . . ."

"Emma sat up all night, watching the house."

"And she didn't see him?"

"That's right," said DeDe. "He never showed up."

Buffaloes in London

AFTER LEAVING PRUE'S APARTMENT, DEDE AND MARY Ann took the twins to breakfast at Mama's in Gramercy Towers. A hot meal and the sound of laughing children did wonders for Mary Ann's faltering spirits.

The ordeal, she realized, was finally over.

"It's a great story," she remarked, "even without . . . him."

DeDe wiped a blob of jelly off Edgar's chin. "I'll do all I can to help. Give us a few days, O.K.?"

"Sure."

"Do you still want to do it on your movie show?" asked DeDe.

"I'm not sure about that," said Mary Ann. "Do you mind including the children, by the way?"

DeDe hesitated, then smiled. "Of course not. Not after what you've done." She turned to the twins. "Hey, you guys . . . wanna be on TV with Mary Ann?"

The children cheered.

"There's your answer," smiled DeDe.

"Great," said Mary Ann.

Edgar tugged on his mother's arm. "Can Dad be on TV, too?"

After a pregnant pause, DeDe said: "Dad?"

"*Can* he?" asked Anna, lending support to her brother.

DeDe looked from one child to the other, then said quietly: "Do you mean Mr. Starr?"

Both heads nodded, eyes wider than ever. Mary Ann turned and waited with them for DeDe's answer.

"Darling," said DeDe, "Mr. Starr has gone back to London. We won't be seeing him for a while."

"*Why?*" asked Anna.

"Well . . . because that's where he lives. He was just on vacation when you met him on the ship. His house is in London."

"His house is *neat,*" said Anna.

DeDe stared at the little girl. "*What,* darling?"

"He has chipmunkies," said Anna.

Edgar corrected her. "*Chipmunks.*"

Anna stuck her tongue out at her brother. "And buffaloes," she added defiantly.

"And a great big windmill," said Edgar, upping her one.

"It's in Japan," Anna revealed. "He has a bridge in his yard that goes way high up in the air."

"Right," said DeDe. She cast a wry glance in Mary Ann's direction. "There's no telling *what* that bastard told them." Then she turned back to the children. "You guys ready to go home?"

"Where?" asked Edgar. A damn good point, thought Mary Ann.

"To Gangie's house," replied DeDe.

The children said yes.

They spoke their parting words in the garage next to L'Etoile. DeDe waited there for her Mercedes—Mary Ann, her Le Car.

"You've been an angel," said DeDe, sounding oddly like a clubwoman from the peninsula.

Mary Ann smiled ruefully. "Glad to help."

"Right," grinned DeDe.

The Mercedes arrived. DeDe held the door while the twins scrambled into the front seat. When she slid behind the wheel, Mary Ann leaned down and spoke to her.

"You're not going to tell me, are you?"

"What?" asked DeDe.

"You know. If we got the right guy."

DeDe shook her head.

"Why? Because we didn't?"

DeDe smiled. "If we didn't, I don't want you to suffer because of it. You've done enough already."

"What if we did?"

DeDe shrugged. "I don't want you to be tempted."

"Tempted?"

"You know," said DeDe. "By the story."

"DeDe . . . I'm your friend. I would never betray the trust. . . ."

"I know. And you'd never forgive yourself either. How could you? You're a journalist."

"I am?"

DeDe grabbed her hand and kissed it. "You are."

"Thanks," said Mary Ann.

"Don't mention it," said DeDe.

It was almost noon when Mary Ann dragged herself up the stairway at 28 Barbary Lane. As she slipped her key into the lock, she heard Mrs. Madrigal's distinctive footsteps behind her.

"Dear . . . is that you?"

"It's me," said Mary Ann.

The landlady's eyes were bloodshot.

"Good God," said Mary Ann. "Is something . . . ?"

"I'm sorry," said Mrs. Madrigal. "I have something unpleasant to tell you."

Lucking Out

A SENSE OF *DÉJÀ VU*, ALMOST INDISTINGUISHABLE from nausea, swept over Mary Ann as she and Mrs. Madrigal strode through the lobby of St. Sebastian's Hospital.

It was here that Michael had been treated for Guillain-Barré almost five years before. Here, too, was the sinister flower shop where the man with the transplant had secreted body parts for the cannibal cult at Grace Cathedral.

The most macabre memory, however, was a fixture of the hospital itself: an antique portrait of St. Sebastian, shot through with arrows, proudly displayed on the wall above the reception desk.

Mrs. Madrigal took Mary Ann's arm and steered her away from the holy man. "C'mon, dear. I know the way. This place is too Catholic for words."

They rode the elevator to the third floor. When they emerged, Jon was waiting for him. The very sight of him cracked the bland veneer that Mary Ann had assumed for the ride to the hospital.

She fell into his arms, weeping.

"A helluva way to come home, huh?" He laid his hand gently on the crown of her head.

"Are they awake?" she asked.

"Brian is," said the doctor. "Michael nodded off about an hour ago." He turned to Mrs. Madrigal. "Did you fill her in on the particulars?"

"As best I could," said the landlady.

"His lung was punctured," Jon told Mary Ann. "That was the worst part. It was a surprisingly small puncture, though . . . all things considered."

It sounded awful to Mary Ann. "Did they sew it up or what?"

Jon shook his head. "It wasn't that bad. It should heal on its own. He's got a tube in him so that can happen. It isn't as bad as it looks, Mary Ann. That's the main thing you should know."

"But I thought they . . . did it three times." She couldn't bring herself to say the word.

"Two of the blows glanced off his ribs," said Jon. "There were plenty of stitches, but they were all in the chest wall. He's breathing normally now. . . ." He smiled at her. "I expect that'll change when he sees you."

"What about Michael?"

"An enormous goose egg, mostly. Half-a-dozen stitches. He's O.K. . . . or he will be soon." He looked at Mary Ann earnestly. "We lucked out, didn't we?"

"If you can call it that," said Mary Ann.

"We can," said Jon. "We have to."

Brian's head was turned towards the window when Mary Ann entered the room. His chest was a mass of bandages. The tubes sprouting from the hole in his side led to a sort of suction cannister on the floor beside the bed.

As he breathed, a thing that looked oddly like a Ping-Pong ball bobbed about erratically in the canister. Another tube (an IV, she presumed) led from a bedside pole into Brian's arm.

Michael was sleeping in the other bed, an enormous bandage crowning his head.

"It's me," said Mary Ann.

Brian rolled his head over and smiled at her. "Hi, sweetheart."

Mary Ann moved cautiously towards the bed, feeling his wounds with every step. "Is there anything I can kiss?" she asked.

A large tear rolled down Brian's cheek. "Just stand there and let me look at you."

She stood there awkwardly, hands at her sides. "How's this?"

"Just fine," he smiled.

"Shall I show a little leg?"

She had never seen a grown man laugh and cry at the same time. "Jesus," he sobbed, "I love you so much!"

"Brian, damnit . . . if I start blubbering . . ."

"I can't help it. I've never been so goddamn glad to see somebody in my whole life!"

She grabbed a Kleenex from the bedside table and stood over him, blotting his cheeks. "Hush now . . . I'm back. I'm so sorry I wasn't here, Brian."

"What are you talking about? How could you have known?"

"I know, but you needed me and . . ."

"To hell with that. Did you find the kids?"

Mary Ann nodded. "We found them."

"They're O.K.?"

"They're fine," said Mary Ann.

"Then you did good."

Mary Ann turned the Kleenex on her own face and blew her nose noisily. "How long will they keep you here?" she asked.

"Two weeks," said Brian. "Maybe three."

"Then, let's do it here."

"What?"

"The wedding," said Mary Ann. "Remember?"

"Sure . . . but . . ."

"Yeah?"

"Well, you wanted a garden wedding."

"Fuck the garden. I wanna be married to you. Do you wanna be married to me?"

"I do," said Brian.

Mary Ann beamed. "I'll tell Mrs. Madrigal."

Michael's Doctor

ICHAEL SLIPPED INTO THE HALLWAY TO FIND JON reading a *Highlights* magazine next to the nurse's station.

"Hey," said the doctor, "you're supposed to be prone, sport."

Michael sat down next to him, wearing only his hospital smock. "Whoa!" he yelped, stiffening as his bare butt collided with cold plastic.

Jon grinned. "They're not for patients."

"What? The chair or the dress?"

The doctor pointed to Michael's room, admonishing him with his eyes.

"In a minute," said Michael. "I thought the lovebirds could use a little privacy. Anyway . . . stop being such a doctor."

Jon shrugged. "I'm not in white, am I?"

"You're on the verge . . . I can tell. Why don't you get some sleep, Jon? How long have you been here, anyway?"

"I'm all right," said Jon. "I'll go home with Mary Ann when she leaves."

"Did Mrs. Madrigal go home?"

Jon nodded. "It's past time for Bambi's lunch."

"Jesus," groaned Michael. "I completely forgot about that little drama!"

"Didn't we all?"

"Mary Ann says that's next on her agenda . . . now that the twins are back. Did you hear from the police, by the way? Anything new, I mean?"

Jon shook his head. "I don't expect there will be. No license number, no solid description. The people who found you didn't reach the police until half-an-hour after the attack. I think we've got to write it off, Michael."

Michael's eyes glazed over.

"Hey," said Jon. "You with me, sport?"

"Yeah."

"It was an awful thing, Michael, but you can't let it get the best of you. Don't let those bastards change the way you look at life. Hey, sport . . . look at me."

Michael's lower lip was trembling uncontrollably. Tears flooded his face. "I know, Jon . . . it isn't that. It's just . . . ."

"What?"

"Do you think they blame me?"

Jon blinked at him, uncomprehending. "Who?"

"Mary Ann and Brian."

"Michael . . . what in the world are you talking about?"

"Well," answered Michael, his voice quavering. "Those guys who jumped us . . . they thought we were *both* gay . . . and . . . if I hadn't been there . . ."

"Jesus," muttered Jon.

"No, listen . . . they were just plain wrong about Brian. They had even less reason to attack him than me. But he got the worst of it. He . . ."

"Even *less* reason, huh? Meaning, I suppose, that they had at least a marginal reason to attack you? Is that what you think, Michael? Do you really believe that you deserved to get it more than Brian did?"

"Jon . . . I don't . . ."

"Goddamnit, Michael! How dare you talk like that? Brian doesn't think that. Mary Ann certainly doesn't. You're the biggest homophobe in the family. What the hell does gay have to do with anything?"

Michael looked at him imploringly, eyes brimming with

tears. "Jon . . . please . . . I came out here for a hug."

A hug was what he got. "Listen to me," said Jon, speaking directly into Michael's ear, "you taught me everything I know about being happy with myself. Don't poop out on me now, kiddo."

"Jon, I just can't keep . . ."

"Yes you can," said the doctor. "You're the toughest little fucker I know. You're right out there on the battle lines . . . and that's where I want you to stay. Christ, Michael . . . I'm the guy who wouldn't let you kiss him in airports."

Silence.

"I'm different now," Jon added. "You're the one who changed me."

Michael pulled away from him and looked into his eyes. "Who have you been kissing in airports?"

Jon faked nonchalance. "Oh . . . lots of people."

"I'll bet."

"Wanna try for a hospital?"

They kissed for almost half-a-minute until the head nurse returned to her station.

She cleared her throat noisily. "If you don't mind, gentlemen."

Jon looked up at her and smiled. "It's all right," he said. "I'm a doctor."

Options

WHEN MARY ANN DESCENDED THE STAIRS TO THE basement, she found Bambi curled—no, *coiled*—on an ancient sofa Mrs. Madrigal had provided for her comfort.

She looked up sullenly, a long shadow falling across her face.

"You're gonna pay for this," she said ominously.

"I suppose so," said Mary Ann.

"I'm not talking job, lady—I'm talking criminal action. Your ass is grass, Mary Ann."

It was creepy to see how much of Larry Kenan's pig lingo Bambi could appropriate for her own use.

Mary pulled up a chair. A safe distance away. "I thought we should . . . discuss things first."

"Tell it to the police," snarled Bambi.

"Do it yourself," countered Mary Ann. "The door is open."

The anchorwoman cast a quick glance up the stairs.

"You're free to go," said Mary Ann.

Bambi's eyes narrowed suspiciously. "This is still a kidnapping, you know. Just because you're turning me loose doesn't mean . . ."

"I know."

"And just because somebody else did it for you . . ."

"I know that, too." Mary Ann smiled sweetly. "So, haul ass, lady." She jerked her head jauntily towards the stairs. "Give my love to Larry . . . while you're at it. The poor jerk thinks you're out on a hot story. I'd hate to be the one to disillusion him."

"You're gonna hate it even more when . . . What did you tell him?"

"Just that," shrugged Mary Ann. "That you and I were out chasing the scoop of the year."

"DeDe Day?"

Mary Ann nodded, smiling.

"I Xeroxed those notes, you know." Bambi's sneer was almost obscene. "Stealing my purse was the stupidest thing you could've done. That story is still ours, Mary Ann. All it takes is a phone call to the station."

"What a coincidence," said Mary Ann. "Those were my exact words to DeDe."

Silence.

"We were talking about a different station, of course."

Bambi glared at her murderously. "You wouldn't do that."

"Why not?" said Mary blithely. "My ass is grass, right? I'd get a much warmer reception at Channel 5. And let's face it . . . there *is* no story without DeDe and the kids. *Is there?*"

Silence.

"That's why I thought we should have a little discussion first. I wanted you to know what your options are . . . before you screw this up completely." Another smile, more sugary than the first.

"Go ahead," muttered Bambi.

"Well," said Mary Ann, "you can press charges, like you said. That'll simply force me to explain publicly why we felt a moral obligation to hold you here until DeDe was certain that her children were out of harm's way. That won't look very pretty, Bambi. It wasn't your story in the first place. That's easy enough to prove."

355

"A story is a story," growled the newscaster.

"Exactly," said Mary Ann. "And I'm prepared to share this one with you."

Bambi gave her a long distrusting look. "You are?"

"With you or Wendy Tokuda. Take your pick."

The coil tightened. "I wanna know what 'harm's way' was."

Mary Ann blinked at her. "Huh?"

"You said, 'when the children were out of harm's way.' What possible threat could justify your locking me in a cellar for three days?"

"The threat was *you!* The press! DeDe is my friend. She's made some dumb mistakes, but she's a good woman and I like her. She wanted time to breathe, that's all. A month of serenity with her mother and children. Is that too much to ask for a woman who escaped from Guyana in a fish barrel?"

"What about that double, then?"

"What about him? She says an imposter was trained while she was still in Jonestown . . . but she left days before the massacre. It's definitely worth mentioning. I'd count on being shot down, though."

"Why?"

Mary Ann nailed her with a glance. "Do *you* think Jim Jones is still alive?"

Bambi scowled and looked away. "So what do you want to do about this?"

"All right: I want you to sign a paper certifying your willing tenancy at 28 Barbary Lane over the past few days . . ."

"Just a second!"

"I'm not finished. Since it's obvious that you and I have been out interviewing DeDe for the past few days—got that—you couldn't possibly have been locked in the basement of 28 Barbary Lane. This was simply your command post. I think that sounds pretty damn glamorous myself."

"What about air time?"

"We'll share that," said Mary Ann. "I don't care if you do the announcing. You can interview me."

"I'm ever so grateful."

"You should be. I've been leaning toward Wendy lately. The book rights are mine, incidentally." Mary Ann smiled. "Not that you'd pose any threat there."

"So . . . you weren't in Cleveland, then?"

"Of course I was in Cleveland!" Mary Ann's indignation was heroic. "Do you think I would lie about my own grandmother?"

A Garden Wedding

AFTER SLEEPING FOR ALMOST FIFTEEN HOURS, MARY
Ann awoke at 9:00 A.M. and hurried downstairs
to Mrs. Madrigal's apartment. The landlady was
in her kitchen, baking a cake.

Baking *the* cake.

Mary Ann pecked her on the cheek. "You're so sweet to be
doing that. What are those little brown specks in the batter?"

"Carrots," said Mrs. Madrigal.

"You're lying."

"Then don't ask impertinent questions. I take it you
worked things out with Bambi?"

"Completely."

"Good girl. Have you called your mother yet?"

"After the ceremony," said Mary Ann. "I want this to be
just family. I mean . . . my family here."

The landlady smiled lovingly. "I knew what you meant."
She held out a spoon for Mary Ann to lick.

"Yum-hum," said Mary Ann. "Carrots!"

* * *

DeDe phoned at eleven o'clock.

"I just saw the papers," she said breathlessly. "I'm so sorry about Brian!"

"Thanks."

"You poor thing! You must think this week will *never* end!"

"It can't," said Mary Ann, "until tonight."

"Jesus. I'm afraid to ask."

Mary Ann laughed. "No. It's good this time. We're getting married tonight. At the hospital. I'd love it if you could come."

"Of course! How exciting! Can I bring the children?"

"That would be marvelous!"

"What about the show?"

"You mean our debut on the news?"

DeDe laughed. "Yeah."

"Is Monday all right with you?"

"Sure," said DeDe. "Fine."

Mary Ann giggled. "It sounds like we just made a date for lunch or something."

"Well . . . we can do that, too."

By mid-afternoon, Mary Ann was back at the hospital. When she opened the door to Brian and Michael's room, the sight that confronted her took her breath away.

"My God!"

Michael beamed at her from his bed. "Pretty neat, huh?" The room was a veritable jungle of greenery and flowers—most of which were obviously not indigenous to the hospital florist. Both beds were framed by boxwood bushes, passion vines trailed along the window sill, and a bright pink fuchsia drooped luxuriantly from Brian's IV pole.

"They're on loan," said Brian. "Ned and a friend brought them by a little while ago."

Mary Ann was undone. "What a sweet thing!"

Brian nodded. "You get your garden wedding, after all."

"Where is he?"

"Who?"

359

"Ned. I want to call and thank him."

"They'll be back in a minute," said Brian. "They went to get coffee."

"Anyway," said Michael, "we've got some questions to ask you."

"If you mean Bambi, I've taken care of that."

"What did you tell her? That the whole damn thing was a wild goose chase?"

"She doesn't know about the kidnapping," said Mary Ann. "She doesn't even know about my trip to Alaska. She thinks we locked her up to prevent early release of the story." She looked earnestly at both men. "I don't want her—or any-body—to know about Mr. Starr."

"Why?" asked Michael.

"Because that whole thing was a big fiasco. It's embarrass-ing. It makes DeDe and me both look a little drifty."

A smile flickered across Brian's face. "What were you doing up there, anyway? Chartering dog sleds? Chasing Eskimos across the ice?"

"Brian . . ."

"And this Starr guy?" asked Michael. "You have no idea where he went after he dropped the kids off at Prue Giroux's house?"

"None," said Mary Ann.

"In other words, it was just Mrs. Halcyon's dumb mistake. There was never a kidnapping. There was never a real threat of any kind. Slow curtain . . . The End."

Mary Ann nodded vaguely. "That's about it, I'm afraid."

Michael addressed his next question to Brian. "Why do I have such a hard time believing that?"

Brian gazed lovingly at Mary Ann. "It's all right," he said. "She never lies to us about the important stuff."

A bald head poked through the doorway.

"Ned!" exclaimed Mary Ann, grateful for the interruption. "This is the sweetest thing anyone has ever done! We've *definitely* got to get a photographer now! Those fuchsias are the most wonderful . . ." Her gushing stopped when she saw the man shambling into the room behind Ned.

Brian took it from there. "Mary Ann, this is ____ ____."

"Yes," she said, "I see."

"He and Ned are staying for the wedding." Brian winked at his bride-to-be. "I figured you wouldn't mind."

Back in Her Own Backyard

FRANNIE HALCYON WAS HELPING HERSELF TO MORE cinnamon toast when her daughter joined her for breakfast on the terrace at Halcyon Hill.

"How was the wedding, darling? Did everything go off all right?"

DeDe sat down and poured herself a cup of coffee. "Very sweet," she said. "In some ways, a lot like mine. The minister even read from Gibran."

The matriarch's brow wrinkled. "Oh, dear. Are they *still* doing that?"

DeDe smiled. "_____ _____ was there, by the way."

"Really? What on earth for?"

"He's a friend of the family," smiled DeDe.

"Oh."

"And Mary Ann sent you a piece of the wedding cake . . . along with her love."

"Bless her heart," said Frannie. "She's had a dreadful time of it, hasn't she? All that frantic dashing about with you . . . and then her fiancé is mistaken for a homosexual."

DeDe scowled at her. "That is hardly the point, Mother."

"Well," said Frannie merrily, "all's well that ends well, I

always say. One look at my grandchildren is proof enough of that."

"Are they up yet?" asked DeDe.

Frannie pointed to the edge of the garden. "They're out there keeping Emma company." She smiled benevolently at the distant figures, then turned to her daughter with a sigh. "You know . . . I feel awfully silly about all that."

"All what?" asked DeDe, buttering a piece of toast.

"Well . . . not checking to see if Mr. Starr had come back to the ship. We maligned him dreadfully . . . when you come to think of it. We assumed the very worst about him."

DeDe took a bite out of the toast. "That was a perfectly natural reaction."

"I know. Just the same, I wish I could write him a thank-you note. Do you think he left a forwarding address with Prue?"

DeDe shook her head and continued to eat.

"He must think us awfully stupid," added Frannie. "I mean . . . leaving the children like that. Think how it must have looked to *him.*"

"I wouldn't worry about it," said DeDe.

"He was always such a gentleman," said Frannie, closing the subject once and for all. She turned her gaze to the garden again, then shook her head in admiration. "Emma's such a marvel, isn't she? Just look at her out there! She's absolutely obsessed with that new azalea bed of hers."

"Uh-huh," said DeDe.

"You can't help admiring her," said Frannie. "Starting a new hobby at *her* age."

DeDe nodded. "She loves this family very much."

"I don't care what they say," declared the matriarch. "You can't get help like *that* anymore."

When the phone rang, DeDe took it in the kitchen.

"Halcyon Hill."

"Uh . . . Emma?"

"No. This is DeDe." *At last,* she could say that.

"I thought so! Thank God!"

"Who is this?"

"Who else? The Red Menace."

"D'or! Where are you? You sound different."

"It must be the ambience. I'm in Miami."

"What?"

"At the Fontainebleau, no less. When I sell out, I don't fuck around!"

DeDe laughed. "I've missed you so much."

"Yeah? Wanna see me?"

"Are you kidding? How soon can you get here?"

"Gimme a day or so. Listen, hon . . . what about your mother?"

"I'll take care of that," said DeDe.

Five minutes later, she hung up the phone and went out to take care of it.

Six Weeks Later...

ARY ANN AND BRIAN CHOSE GOLDEN GATE PARK AS the site of their unofficial "honeymoon"—a lavish picnic lunch that marked their first venture into the outdoors since the knife attack. At the last minute, they asked Michael to join them.

"You know," said Mary Ann, smearing Brie on a chunk of sourdough bread, "there's only one thing missing today."

"What's that?" asked Michael.

Mary Ann smiled and handed him the morsel. "Jon," she said.

Michael popped the bread into his mouth and turned to Brian. "Will you please tell the Little Woman to lay off for a while? She's determined to make us Lucy & Ricky & Fred & Ethel."

Brian grinned. "Does that make me Fred or Ricky?"

"Don't press your luck," said Michael. "You might be Ethel."

"When does Jon's ship get back?" asked Mary Ann.

"Tomorrow," said Michael. "Pass the smoky cheddar, please."

Brian shoved the cheese board in Michael's direction. "Remember when you and I were here last?"

"Yeah?"

"You told me to hurry up and marry Mary Ann."

"He *did?*" Mary Ann stopped spreading Brie and looked up. "That's so sweet, Mouse."

"Well," continued Brian, still talking to Michael, "I think it's time you married Jon."

Michael lopped a strawberry into his mouth. "I've done that already."

"Then, *re*marry him." This was Mary Ann, putting in her own two cents' worth.

Michael looked at them in succession. "You guys want *everybody* to be married."

"But, it would be so wonderful, Mouse. We could all plan trips to Yosemite together . . . and *family* things. You've been looking for two years, Mouse. Have you ever found *anybody* better than Jon?"

Michael pretended to search for another strawberry.

"Everybody but you can see that. Jon is your Christmas tree man."

"My *what?*"

"You told me that, once. Before you met Jon. You said you didn't expect that much from a relationship . . . just somebody nice to buy a Christmas tree with. That's Jon, Mouse! He doesn't even mind it when you sleep around."

"Oh?"

Mary Ann nodded. "He told me so himself. He *loves* you."

"He sleeps around himself," said Michael. "Why do you think he's on that ship?"

"Then you're *perfect* for each other! Like me and Brian."

Brian gave his wife a funny look. She squeezed his leg to reassure him.

"Are you meeting his ship?" she asked Michael.

A long pause, and then: "Yeah."

Mary Ann smiled triumphantly, giving Brian's knee a healthy shake. "You see . . . you see?"

"See what?" asked Michael.

"Nothing," grinned Mary Ann.

"You're impossible," grumped Michael. "What did you do with the Dijon?"

But his smile betrayed him again.

High on the ridge above them, Prue Giroux made her way carefully through the rhododendron dell, disregarding once again the admonitions of her priest.

She had not set foot in Luke's shack since her escape with the children.

Something strangely akin to remorse engulfed her as she pushed open the door of the little house and perused its scattered contents.

The walls had been horribly vandalized with spray paint. The foam rubber "sofa," once the scene of her happiest moments, was littered with alien condoms.

"Animals," she muttered.

Very little remained except the handmade plaque, now rudely splashed with crimson:

THOSE WHO DO NOT
REMEMBER THE PAST
ARE CONDEMNED
TO REPEAT IT

She couldn't bear the thought of leaving that sentiment behind, so she removed the plaque from the wall and slipped it lovingly into her tote bag. Before the tears could come, she hurried out into the sunlight again and scaled the slope to the rhododendron dell.

She was halfway across the dell when she spied a familiar figure emerging from one of the enormous bushes.

"Oh . . . uh . . . Prue, darling." It was Father Paddy, looking unusually flustered.

Prue tried to sound breezy, hoping he hadn't deduced the reason for her visit to the dell. "Isn't it a gorgeous day, Father?"

"Yes, indeed! God's in his heaven, all right!"

"Mmm."

"What are you . . . uh . . . doing in this neck of the woods?"

"Just walking Vuitton," said Prue.

"Oh . . . well, it's a lovely day for . . ." Before he could finish, another man emerged from the huge shrub. He greeted Prue by name, winked at Father Paddy, and sauntered off down the path, whistling contentedly.

"I didn't know you knew Officer Rivera," said Prue.

Father Paddy hesitated. "Actually . . . we just met."

"He's so conscientious," observed the columnist. "It's nice to know that there are policemen like that."

"Yes," said the cleric. "Yes, it is." He took Prue's arm suddenly. "I don't know about you, darling, but I'm *famished.* How about a little lunch somewhere?"

"I'd adore lunch," said Prue. "Help me find Vuitton."

The priest scolded her with a glance. "You've lost him again?"

"Of course not," said Prue. "He's around here somewhere. Vuiiiiton! Here, boy! *Vuiiiiiton! . . .*"

The TALES OF THE CITY *Series*

TALES OF THE CITY
A bewildered young secretary forsakes Cleveland for San Francisco, tumbling headlong into a brave new world of laundromat Lotharios, cutthroat debutantes, and jockey shorts dance contests. This is the book that became the smash hit PBS miniseries. *American Playhouse.*

Fiction/Literature
ISBN: 0-06-092480-2 $12.00   Audio ISBN: 1-55994-203-7 $15.95

MORE TALES OF THE CITY
The divinely human comedy that began with *Tales of the City* rolls recklessly along as Michael Tolliver pursues his favorite gynecologist, Mona Ramsey uncovers her roots in a desert whorehouse, and Mary Ann Singleton finds love at sea with the amnesiac of her dreams.

Fiction/Literature
ISBN: 0-06-092479-9 $12.00   Audio ISBN: 1-55994-208-8 $15.95

FURTHER TALES OF THE CITY
While Anna Madrigal imprisons an anchorwoman in her basement, Michael Tolliver looks for love at the National Gay Rodeo, DeDe Halcyon Day and Mary Ann Singleton track a charismatic psychopath across Alaska, and society columnist Prue Giroux loses her heart to a derelict living in a San Francisco park.

Fiction/Literature
ISBN: 0-06-092492-6 $12.00   Audio ISBN: 1-55994-301-7 $15.95

BABYCAKES
When an ordinary househusband and his ambitious wife decide to start a family, they discover there's more to making a baby than meets the eye. Help arrives in the form of a grieving gay neighbor, a visiting monarch, and the dashing young lieutenant who defects from her yacht.

Fiction/Literature
ISBN: 0-06-092483-7 $12.00   Audio ISBN: 1-55994-276-2 $15.95

SIGNIFICANT OTHERS

Tranquillity reigns in the ancient redwood forest until a women-only music festival sets up camp downriver from an all-male retreat for the ruling class. Among those entangled in the ensuing mayhem are a lovesick nurseryman, a panic-stricken philanderer, and the world's most beautiful fat woman.

Fiction/Literature
ISBN: 0-06-092481-0 $12.00   Audio ISBN: 1-55994-300-9 $15.95

SURE OF YOU

A fiercely ambitious TV talk show host finds she must choose between national stardom in New York and a husband and a child in San Francisco. Wistful and compassionate, yet subversively funny, *Sure of You* is a triumphant finale to one of the most entertaining series of novels ever written.

Fiction/Literature
ISBN: 0-06-092484-5 $12.00   Audio ISBN: 1-55994-299-1 $15.95

The TALES OF THE CITY series is also collected in two deluxe hardcover editions.

28 Barbary Lane
Fiction/Literature
ISBN 0-06-016466-2 $27.50

Back to Barbary Lane
Fiction/Literature
ISBN 0-06-016649-5 $27.50